STONE'S

L.A.S.T. DEFENSE

THROW

PATRICIA D. EDDY

Editing by: Michelle Fewer

Proofreading by: Book Dweller Proofreading

Cover Design by: Deranged Doctor Design

Cover Photography by: CJC Photography

Cover Models: Dominic Calvani & Sky Simpson

CHAPTER ONE

AJ

"STONE. Blade. Get your asses in here." Chief Harris stalks into his office, his bad attitude following him through the station like a cloud of Axe body spray in a sauna. *Shit*. Ten more minutes and I would have been on I-35 headed home.

I push up from my chair as Jasper shoots me a look I know all too well. We ain't gettin' out of here on time. We'll be lucky to get out of here at all.

"Keep the piss and vinegar to yourself if you don't want to spend the next month doing the chief's paperwork," I mutter.

My twin brother snorts. "You're the one gunnin' for captain. I'm going fishing tomorrow."

"We'll see about that, *little* brother. I'll pull rank if I have to."

"You're *five minutes* older than I am, AJ. That don't mean shit and you know it," he grumbles.

"Maybe not, but the chief likes me more. Or *dislikes* me less."

"Shut the goddamn door." Harris barely glances up from his computer until the din from the bullpen falls away. The scent of stale coffee in here could choke a hog. He doesn't ask us to sit down, a sure sign we ain't gonna like what he has to say.

"The Cordova Cartel is making moves again. One of Marvin's CIs thinks they're running some distribution operation off Rundberg. Shipments goin' in and out of a strip mall at all hours of the night."

"Marvin hasn't had a reliable CI since Jasper and I were in college." I glance at my brother. "You hear any chatter about a strip mall op?"

"Nope. Dead silence." Jas holds his hand to his ear. "I reckon that was a pin droppin' in the break room."

"You're a goddamn comedian now?" Harris barks.

"No, sir." Jasper shoves his hands into the pockets of his jeans and stares down at his boots.

Fuck. We're gonna be on the chief's shit list for months if we ain't careful. "What my brother means, sir, is that *our* CIs say the cartel's been quiet the past few weeks."

"And quiet usually means they're up to somethin'. So you're gonna work on your jokes while you run stakeouts for the next two nights."

I shake my head. "Chief, I'm takin' Grace up to Lake Livingston this weekend. We're fixin' to leave in a couple hours."

"Not anymore."

He slides a piece of paper across his desk. I have to squint to make out his messy scrawl. With that handwriting, he should have gone to med school.

"Stone, take McGrath to location Alpha. Blade, you're with Billings on location Bravo. I expect a full report from each of you by ten a.m. tomorrow. Now get the fuck out of my office."

"Goddammit." I punch Jasper in the upper arm once we're back in the bullpen and out of the chief's earshot. "Next time, keep your wisecracks to yourself."

"This wasn't my fault and you know it," Jasper snaps. "Marvin's had it out for us since I pranked him last year. That idjit can't take a fucking joke."

"You spiked his coffee with ghost pepper extract. He was shitting fire for a week! Thanks to you, I gotta tell Grace we can't go up to the cabin this weekend."

Jasper cringes. "Fuck. I'm sorry. But Grace knew what she was signing up for when she married you. She'll understand."

"Not this time." I pull my phone out of my back pocket and stare at the screen. Grace smiles back at me from the finish line of last year's Austin Half Marathon. "She taught her final class of the term yesterday. We were goin' up to the cabin to celebrate."

"So you'll go next weekend." He waves Billings over from across the bullpen.

"Can't. She's got the Austin Marathon in two weeks and she keeps talkin' about carb loading and taper runs. Apparently, her sleep schedule has to be 'on point.' Whatever the hell that means. Once this weekend's over, she won't touch a single drop of alcohol til she crosses that finish line. Then she's back to a full teaching load. Including summer session. This was our last chance to get away until Christmas."

"Shit, man. I'm sorry." Jasper checks his watch. "But if we don't start to look like we're takin' this assignment seriously, Harris is gonna have our asses. Call Grace so we can get to work."

A few feet away, McGrath pushes back from his desk and grabs his jacket.

Fuck.

"McGrath, don't even *think* about leaving. We're pullin' an all nighter."

The guy snaps to attention, drops the jacket on his chair, and follows Billings over to us.

"What's going on, lieutenant?" He's practically bouncing on

the balls of his feet, he's so goddamn excited. He and Billings have only been on the job a little over a year, but they're both solid. They're also kids. McGrath is only thirty-two and Billings might be even younger.

Jas and I are north of forty, and the prospect of no sleep has my back aching already.

"Stakeout. Chief's orders. You're with me. Billings is riding with Jasper. Head down to the motor pool and pick up two sedans. Then go to Siren Coffee for traveler boxes. Be back here in thirty."

"On it." The two of them double-time it out of the bullpen like their asses are on fire.

For the next twenty-seven minutes, Jas and I go over every line of the file Marvin put together. His source provided nothing but vague rumors that don't stand up to a lick of scrutiny.

"This is horseshit," I say as Jasper shrugs into his jacket.

He shakes his head. "Tell that to the chief. Marvin's so far up his ass, he can tell you what Harris had for breakfast."

I choke back a snort, but my brother isn't done.

"The fucker ain't been on his game since that failed drug bust last year. He's got more CIs than a centipede has legs, and none of 'em can ride and chew at the same time."

"Tell me how you really feel, Jas."

He gives me the side-eye as we wait for the elevator down to the garage. "You call Grace yet?"

"Fuck." Billings and McGrath are due back any minute, and if we don't get a move on, we'll never hear the end of it.

Jasper cringes as I thumb out a quick text message.

AJ: Caught a case. Jasper and I are on stakeouts all night. Tomorrow too. I'm sorry, but we gotta cancel our trip this weekend. I'll make it up to you. I promise.

My phone rings less than sixty seconds later. I'll catch hell for it tomorrow, but I tuck the device back in my pocket and let the call go to voicemail.

"AJ, you're playin' with fire. Grace is as easy goin' as they come, but ignoring her? She's gonna have your ass in a sling for months."

My brother's right. I should call her back. Apologize. Grovel, even. But she's been looking forward to this trip all winter. Hearing the disappointment in her voice might do me in.

AJ: About to get in the car. We'll talk in the morning. I promise. I love you.

The message status changes to *Read*, but Grace doesn't reply. Or call again. It's gonna be a long damn night. And an even longer morning.

CHAPTER TWO

Grace

A WET NOSE pulls me from the comfort of sleep. The shower's running.

Well, ain't that just grand.

AJ came home from his stakeout and didn't bother waking me. At least he *knows* he stepped in it last night.

Belle, my Australian Shepherd/Bernese Mountain Dog puppy, puts her swollen paw on the bed and whines. "I know, sweetie. Wasp stings are no fun at all." The poor dog stepped on one of the mean little shits out on the deck yesterday morning, and she's been favoring her foot ever since.

I glance at the bathroom door with a sigh. "He didn't feed you, did he?"

She limps out into the hall, then stops and peers back at me.

That's a no. While Belle loves AJ, she's bonded to me something fierce. Pretty sure this dog would throw herself in front of a whole swarm of wasps for me—even after getting stung and visiting the dreaded *v-e-t*.

"Come on. Mama's got you." I slip into my robe and pad out to the kitchen. My knees crack and pop for the first few steps. Six months of training for the Austin City Marathon have left me in the best shape of my life—except for my knees. They're not pleased with me. But one more long run, and I can start my taper.

Belle limps along ahead of me. She's barely putting any weight on her bad paw. If it's not better by tonight, she's going back to the vet.

At least the pain isn't affecting her appetite. She wolfs down her breakfast in record time, then stays by my side while I make a pot of coffee for AJ and a cup of instant Cafe Vienna for myself.

The early morning light peeks over the hills, creating a scene worthy of an oil painting, but I can't appreciate it. Not today.

Tossing and turning all night left me completely raw. Being the wife of a Ranger isn't for the faint of heart. But he's never refused my call before. Never canceled plans by text message. Never failed to wake me up when he got home from a stakeout.

His steady footsteps slow as he reaches the kitchen. And though my morning coffee ritual usually soothes me, tension gathers in my shoulders instead.

Yet, I pass him my mug, the rich scents of cinnamon and vanilla wafting between us.

"You're up early," he says quietly.

"I never sleep well when you're on a stakeout."

"Grace—"

His tone grates on my last, frayed nerve, but when I feel the heat of him seep into my back, I turn.

It's the silly little habits you develop after so long together that often mean the most. AJ thinks my coffee tastes like flavored water, but we share this moment of connection almost every morning.

His arm snakes around my waist as he takes a sip of my Cafe Vienna. I can't help but melt against him. Even when I'm angry—or hurt—his quiet strength still grounds me.

"I'll never understand how you drink this stuff," he says. The affection in his tone softens a fraction of my anger.

"Because it tastes like cinnamon and vanilla and everything good in this world."

"I should have said no, darlin'. I'm sorry."

Resting my head on his shoulder, I try to find the right words to put us back on equal footing. Or at least make him understand why I was so angry with him.

"I don't care that you have to work this weekend, AJ. Yes, I was looking forward to a little getaway. We haven't had much time together the past few months. But you couldn't even call me to let me know?"

He pulls back and stares down at his boots, a flush creeping up his neck to his cheeks. "Jasper warned me you'd be mad as a wet hen."

He's digging himself a deeper hole with every word. I straighten my shoulders and give him my best glare. "Maybe next time you'll listen to him. I don't like going to bed without you. But going to bed angry because you were too much of a coward to answer the phone? That was so much worse."

He flinches, his gaze pinned to the floor. "One more big case —maybe two—and I'll make captain. Then I'll be handing out the shit assignments and comin' home on time every night."

I choke out a laugh. "Promises, promises. You'd never ask your people to do anything you wouldn't do yourself."

He stiffens, his expression shuttering. As much as I want him to own up to his mistake, I can't handle spending another minute with this still simmering between us.

Cupping the back of his neck, I pull him down to brush a kiss to his lips. "After fifteen years of marriage, I *know* you, AJ. This is who you are. Who you've always been. I don't want or need you to change. But we work because we're honest with one another. Always."

His gaze softens, silver flecks glinting in his bloodshot blue eyes. After a beat, he rests his forehead against mine. "How about, 'I'll come home on time more often'?"

"Better." I brush the backs of my fingers along his cheek. He hasn't shaved. Or slept. If I had to guess, he only came home because the showers at the office have no water pressure. "You're exhausted."

"We waited all fucking night outside of one of the strip malls down by the river, and nothin'. Either Marvin's CI got bad intel or they made us. Fuckers. I could have been in bed. With you. Instead, I had to hear McGrath snore every time he nodded off for more than five minutes. Harris is gonna shit a brick when he finds out we came up empty. We'll be lucky if he doesn't put us on traffic duty for the next month."

"Is he expecting you right away?" Even after so many years together, when we're this close, my nipples tighten and something flutters in my core.

The corners of his eyes crinkle, and his voice takes on a smoother tone. "I got an hour."

"Then come with me." I link our fingers and lead him down the hall to our bedroom.

"I had a whole romantic evening planned up at the cabin tonight," he says as I let my robe drop to the floor at the foot of the bed. "Bubble bath, rose petals, champagne, chocolate-covered strawberries..."

I have to stifle my snort with my hand. "In that tiny-ass tub? We have a much better one here."

His hands frame my breasts through my thin tank. "Yeah, but the cabin don't have a landline. Or a single reliable cell tower within fifty miles."

Dropping to one knee, AJ presses a kiss to the black cotton panties covering my mound. Goosebumps race over my skin.

"God, you smell like rain," he whispers against me. "Lie down so I can taste you."

AJ

Grace curls her fingers around my tie and pulls me to my feet. "Get naked first, handsome."

"Yes, ma'am."

The Ranger double belt looks cool, but times like this, I curse the damn thing. My zipper is strangling my dick by the time I get it loose.

Grace's deft fingers flick open the buttons on my dress shirt one by one until she can press kisses across my chest. Her nipples strain against her thin tank, hard points I ache to wrap my lips around.

Instead, I sink my hands into her dark blond hair and crush my mouth to hers.

Fuck.

Boots.

I stumble and almost fall on my ass—with Grace on top of me—trying to get the damn things off without the use of my hands.

"Careful there." Her voice takes on a sultry tone, a hint of Texas twang infusing her words, as she grabs my hips to steady me. "Unless you *want* to do it on the floor."

"Perfectly good bed...right behind you," I manage as I tug at her panties. "But these have to go."

Her blond curls glisten with arousal as she lies down and spreads her legs for me. The first light touch of my tongue is like coming home in every way. Her scent, her taste, the sound of her breath catching in her throat...even the slight tremble of her thighs is perfection.

I find my rhythm quickly, tracing patterns over and around her clit until her heels start to dig into the mattress.

"Aaron...please..."

She only uses my first name when she's about to come—or when I'm being a complete jackwad—and I reach up to give one of her nipples a hard pinch. It's enough to send her flying over the edge. Her body coils like a spring, her back arches, and her moan turns into a keening cry.

I slow my strokes, lapping up her release like it's water in the hottest desert until her tremors fade.

At forty-three years old, I shouldn't be this close to blowing my wad in my briefs, but precum leaks from my crown as I strip off the dark blue cotton.

"Turn on your side, darlin'." Positioning myself behind her, I wrap my arm around her waist. Her channel's tight, and I kick myself for all the overtime I've put in this month.

Slowly, I start to move my hips. Grace matches me thrust for thrust. Her hair tickles my nose as I kiss my way up the curve of her neck to her ear.

"Touch yourself, darlin'. I want you to come again."

From this position, I can't see her face, but when she fondles her clit, her soft breaths quicken.

I don't deserve this woman. I never have. I never will. But by some miracle, she's never given up on me—even when I'm being a fucking idiot.

Under my hand, her abs start to quiver. "Harder," she moans.

Anything she wants, I'll give her. Each thrust brings us closer. The ache in my balls turns into an all-consuming fire.

"Fuuuuck."

With one last thrust, I let go, and Grace comes with me.

THE MINUTES SLIP AWAY TOO QUICKLY. DELAYING the inevitable just a little longer, I trace the lines and curves of her tattoo with my fingers. The phases of the moon arch over a cluster of pink, white, and red oleanders—the official flower of Galveston, where we were married.

Our legs tangle under the sheets. I'll have to go soon, and she'll spend the rest of the weekend alone. Fuckin' job. At least on stakeout, we shouldn't be in any real danger. This is an intel-gathering op only.

Grace rubs her foot up and down my calf with a sigh. "Will I see you at all tonight?"

"Not unless we can convince the chief that Marvin's intel is as worthless as teats on a bull. You painting this weekend?"

"Maybe tomorrow." She stretches, and her nipples tighten under the sheet. "One of my students wants to turn in his final project early. I told him no the other day, since we were supposed to be gone, but I emailed him back last night. I'll meet him at the community college a little after noon. If I start my run there, I can get in a flat, eighteen-miler that takes me around part of Lady Bird Lake."

I trail kisses along her shoulder. "There ain't a lot of traffic out that way. You'll take Belle, right?"

Grace turns to face me, disappointment churning in her blue-green eyes. "She stepped on a wasp yesterday. I left you a voicemail. The vet doesn't want her running for at least a few days—if not a week. I'll drop her at Bark Away so she doesn't destroy another pair of my shoes."

"Dammit. I *did* listen. Fucking all nighter is messing with my head. But I don't like you running out there all alone."

"Aaron—"

I cringe at her tone and hold up a hand. "I know, I know. You're a grown-ass adult who can handle herself. But...take your pepper spray and your whistle. Please. And call me when you're back in the car."

Her expression softens, and her palm against my cheek is reassurance we're *mostly* square after my fuckup.

"I'll be done by five. Don't worry."

I press a kiss to her forehead and get to my feet. "Darlin', I *always* worry."

STRAIGHTENING MY TIE, I stand in front of the mirror and cast a glance over my shoulder at Grace. She's still in bed, Belle curled up next to her. God, she's so fucking beautiful.

"I know we ain't supposed to go to bed angry, but the make-up sex is pretty damn hot."

She throws her head back and laughs, then narrows her eyes at me. "AJ Stone, if you pick a fight with me again tonight, there won't be any 'make-up sex' to be had. Now get out of here before the chief comes banging on our door looking for you."

CHAPTER THREE

Grace

I CIRCLE the community college parking lot for fifteen minutes before a space opens up. I should have remembered that Austin Pride was using our quad as staging grounds for today's parade. It's a good thing I don't plan on leaving anytime soon.

By the time I finish my run, the parade will be long over. I'll get to see a bit of it on my way to the lake. Maybe all that positive energy will help keep me from bonking at mile fifteen like I have on every single training run the past two months.

The comforting scent of drying oil paint surrounds me when I step inside my classroom. Several of my students' final projects are still in progress along the fringes of the space. Others are finishing theirs up at home.

My fingers itch with the need to create something—anything. I love painting. But drawing is where my heart is.

Maybe I'll break the seal on my new sketchbook tomorrow. Training and teaching have stolen every ounce of my creativity the past few months, and I've missed spending all day in my studio bringing something beautiful to life.

I had no clue when I signed up how much this race would eat me alive. Last year's half marathon was a walk in the park—fun, even. But twenty-six-point-two miles? That ain't just twice the distance. It's twice the pain, four times the blisters, and a whole lot more cussin' at myself for *ever* thinking this was a good idea.

A gentle knock on the open door pulls me from my little pity party.

Joshua, twenty years old and built like a semi-truck, fills the doorway with a black portfolio clutched in one hand. His smile wavers for a beat, but then brightens.

"Hey, Ms. Stone. Thank you so much for meetin' me today." He lifts the case a little higher. "You're saving my bacon. Otherwise, Ruth and I were gonna have to wait a whole *month* to get married!"

He's so earnest. Like waiting four short weeks would wreck his whole world. Though, I can still remember how excited I was when AJ proposed. And how our one year engagement was eleven months and twenty-nine days too long.

"Come on in, Joshua." I tug the hem of my running tank down a little lower to cover my ass. I often hold office hours on Saturdays, so half the class has seen me in my running clothes before, but today's shorts leave very little to the imagination. "Did you have any problem finding a parking spot?"

He frowns. "I thought it'd be empty on campus today. My pop is in the loading zone waitin' for me." His gaze flicks to the window, then back again. "You're not gonna miss your run because of the parade, are you? Shoot. I should have worked faster and turned this in yesterday."

"Don't worry about it. I'm trying the eighteen mile loop around Lady Bird Lake again."

He lets out a low whistle. "When I used to help Pop at the ranch, we'd walk a good five miles a day, but that toasted my hide somethin' fierce."

"Well, you were probably doing a lot more than walking. Feeding the cows, running the tractor, bailing hay? It's just me, my water bottle, and six months of training. I can't wait to have my weekends back when the marathon is over."

Joshua shifts, the portfolio tight against his chest. "Uh, don't open this until later, okay? If it ain't good, I don't want to know until after the wedding."

"You're incredibly talented. If the rest of your work this semester is any indication, you'll be just fine. But I'll log it in today and grade it on Monday with the rest of the class. Promise."

His shoulders sag in relief, and he backs toward the door. "Thanks, Ms. Stone."

"Congratulations on your wedding!" I call once I lock the portfolio in the old cabinet at the very back of the room, but he's already gone.

Why was he so nervous? He's always been quiet in class, but he has some real talent with oils. Curiosity gets the better of me, so I return to the cabinet and take a quick peek.

"Oh, my God."

The midnight sky blazes with stars. A swollen moon hangs in the corner of the canvas, so luminous, it spills silvery light across everything beneath it.

At the center, a woman rises above a crowd. She's framed by tall poles, each with a lantern glowing gold against the darkness. Flowers bloom at her feet, twining up her arms, all the way to a crown of blossoms around her head.

Her hands stretch skyward, palms open, as if she's drawing the light of the moon down into her body. Her blond hair flows behind her in a rush of motion.

The whole scene pulses with reverence and awe. It's less like paint on a canvas and more like a song caught mid-verse. Something so hauntingly beautiful, it's hard to look away.

It's stunning. Moving, even. The kind of painting that makes you believe in something *more*, even if you never thought your-self capable of faith.

I'll write up some notes for Joshua on Monday, but his final grade is already set. This piece is, without question, an A.

———————

EIGHT MILES into the run and I feel like I've just started out. My endorphins kicked in right away—the energy of the crowd marching from the college was electric. For the first thirty minutes, I ran along the parade route, and while I've left them far behind by now, I got enough "lookin' great" and "you go, girl" comments from the drag queens to put me on cloud nine.

Add in the view of the lake on this beautiful, clear day, and I'm practically floating through the miles.

Pulling a fuel packet from my tiny hip pouch, I tear it open with my teeth and choke down the vaguely chocolate pudding-flavored energy gel. Trying to run while shoving the crumpled foil into my pack is awkward as all get out, but I manage to tuck it away as I turn off the trail and onto the road that leads back to town.

This is the perfect training loop. Traffic is almost non-exis-tent, there are plenty of trees for shade, and a convenience store at mile twelve has clean bathrooms. One of the other teachers told me about this trail a couple of months ago, and I've been in love ever since.

A quarter mile ahead, a white cargo van is parked across all three spaces in a little pullout area by the side of the road. Instinctively, I move further onto the opposite shoulder and my hand brushes over the pepper spray clipped to my running belt.

The van's engine rumbles to life. The driver flashes me a peace sign, and I reply in kind—rules of the road no matter how you're getting from one point to another.

But as I pass, he leans out the window with something in his hand. Two little wires fly toward me, and twin jolts of pure, unadulterated agony spread out from my stomach.

My vision goes white. Black spots burst amid the blinding *nothingness.*

Every muscle seizes at once. Do I scream? I should scream. But...I...can't hear anything over my pounding heart.

My head slams into the dirt. Rocks scrape against my bare arms.

Confusion gives way to terror, but no matter how hard I try, I can't move. Or fight. Only panic as I struggle to breathe.

Nothing makes sense. Not the deep voices on either side of me. Not the pressure around my arms and legs. Not the loss of the sun's warmth on my skin.

I hit another hard surface, but there are no rocks this time. Only the vague scents of sweat and motor oil.

Someone grabs my ponytail and forces my head back.

"Drink!"

The rough command sends an icy chill through me. Liquid flows over my lips. Water? No. It's...bitter.

I try to spit it out, but thick fingers pinch my nose. I don't want to do this. But...I'm running out of air. Wheezing, I choke down a large gulp of the liquid, only to be forced to do it again and again.

The dark spots start to fade. Fuzzy shapes coalesce into people. Dark gray walls and black canvas upholstery. I'm *inside* the van. Pushed into a bucket seat. A plastic zip tie binds my hands together.

I try to lift my arms, but they're so very heavy. Why are they so heavy?

"Dump her phone in the ditch, Brother Malone," the man in front of me growls. His face is vaguely familiar. Where do I know him from?

After a sharp, metallic sound, my left wrist starts to burn.

Blood wells across the spot where my GPS watch used to be.

"Wha...?" My lips are going numb. My fingers. My toes. My entire body is floating away.

Do something...

The thought pings around in my head, but it's a whisper, when I *know* it should be a scream. Why don't I scream?

The man forces the last of the water down my throat. I should fight him. Do something. *Anything.*

"Prophet, I've destroyed the watch and tossed her phone," another man says from the passenger seat. "I'll burn the rest later. We should go. Now."

The one in front of me—Prophet?—kneels and pins my ankles together. Someone else slips a plastic tie around them. The sound of it tightening should terrify me, but the world has gone soft. A gentle haze covers the inside of the van. My thoughts are hazy too.

The two men lift me out of the bucket seat and lay me down on the floor. The vibration of the engine rumbles against my back. I can't squirm. My body won't listen to me. The older man covers me with a blanket from my head to my toes. As the light fades, I moan.

"AJ..."

CHAPTER FOUR

AJ

"YOU STARE at that phone any harder, your eyeballs are gonna pop right out of your head. Just call her for fuck's sake. It's worth interrupting her run to tell her the news." Jasper drains the last of his coffee with a grimace. "Unless you don't think she'll be happy your promotion came through, *Captain Stone.* Or maybe you're too chickenshit to tell her Harris wants us out there again tonight."

My brother's lucky we have witnesses or I'd be tempted to punch him.

"She knows we're workin' tonight. And I ain't scared, asshole. We made up this mornin'." I don't tell Jasper I've already snuck off to the break room to call Grace three times this afternoon, but she hasn't picked up. "She's probably asleep on the couch with Belle stretched across her legs. We've got a couple of hours before we head out. I'm gonna run home by way of Whataburger. Grace always craves fries after a long run. Cover for me if Harris gets his britches in a bunch."

"Be back by eight and I won't have to," Jasper says as he

ambles off to the break room for yet another cup of what passes for coffee around here.

I stifle my yawn as I slide behind the wheel of my SUV. The two hours I caught in one of the bunks this afternoon wasn't near enough. A large Dr. Pepper *might* keep me awake until McGrath and I park outside that goddamn strip mall for the second night in a row.

Any other day, my promotion would have gotten me out of this shit assignment. But Jasper just *had* to get pissy in his report this morning. The man has no sense of self-preservation. Or he don't give a crap about his career. Or both.

I shouldn't have to suffer because of his attitude, but Harris likes to punish us both equally. I'd tell him we're twins, not the same goddamn person, but that'd just put me on his shit list permanently.

I'm next in line at the drive-up window when my phone rings. I don't bother checking the screen. Probably McGrath asking what I want him to pick up for tonight.

"AJ Stone."

"Mr. Stone? This is Misty with Bark Away Day Care. We close in fifteen minutes and no one's come to pick up Belle yet. Mrs. Stone said she'd be back for her by five-thirty, and it's nearly seven. We've left several messages, but she hasn't returned our calls. I just need to confirm that one of you is on the way."

The hairs on the back of my neck stand on end. There's no fucking way Grace would forget to pick up Belle from doggie daycare. Something is *very* wrong.

"I have to call you back." I hang up and open the runner tracking app Grace uses to share her location. The little blue dot on the map punches me in the gut so hard, I can't breathe.

She hasn't moved since 2:37 p.m.

Flipping on the lights and siren, I lay on the horn until the car in front of me gets the hell out of the way. "VoiceAssist, call Jasper."

"Grace tell you to stick those fries where the sun don't shine?" he drawls.

"She never picked up Belle, Jas. Her phone's still out by the lake. It's *been* there for almost five fucking hours. Issue a BOLO and meet me at the end of Pendernales Road, ASAP."

"Fuckin' A. I'm already out the door," he says.

"Wait!" I call before he can hang up. "Get McGrath to pick up Belle from Bark Away Day Care and bring her to the station. Our security code is 8751. They close in fifteen."

"On it."

The twenty-five minutes it takes me to reach Grace's last known location might as well be an eternity. Why didn't I check the GPS earlier?

Because Grace is always careful.

And she always has Belle with her.

But not today.

If I hadn't been so distracted—and exhausted—by that goddamn stakeout, I might have remembered that the dog stepped on a wasp and couldn't run. I would have checked her location every hour on the hour. Hell, I would have kept the app open the entire fucking day.

"Please be okay, darlin'. Please..."

Even as I say the words, I know she's not. She can't be. Her phone's still on. If she were injured, she would have called someone.

Please, Grace. Please be...alive.

THE WILLOW TREES swaying in the breeze cast long, ghostly shadows across the asphalt as the sun sets behind them. This street dead ends at the Butler Trail, the group of three parking spaces full up. I jump out of the SUV, the engine running and lights still flashing. My boots crunch over the dry grass at the side of the road.

Her phone should be *right* here.

A few more steps, and I can make out a siren in the distance. Jasper. Thank fuck. I can't do this alone.

A narrow ditch on the other side of the crumbling parking lot is overgrown with weeds and wildflowers, but something neon orange flashes amid the multi-colored petals.

Grace's water bottle. Nothing else in this world is that ungodly bright. My heart stutters, then pounds so hard, I feel it in my temples.

I drop to my hands and knees. The bottle is warm, no longer sweating from ice melting in the heat of the day. A single scuff mars one side, but it's otherwise pristine. Same with the ditch. No trampled flowers, no rocks kicked onto the pavement, no blood.

Tires squeal as Jasper slams on his brakes. "AJ! Where you at?"

"Here!" I push up enough he can see the top of my head, then crouch down again. Her phone has to be close by. I check my own screen. According to the flashing blue dot, I'm right on top of the fucking thing. "Voice Assist, Call Grace."

The ringer is faint—but close.

Running my hands over the ground, I wince as the sand spurs slice at my fingers. But when I find the device, the pain fades, and my entire world comes crashing down around me. The screen has a single crack—and a dozen missed calls and texts.

Bark Away Day Care, the college, her friend Cristina, and me.

She's gone. My Grace is gone.

The firm grip on my shoulder shocks me out of my fog. "Give me the phone, AJ."

I stare up at my brother—at the evidence bag in his hand. "No. It's...what if she calls?"

"If she calls, she's gonna call *you*, dipshit. Not her own number. Give me the goddamn phone. Water bottle too."

My brother doesn't pull out the "I could have been the older one" tone very often, but maybe that's why it's so fucking effective.

I pass him the phone and water bottle, then cringe at the sound of rustling plastic.

Jasper seals the bags, then walks the length of the ditch without leaving the asphalt. "Don't look like anyone disturbed the scene. No signs of a struggle. No blood. We need forensics out here. The whole fucking team. Canvas the area, find any security cameras with a view of this spot...a helicopter if we can get one."

He's all business, like this is an official investigation.

I land on my ass in the weeds. *Fuck.* It is.

My wife. My best friend. She's gone. Someone took her.

CHAPTER FIVE

Grace

THE VAGUE SCENT of soap surrounds me. But it's not mine. My soap smells like gardenias and jasmine. AJ's is good, old-fashioned Irish Spring. This is almost...industrial. Harsh, with a bite of lemon that burns my nose.

My lids are so heavy. I force them open, catching a quick glimpse of a wood ceiling before they close again.

Wood? Our bedroom is a light beige. Where am I? This pillow is too thin. Lumpy. Same with the mattress.

The headache splitting my skull makes it hard to think. I don't remember how I got here. I was out on a run. I left the lake behind. Then...?

I try for another peek at my surroundings. God, the light makes my head pound even harder.

"Drink!"

The memory of that harsh voice, of someone holding me down, is too much. I roll onto my side, bile crawling its way up my throat. It's only the shock of what I'm wearing that stops me from vomiting.

My running clothes are gone. I'm braless, barefoot, and clad in a white cotton dress that buttons all the way up to my neck.

Scrambling back, I kick at the sheet and blanket. I'm so dizzy, but when I bring my hands to my mouth, I realize I'm... *clean.*

Someone kidnapped me, brought me here—wherever *here* is—bathed me and dressed me. I reach between my legs and find a pair of simple cotton panties. They're dry. Nothing hurts *down there.* But the idea that I could have been raped while I was unconscious...

The nausea hits again, so strong I dry heave over the side of the bed until my stomach muscles ache and sweat dots my brow.

Collapsing back against the thin pillow, I struggle to clear the fog muddling my thoughts. There was a van. Then pain. But after that, nothing.

The room is still blurry, and I rub my eyes until tears gather at the corners. They're so dry. My throat too.

This time when I sit up, the dizziness isn't so bad. An old, beat-up desk and chair sit against the wall to my left. On the other side, two solid wood doors. One is open a crack.

You can do this, Grace. Get up and find a way out.

Feet on the floor. A hand on the rough-hewn headboard to steady myself. And I'm standing. Wobbly, but upright. Slowly, I shuffle toward the open door.

Stark white walls, a simple tile floor, a toilet, sink, and tiny shower.

For a few seconds, I stare at the faucet. If I turn it on, someone could hear. But I'm so dehydrated, I won't last much longer without water.

As I reach for the handle, the world tilts. The next thing I know, I'm on the floor, my cheek pressed to the cool, white tile. The side of my head throbs, and tears leak from my eyes. Everything hurts. Panic tightens my chest. I'm shaking.

"Move, darlin'. You can do this. Try that other door. Now."

It's not my voice I hear in my head. It's AJ's. Does he know I never made it home? He'll search for me. He'll *find* me. But I can't just lie here and wait. Whoever took me did it for a reason. I don't want to find out what it was.

Wrapping my fingers around the edge of the sink, I pull myself up, holding on until I'm mostly steady. Each step feels like a mile until I make it to the other door. But the knob only rattles when I try to turn it.

A dull thudding sound gets steadily louder. *Shit.* Someone's coming.

I stumble back until I hit the far wall. My heart pounds so hard, I can barely breathe. My legs tremble. Fear and the after-effects of whatever they gave me combine until I'm sure I'm about to collapse again.

A key rasps in the lock, and the door swings open. The man who enters is tall and solid. Dressed in a pair of black pants and a gray shirt. The collar almost looks like it belongs to a priest, but there's no telltale white boning in the center. Gray threads his black hair and full beard.

"Blessed day, Nova," he says with a small smile. His voice is familiar. It terrifies me, despite the warmth in his tone.

A vague memory fights its way free from my addled mind.

Sweat. Stifling heat. Fear. And that one word.

"Drink!"

He's the one who took me. *Fuck.* The way he's looking at me is almost...reverent, and that's the most terrifying thing of all.

"I said, 'Blessed day, Nova.'"

The warmth is gone now. His dark brown eyes narrow on me as he approaches. Backed into a corner, there's nowhere for me to go, and he captures my chin in a bruising grip.

"You will answer when I speak to you, Nova."

"You're...hurting me." My voice crackles weakly, rasping over my dry throat.

He holds fast as another man, this one younger and bigger, carries a tray into the room and sets it on the desk. Eggs. Hash browns. A glass of water. A cloth napkin. And a plastic spoon.

"Wait outside, Brother Malone," he commands.

The second man nods, his eyes downcast, and shuts the door behind him.

"We're going to try this again. 'Blessed day, Nova.'"

He shifts his hand to my throat. His fingers stay loose, but the threat is there.

"Who the hell...is Nova?"

The slap comes so quickly, my vision blurs as fire blooms over my cheek. My knees buckle and I slide to the floor.

"Members of the Blessed Flock are not allowed to swear, Nova," he snaps. "We keep ourselves pure in service of the Glorious One."

I'm hallucinating. It's the only thing that makes sense. Heat stroke. A head injury. Whatever drug they gave me.

"My name is Grace."

He hauls me up by my arm and shoves me against the wall. "Your old life was without purpose. Now, you are Nova, the bright light to banish all darkness and bring about the Glorious One's return."

"Look, asshole, I don't know who the fuck you are—"

His hand flies to my throat again, but this time, he squeezes hard enough I can barely breathe.

Desperate, I claw at his fingers, but the world is getting dimmer by the second. Until he suddenly lets go. Coughing and wheezing, I try to put some distance between us, but the room is so small, he's on me again in a heartbeat. This time, he wraps his arm around my shoulders like he's trying to *comfort* me.

"I should have introduced myself before. I am Prophet Zeke, the head of the Blessed Flock. Sit down. Eat, and I will explain everything."

This guy is out of his gourd. He's bouncing between sweet and enraged so quickly, it would leave me dizzy—if the room weren't already spinning. He guides me into the chair. My stomach rumbles loudly, but I push the plate away.

"You kidnapped me! You *drugged* me. I'm not eating this."

Zeke plucks the spoon from the desk and takes a bite of the eggs. "The rohypnol was to ensure your safety—and mine—on the journey. And to protect my wives when they bathed and dressed you."

"W-wives?" Oh, God. This is some sort of cult. "What else did you do to me?" I squeeze my legs together and wrap my arms around myself tightly. "Did you...? Did anyone...?"

"No!" he shouts, his lip curling in a look of pure disgust. "*That* is not allowed here."

The relief only lasts a moment. "But kidnapping is?"

Knowing the slap is coming doesn't make it hurt any less. I taste blood, and it turns my stomach.

He composes himself, and the small smile reappears.

"I did not kidnap you. I freed you from a life without purpose."

Oh, hell no.

"Taking someone against their will is kidnapping, asshole. And you picked the wrong woman. My husband is a Texas Ranger. He'll find me. And when he does, you and your entire *Blessed Flock* will go to jail for the rest of your lives!"

Zeke throws his head back and laughs. "We're more than seven hours from Austin, *Nova*. No one will ever find you here."

"Seven...hours?" A tear tumbles down my cheek. The food. It's...*breakfast*. Sunday breakfast.

"We're less than a hundred miles from the border. Now, please eat."

I'm starving. My stomach is hollow and my mouth feels like cotton. I don't trust the water, but I force a bite of the eggs because if I don't get something in me, I'll be useless.

Zeke sits on the edge of the bed, looking absurdly pleased with himself, like we're having some kind of demented picnic.

"When my son told me he'd found you, I admit I did not believe him at first. Joshua has a flair for the dramatic. But then he sent me the photo of your tattoo."

The spoon clatters against the plate. "Joshua? Joshua Nichols is your *son*?"

He beams. "Yes. My Joshua. He and his betrothed will be wed this evening, and he will take his place as my newest junior cleric."

The room tilts. This wasn't random. Joshua knew where I'd be running yesterday. He knew I'd be alone. Vulnerable. Icy fear and dread churn in my stomach. The whole world narrows to the pounding of my heart.

Zeke chose *me*. All because of the ink on my skin?

As surreal as it is to be having a conversation with a deranged kidnapper, I have to convince him that he made a mistake. "Millions of people have tattoos like mine. I'm not your Nova."

Zeke's expression hardens. "Open the drawer."

His tone carries a sharp edge that warns another slap will follow if I don't obey. So, I wrestle the drawer open. A heavy, leather-bound book with words burned into the cover sits in the center. "'The Doctrine of the Blessed Flock as told to Prophet Zeke by the Glorious One'?"

He has *got* to be kidding.

"Take it out and turn to page thirty-three." The *Doctrine* is heavy enough, I might be able to chuck it at him and do some damage. But if that Malone guy is waiting right outside, what good would it do me?

I'm so lost in my own scattered thoughts, I don't move. Zeke loses patience with me, snatches the book from my hands, and slams it down on the desk.

With a hoarse yelp, I shove the chair back and run for the

door. The dress tangles around my legs, and I'm too slow. Too clumsy.

Zeke catches me with an arm around my waist and drags me back to the chair. He tries to shove me down, but I spin and drive the heel of my hand into his nose. The crunch of cartilage is oddly satisfying. As is the blood dripping down his chin.

"Fuck you *and* your Blessed Flock."

He wipes the blood from his upper lip with his sleeve, his face a mask of calm, as if getting his nose broken is an everyday occurrence. "Page thirty-three, Nova. Or you will learn that actions have consequences."

"No." I won't give him the satisfaction. Even if we *are* seven hours from Austin, AJ will find me. He'd burn down the entire world before he'd let anything keep us apart. The kind of love we share—the kind we've worked so hard to keep—doesn't surrender to the whims of a madman.

Zeke grabs my shoulders, slams me down into the chair, and opens the book himself.

"Oh, my God." Lines of text cover the parchment in a bold, heavy scrawl. But it's the image in the center that terrifies me.

My tattoo. Not a vague representation, but an almost exact replica down to the way the phases of the moon curve over my shoulder and the curl of the ribbon around the stems of the delicate oleander flowers.

"Read it," Zeke snaps, his finger jabbing the first paragraph.

"Th-the Prophet will find the one who b-bears the m-mark of the Blue Moon over the most sacred of oleander flowers. Sacri—oh, God—sacrificing the Nova on a Blue Moon will honor the Glorious One. He w-will grant the Prophet and his entire flock eternal...life."

"You...you're g-going to k-kill me?"

I have to get out of this room. Surely there's someone in this *Blessed Flock* who doesn't condone murder.

"On the next blue moon, yes. In two years, eleven months,

and one day. Until then, you will be a revered member of my flock."

Killing me isn't enough? He's going to keep me prisoner for almost three years?

None of this is real. I have to be in a coma. Or dead. That's it. I'm already dead and the afterlife is some massive mind fuck that never ends. Except, my cheek still throbs where he slapped me. My mouth is so dry, I can barely swallow.

The way Zeke is looking at me...he truly believes this. All of it.

I grab his sleeves, ready to beg if I have to—even though the idea of touching him disgusts me.

"Let me go. Please. I won't tell anyone you took me. Not even my husband. I'll...make something up. I hit my head. Blacked out. Ended up across town sleeping in a bus station or something."

"No. This is your home now, Nova." Zeke shakes off my hold, then strides for the door. He pauses with his hand on the knob. "Read the book, Nova. All of it. Then you will understand there is no going back. You are the Flock's salvation."

For what feels like hours, I stare at the plate. If I don't eat, I won't have the strength to escape. But if any of the food is drugged, I could lose another day. Or more.

I dump the water in the sink, wash the glass with that awful lemony soap, and fill it directly from the tap. The first few sips are pure heaven.

Returning to the desk, I risk a bite of hash browns. They're cold, oily, and disgusting, but I don't care. If I still feel okay in a few minutes, I'll have more.

"Read the book. All of it."

Hell, no. I'm not reading the delusions of a guy who thinks killing me will give him eternal life. Instead, I pick up his precious *Doctrine* and throw it across the room.

CHAPTER SIX

AJ

THE BULLPEN'S a storm of noise—phones ringing, boots pounding the linoleum, whispered conversations, squawks from the radios, the occasional shout.

My feet ache, blisters broken open twice over from walking miles of the trail more than a dozen times in the past twenty-four hours. I brace a hand on my desk, too tired to even sit down—because I'll never get back up again, and Grace needs me out there.

Marvin's posted up near the back wall, arms folded, watching the chaos. When his gaze lands on me, he straightens and beelines for my desk.

Fuck.

"Stone," he says, his tone almost gentle. "I'm real sorry about Grace. If there's anythin' I can do..." Shaking his head, he adds, "We'll find her."

I've had it with the empty reassurances everyone's been feeding me since she vanished. We don't have a single goddamn lead. If Marvin really wanted to help, he'd be out there. Looking for her. Still, I give him a sharp nod. If I open my mouth, I'll unload every ounce of rage boiling in my chest.

If it weren't for his CI's bullshit intel, we would have been up at the cabin. And no one would have dared touch her.

"Stone!" Harris shouts, stalking toward me. "I told you to go home!"

"Go home?" I shove past Jasper and beeline for the chief. "My wife is fucking *missing*! If you think I'm goin' home, you're a goddamned idiot."

"You fixin' to fight me?" Harris asks, then shakes his head and turns his focus to Jasper. "Blade, get your brother out of here before he talks himself right into a demotion. Or a suspension. Or both. Austin PD is taking over the case."

"Like hell they are," I grit out. "Those jackoffs wouldn't know a clue if it jumped out of the ground and bit them in the ass."

"You're on thin fuckin' ice, Stone," Harris warns. "This wasn't my idea. Orders came all the way from the top."

This can't be happening. APD will shut us out before we know what hit us. Grace will be one woman in a sea of missing persons to them. But here, she's family. To me...she's *everything*.

"Chief—"

Jasper grabs my arm. "Harris ain't got a choice. And neither do you, dumbass. I'm taking you home. We've been up for almost forty-eight hours. We ain't worth spit to Grace without some sleep." He's calm as fuck, which sets me off even more.

"She's out there somewhere," I spit through clenched teeth. "She could be hurt. Or...worse."

"Aaron." Jasper tightens his grip until I meet his gaze. Fuck. It's like looking in a goddamn mirror. His hair's a little lighter, and he favors a full beard while I shave every couple of days. But we're more alike than not in every other way. Down to my haunted look reflected in his eyes.

He's followed every lead right along with me. Called in

favors at APD, even the FBI. I know he's right. But how can I sleep when I don't know if Grace is even still alive?

"I'm goin' back to the trail. We missed something."

I pull my phone off the charger and check it for the thousandth time. No messages from Grace. And worse...no ransom call.

"The only place you're goin' is home," Jas says. "Hand over your keys. I'll drive you and bunk at your place tonight."

"I don't need a babysitter."

"Oh no?" His brows shoot up. "You're holdin' that phone upside down."

Fuck.

I'm worse off than I thought. Suddenly, I can't string two words together without feeling like I'm clawing my way through quicksand. My shoulders slump as I follow Jasper out to my SUV. One of Grace's sweaters is still in the passenger seat, and I clutch it so tightly, the fibers stretch almost to their breaking point. She's gonna tear me a new one if I ruin it. I'm half tempted to rip it to shreds so she'll come back and do just that.

Instead, I hold it to my nose and inhale deeply.

Jasmine and gardenia. She's worn the same perfume for our entire relationship. It's my favorite scent in the world. What if I never smell it on her again?

"AJ, we're gonna find her." The strain in Jasper's voice isn't reassuring. I'm usually the one who talks to victims and witnesses when we work a case together. My brother ain't a people person.

"She's been missing for thirty-one hours." The lump in my throat threatens to choke me. "We don't know if she's even still in the country. Whoever took her ain't interested in ransom. They would've called me already. Released their demands to the media. Something." My tears spill over. "What if she's already dead?"

"She's not. You'd know. You'd feel it," he says.

Would I? We've been together so long, we can finish each other's sentences. But soulmates? Neither of us ever put much stock in the concept.

I close my eyes, picturing her and Belle as they lounged in bed Saturday morning. The soft smile curving her lips. The light in her eyes.

Did I tell her I loved her before I left?

Fuck.

I didn't.

Please, God. If you're up there, bring her back to me. Give me a chance to be a better husband. To tell her—to show her—that I love her. Every damn day.

I haven't prayed in over a decade, but now it's all I can do. That...and hope somewhere out there, she's doing the same.

THE REST of the drive passes in a blur. Light spills from the front windows of the house, and it takes me a full minute to remember that McGrath kept Belle overnight, handing her off to one of his State Trooper friends early this morning. The woman brought the dog back here so she'd be somewhere familiar.

As soon as I step over the threshold, Belle bounds through the house, her nails scratching noisily across the tile. She skids to a stop and whines once she sees Grace isn't with me.

"Dammit. I only got her away from the door ten minutes ago." A petite, blond woman dressed in a pair of jeans and a loose red tank top comes in from the kitchen, a dish towel slung over her shoulder, and holds out her hand. "Captain Stone? Lieutenant Blade? I'm Parker Elmore."

"Jasper. And that's AJ," Jas says as he shakes her hand.

"You're doin' us a favor, Parker. Not reporting for duty. Did Belle give you any trouble?"

"She's a good puppy." Parker drops to one knee and scratches the dog behind the ears. "But she sat by the front door all day. I tried a tennis ball, her rope toy, even treats. At least she finished all her dinner. If you two are hungry, there's a tray of enchiladas on the stove that should still be warm."

"You...cooked?" I run a hand through my hair. Fuck. I need a shower. I can't remember the last time I ate. Yesterday?

Parker shrugs. "Didn't think you'd be up for it, and I rarely have the time. My mama was a chef in El Paso for twenty years. I've got all her secret recipes. You need me back here in the morning?"

I can't think that far ahead. Fucking hell, I can't think at all. Somewhere in the background, I hear Jasper telling her to show up at ten.

Bypassing the stove, I move to the wet bar and dig out the bottle of Pappy's I was savin' for when I made captain. I stare at it for a full minute before I shake my head and pour myself a glass of Maker's Mark instead. Grace and I were supposed to open the Pappy's together.

"Nope." Jasper eases the glass from my grip. "You ain't touching a drop until you eat something."

"Fuck you." I don't have the energy to throw any malice behind my words. Plus, deep down, I know he's right. The bourbon would go straight to my head. I *want* it to. I *need* it to. Otherwise I'll be staring at the ceiling all night thinking about the horrible things Grace could be going through.

"Sit down. I'll get the food. Eat two enchiladas and I'll give this back to you."

When he returns with the plate, I grunt my thanks. Parker's a damn good cook, and the food clears my head a fraction.

Jasper and I sit in silence until I can't keep my eyes open another second. He knows where the guest room is.

I make it as far as the bedroom before stopping cold. Our bed still smells like her, still holds the shape of her body. I can't. Not tonight.

So I grab a pillow and blanket, dragging them into Grace's studio. At least here I'm surrounded by her—her colors, her brushstrokes, the way she sees beauty where the rest of the world sees only broken things.

I stretch out on the couch and press my hand hard over my mouth. The sobs come anyway, raw and ugly.

Belle pads over and rests her head on my thigh. Her big blue eyes are wrecked with the same question burning me alive.

Where is she?

I curl an arm around the dog's neck, bury my face in her fur, and press a kiss to her head.

"We'll find her, girl." My voice cracks, hoarse from calling Grace's name for hours while walking the trail. "On my life, we'll find her."

CHAPTER SEVEN

Grace

CURLED into a ball under the thin blanket, I sob until my eyes are so swollen, the small room blurs into nothing but shapes and shadows. The sound of my ragged breathing is the only break in the silence, yet it's too loud. Too fragile.

After Zeke left, I examined every single inch of the room. The walls, the corners, the baseboards...even under the small sink and behind the toilet. No cameras—unless they're *really* well hidden. Nothing I can use as a weapon except the heavy desk chair. But my arms tremble so much I doubt I could even lift it, let alone swing it.

The eggs and hash browns are gone, stretched into tiny bites over what felt like hours, maybe an entire day. I don't think they were drugged. Though I'm still so hungry that my stomach is gnawing at itself. Hunger is the worst kind of enemy, I think—it eats your strength, your fight, every second.

Zeke's *Doctrine* lies open at the foot of the bed, his arrogant scrawl mocking me. If I close my eyes, I might sleep. But what if I don't hear the door when it opens, or the footsteps when they come for me? What if I lose my only chance at escape because I let myself rest?

So I read page after page, until, hours later, I'm crying again.

If I weren't locked in this tiny room waiting for him to murder me in some ritual sacrifice, I'd laugh at the damn thing. The Glorious One is some twisted cocktail of God, Zeus, and Q from *Star Trek*—a cosmic tyrant who supposedly speaks only to the *Prophet*. And Zeke is a delusional megalomaniac with daddy issues, so drunk on his own power, he thinks the sun rises and sets by him.

From the list of the cult members I found in the very back of the book, over four hundred men, women, and children have bound themselves to him. Some by choice, but most—I'd bet—by fear. While a lot of them live on this compound, more than a hundred are spread out all over Austin, Dallas, and El Paso.

With that many members across the state, even if I can escape, will I ever be safe again?

My entire body jerks. *Shit*. I fell asleep. But for how long? What I wouldn't give for a window. Any way to tell time.

I force myself out of bed and lug the book back to the desk. Maybe it'll be easier to stay awake in that uncomfortable chair.

The beginnings of the book are too fantastical to take seriously, so I flip through it until I find a list of more than a dozen rules the Blessed Flock has to live by.

All men over eighteen carry the title of Brother. Women earn no titles of their own until they marry, and then they become Sister.

In the presence of the Prophet, or any Brother, women are forbidden to speak unless spoken to. Their voices belong to the Flock, not themselves.

Members of the Blessed Flock must keep themselves pure. There will be no swearing, no carnal acts outside of marriage, no lying, cheating, or stealing.

"No stealing? But kidnapping is totally okay," I mutter with a little snort.

At eighteen, men are sent beyond the Flock's lands for one to three years to find a wife.

Once married, women are forbidden from ever leaving the Flock again.

A fresh tear rolls down my cheek. The women are trapped. Every one of them. Do they care? They must. Some of them must. If I can find even one...maybe we can get out of here together.

BANG.

The door flies open, and I scramble up. Or try to. I fell asleep at the desk, and everything hurts. Tripping over my own numb feet, I land on my ass against the wall.

"Blessed Day, Nova," Zeke says with one of his bland smiles.

Malone follows with a plate of eggs and country potatoes. My mouth waters before I can stop it. He sets the plate on the desk, then backs out into the hall without a word.

"He'll stand guard until I leave and lock you in again," Zeke says smoothly. "Run, and you'll be caught before you make it ten steps."

"Screw you."

His lips curl like I just spit in the holy water. "We do not swear here, Nova."

Using the wall for support, I wobble to my feet. "I'm not a member of your *flock*."

"You are now." He gestures to the open book on the desk. "Did you find my Doctrine enlightening?"

"I found it delusional as fuck."

He backhands me—what is this, the third time?—and the

taste of blood in my mouth is becoming a regular thing. But I'm not done.

"You treat your women like property. Trap them here? No formal schooling beyond what *you* teach them? Silenced unless you grant them *permission*? Do you make them wear muzzles and chastity belts too?"

His smile vanishes, voice dropping to a dangerous calm. "I will forgive your outburst this one time, Nova. You are still new here. Still learning. But consider this your final warning. If you continue to disobey, the consequences will be severe."

He snatches the plate from the desk, spins on his heel, and strides from the room. The lock *thunks* so loudly, I flinch, and two sets of footsteps retreat down the hall.

Solitary confinement is a torture technique, isn't it? The walls are nothing but plain wood, the bathroom almost pure white. There's nothing to look at. No way to distract myself other than his damn *Doctrine*.

I can't even pace. It's only six steps from one side of the room to the other. And I haven't eaten in so long. Much longer, and I won't be able to think straight. But that's what he wants, isn't it?

Zeke is so concerned with purity and swearing? I'll give him swearing.

"Hey, asshole!" I scream and pound my fists against the door. "I can't be your fucking sacrifice if you starve me to death first!"

When I don't hear any telltale footsteps approaching, I try again. And again. It's all I can do. That...and pray my husband finds me.

IT'S BEEN HOURS. I'm so hungry and weak, I can barely stay awake. I tried some sit-ups and pushups a few minutes ago, but gave up after I got so dizzy, my head hit the floor. Now, I sit on the bed with my knees drawn up and my arms wrapped around my shins like I can somehow keep myself from falling apart.

I'm so tired, I don't even fully register the soft thud of footsteps.

Three knocks. A pause. Then the lock *thunks*. This...is new. If Zeke thinks knocking is going to change my attitude, he's sorely mistaken.

"Shit!" I leap up as Joshua's bulk fills the entire doorframe.

"Blessed Day, Nova."

"Enough with this 'blessed day' crap. And don't call me Nova. You know that's not my name," I snap. "I'm Grace Sto—"

His hand clamps around my arm, his grip unbreakable as he drags me into the hall. "Prophet says you're going to the box."

"The b-box? What's the box?" I try to resist, digging my heels into the rough wood, but it earns me nothing but splinters. "Please, Joshua. Don't do this."

"It's Brother Joshua," he grits out. "And Prophet knows what's best for you."

Where is the sweet, awkward kid from my painting class? The one who blushed when I praised his technique? Who laughed nervously when I asked about Ruth, the fiancée he said he couldn't live without?

Now, all I see is a zealot.

I sweep the hall with my gaze, searching for anything—an open door, a shadow I can dart toward—but Joshua locks my wrists together in one of his big hands. He drags me down the stairs like I weigh nothing at all.

"Did you get married, Joshua? Her name was Ruth, right?" My voice shakes, but I keep pushing. I have to find the boy I knew in my class—the one buried under all this fanaticism.

He doesn't answer. Doesn't even blink.

Women are forbidden to speak unless spoken to.

"Brother Joshua," I try again, softer this time. "I know I'm not supposed to talk, but...please. Just one question? I know the rules. I'm just...scared."

He halts in the living room—so sparsely furnished, it feels like it belongs in a prison. Just two sagging couches, a fireplace, and a pile of board games stacked in the corner like an afterthought.

"What is it, Nova?"

"Did you get married?"

His eyes brighten, his whole face softening for a heartbeat. "Yes. Ruth is helping the other wives cook supper now. She loves it here."

I swallow against the bile rising in my throat. "Brother Joshua, I have a husband. We've been married for fifteen years. He's probably out of his mind looking for me. You love Ruth, don't you?"

"She's perfect," he says, almost dreamily.

"If she went missing, what would you do to get her back?"

"Anything. I'd die for her."

The flicker of humanity breaks me open. "Then please. Call the Austin field office for the Texas Rangers. Ask for AJ Stone. Tell him where I am. He'll protect you and Ruth. He'll keep you safe from your father."

Joshua's entire body goes rigid, and the brief spark of humanity fades into pure evil. He jerks me forward so violently I stumble and nearly crash into him. "You'll address him as *Prophet*. And when I tell him you tried to turn me against him, he'll double your time in the box."

"Brother Joshua—"

"You will not speak to me again!" His shout hurts every bit as much as his father's blows.

He wrenches me through another door and into the sunlight. It sears my eyes after two—or is it three?—days locked in that dimly lit room. The ground is rough, sharp pebbles slicing my bare feet with every step.

The pain is nothing compared to the terror of what could be coming next. Zeke was already willing to hit me for the smallest infraction and starve me without a second thought.

Why didn't I read more of that fucking book? Maybe then I'd know what this box is.

It's so hot, sweat slicks my skin. Whispers from all around us raise the hairs on the back of my neck.

"Nova's going into the box?"

"Good. She broke Prophet's nose. He should keep her in there for a week."

"My wife hasn't raised her voice to me once since she came out. I hated doin' that to her, but she knows her place now."

Pure panic takes over. My body goes rigid, but Joshua just tosses me over his shoulder, an arm banded around my legs.

"You don't have to do this! Take me back to my room. Please!"

He doesn't say a word. My eyes have adjusted, and I realize we're surrounded. Men. Women. Even children. Some are stern, others have a hint of pity in their gaze. But not a one moves to help me.

Joshua sets me down in front of a small, wood building backlit by the late afternoon sun. It can't be much larger than a closet, with a massive padlock dangling from a heavy metal hasp on the outside of the door. Zeke waits for us, arms folded, a king ready to dispense judgement.

"Prophet, Nova spoke without permission and tried to convince me to call the authorities."

Zeke digs into his pocket and comes up with a set of keys. "Nova knows the rules. And yet, she continues to break them. This is unacceptable. As the arbiter of justice, I sentence her to four days in the box."

The very idea that he's the arbiter of *anything* turns my panic into anger.

"Fuck you, asshole. My name is Grace Stone, you're a kidnapper, and your cult is going straight to hell."

Zeke grabs my arm with such force, my knees buckle from the pain. "Five days," he growls as Joshua yanks the door open.

The heat hits me first. A wall of it, hotter than any oven. Inside, it's blindingly white. Thick cloth is stapled to every wall, the floor, even the ceiling. No bed. No chair. Only a dented plastic jug of water and a camping toilet shoved into the corner.

It's so small. I'll go mad in there. I'll *die* in there.

"Don't. Please," I beg, my voice cracking into pieces. "I'll be good. I'll do anything. I promise."

"I told you actions had consequences," Zeke says as he shoves me inside. "After this, you will never fight me again."

The door shuts with a bang.

I hurl myself at the wood. Kick. Punch. Slam my shoulder into it until fire shoots down my arm. It doesn't budge.

Sweat stings my eyes. A bead of it crawls down my spine. The air is heavy, thick, and suffocating. I'll roast alive in here.

Then it starts. A low hum. Subtle at first, then swelling until the walls themselves vibrate. My teeth buzz in my jaw. My ribs ache. It feels like the sound is *inside* me, trying to claw its way out.

I scream obscenities—at Zeke, at Joshua, at every last twisted member of the Blessed Flock—until my throat is shredded raw.

No one answers.

No one cares.

No one comes.

I DON'T KNOW if it's been hours or days. Time is an endless circle, twisting and turning until I can't remember anything but *this*.

The heat scorches me alive until I'm gasping, clawing at my own throat, desperate for air. Then the cold seeps in, turning my sweat to ice, leaving me shivering so hard my teeth ache. There's no in-between. No relief.

The constant, white glare burns through my eyelids no matter how tightly I squeeze them shut. I try covering my face with my hands, curling in the corner, but it finds me there too.

And the sound. God, the sound. It's vibrating my very soul, crawling inside my chest and throwing my heart off its rhythm. Sometimes it fades, only to be replaced by Zeke's voice. He reads from his fucking book, and his tone is so calm, so tender, so comforting, I find myself *wanting* to listen.

Nova. My Nova. Your sacrifice will save us all. You are the chosen. Surrender, and the pain will end. You will know only peace. Only love. Only your divine purpose.

The first few times I heard his voice, I cursed him. Spat venom through a dry, cracked throat. Now? I don't have the strength. My tongue sticks to the roof of my mouth. My lips split when I try to speak.

The jug of water is almost empty. I tried to ration it, but I must have failed. I don't remember. My stomach twists, hollow and aching, but hunger is nothing compared to this endless thirst.

I think about AJ. Belle. My friends. My students. The sound blurs the memories until there's nothing but pain and despair and endless fear.

"AJ. I love you. Please...find me."

"WHAT IS YOUR NAME?" The words filter through the fog in my head. I roll onto my back and blink my dry, bleary eyes. Is that...Zeke? Or another cruel trick of the lights and the heat and the inescapable sound?

"Your name!"

"Nova," I whisper. I know that's not right, but I'm so tired, so weak, it's the only answer I have.

Zeke snaps his fingers, and another man appears at his side. "Bring her back to her room. She has learned her lesson."

GIVING up my name shattered my soul. But in return, I got a shower, a plate of food I barely tasted before it was gone, and sleep. The trade wasn't close to fair. If only I'd had a choice.

Even after a night plagued by terrifying dreams, my ears still ring. My body aches, and I can't muster the strength to sit up—let alone get out of bed—when Zeke comes in with my breakfast.

"Blessed Day, Nova."

"Blessed Day, Prophet," I whisper. The words taste like ash and despair.

"I trust your time in the box has brought you clarity."

"Yes, Prophet."

With every little submission—calling him Prophet or following one of his *rules*—I break a little more.

"Good." He sits on the edge of the bed, but doesn't touch me. Thank God. I don't believe for a minute that rape is forbidden here. It's a cult for fuck's sake. His doctrine says he's allowed four wives. How long until he tries to make me one of them?

"We are a family here, Nova. Families eat together. They pray together. And they work together. You will spend the next two days resting. After that, you will be allowed to take breakfast and dinner with the flock. Brother Malone or Brother Vincent will retrieve you from your room, bring you to the dining hall, and return you here when the meal is done.

"You will spend the rest of your time learning the Doctrine. In one week, I will test your knowledge. If you pass, you will be assigned to the greenhouse with my wives. There is much planting to be done before winter."

My breath hitches. *Other people.* Even if it's just meals. Even if it's only work. The chance to look another woman in the eyes —to whisper one word, to find one ally—it's more freedom than I thought I'd ever have again.

Zeke frowns, his expression cooling in an instant. "If you violate a single rule, Nova, you go back to the box. Do you understand?"

Tears swim in my eyes. He knows I'm not totally broken. Not fully *his*. I have to be more careful.

"Yes, Prophet."

Once he leaves, I curl into a ball and pull the blanket over my head. "My name is Grace Stone. Zeke Nichols will *not* destroy me."

The words sound so hollow. I don't know how to make myself believe them. I've watched enough true crime shows to know my fate. Before long, I'll shatter completely.

Cults don't break people overnight. They grind them down. Strip away every scrap of identity until there's nothing but obedience.

Zeke has another two years, ten months, and...I can't even be sure how many days. Not anymore.

If I survive—if *Grace* survives—until Zeke kills me, it'll be a miracle.

CHAPTER EIGHT

Six Months Later

AJ

BELLE JUMPS UP, her tail wagging for all of five seconds before she realizes I'm alone. Then it's like someone let all the air out of her sails. She sniffs me, whines once, and parks her ass back down, staring at the door.

She doesn't understand why her best friend abandoned her.

A single scratch behind her ears is all I can manage. She's Grace's dog through and through. From the moment we met her at the rescue, Belle knew she'd found her person. She was Grace's shadow, her protector, and her security blanket for six months. Hell, the last photo I took of my wife was with Belle out on the back deck at sunset.

It's my phone's lock screen. In a frame on my desk at work. And that moment—that one perfect moment when Belle put her paws on Grace's shoulder and licked her ear—haunts me. Because I keep trying to picture Grace laughing like she did that day, but I can't. Whenever I close my eyes, all I see is my wife alone, broken, and in pain.

I kick off my boots and trudge into the bedroom. It's the only room that still smells like Grace. Every Saturday, I walk ten miles of the Butler Trail around where she disappeared, and when I get home, I shower with her soap and add a single spray of her perfume to her pillow.

For six months, my sanity has been tethered to that fucking pillow.

Stripping off my jeans, tie, and dress shirt, I sink down onto the bed and drop my head into my hands, fingers digging into my scalp as if I can pull the pain out of me.

Austin PD suspended their investigation into her disappearance today.

My wife is officially a "cold case."

If it weren't for Jasper, I'd probably be in jail right now. Having to stand next to those APD assholes as they announced there'd been no new leads since early summer did me in. I was about to lose my shit when my brother clamped a hand down on my shoulder.

"AJ...don't."

I wanted to punch every cop at that fucking news conference. Every cop who worked the case and failed to find even a single goddamned lead.

But most of all, I wanted to wrap my hands around Lieutenant Davy's neck and squeeze the life out of him for saying that whoever took Grace was clearly "a professional"—the universal code for "human trafficker."

My beautiful, smart, talented wife is probably some demented asshole's personal sex slave—if she's even still alive.

Belle's cold nose swipes along my neck. Hoarse, gut-wrenching sobs catch in my throat. I slide to the floor, wrapping my arms around the dog and letting six fucking months of pain cut me so deep, sixty pounds of fur and sadness is all that's holding me together.

————————————

JASPER CALLS me three times before I pick myself up off the floor and dump food into Belle's bowl. I should make myself dinner—something besides a frozen burrito and tater tots—but I only enjoyed cooking when Grace was here to eat with me.

Still, if I aim to keep walking the trail week after week, I'm gonna need to start eating more. I had to punch a fresh notch in my belt this morning—the second since she disappeared.

While the burrito and tots heat up, I head for my home office. APD froze me out of the case after only three days, so I took matters into my own hands.

The bulletin board takes up half the wall. Grace's photo is tacked dead center, and every lead I uncover goes on an index card, scrap of paper, or torn napkin—whatever I have nearby. And there are dozens of them. All cataloged by time, location, potential suspect.

Three separate security cameras caught images of Grace in the hour before her GPS signal stopped moving. Five other runners remember seeing her that day, but I haven't found a single fucking person who was on the trail between two and three p.m.

That lake is one of the most popular recreation areas in Austin. How was she out there all alone on a sunny day in April?

Grace's last email is tacked in the upper left corner of the board. One of her students asked if he could turn in his final art project early.

Joshua,

Looks like I'll be in town after all this weekend. If you can meet me at my classroom at noon on Saturday, I'll be happy to grade your painting for you.

-Professor Stone

APD couldn't interview the kid for almost two weeks. He'd been on his honeymoon. But half a dozen of his friends and one of the local bar owners alibied him. Apparently he'd gone right from the community college to his bachelor party.

The wind starts to howl, and fat raindrops pelt the windows. With a low hum, the heater kicks on, and I wonder if Grace is somewhere warm.

She could be cold. Wet. In pain.

Or dead.

"I'll find you, Grace. If it's the last thing I do, I'll bring you home."

Belle starts to bark, and a few seconds later, the doorbell rings.

I race to the foyer, half-convinced Grace heard me and is waiting outside. But it's only my brother. The dog lets out a loud sigh, then stares up at Jasper like it's *his* fault she's so damn disappointed.

"What do you want?" I ask, too weary to force any strength into my tone. "I'm busy."

"You gonna invite me in? It's rainin' hard enough to strangle a toad out here."

"Not if you're fixin' to give me a lecture. I'm walking the trail tomorrow. End of discussion."

"For fuck's sake, AJ. What do you expect to find out there? The assholes who took Grace ain't gonna drive right by you with a 'Want to get kidnapped? We can help!' decal on their window."

"Last I checked, you weren't my goddamn keeper. My Saturdays are my own. If I want to walk the trail, I'm walkin' the trail. It's no skin off your nose what I do with my time. You ain't gone with me in six weeks, and I sure as shit don't expect you to start up again now."

Jasper stiffens, his blue eyes taking on the same frustration I feel deep in my soul. "I stopped going because I can't stand seein' what it does to you."

"I don't matter here, Jas. Grace does. If she were here—if I were the one missing—she'd be out there every fucking day looking for me."

"And so would I," he says, his shoulders slumping in defeat. "You're so deep in your own head, you can't see I'm on your side."

The smoke alarm blares. *Fuck.* The tots.

I race into the kitchen, grab a pot holder, and yank the tray from the oven. The tots are petrified bits of ash, and the burrito exploded in a mess of burnt and blackened cheese.

"Pizza will be here in forty-five minutes," Jas says from behind me and tucks his phone back into his pocket. "You got any beer?"

"No."

He opens the fridge and snorts. "You always were a terrible liar."

I give him the side eye. "I'm a damn good liar as long as I ain't talking to someone I've known since conception."

Twisting the tops off two bottles of Shiner, he chuckles, then hands me one. "Harris is losin' patience with you, AJ. You're dangerously close to getting shitcanned. How many days have you called in sick this month?"

With a shrug, I take a long pull of my beer. If he's asking the question, he already knows the answer.

"Nine," Jasper says. "Billings, Schaffer, Urbanski, and I are all workin' overtime to cover for you—unpaid, by the way—but Harris ain't gonna let this go on for much longer."

"*This?* You mean my wife in the hands of some fucking trafficker? Being tortured as someone's sex slave? Or her body rotting in some unmarked grave?" I get right in Jasper's face, but we're the same height, and after the past few months, he's got an extra twenty pounds on me. "If Harris would like to put a stop to it, I'd be much obliged."

"Dammit, AJ. Those Austin PD jackoffs should never have closed the case. Hell, they shouldn't have opened it to begin with. It should have been *ours*." Jasper scrubs his hands over his face, then sighs. "Billings has friends there who'll keep investigating on the down low. No one's givin' up on Grace. But you gotta come back to work. It's been six months—"

I grab the bottle out of his hand and heave it at the sink. It lands with a solid *thunk*. "Get out."

"AJ—"

"No. You just told me to *move on*, asshole. Fuck you!"

Belle bounds into the kitchen with a quiet growl. Leaning against my legs, she stares at Jasper like he's her mortal enemy.

My brother doesn't move for what feels like forever. I should care that I put that hurt in his eyes.

I don't.

When he finally shuffles out of the kitchen, I follow him all the way to the door, just so I can slam it in his face as he turns to say goodbye.

Belle circles the bed in the foyer three times, then plops down with a heavy sigh. She'll stay there until I turn in. Always waiting. Always hoping. Despite taking my side earlier, her big, blue-eyed gaze doesn't pull any punches. She blames me.

She ain't the only one.

Grace's dad hasn't spoken to me in months. Not since he found out it was that goddamn stakeout that put her on the trail in the first place.

The house is too silent. Too still. The weight of it crushes me. Grace's laughter used to be a constant melody. Now only ghostly whispers linger in the dusty corners.

I should smell enchiladas, tamales, or grilled cheese and tomato soup. Instead, it's nothing but stale air and burnt tots.

Reaching under my shirt, I curl my fingers around her wedding ring. She never wore it running, and I found it in her jewelry box two days after she disappeared. I've worn it on a chain ever since.

Her favorite mug sits on the counter, waiting for her. The only coffee I drink at home now is Cafe Vienna. But it tastes like shit when she's not here to share it with me.

How much longer can I do this? Keep pretending that one day, she'll come home.

My legs give out and I'm on my ass on the floor, the back of my head slamming into the cabinet for good measure. A raw, guttural scream escapes, and my eyes start to burn.

The neighbors are too far away to hear—I think. But I wouldn't care even if they did.

I'm broken. Without Grace, there's nothing left of me to fix.

"Please come back to me," I beg the universe. Or God. Or maybe Grace.

But only silence answers, and it's louder than any words.

CHAPTER NINE

Grace

THE INKY BLACKNESS of a moonless night stretches for miles beyond the small window over the desk.

Sometimes, I watch the stars or the rain long enough, I can almost convince myself AJ is seeing the same sky. That he's caught in the same storm.

Other times, the darkness swallows me whole.

After months of *pious devotion*—Zeke's term for complete and total acceptance of my fate—he moved me into this slightly larger room where I can see the sky.

His bedroom is down the hall, with my former cell in the middle—a reminder that he can take away what little I have in an instant. His four wives and nine children have their own house next door. Each night, he brings a different wife into his bed. None of them complain. Some even look eager. But I can't be sure if that's devotion or survival.

I'm rarely allowed to speak to them. Even in the green-houses, where we tend to herbs and vegetables, or endless rows of oleander bushes, their blooms so sickly sweet, the scent is permanently etched on my skin, the men stand watch.

The only time I talk to anyone is in the dining hall. The women and children all eat together, but most of them talk *about* me, not *to* me. I don't say much more than, "Blessed day," or "Please pass the potatoes."

Zeke tests me on the Doctrine every week. If I answer correctly, I'm rewarded. A second pillow. A heavier blanket for winter. But never any semblance of freedom. I'm watched, always. And at the end of the day, Zeke or Malone lock me back in this room.

I press my ear to the door, holding my breath. Silence. No footsteps, no murmurs. Nothing but the thrum of my own pulse and the faint whistle of the winter wind threading through the boards.

Though I don't have any way to tell time, it's been hours since Zeke bade me a blessed night.

Turning on the lamp would be too dangerous, so I feel my way back to the bed. Weeks ago, while scattering feed for the chickens, I spotted two thin scraps of wire. I pocketed them like contraband, tucked them under my mattress, and prayed no one would search my room.

AJ taught me how to pick locks one weekend when a winter storm left us snowed in. It was a fun diversion. I never thought the knowledge might save my life.

The mere thought of my husband makes my chest ache. Is he still looking for me? Or has he given up?

For a while, I tried to keep track of the days, but now...I only count the moons. Eight times, Zeke has gathered everyone around the altar in the center of the compound, forced a crown of oleander blooms onto my head, and made me lie on the hard stone—no matter what the weather—so he could rehearse my death.

The box was hell, but at least it's over. This...this is a

promise of what's to come. Only at the end, he won't stop the knife an inch away from my skin. He'll drive it deep into my side so my blood "purifies them all."

"Stop it, Nova."

My legs give out, and I collapse onto the thin mattress. Silent tears tumble down my cheeks. Despite Zeke's constant repetition of Nova, Nova, Nova, my inner voice has never forgotten who I am. Until now.

I dig my fingers into my thighs hard enough to leave bruises. "No. I'm Grace. Grace Stone. I have a husband, a father, a dog, and friends back in Austin. A job I love. A whole *life*."

I'm not Nova. I'm not a *sacrifice*. I'm a person.

Swiping at my eyes, I realize how wrong I am.

I *was* a person. Now, unless I can run more than twenty miles before dawn, I'm nothing.

The day Zeke took me, I was planning on eighteen. But that was after months of marathon training. I haven't run a step since. I've lost so much weight. The meals here are small. Bland. Some days, I can barely force them down.

But every night, I pace the room for hours, do sit-ups until I want to vomit, and go through a series of post-running stretches to keep myself in shape.

I'll need a miracle to make it off the flock's lands. But I have to try.

First step? Get out of this room.

I've picked the lock every night for the past week. I can do it no matter how hard I'm crying. Or how dark it is on the new moon.

Interior door locks have six pins. Six steps closer to freedom. Or...the start of it.

The first is easy. Two and three are more difficult. Four, five, and six click into place, and the door opens a crack. The brief moment of joy is shattered by a loud creak from the hinges.

Shit.

Zeke is going to come running down the hall any second. I should shut the door and get in bed. But this cold, moonless night is my best chance. So I count to sixty.

The house is still utterly silent.

I skip the third and eighth stairs—the ones with loose boards—and slip out into the frigid night. I'd give anything for my running shoes. Or my sports bra. But all I have is a simple, white cotton dress, a light gray sweater, and hand-me-down work boots with thin socks. I'll be lucky if I don't freeze to death before I make it past the first hill.

I press myself to the back wall of the house and try to quiet my breathing. When my heart stops pounding, I peer around the corner.

Four lookout towers topped with tiny shacks surround the main part of the compound. Zeke is so paranoid about security, they're manned twenty-four hours a day. But with the biting cold, the sentries will—hopefully—be huddled in front of the space heaters inside. If any of them see me, I'm done for. Zeke will send me back to the box, and I doubt there will be anything of *Grace* left when I come out again.

I'm almost to the edge of the cluster of houses when voices drift over the air.

Shit.

Zeke has a strict curfew for his flock. The morning bells go off at six a.m. Everyone works. From feeding the cows and chickens to planting and picking crops in the greenhouses, cooking, cleaning...even the children have assigned chores. So by eight p.m., no one but the sentries are supposed to be outside their homes.

Ducking behind a small shed, I hold my breath.

"Prophet wants this next shipment ready to go by the end of the week," Malone says.

"He wants a lot of things. That don't mean they're possible," the other man grumbles. "We're short thirty-two firin' pins, eighteen slide rails, and a hundred trigger assemblies. Unless tomorrow's delivery truck has some new 3D printers on it, we're buzzard bait."

Malone mutters something under his breath, then asks, "You got enough people to run overnight til Friday?"

"Not unless Prophet lets another three brothers in on the flock's side business. I'm gonna light a fire under the night shift, but that'll only get us so far."

"I'll talk to him, Brother Nolan. Brother Joshua can be trusted. Brother George as well. I'll need to make sure Sister Johanna doesn't say a word to the other wives, but I can help out starting tomorrow."

The men move out of earshot. Holy shit. Firing pins and trigger assemblies? The flock is manufacturing *guns*? Here? Why?

Some Waco-type standoff? Zeke is certainly paranoid enough. No. Malone said they were shipping them somewhere.

For months, I've wondered how Zeke affords this place. Sure, the couple hundred people here all work the land. The women sew and mend clothing. Solar panels cover every roof top. But farm equipment breaks down. Plumbing fails. Storms uproot trees. No one's spinning cotton or wool for clothing. Or mining copper for wiring.

From my window, I've seen trucks coming and going from time to time, but they stop so far away, I've never gotten a good look at what's inside them.

Is this how they make their money? Guns?

Stop.

It doesn't matter what Zeke is doing or how he's doing it. If I can run far enough by morning to get off the flock's lands, I'll be free.

A BLISTER BURSTS on my heel with a quick, sharp sting. My lungs burn. I haven't run in so long, my body is failing me. The rain doesn't help. Cold needles slice at my skin, turning the prairie into a mud pit. Hours—God, it feels like hours—and I have no idea how far I've gone. Six miles? Ten? What if it's only three?

With no stars to guide me, I might not even be running in a straight line. I pick a tree in the distance, run until I reach it, then collapse against the trunk for a count of sixty before I choose another. My legs feel like they're made of lead, and my boots sink so deep into the muck, I might as well be running through quicksand.

A bolt of lightning tears a hole in the sky. Thunder follows —so loud, it rattles my teeth.

The second strike hits the tree I was keeping in my sights. For a moment, I can't see a thing. Another rumble. But this one...sounds wrong. Lower. Closer. Longer.

Not thunder. *Horses*.

Ice floods my veins. Panic squeezes my chest so tightly, I can barely breathe, and I push my legs harder.

"There she is!" a man shouts. Vincent, I think. He was on guard duty tonight. Flashlight beams sweep through the rain, slicing across the field until they blind me.

"Give it up, Nova. You can't outrun us!" Malone's rage lashes at me through the storm. He's the meanest of Zeke's clerics. The only one besides the deranged prophet who truly scares me.

I've failed.

All my planning. Every "Blessed day" and "Yes, Prophet" and "Praise to the Glorious One" I uttered as my soul fractured into pieces. The blisters on my feet and scratches on my legs from running through the fields for hours.

But it's the loss of hope that sends me to my knees.

The two men circle me several times, their horses kicking

mud in my face. When they finally stop, Vincent keeps his flashlight trained on me, while Malone dismounts with a wide smile.

"Prophet said if you wanted to run twenty miles, we should help you do it." The asshole pulls a length of rope from his saddle bag, as casual as if he were about to tie down a bale of hay. "We've been followin' you for a couple hours now. I reckon we coulda' let you go on for a little longer, but the storm's rough, and it ain't fair to the horses."

The light wavers as Vincent swings his leg over the side of Bonnie, his favorite mare. She shakes her head and paws at the wet ground, her gentle eyes on me like she knows what's about to happen won't be good.

Vincent grabs me and hauls me to my feet. I thrash, weak as I am, but he pins my arms in front of me easily.

"Get y-your f-fucking hands off m-me," I scream. I'm so cold, my teeth chatter, but fury keeps me from cowering—from giving in completely.

"Swearing, Nova? After all Prophet's given you? Tsk, tsk, tsk," Malone says. He loops the rope around my wrists, snug and merciless, then ties the other end to his saddle.

"No," I whisper, horror clawing at my throat. He wouldn't be so cruel—

The sound that tears from my lungs isn't a scream. It's the death of every prayer. Every good thing I've ever known. Every small shred of hope I've clung to these past months.

Another bolt of lightning illuminates Malone's grin a second before his fist slams into my stomach.

I collapse, fingers clawing uselessly at the muddy soil as if it can somehow protect me from what's coming.

From the pain.

The humiliation.

The box.

The men mount their horses.

I have to get up. If I don't...

With a soft *chi-chi*, Malone urges his horse forward a couple of steps. The rope pulls taut, and my shoulders beg for mercy.

"Please!" I gasp. "D-don't...d-do this!"

Malone chuckles. "I'd get a move on if I were you, Nova. Or I'll let Thunder drag you 'til your shoulders pop clean out. You'll live. But you'll wish you hadn't."

I force my legs under me. Somehow, I rise, trembling, swaying, but on my feet. The rope burns as I wrap it around my hands, a desperate attempt to hold on—to keep myself from the worst of the pain.

"You're a sadistic asshole," I scream into the wind. "And my name is Grace!"

Neither man scolds me for swearing. Not this time. And that scares me more than anything.

Hoods pulled low against the storm, they dig their heels into their horses' sides.

Malone gives me one last glance over his shoulder.

"Time to see how fast you can run, *Nova*."

<hr>

MUD CLOGS MY THROAT. Scratches at my eyes. My mouth tastes like blood and grit.

"I'm gonna count to five, Nova," Malone taunts. "One. Two..."

I stagger upright, searing pain shooting from my right knee all the way up to my hip. Blood drips from the deep welts around my wrists. Through my tears, I catch sight of the houses beyond the next rise. The faint glow of the morning sun behind us casts the compound in an eerie reddish light.

It stopped raining somewhere along the way. I don't know when. Time is gone. Stolen by a sea of endless pain. I fall. Again.

The first time, the sharp edge of a rock tore my cheek open. Another, I dislocated my knee. Vincent held me down while Malone shoved it back into place. I screamed until my throat was raw.

At least once, I blacked out. When I came to, I was on my back, being dragged across a soggy meadow of slick mud and sharp stones, my body bouncing like a rag doll. My dress is ripped to shreds. The brisk wind burns my raw skin.

"P-p-please." My teeth chatter so violently, I can barely form the words. "I n-need a m-minute."

"You'll get what you need as soon as you're standin' in front of Prophet. Until then, keep runnin'." Malone spurs Thunder to take off at a slow trot.

I never ran this fast when I was training. But the terror of being dragged—again—is enough for me to try. Even if every step brings me closer to a punishment I'm sure will make this look like a walk in the park.

My chest caves in with the crushing weight of dread. Zeke waits by the box, surrounded by all of his senior clerics. Nolan, Richie, Ollie, and Harold form a grim wall of gray–shirted muscle behind him.

Malone jerks the rope from Thunder's saddle. I collapse at Zeke's feet.

"I've been too lenient with you, Nova," Zeke says, shaking his head slowly. "You think I'm an idiot?"

"No, Prophet." I force myself to look up at him. If this is the last time I have the strength to resist, I'm going to do it with my whole heart. "I think you're a delusional, sadistic fuck."

His kick catches me in the hip, and I see stars.

"You spent five days in the box once." Zeke passes a set of keys to Nolan. "This time, it will be ten."

"I'll f-freeze to d-death, asshole. You're just p-proving my p-point. Or d-don't you care about your p-precious sacrifice any more?"

If I weren't already terrified, Zeke's laugh would chill me to my core.

"The box has heat, Nova. Just enough to keep you alive." He grips the rope still knotted around my wrists and drags me inside like a bag of trash. I barely notice the pain.

Ten days without food or sleep...I won't survive it. This...will be the end of me.

"Prophet, I have the MREs you asked for." Joshua stands in the doorway with three silver pouches clutched to his chest. His gaze lands on me and, for one fleeting second, I think he might actually feel a shred of pity.

Zeke points, and Joshua throws them into the corner. "I suggest you ration these carefully, Nova. The water too. You will not get more."

The door slams shut. The lock clicks.

I can't move, my wrists still bound, staring at the food I won't have the strength to eat. The speakers rumble to life, and I realize...I don't even have the strength left to cry.

CHAPTER TEN

Grace

GENTLE FINGERS PRESS to my neck. "Can you open your eyes, Nova?" The voice is quiet. Kind.

I force my heavy lids to move, but can't make sense of what I see. I'm back in my room. Outside the window, snow falls steadily. How did I get here? The last thing I remember is trying to open an MRE with bound, shaking hands while the deafening vibrations tore me apart.

I don't know how long it took for my body to stop feeling like mine. Hours? A day? I couldn't even work the rope free from my wrists.

The torturous sound never let up. Or...did it? Every time I tried to move more than a few inches, I passed out. Sometimes, I thought I heard Prophet whispering. Promising me the pain would end if I'd just let go. I...almost believed him.

The man leaning over me looks so much like Prophet, I whimper until I see his full head of white hair.

"Shhh." He tucks the blanket up to my chin with such gentleness, I want to cry. "You're safe for now. I won't hurt you.

Your fever was a hundred and three when my son finally let me check on you. It's down to a hundred now."

"Your...son?" The words take every ounce of strength I have. My cheek aches, but that's nothing compared to the pain in my shoulders. My legs. My wrists. My heart.

"I'm Abe," he says quietly. "Prophet Zeke is my son."

FOR THREE DAYS, Abe brings me meals and sits with me. I'm too weak to leave the bed. Too humiliated when I need his help to use the bed pan. Too broken to do anything more than stare out the window at the falling snow.

He treated the infected slice to my cheek, dressed the rope burns around my wrists, the gouges on my legs and back. He told me my knees were so damaged, I'd never run again. I sobbed like a child in his arms.

If Prophet hadn't let Abe check on me after eight days, I'd be dead now. The fever would have killed me. I think...I wish it had.

Abe sets a tray on my lap. Creamy potato soup and crusty bread. I don't move. My hands shake. They always shake now.

"You should have let me die."

Is that a tear shining on his cheek? Kindness in this place can't be trusted. I've learned that lesson a hundred times over. But God help me, I'm so starved for it.

I lost myself in that fucking box. Exhausted, injured, with mud caking my skin and fingers so numb, I could barely rip a single pouch open, I begged for death. Prayed for it.

I even started reciting parts of the Doctrine. I told myself if Prophet heard me, he'd have mercy, but I knew that was a lie.

The box broke me. I *wanted* to believe in the Glorious One. In everything Prophet wrote in his manifesto. And toward the end...I think I did.

Abe presses his ear to the door for a moment before his shoulders relax. "Brother Malone is talking to my grandson."

I stare at the soup, terrified of saying the wrong thing—of saying anything at all.

"Nova—" Abe grits his teeth hard enough I can hear them grinding together. "What's your real name?"

"Nova, Brother Abe," I say automatically.

"That's not the truth, and you know it." Leaning closer, he drops his voice to a fierce whisper. "I can't save you. I wish I could. You're Nova now, and my son will sacrifice you at the next blue moon. But you were someone else once, and I want to know who she was."

"Why, Brother Abe?" The words burn my throat.

"Because someone should remember her name when she dies."

Abe swipes at his eyes, but a few tears escape his sleeve. "And I'm not anyone's brother. When no one's around, you can call me 'Abe.'"

He holds out his hand like he wants to shake. Oh, God. He does.

"Hello. I'm Abe. And you are?"

My whole arm trembles. I try not to look at the blood-stained bandage around my wrist.

"Grace."

CHAPTER ELEVEN

Present Day

Grace

A PUFF of steam escapes with every breath. It might be mid-afternoon, but it's only the first of March, and one of the clerics said it was going to snow tonight.

I turn toward the eastern horizon—drawn more by instinct than intention—where the pale moon is just now rising. Does Prophet know that the full moon doesn't happen at midnight? That it's a different time *every month*? That today's moon probably reaches its apex long before dark?

My little bout of pettiness brings a hint of a smile to my face. The sensation is so foreign. I cling to it, try to draw it deeper inside me. When did I stop smiling? When did I stop feeling anything at all? And why?

The scar across my cheek pulls, and now I remember. All of it. The taste of mud in my mouth. The blood dripping from wrists rubbed so raw, I'll never escape the ropes they used to bind me. I've tried to forget. But it all comes back in a rush.

And the world tips sideways.

As if she senses I'm going down a deep, dark hole, Marley, a sable American Quarter Horse, bows her head over the paddock fence and nuzzles my hand with her velvety nose.

For a blink, I see another horse caked in mud. My fingers twitch, instinctively curling into her mane. One of her braids tickles my wrist. The sensation pulls me out of the memory. I stroke up and down her nose, letting her warm breath ground me.

"I'm okay, pretty girl. Want a carrot?"

She sniffs around my closed palm, her nostrils flaring. Unfurling my fingers, I lean against the fence and wait for her to pluck the treat from my hand.

"Nova! Your time's up!" Brother Malone shouts from the top of the hill.

I stifle my yelp. In my panic, the carrot slips from my fingers and tumbles to the grass.

"*Shit.*"

I realize my mistake when a heavy hand clamps down on my shoulder. "Swearing *again*, Nova? Prophet ain't gonna be pleased. It's time for you to start preparing for the ceremony."

Most days, Brother Malone is the one Prophet sends when they need me moved—from my room to the greenhouse, the classroom where I help the children smear fingerpaint on paper, or the dining hall where I sit at the end of a long table, barely eating, not speaking, only *existing*. Like a piece of furniture.

His fingers dig into the space where my neck meets my shoulder, a precise squeeze that sends white-hot pain racing down my arm. I stiffen, my breath caught in my throat, eyes lowered. Crying only makes it worse. Crying reminds me I used to be...human.

After my failed escape attempt, Prophet destroyed any illusion I'd ever be free again.

I'm almost never alone unless I'm locked in my room. During my time in the box, someone replaced the door. It's heavier now, the hinges reinforced, and the knob completely without a keyhole. Instead, two heavy latches with padlocks secure the outside.

Brother Malone leans closer, his breath damp against my ear. I don't hear his words—they're all the same anyway—as my full focus is still on the moon.

The first tear stings my eye. No. Not here. Not with *him*.

Just as it's about to slip down my cheek, a shadow moves in my periphery. Something shifts in Brother Malone. His hand falls away, the pressure gone so fast, my skin still burns with the sting of it.

"I'll walk her back to her room when she's done here, Brother Malone. Marley needs her hooves checked, and Nova keeps her calm."

Abe crosses his arms over his chest and practically *dares* Brother Malone to defy him. He never gives orders. He just... shows up. Quietly. And when he does, the air is somehow breathable again. I'm not safe—nothing and no one here could give me even the illusion of safety—but with him around, I'm almost...alive.

"Yes, Father Abe." Taking a step back, Brother Malone pins his gaze to the center of Abe's chest. "But I'm still tellin' Prophet about the swearing. She knows it's against the rules."

Of course he will. Obedience here is as valuable as gold. And Prophet will dole out another punishment with a gleeful smile. I wonder what he'll take from me? My thickest pair of socks? No. Probably my time with the children. Prophet knows it's the only thing in this place that truly brings me joy.

Brother Malone might be top cleric, but all the men respect Abe. The older veterinarian spends his days in the barn alone —whether by choice or by exile, I've never been brave enough to ask—unless someone gets hurt. Then, he's the closest thing the flock has to a doctor.

He treated my injuries after my escape attempt left me with a dangerously high fever. For three days, he sat by my bedside. Giving me fluids, cold compresses, and antibiotics. He probably saved my life.

And when I was strong enough to walk again, he brought me down to the barn to meet Marley. I didn't want to *see* a horse, let alone touch one. Not after being tied to Thunder and forced to run or be dragged more than eight miles back to the compound.

But Marley is such a gentle soul. Damaged. Broken. Like me.

Abe takes another step toward Brother Malone, his voice low, controlled, quiet. "No. You'll say nothing about Nova's swearing. Or you won't ride Thunder for a week. It's the full moon. Her *last* full moon before the end. Hand on the Doctrine, you will not punish her for this."

Last full moon before the end.

The reminder lands like a weight on my chest. Twenty-nine more days, and nothing will matter anymore. I'll be dead, and Grace will be truly gone.

Brother Malone grumbles his agreement, scowling, but not brave enough to challenge Abe. "Thunder is the only horse who doesn't try to buck me off every time. All right. You get one pass, Nova. But if it happens again..." He draws back like he's about to slap me.

I lower my gaze to his heavy work boots and nod. After a moment, his footsteps fade away.

"Is he gone?" I ask softly.

"He's gone, Grace."

I'm so broken, hearing my real name raises a lump in my throat. In a feverish moment of weakness, I shared it with Abe.

And sometimes—if he knows it's safe—he'll use it, and I remember who I used to be.

If it weren't for him, I'd have shattered completely. The days I spent in the box after my escape attempt left me utterly without hope and unwilling to risk even a hint of rebellion ever again.

I haven't let myself think about my life *before* in months. My husband's face is faded now. His voice...I can't remember what it was like to hear him say, "I love you." Or feel his arms around me. My friends, my family, my dog...they've all slipped from my grasp, dreams dissolved in the light of day. Sometimes I wonder if any of it was real, or if I just imagined it to survive this place.

Knowing I was less than two miles from escaping the flock's property was bad. Realizing Brother Malone and Brother Vincent were following me the whole time was worse. But they turned running from one of my passions to something I'll never want— or be able—to do again. I don't even run in my dreams anymore.

"I can give you ten, maybe fifteen, minutes," Abe says. "One of the cows is gonna calf soon, but there's a bit of time yet."

My heart lodges in my throat as I rest my forehead against Marley's. "You'll miss the ceremony tonight?"

"No, no, dear. I'll be back in time. It's only three." Abe approaches slowly, careful not to spook the gentle horse. "You won't be alone."

I wrap one hand around the top of the fence and ease myself down to retrieve the lost carrot. My knee pops, and the pain brings tears to my eyes.

"Abe!" I gasp. "My leg..."

He's at my side before I fall, taking my elbow and helping me limp over to a bench next to the paddock.

"Deep breath, now. The kneecap probably dislocated again. I'll get it back into place, wrap it up tight, and give you a shot of morphine."

How can the one man here who seems to care for me at all be the *father* of the sadistic fuck who stole me from my home, my husband, my life? From the sun-drenched mornings in Austin where I'd share a cup of coffee with AJ, believing my little slice of the world was basically good and safe?

Abe crouches down in front of me. Panic tightens my chest. I hear my heartbeat in my ears.

"It's okay, Grace. Let me see."

I pull the hem of the white cotton dress up as far as I dare. It's already swollen, the angle of the kneecap unnatural. My stomach flips at the sight. "I've been so careful the past few months."

"Look away now," the older man says softly. "Deep breath."

Screwing my eyes shut, I nod.

Pop. The terrible, sickening snap as the kneecap slips back into place shatters the tenuous control I've kept over my tears, and the first one traces a hot trail down my cheek.

"There we go," Abe murmurs softly. "Stay right here. I'll be back in two minutes."

"Hurry." My voice cracks on the word. "If Malone comes back and finds me still here..."

Abe rushes off and the cold wraps around me like a shroud. It's barely forty today. I rub my hands up and down my arms, the motion causing one of my sleeves to ride up. The scar around my wrist flashes in the weak sunlight, thick and pale, like wax melted over my skin.

"Time to see how fast you can run, Nova."

Abe returns seconds before the memory swallows me whole.

"This won't take long at all," he says. Before I can look up at him, he jabs the needle into my upper thigh.

"The hiss escapes from between gritted teeth. "You could have warned me."

"It would have hurt more if I had." Abe wraps my knee with an ACE bandage, then offers me his hand to help me up. The morphine is already turning the pain into a dull, hazy memory as we shuffle away from the barn.

"These ceremonies are bullshit," he says after a few awkward steps.

"What?" I stop, certain I misheard him.

He sighs, scanning the path and the barn to be sure no one's close enough to hear. "I loved my son once. I suppose a part of me still does. But he's off his fuckin' rocker."

For the first time in more than two years, a sliver of hope shines through the despair. Dangerous, aching, *real* hope. I grab Abe's arms, tears lending a shimmer to his lined face. "Can you talk to him? Or...help me? Call my husband. AJ Stone. He's a Texas Ranger. Tell him where I am. He'll protect you."

I knew Abe didn't care if I followed all of Prophet's rules, but I thought he was a believer.

His expression shutters, and he shakes his head. "That boy had me declared mentally incompetent seven years ago because he needed someone to keep his animals healthy. He won't let me anywhere near the phones or the cars. Believe me...I've tried."

The fragile sliver of hope I'd grabbed onto slices deep, then shatters into dust.

Abe starts to guide me up the gentle hill, his hand around my elbow so I don't fall.

Tears clog my throat. I don't want to die. This is my final fake ceremony before the end. In twenty-nine days, Prophet will drive a knife through my side. Someone will bury my body on the flock's land, and Grace Stone will never be heard from again.

Dying will be easy. Quick. I'll bleed out in a few minutes— or so Abe says. In my nightmares, it's only a single flash of pain.

Then vast, unending nothingness. I'm almost looking forward to it.

But disappearing forever—with no one left to remember me—terrifies me.

CHAPTER TWELVE

Grace

As we turn the corner, Prophet races out of the house, his eyes wild. "Nova! Inside. Now. Run!"

Abe tightens his hold on my elbow. "She ain't runnin' anywhere, son. Her knee gave out today. She'll walk. Slowly."

Prophet doesn't listen. He never does. Grabbing my free arm, he tries to drag me back to the house like some disobedient child.

But his father stands tall, fury flickering in his eyes. "You *brought* me here to keep the flock healthy," he says, his voice sharp enough to cut stone. "This is how I do it. Let. Go."

Prophet's face twists—rage collapsing into something I never expected to see. Fear.

A low hum rises on the wind, steady and mechanical. Wrong for this place. It's oddly familiar, but it takes me several seconds to understand what I'm hearing.

Oh, my God.

Cars.

Two black SUVs crest the ridge and glide down the dirt

road winding through the fields. They don't belong here. Prophet would never allow all that sleek precision. His world is rusted-out pickups and boxy white vans.

My heart slams into my ribs.

Outsiders. They'll see me. They'll help me.

Prophet barks orders, shoving me toward the house, but I wrench my arm from his grasp. Pain tears through my knee. I ignore it and force myself to take another step. I've been trapped in his cage for too long. Hope is twenty feet away and I'll crawl to it if I have to.

The SUVs brake hard, throwing up gravel. The front passenger door flies open. A man in a crisp white shirt steps out. The polished Ranger star on his chest glints in the pale afternoon light. But it's the oversized belt buckle—the gaudiest, most ridiculous belt buckle in the whole of Texas—that shocks me the most. I've seen it before. Dozens of times. It was the punchline to so many of AJ's jokes. But now, it shines like salvation.

"Marvin! It's Grace. Grace Stone!" I race for him, falling into his arms when my knee gives out again. "Prophet kidnapped me—"

"Nova! Get back here right now!" Prophet shouts.

Marvin freezes. His grip clamps down, not to reassure, but to contain. I see it. The flash of shock, the slight tremor of fear. He wasn't expecting me to be outside. In the open. Where I could be seen.

"Marvin, please! Help me!"

His hand slams over my mouth. "Shut it," he hisses, his voice tight with fear. Rough fingers dig into my jaw as his eyes dart to the SUV.

The rear door opens. A man steps out with the kind of presence that warps the air itself. Crisp suit jacket, revolver at his hip, flanked by four men with AKs. Authority radiates from him like heat off asphalt.

His gaze slices from Prophet to Marvin, to me—pinned and trembling against the SUV. His lip curls in disdain. "The Ranger captain's missing wife. Here. All this time?"

Marvin's hand trembles where it grips my jaw. "Jefe, she's no one. A woman Prophet took in. She answers to Nova now."

This isn't happening. He's...he was...a friend.

I shake my head violently, trying to scream around his palm, but it comes out as nothing more than muffled sobs.

Jefe doesn't spare me a single glance. His eyes stay locked on Marvin. "Do you take me for a fool? I remember her face on the news. Half the state was searching for this woman. And all the while, you knew she was here. You fed me lies while you played lapdog to this false prophet."

Prophet steps forward, chin lifted. "She is Nova, chosen by the Glorious One. She was never Grace Stone. Her sacrifice—"

"Silence!" Jefe snaps. Prophet flinches.

Jefe turns back to Marvin. "Give me one reason I should not put a bullet in your skull right now."

Marvin's face goes pale. He lets me go, and I crumple to my knees in the mud, arms wrapped around myself as if that could somehow shield me.

"Because...she's...she's broken. She only answers to Nova now. The Rangers have no idea where she is. Let Prophet finish what he started, and in a month, the problem disappears forever."

Jefe regards me with cold detachment. His hand rests on the grip of his revolver.

"The only problem," he says softly, "is that Captain Stone still breathes. A man like that does not stop searching. Not until he finds his wife. Not until he buries every man who stood in his way."

Hot tears tumble down my cheeks. Not from pain. From knowing AJ hasn't given up on me. Of course, he hasn't. He's a hurricane in boots and a Stetson. Once he gets his teeth into something, he never gives up.

God, I'd give anything to see him again. To feel his arms around me. To tell him I love him. I can almost hear him calling my name.

Not Nova.

Grace.

"Kill her. But don't get any blood on the cars," Jefe says coldly.

Prophet lunges, dragging me upright. His voice sharpens with desperation. "No! Let me perform the ceremony tonight. It is a full moon. The flock will accept it as my Doctrine. So will the Glorious One. You'll see the truth with your own eyes, Jefe. And afterward, you may dispose of her body as you wish."

One of Jefe's men cocks his gun.

"Please," I beg, my gaze level with Marvin's ridiculous belt buckle.

Of all the things to see as I die, why does it have to be *this?* I thought it would be the night sky. Something...peaceful. Not a hunk of metal with a golden man, his cowboy hat held high in one hand, riding a bucking bull. But it's the diamonds spelling out "Fort Worth Rodeo" that make it so damn ugly.

"No!" Prophet shoves Marvin back and shields me with his body. I can't see his face, but his entire presence shrinks as he turns to Jefe. "If you kill her now, you lose everything. The flock, the future. Nova guarantees our strength forever."

Jefe snorts. "As long as the guns arrived, I let you have your delusions. But this? It is dangerous." He gestures at the men behind him. "They will inspect your facilities until midnight. If you can complete your ceremony before then, fine. If not, she dies now."

Brother Malone inches closer. "Prophet's Doctrine requires a blue moon. That's at month's end."

"What the fuck is a blue moon?" one of the enforcers behind Jefe asks.

"It's the second full moon in a single month. Today is the first. There's another on the thirtieth," Prophet explains, the words spilling from his lips faster and faster. "Nova was supposed to be upstairs when you arrived. You were...early."

Jefe answers with his fist. Blood spatters as Prophet hits the dirt next to me. "So you knew. And you hid her. Victor—end her. Now."

"No!" Prophet scrambles up, his eyes wild. "I will perform the sacrifice tonight."

Marvin leans in to whisper in Jefe's ear. I can't bring myself to move. Hours. I only have hours left to live. How could I have gone from such intense hope to...*this*...so quickly?

"You may have your ritual," Jefe says. "But once she's dead, Marvin will dispose of the body. He can dump her over the border on the Sandoval Cartel's land. When her corpse is found—*if* it's found—her husband will assume she was caught up in Sandoval's flesh trade. Marvin will help sell the story. Get one of his CIs to reach out with some damning information the Ranger chief can't ignore. Maybe it'll even keep him off our backs for a few months."

The biting wind cools the tears as they hit my cheeks. AJ will believe him. Marvin is...a friend. Or at least we always thought he was.

"You won't regret this. Once you see how the flock responds to her death, you'll understand. You'll...believe," Prophet says.

His elation sickens me. I thought I was immune to it. To feeling anything at all after almost three years in this place. But one fleeting moment of hope was all it took.

Prophet snaps his fingers. "Brother Malone!"

"Yes, Prophet?" Brother Malone says, suddenly right behind me.

"Take her upstairs to prepare."

Through deep, choking sobs, I look up at Marvin. "We've known you for years. AJ...he's your friend. I thought you were a good man."

He shrugs, shoves his .45 back in the holster, and adjusts his belt buckle like it's tied directly to his dick. "You thought wrong."

Brother Malone grabs a fistful of my hair. "Get up, Nova. Now."

I don't fight him. There's no point. I just hope the end is quick.

CHAPTER THIRTEEN

Grace

OUTSIDE THE WINDOW, tiny snowflakes swirl in the light from dozens of lanterns surrounding the altar.

Did Prophet do this on purpose? Give me a room where I'm forced to see the spot I'll die?

Probably. He's just *that* demented.

The adults gather around the altar—a few at a time—all wearing heavy coats, scarves, and gloves, while I shiver in the thin, white silk dress Prophet delivered in a fancy box not long after he brought me dinner.

He threatened to strip me himself if I didn't put it on. So, I did. But now I regret not fighting harder.

The plate of chicken and rice sits untouched on the desk. Every time I've even *looked* at the food, I've wanted to throw up.

For hours after Brother Malone locked me in here, I beat my fists against the door, screaming for someone—anyone—to help me. My fingers are swollen and bruised, my voice almost gone.

Now, I can't step away from the window. Can't pull my gaze

from the altar. The last time it was this cold on a full moon, I passed out before Prophet finished ranting about my *divine purpose*. Will the knife hurt much? Or by the time he plunges it into my side, will I be unable to feel anything at all?

The click of the lock might as well be a gunshot, yet I don't flinch.

"It's time, Nova," Prophet says as I turn around.

He and Brother Malone are both dressed in their best black wool coats. Figures. They'll be warm and cozy as I turn into a sacrificial popsicle. They each take one of my arms and march me out of the room and down the stairs.

I should beg. Plead for my life. But it won't do any good. Splinters dig into my bare feet as they drag me into the middle of the living room. The pinpricks of pain are enough to give me one final burst of strength they don't expect, and I wrench my arms free, whirl around, and glare at the man about to murder me.

"You're no prophet," I hiss. "You're a power-hungry, delusional asshole who made up some bullshit gospel because he needed to feel *special*."

He snarls, wraps his hand around my throat, and squeezes until I can't breathe. I claw at his fingers, drawing blood, but he only tightens his grip. "Swear again, and I'll make your death ten times more painful. How would you like a hundred small cuts before the end, Nova?"

His fingers loosen, a challenge in his cold, brown eyes. I gasp and wheeze as he pulls a handkerchief from his pocket and dabs at the blood welling on the back of his hand.

I'm beyond caring what he does to me. In minutes, nothing will matter ever again.

"What do I have left to lose, you piece of shit?" I ask, my voice rough, but strong. "I'll still be dead. Your entire flock is going to hear how you kidnapped me because of a tattoo. That's not religion. That's a fucking coincidence!"

The slap sends me reeling right into Brother Malone. His scratchy wool coat against my bare arms makes my skin crawl.

"Prophet?" Sister Mary, Prophet's youngest wife, slips into the room from the kitchen. "I finished braiding the ceremonial ties."

In her pale fingers, she holds a length of white and gold rope with oleander flowers woven into the strands. She doesn't look her husband in the eye, just sets the offering in his hands and backs away.

"Excellent. Where is my father with the wine?" Prophet asks.

Wine?

Prophet doesn't allow his flock to drink anything but water, milk, and juice. No tea. No coffee. And certainly no alcohol.

Fear flickers over Sister Mary's face briefly until Abe shuffles through the front door. He carries a cup of purple liquid in his aging hands.

"You're late." Prophet takes the glass from his father. "The rest is at the altar?"

Abe nods, his eyes meeting mine for a single moment before he pins his gaze to the floor.

Brother Malone grabs a fistful of my hair and yanks my head back. The fingers of his free hand dig into the sides of my jaw.

No. God, no.

He's going to drug me.

Prophet pours half the liquid into my mouth, then slaps his hand over my lips while Brother Malone pinches my nose.

Swallowing the bitter grape juice is just another in a long line of deaths. My freedom. My voice. My hope. When he gives me the rest, I don't resist. Maybe...it's better this way.

"How long will it take?" Prophet asks.

Abe swipes a tear from his cheek. "She'll start to feel the

effects almost immediately. After she drinks from the goblet at the altar, her heart will give out in less than ten minutes."

Prophet turns back to me, and Abe mouths, *"I'm sorry."*

My stomach cramps with such force, it steals my breath. The room starts to spin. "What...did you...give me?" I manage through clenched teeth.

"A concentrate of oleander nectar." Smug satisfaction drips from Prophet's every word. "The plants hide the flock's land from view. They serve as our protectors. Their flowers led me to you. And now, they'll speed your journey to the Glorious One."

I can feel my heart skipping beats against my ribs. "You... fuck...ing...bast—"

A wave of intense pain turns the world fuzzy. My legs tremble. How long until I can't stand on my own? Until I don't care? About anything?

Already, it's getting harder to see. Black spots and bright, white halos float all around me.

Brother Malone spins me to face him, then ties my wrists with the braided rope. The scent of the blooms is so sweet I want to vomit. A flash of pure terror sends sweat breaking over my skin. *No. Not again.*

Thunder isn't here. It's not raining. I'm inside. Aren't I? The white and gold are almost...pretty against my skin.

Am I drunk? It feels like I'm—no. The poison. The ceremony is about to start. I'll die soon. I'm ready. Just a little pain and then...nothing.

Prophet tugs on the rope. I don't fight. Just stumble after him with slow, awkward steps. Biting cold stings my cheeks. It's darker now. My toes go numb. I can't tell if the trembling in my limbs is from the freezing air or the poison.

Men and women start to chant and sing all around me. I can't make out the words. The sound grows louder until each beat is like a physical blow to my chest. Or maybe that's my heart giving out. Abe said...

Someone lifts me up onto the altar. Prophet shoves a crown of oleander blossoms onto my head. The stems scratch at my temples. Panic sharpens my vision for a brief moment. A silver goblet glints in the lights from the lantern. It's so cold against my lips. More bitter juice. I swallow every drop, hoping the end comes quickly.

"The Glorious One will welcome our precious Nova home tonight! Her sacrifice will please Him so greatly, He will bestow upon me—upon all of us—life everlasting!" Prophet shouts.

With every passing second, I feel less and less.

The snow is so pretty falling around me. A hand cups my neck, easing me onto my back. My arms are pulled over my head.

The next cramp is so strong, I try to curl onto my side, but I can't move, the ropes and my own muscles locking me into place.

Prophet's voice is getting softer now. What's he saying? Is it time?

I'm not cold anymore. Sweat prickles along my brow. My chest tightens as warmth bursts over my skin.

Shadows surround me. No. Those are men. Black coats. Black hats. Prophet's clerics lay their hands on me.

Another burst of pain spreads out from my stomach. "Please," I whimper. "Make...it...stop..."

I can't hear my own voice anymore. I can't hear anything at all.

I'm so hot. Who turned the heat on? It's unbearable. I struggle to lift my head, but lose the battle.

Prophet pulls a shiny blade from inside his coat.

I can't summon the strength to be afraid. Each wheezing breath is harder than the last. I'm burning up. And so tired. If I close my eyes, I'll drift away. Maybe I'll do that. Fall asleep and never wake up.

AJ. I want to see AJ again. One last time. His face is only a blur in my memories. Dark hair. Blue eyes. The rest...he's gone.

"Aaron, I'm so sorry..."

The darkness draws closer. It's calling to me. Telling me it's okay to sleep. To stop fighting.

I close my eyes.

White hot pain pierces my side. I feel nothing but the burning agony spreading through my stomach and chest. My arms and legs are numb. I can't scream. Can't see. Can't move.

All of a sudden, I'm cold again. So cold. Too cold to shiver.

"I love you, AJ."

There's nothing now. No light. No sound. Only the sensation of the last, slow beats of my heart fading away.

CHAPTER FOURTEEN

Grace

MACHINES HUM ALL AROUND ME, along with a beeping that matches the throbbing in my temples.

My throat burns. Rough and raw, like I've been screaming for hours—or days. Something is wrapped around my head. I want to touch it, but I'm too weak to move.

Little twitches—my fingers, toes, lips—are all I can manage.

The beeping quickens.

What's going on? Where am I? My stomach twists in on itself. Bile burns the back of my aching throat.

"Señora?" The man's voice is soft, with a thick Mexican accent. Gently, he lifts one of my eyelids, blinds me with a bright light, and repeats the process with my other lid.

A tiny whimper from close by sends panic prickling over my skin. Until I realize it came from me.

"Shhh. You are safe here."

He's close enough to rest his hand on mine. The beeping is so fast now, it's almost a constant tone.

"You must stay calm, señora. *Manda la calma.*"

No.

I'd scream the word if I could. Stay calm? I can't move. Can't open my eyes. And there's a strange man *touching* me. I have to get out of here. He'll hurt me. He'll lock me away and I'll disappear forever.

It takes all the strength I have to open my eyes. I have to know who this man is. But everything's blurry. Hazy. Like I'm looking through a dirty window.

Brown hair. Tanned skin. Stubble. A white coat.

"¿Señora? ¿Habla ingles? English?"

English. Yes.

I nod. Big mistake. The room starts to spin. Squeezing my eyes shut, I will myself not to throw up. It...mostly works. More bile coats my tongue. The bitter taste makes me gag, which sends shooting pain spiraling out from my side.

"Breathe," the man says softly. "I do not want your stitches to tear."

Stitches?

The beeping eases a fraction as I drag air into my lungs.

"Better. You must be frightened, but I swear, you are safe, señora. Injured, but safe. I am Dr. Alejandro Reyes. This is my clinic," he says and perches on the edge of a chair next to the bed. "If your blood pressure rises any higher, I will have to sedate you."

My vision has cleared enough for me to make out the doctor's face. His brown eyes are kind. A jagged scar runs from his ear down his jaw and across his throat.

"Do you understand?" he asks. "Please say something. Or tell me your name. You had no identification on you when you were found."

I blink up at him. It's a simple request. My name. It's...it's...

Tears slip down my temples.

"I...don't...know. Why...don't I...?"

Reyes curls his fingers around mine. "You suffered a serious head injury. A cranial fracture. Your brain had already started to swell when you were brought here. I operated to repair the broken bone, then put you in a medically induced coma to let the swelling go down. I did not know if you'd be able to speak —or even wake up—until a few minutes ago."

I search for a memory—*any* memory—but my entire life is...gone.

"Can't...remember...anything." My rough, dry throat seizes, and I start to cough. The pain in my side is so intense, my vision goes white.

Reyes presses a straw to my chapped lips. "Water. Slow sips. You were intubated for almost forty-eight hours."

"M-my...side..." I whisper once I can breathe again. "Hurts."

His warm brown eyes shift to the floor. "Señora, you need to rest. I will explain everything, but I am afraid you are not strong enough yet to hear it."

I have to prove him wrong. Gritting my teeth, I reach for him and wrap my fingers around his wrist. "Who...am...I?"

His voice takes on such a sorrowful tone, I want to cry. "I do not know. But the brain is a wondrous thing. You could wake up tomorrow and remember everything."

I turn my head—as much as the throbbing pain allows— and see a shock of blond hair draped over my shoulder.

Shit.

I don't even know what I look like.

How do you forget *who you are?*

"Mirror," I croak. "P-please."

Reyes stiffens. "Are you certain? There is significant bruising."

I've never been more certain of anything in my life. Or...I don't think I have. "Yes."

The doctor pulls out his phone and opens the camera app. "Here."

My hand shakes too much, so Reyes does his best to get the angle right. The white bandage around my head shocks me, but it's nothing compared to seeing myself for the first time.

Dark circles swell under my blue-green eyes.

The deep purple bruise on the left side of my face almost looks like...a boot print. A long scar follows the curve of my right cheekbone.

"I don't know her." The words fall from my lips like dust. Gritty and in so many pieces, I'll never put them back together again.

Carefully, I ease my head back down to the pillows. The throbbing gets so much worse.

"You are not alone, señora. Not anymore. I will do whatever I can to find out who you are." Reyes gives my shoulder a gentle squeeze. "A white, American woman missing will have made the news. Somewhere."

I want to believe him. But panic swells in my chest and the beeping gets faster and faster until the pain in my head is overwhelming.

I want to ask more questions, but the words won't come. They're all tangled together like someone took the letters, scrambled them in a bowl, and dumped them out on the floor in front of me.

Reyes injects something into the IV—how do I know what an IV is, but not my name?—and within a few seconds, my body starts to float.

Closing my eyes, I give into the gaping emptiness of where my life should be.

CHAPTER FIFTEEN

AJ

I PULL the cord on the old banker's light on my desk. Too many late nights and too much fucking paperwork. My neck is killing me.

Spinning around in my chair, I rub the stabbing pain until it turns into a dull ache. From the credenza against the wall, Grace laughs from the last photo I took of her. Two seconds before I'd snapped the picture, Belle had stuck her tongue in Grace's ear.

The dog has never been the same since Grace disappeared, but she no longer sits by the door all day, hoping her person will finally come home. And while I still run the trail every fucking Saturday, Belle and I spend our weeknights in a cheap studio apartment only two blocks from the station.

More than once, I've thought about selling the house at the lake, but I can't face the prospect of living somewhere Grace has never been. And Belle needs the space to run on the weekends. The apartment was a compromise. A way for me to sleep at night in a bed that doesn't constantly remind me of all I've lost, while keeping the house we bought together in case, by some miracle, Grace comes home.

She should be waiting for me right now. Steam coming out her ears. Ready to remind me what I'd promised the day she disappeared. That when I made captain, I'd come home on time more often.

Shit.

I gotta get out of here if I don't want the doggie daycare to read me the riot act. Again.

"I miss you, darlin'." Picking up the photo, I crush the wood frame to my chest and give myself a count of five to wallow in my grief. "I'll never stop lookin' for you. There ain't been one single moment I've forgotten you. And there never will be."

My eyes burn. I haven't cried in at least a month, but the anniversary of Grace's disappearance is in a little over three weeks. And the closer it gets...

I already put in for time off. I'll let Elmore take Belle so I can spend a solid forty-eight hours drowning myself in a bottle of tequila.

I'd ask Jasper to take the dog, but the few times I've talked to him this past year, he's told me to start dating again, and I ain't ready.

I'll never be ready.

The fucker found the love of his life a few months ago. After nearly dying last year in the explosion that ended his career, he's so happy most of the time now, it's hard for me to be around him. Hell, I had to stop watching Channel 5 News because his girlfriend is one of their on-air reporters.

She's damn good at her job, but seeing her reminds me of all I've lost. So now I'm a Channel 10 devotee—even though their coverage sucks ass.

I spin my wedding ring around on my finger. Grace's ring is tucked under my shirt on a chain. Maybe one day, I'll take it off, but it sure as shit ain't gonna be today.

Setting the photo back on the credenza, I let out a heavy sigh. It's quiet at the station this late. Elmore is still around here somewhere. She drew the short straw this week. Hardison, her partner, got to go home early while she finishes up all his paperwork.

Before I can grab my coat, my desk phone rings.

Ignore it. Belle's waiting for you.

But I've never been very good at listening to my inner voice. So, I pick up the receiver. "Stone."

"Captain AJ Stone?" a man with a thick, Mexican accent asks.

"That's what I said. Mind tellin' me who you are and why you're callin' so late on a Friday night?"

"My name is Dr. Alejandro Reyes. I work at a small clinic outside of San José de Carranza in Mexico."

"Doc, Mexico ain't in my jurisdiction. Call your National Guard." I don't have time for this. It's been a long damn day and I won't let Belle think I forgot her.

"I do not need the assistance of law enforcement. I am calling specifically for you. Four days ago, a woman's body was dumped at my clinic's back door."

My knees give out. I land in my desk chair—hard—and the fucking thing rolls back and hits the credenza. Panic, grief, and despair squeeze my chest tight enough it's hard to breathe. This is the moment I've dreaded for two years, ten months, and six days.

"B-blond hair, five-foot—fuck—five-foot-six, a hundred and forty pounds?" The stats I've rattled off a thousand times since Grace disappeared are so much harder to force from my lips when there's a real possibility I'll never have to say them again.

"Captain Stone, I found the website you set up after your wife's disappearance with all of that information. It is why I called you. But...if I am to be certain this is your wife, I need to know if she has any tattoos or birthmarks."

"The phases of the moon on her right shoulder over a spray of oleander flowers. Look, Reyes, if you ain't about to confirm I can finally lay my wife to rest, hang up now or I'm fixin' to come down there and beat the everlovin' shit out of you."

If this is a prank call—or another asshole only interested in the fifty thousand dollar reward—it's gonna set my last fuck on fire.

"What about her *left* ankle?" Reyes asks.

The chair is the only thing that keeps me from ending up in a puddle of grief on the floor. "A semi-colon tattoo. As part of a b-butterfly. We kept that detail out of the news," I whisper. "When can I pick up Grace's body? And where?"

"Mierda. Captain Stone, I am not explaining myself well. When I found her, she had been stabbed, poisoned, and kicked in the head with such force, her skull fractured. My clinic is small—only a single operating room—but I was trained at the Universidad Autonoma de Guadalajara. It is the best medical school in the country."

I don't understand why he's telling me this. Hearing how my wife suffered before her end is only going to make my nightmares that much worse.

"I was able to repair the skull fracture, but her brain was swelling, and I had to put her in a medically induced coma for two days. She woke up yesterday morning."

Woke up...

Hope thaws the ice around my heart, the flames building so hot and fast, I can't catch my breath. "Grace is...alive?"

"Sí. She is. But she has no memory of her name, her life, or what happened to her since her disappearance."

Fucking hell.

"Can I talk to her? Where did you say you were again? I'll get in the car right now. Drive. Fly. Both. Whatever I need to do."

"Captain—"

"AJ. You found my wife. Alive. Call me AJ."

"Gracias, AJ. Grace is confused and very scared. Her injuries are serious, and my responsibility—as her doctor—is to keep her as calm as I can. Seeing you in person...well, I believe it would be the better option."

"I'll get in the car as soon as we hang up the phone. Just need to get one of my lieutenants to take care of my dog for a few days. Where did you say your hospital was?" My hands shake as I reach for my cell phone.

"Twenty miles west of San José de Carranza. There is only one road in and out of town. You will not miss it."

"San José de Carranza?" My phone gives me directions to the middle of fucking nowhere. "How small is this *clinic* and why haven't you transferred Grace to a bigger hospital?"

Digging my fingers into the arms of my chair hard enough my knuckles crack, I wonder if this sombitch is even a doctor. I wouldn't know a Mexican medical school if it bit me in the ass.

He sighs, his voice weary. "AJ, forgive me for being so insensitive, but your wife was stabbed, poisoned, and left for dead in a burlap bag. She was suffering from hypothermia, and I believe that is the only reason she is still alive. Whoever hurt her clearly wanted her dead. What happens when they realize they failed in that endeavor? If I transferred her to Chihuahua, it would not be long at all before she was identified. She has no defenses. The people who tried to end her life could walk right up to her and she would have no idea who they were."

Fuck.

He's right.

"Doc, I don't know you, but if I find out you're lyin', San José de Carranza is gonna be down one doctor."

"I took an oath, *Captain Stone.* Not unlike yours, I believe. I put my patients first. Always."

I can't tell if he's a self-righteous asshole or a truly good man. Not over the phone. But all that matters now is getting to Grace.

"Take down my cell," I say after I unclench my jaw. "If Grace remembers anything—if *anyone* comes lookin' for her besides me—you call. Understood?"

"Sí. Go ahead."

I rattle off the digits, push to my feet, and grab my jacket off the back of the chair. "I'll be there by nine in the morning. If you do tell her anythin' about me, tell her I *never* stopped lookin' for her." It's one of a thousand things I want Grace to know. A thousand things I didn't think I'd ever get to say.

"Very well. But AJ?" The doctor clears his throat and lowers his voice. "I do not recommend telling anyone that Grace is alive. Not unless you trust them with your life. And hers."

———————————

"Elmore!" I call on my way through the bullpen. "I need you to pick up Belle tonight!"

Dammit. Where is she? The mug of coffee on her desk is still steaming, but her computer's off and her coat ain't hanging on the rack by the door.

"Elmore!"

Fuck. I don't have time for this.

The doggie daycare closes in twenty minutes. I'm gonna have to pick up Belle and take her all the way out to the lake with me. I can't go to Mexico without our passports, my personal sidearm, and some of Grace's things.

Pulling out my phone, I text Elmore on the way out of the station.

AJ: Need you to watch Belle this weekend. Got something personal to deal with. Call me. ASAP.

I'm so distracted, I don't notice her leaning against the

driver's door of my SUV until I practically punch her in the gut reaching for the handle.

"Fuck!" My keys slip from my hand, but she catches them before they hit the ground.

"I *know* you weren't fixin' to walk out of the station like it was just any other Friday." Elmore draws up to her full height, hands on her hips. "And you sure as shit weren't gonna drive all night to a tiny town deep in the middle of Sandoval cartel territory, alone."

Yeah. I was. I am.

"Move," I grit out, pushing into her personal space to give her my best glare. "You weren't supposed to hear any of that."

"No shit. Next time you have secrets to keep, use your inside voice. Or close your office door."

"I need you to watch Belle—"

"No." She tucks my keys into her pocket like they belong there. "I'm driving you out to the lake. *You* are gonna call Jasper on the way. Emi can take care of Belle for the weekend while he comes with us."

"Fuck no. My brother and I ain't exactly on speaking terms. And there is no 'us' in this scenario. I'm goin' to San José de Carranza alone. Give me the keys, Elmore. Now."

"You've been here almost"— she checks her watch—"twelve hours now. You think you're gonna be worth spit by nine a.m. tomorrow after driving all night? Get in the goddamn car. And since I'm about to break God knows how many laws keeping you from doing something *supremely* stupid, I think you can call me Parker."

Parker Elmore is the best Ranger I've ever trained. She's also stubborn as fuck and the closest thing I have to a friend. Unsure why I expected her to just...ignore the fact that Grace is alive. But goin' all the way to Mexico? Riskin' her career? That ain't in her job description.

"Fine. You can come. But I ain't callin' my brother."

I trudge around to the passenger side of the car while Parker slides behind the wheel and adjusts the seat. She's a full eight inches shorter than I am.

"If you don't call Jasper, I will," she says as we pull out of the parking lot. "He's probably about to leave to pick up Emi from Channel Five."

"And you know this, how?" I lean against the door frame, exhausted and wired at the same time.

"Emi, Isabel, and I have drinks every couple of weeks." She gives me a quick side-eye. "And if *I* have to call him, you'll never hear the end of it. We need him, AJ. The Sandoval Cartel is serious shit."

She's right. Maybe he won't pick up the phone. I've been enough of an ass to him since Grace disappeared I wouldn't blame him.

So, of course the sombitch answers on the first ring.

"Let me guess. They're givin' you *another* award," Jasper drawls. "Captain AJ Stone makes the news? Again?"

How the hell do I explain the past half hour? Spit it out like it's some movie-of-the-week plot? I didn't think this through.

"AJ?" My twin brother actually sounds concerned. "What's goin' on?"

Parker reaches across the center console and gives my forearm a quick squeeze. It's enough to unstick my tongue from the roof of my mouth.

"It's Grace...she's alive, Jas. I got a call from a doctor in Mexico twenty minutes ago. She's in a small medical clinic outside of Chihuahua."

A rush of air carries over the line. "Holy shit. How?" he asks.

"I don't know. She doesn't...*fuck*. She can't remember anything, Jas. Not her own name, not me, not what happened to her. Belle's at doggie daycare and I need you to pick her up and leave her with Emi for the weekend. Then meet me at the house. But if you ain't there in ninety minutes, we're leaving without you."

"We?" he asks. For all of two seconds, the radio in his truck blasts some sad country song as the engine turns over with a rumble. "Who the fuck—"

"Jasper," Parker says, exasperation roughening her tone. "Ain't no way I was letting him go alone. And since he's as stubborn as both of us put together, I had to steal his keys to do it."

It doesn't take me long to tell my brother everything I know—it ain't much. "We might be down there for a couple of days."

"I'm more concerned with how we get back," Jasper says. "Especially if you don't want the whole world to know she's alive. We can't just stroll up to the border, bat our eyes, and hope for the best."

Fuck.

I didn't think about that. Hell, I haven't thought about a lot of things. What if Grace doesn't want to leave with a stranger? What if she never gets her memory back? What if she does and she's so thoroughly broken, she can't ever trust me again?

"The two of you are ignoring the world's most obvious solution." Parker flips on the blinker and takes the exit for Lake Travis.

"What?" Jasper and I say at the same time.

"Connor."

I shake my head. "Why would I call him?"

Parker shoots me a glance, then huffs. "It's a damn good thing I'm here, AJ. You're not playing with a full deck."

"Connor's a civilian. How the hell is he supposed to help us get Grace over the border?" I ask.

Protecting the former FBI agent, his girlfriend, and her daughter was the last big case Parker and her partner, Hardison, worked with me. But Connor hasn't been on the job in months.

Parker offers me a tight smile. "You need to get out more, AJ. Connor has some powerful friends. And he owes you."

CHAPTER SIXTEEN

AJ

"WHAT THE HELL are you doing here?" I climb aboard the Gulfstream to find Connor Davis sitting in one of the plush, leather seats with a mug of coffee in his hand. It's a little after three in the morning, and waiting almost six hours to leave Austin nearly killed me. But the private plane the former FBI agent was able to arrange will let us bring Grace back into the country without going through border control.

"Makin' sure the plane comes home in one piece," Connor says. "The team out in Seattle tends to destroy the transpos they use. Pritchard would have my ass if he lost his security deposit. It wasn't...small."

I cringe. Austin Pritchard, former head of the United States Joint Special Operations Command, started some sort of rogue mercenary group after he got shitcanned from JSOC, and he's apparently making bank. Chartering a private plane to fly us to Mexico and back ain't cheap. But it's the fastest way to Grace. And the safest way to bring her home.

Jasper shoves his duffel bag into one of the storage lockers at the front of the plane before dropping into the seat across from Connor. "What are you doin' working for Pritchard? And how do I get in on a sweet gig like that? It probably pays a hell of a lot better than...well...the big, fat nothin' I make now."

Frowning, I shoot my brother a glance. "I thought the owner of your building was paying you—"

Jasper's brows shoot up, stopping my assumption in its tracks. "He was giving me a break on the rent, not paying me, asshole. But if you'd bothered to answer the damn phone once in the past three months, you'd know that I moved in with Emi six weeks ago."

His words sting, but all I can think about is what Grace has gone through the past three months...the past three *years*...to steal all her memories away and leave her so close to death.

Parker stows her own gear, as well as the bag she helped me pack for Grace, and finds a seat toward the back of the plane. "Give him a break, Jas. He's had a hell of a day."

I appreciate Parker having my back, but Jasper ain't about to let me off the hook that easy.

Connor leans across the aisle and passes my brother a business card. "Give him a call. It's not steady work." He grimaces and pinches the bridge of his nose like he's in pain. "Not sure that's what you're looking for, but it suits me just fine. My head's still fucked more days than not."

Six months ago, a couple of dirty cops in Dallas beat Connor within an inch of his life, then dumped him in Flash Flood Alley for a storm to finish him off. Jasper got to him in the nick of time. I never asked how Pritchard knew Jas was close enough to find him, or why the man then called *me* to check on Connor in the hospital. Pritchard and I only met once, and that was a dozen years ago when he was visiting Bergstrom Air Force Base and took a tour of the Ranger station.

The pilot emerges from the cockpit and scans our small group. "This everyone?" he asks.

Connor nods. "Yup. We're good to go."

"It's a two-hour flight. Vehicles will be waiting for you at the airstrip. I need four-hours' notice when you want to leave Chihuahua and return to Austin. Understood?"

If the pilot ain't former military, I'll eat my Ranger star and my Stetson.

"Copy that," Connor says. "Won't be a problem."

I don't hear the rest. All I can think about is Grace. My hands clench into fists on my thighs.

Hold on, darlin'. I'm coming.

———

Grace

The shadows in the corners of the room won't stop flickering.

I try to tell myself it's just the old heater stirring the air. It pops and cracks, the vague scent of hot metal always lingering just under the antiseptic.

Every time I move, the stitches in my side itch. I touch the bandages gingerly, then wince at the dull ache.

The nurses are kind. They smile as they check my blood pressure and bring me small meals I think they've cooked themselves. But I see the questions in their eyes.

How could she forget her own name?

What is an American woman doing in the middle of nowhere, Mexico?

Is she about to snap?

I think I already have.

Sleep never lasts long and always brings something dark with it. I wake up gasping, my heart racing, tears streaming down my face. I never remember dreaming—just the feeling left behind. Like I'm trapped. Like I'll never be free again.

How could I have forgotten my entire life? My name. My

childhood. My parents. Have I ever loved someone? Has someone ever loved me back?

The thick scars around my wrists catch the dim light from the bulb over my bed. I sobbed so long and so hard when I first saw them, Dr. Reyes worried I'd tear my stitches. They're ugly, but it's more than that. How evil were the people who took me that they had to—what?—tie me up or chain me for days or weeks? And what happens when—or if—I remember the horrors that left them?

Everything's fuzzy. Like I've had half a dozen shots of tequila on an empty stomach. When I move, my head fills with static that builds and builds until I feel like I'm about to fall out of bed—despite the rails on either side of me.

Exhaustion burns my eyes. The shadows are still there, and every time they move, I'm less and less sure they're just shadows.

Dr. Reyes keeps assuring me I'll get my memory back eventually. But if I do, will I survive knowing who hurt me? And why?

SUNLIGHT SPILLS across the tile floor. But the cold knot in my stomach laughs in the face of its warmth.

"Buenos dias, my dear." The doctor slips into the room carrying a plate covered with tin foil. "I thought you might like an 'American' breakfast today. Eggs and hash browns."

As soon as he pulls off the foil, my stomach lurches. The smell is...*wrong*. Bile burns the back of my throat. "No. God, no."

I can't even *look* at the food without wanting to throw up.

"¡Lourdes, entra aquí! ¡Quita este plato!" Dr. Reyes calls, and the nurse rushes in and snatches the plate from his hand.

Once it's gone, I can breathe again.

Pulling a pen light from his pocket, Reyes checks my eyes and frowns. "Have you been nauseous all night?"

"No." I collapse back against the pillows as another staticky *zap* inside my head turns the world sideways for a beat.

"You had huevos rancheros yesterday. Those did not bother you. I thought something familiar might help trigger your memories. But perhaps your body is remembering what your mind cannot. Pain hides in the strangest places."

I should like eggs. Or...at least be able to eat them without smothering them in salsa. Right? What happened to me that I can't even *look* at them?

Dr. Reyes checks my temperature, then pats my shoulder lightly. "Lourdes made gorditas de harina this morning as well. They are not unlike pancakes. Can I have her bring you some? You must keep up your strength."

Now that I'm no longer about to vomit, I *am* hungry. I nod, careful not to trigger another one of those awful brain zaps.

And when he slides a plate of sweet, crispy griddle cakes in front of me, I eat every bite.

AJ

Fifteen of the longest hours of my life come to an end as Jasper parks the SUV in front of a clay-walled, single story building in the middle of nowhere, Mexico. Connor and Parker pull up right behind us.

My wife is in there somewhere. Injured. Confused. With no idea who she is—or who I am.

I grab the duffel bag with Grace's things—her favorite sweater, the silky pjs she always wore on cold nights, the quilt her mother made for our wedding, and the perfume I've been spraying on her pillow every Saturday night just so I could smell her again—and head for the front door.

Jasper, Connor, and Parker follow close behind.

But my steps slow, then stop too soon. What if the doctor was wrong? What if the woman he's treating *isn't* Grace?

Hope is a dangerous thing. For years, I lived on scraps of it. Barely enough to breathe, let alone survive. But now? I'm bursting with it. If that's not my wife in there, I'll crash and burn so hard and fast, I'll never recover.

"Go on, Aaron," Jasper says, his hand on my shoulder. "We got your back."

I swallow hard. No one calls me Aaron. Not anymore. Even our mama calls me AJ. For years, the only one who ever used my first name was Grace. Even then, she reserved it for sex, or when I was being a complete dumbass.

I should apologize to my brother—for shutting him out when he told me to move on, for ignoring every olive branch he offered after.

When that rich developer asshole tried to kill him and Emi this past fall, he'd reached out again. And again, I'd shut him down.

Yet, one phone call, and he's standing at my side like nothing happened between us.

"What if she's—what if they..." I can't give words to my biggest fear. That the assholes who took her left her so broken, she'll never come back to me.

"What ifs are bullshit," Parker says softly as she takes up post on my other side. "You can what if yourself to death out here, or you can walk through that door and tell your wife you love her."

Ain't that the core of it? Out here, Grace is still gone. In there...I have a chance to get her back.

Despite the faded walls, the dusty roof, and the cracked,

pothole-riddled parking lot, the inside of the building is pristine.

A hint of antiseptic lingers in the air. The old tile floors, though chipped in places, are hand-painted with brightly colored flowers. White plaster walls carry faint cracks, but they've been scrubbed spotless. Even the reception desk gleams.

"Señor Stone?" a young woman asks.

"Yes. Dr. Reyes—"

"Sí, sí. I know. One minute. I will get him for you." She disappears down a hallway, and the urge to call Grace's name—to tear through the clinic until I find her—is so strong, I'm two steps after the woman before I catch myself.

It only takes the doctor a minute to emerge around a corner. "AJ. I am glad—" He stops short, his hardened gaze focused over my shoulder. "Mierda. I warned you not to tell anyone."

"You told me not to tell anyone I didn't trust with my life. And Grace's. Well, these are the people who fall into that category. I sure as shit wasn't gonna go deep into cartel territory without backup."

Jasper sidles up next to me, his hand resting on the butt of the SIG in his holster. "Might as well get this over with," he says, his voice as gravelly and serious as I've ever heard it. "We're the only ones AJ told about Grace. But there's one more guy back in the States who knows where we are. Anything happens to us, we don't check in at regular intervals, and he'll blow your town —hell, the entire Sandoval Cartel—off the fuckin' map."

Reyes gives a small shake of his head. "Miguel Sandoval has no interest in a war with the Texas Rangers. Nor did he have anything to do with Grace's injuries. Of that I am certain."

I study the man for a full minute. "He's tellin' the truth. At least what he knows of it. Stand down, Jas. For now. Reyes, where's my wife?"

JASPER TAKES a seat in the waiting room while Parker walks the perimeter and Connor goes outside to call Pritchard and let him know we arrived safely.

"Come into my office first," the doctor says, his polished smile gone and a weariness to the set of his shoulders. "My nurse, Lourdes, is with Grace now. I have not yet told her anything about you."

"Why the fuck not?" I want to grab the guy and shake him, but he ushers me into a tidy office—bright walls, shelves stacked with medical texts, and a small vase of flowers on the desk.

Reyes takes a seat and steeples his fingers. "Because if you did not show up for any reason, I feared what the disappointment would do to her."

Fuck.

"All I know of you, AJ, came from the website you set up for Grace and a few news articles online. My responsibility is to my patient, not to you."

My anger ebbs slightly, and I take a seat in his guest chair. "You can ask me anything, Reyes. As long as you don't make me wait much longer to see my wife. I've lived without her for two years, eleven months, and five days. I won't last another hour."

He inclines his head with a small smile. "I will save my questions for later. But you should be prepared for her physical and emotional state. When she was left on my doorstep, she had a deep stab wound to her right side. The blade missed all the major organs, and that surgery was simple. Her stitches are healing well, though she will have pain for another week, at least. She had also ingested a toxin that put her heart into arrhythmia. I sent blood samples to a lab in Chihuahua for analysis, but the results are not back yet. It is the skull fracture I was—and still am—most concerned with. It caused her brain to swell. That, along with whatever trauma she experienced at the hands of her abusers, is what led to her amnesia."

"Is it permanent?" The lump in my throat is the size of hell's half acre.

"The brain is the most complicated, delicate, and resilient organ in the human body, AJ. I have no answer to your question. She needs to be seen by a neurologist as soon as possible."

"The minute it's safe for her to travel, I'll get her on a plane back to the States. She'll have whatever care she needs for as long as she needs it."

"A commercial flight would not be advisable for at least a week, perhaps longer," Reyes says. "The air pressure change at thirty thousand feet—"

"What if we go private? We topped out at nine thousand on the way down here."

He nods slowly, a small frown curving his lips. "You could perhaps go as soon as tomorrow then. If she agrees. She is suffering from strong bouts of vertigo, and there is significant weakness along the left side of her body. She cannot—and should not—walk unaided yet. A fall could be catastrophic if she were to hit her head. Physical therapy will be helpful."

I know I need to hear all of this. But every word out of the doctor's mouth does nothing but stoke my rage. When I find the fuckers who took her, I'll be hard pressed not to kill them. Slowly.

"Did they...did anyone...?" *Fuck.* How can I even ask this question? I sure as shit don't want to know the answer, though I need to. "Was she...?"

His dark brown eyes crinkle with understanding. "I saw no evidence of sexual assault. If she had been forced to work the brothels, I would have been able to tell."

Relief prickles over my skin, a feeling so strong and all-encompassing, I'm not sure I can stand for a solid minute. I was never a praying man, but I've said more than my fair share over the past three years.

Dr. Reyes pushes to his feet. "Come with me. I will take you to the atrium. Please let me speak with Grace before she sees you. I believe she trusts me. Well, as much as she trusts anyone at this moment. It may help if I explain how I found you. But do not be surprised if she is scared of you at first."

"Ain't nothin' I can do about her reaction to me, Doc. But I won't push her for anything she ain't ready for. If I have to camp out in one of the SUVs every night for a week—or a month— before she trusts me, I'll do it."

"I live behind the clinic," he says with a sad smile. "If it comes to that, you can stay with me. It is not much to look at, but the couch is comfortable. The others who came with you... we will find couches for them as well."

This guy's the real deal. Kind. Strong moral compass. Dedicated to his job and the people he helps. All the things I used to be before Grace went missing. Since then, I ain't done much worth spit.

"Thank you." I offer him my hand. "I owe you a debt I'll never be able to repay."

"You owe me nothing," he says, then leads me back into the hall and around another corner. An archway painted a bright yellow leads to a large atrium filled with orchids in almost every color.

"Wait here until I call for you." Reyes steps into the room, and my heart stops beating.

Grace sits in a wheelchair facing a large window. Just beyond, roses bloom in large pots, their colors so vibrant, it's like they're *willing* winter away.

Her blond hair is so long now. It cascades down the high back of the chair, halfway to the floor. A thick, white bandage winds around her head, but the rest of her is hidden by the blanket draped over her shoulders.

I ache to go to her. To pull her into my arms and tell her no one will ever hurt her again. But I can't make that promise. Not until I find out who took her.

This—waiting, hovering just out of sight—is the hardest thing I've ever done.

"My dear, I need to ask you a question." Reyes crouches down next to her chair. If he weren't so completely focused on Grace, he could probably see me out of the corner of his eye. "Does the name AJ Stone mean anything to you?"

"No." Her weak whisper shatters my heart into dust. I've longed to hear her voice again, and while it's definitely *hers*, it's also not. Too hoarse. Too hesitant. Too...scared.

"Do you remember the promise I made to you? That I would find out who you are?"

She nods her head slowly.

"Your name is Grace. Grace Stone."

CHAPTER SEVENTEEN

Grace

THE HEATER HUMS in the corner, a low sound that makes my head ache under the bandages. The pain is constant, but I've learned not to try to rub it away.

My hand shakes as I tuck a few strands of hair behind my right ear. The doctor's words play on a loop.

"Your name is Grace. Grace Stone."

The kind nurse, Lourdes, tried two dozen names with me yesterday. Every time she checked on me, she picked a different one. Jane. Gina. Susan. Jill. Christy. Melissa. Jennifer. Brandi. Brooke. Diana. Katherine. I think she looked up American names and made herself a list.

But none of them felt like me.

I'm not sure Grace does either.

"How can you be sure?" I ask, my gaze shifting from the doctor to the blanket covering my legs.

Dr. Reyes glances behind him, then returns his full focus to me. "I found news reports on your disappearance. Photos that look exactly like you. And the website your husband set up when there were no leads. He—AJ—is a captain in the Texas Rangers. He never stopped looking for you. I called him late last night, and he was able to tell me about the tattoo on your left ankle. That was a detail the police never released. And..." Reyes offers me a warm smile, "he is here. Just outside. Would it be okay if he came in?"

My heart lodges itself firmly in my throat. I have a husband? And he came for me?

The doctor's smile fades. "If you are not ready—"

Shit.

"I—I am. Yes."

"AJ, you can come in now." The doctor turns the wheelchair toward the archway, but I struggle to focus on anything more than a few feet in front of me—a side effect of the head injury. So, I hear his firm, steady footsteps before I can see his face.

And then he's in front of me. Frozen. Like I'll simply disappear if he breathes wrong.

My stomach twists into a knot. There's an intensity to his blue eyes that hits me like a punch, but not a single memory floats to the surface.

His dark brown hair is cut short, with threads of silver at his temples. Thick stubble rasps against the palm of his hand as he rubs his mouth.

"Grace." His voice breaks on the word. "It's really you. I...I never stopped lookin', darlin'. Not for a single day."

My eyes burn. Shouldn't he be familiar? Seeing him should trigger *something*, right?

Every moment I don't respond, a bit of the hope fades from his deep blue eyes.

"Grace?"

The first tears tumble down my cheeks. "I d-don't...know you."

He nods like he expected it, but his jaw flexes, and his eyes

—those deep, desperate eyes—shine with something that looks a lot like grief.

"I'm...uh...AJ. I'm your husband. For eighteen years...now."

Husband.

The word detonates inside my chest, but there's nothing behind it. No memories. Nothing familiar. Just a growing ache and hollow panic curling around my ribs and squeezing. Hard.

"I brought pictures. Maybe they'll help?" AJ pulls out his phone, taps it a couple of times, and turns the screen toward me. But it's too small—too fuzzy—for my tired brain to make sense of.

His voice is kind. Gentle. I should be safe with him. So why can't I ask him to come closer? I want—I *need*—to know if the vague shapes in the picture really are...us.

Just say something. Anything.

I dig the fingers of my right hand into my thigh under the blanket and find the tiniest bit of courage. "I can't see...from here."

"Fuck. I'm sorry, darlin'. Can I...uh...sit with you?" He's so serious, his voice soft and almost...hesitant. I may not remember him, but I know the man in front of me is never this unsure of himself.

I think he's trying not to scare me. Does he know I'm scared *all the time?*

"Okay." The word is nothing but a whisper, yet it settles me in a way I can't explain. As does AJ's warmth at my side when he drags a polished wood chair over and sinks down next to me.

Dr. Reyes clears his throat. "Grace, I think you and AJ should have some time alone. But if you want me to stay, I will."

I shake my head softly, and my brain doesn't immediately zap itself sideways at the motion. Maybe it's a sign. I want to trust AJ. I *need* to trust him. I just don't know if I should.

He scoots a little closer, the phone cradled in his hands, and I catch a hint of his scent. Leather and something fresh and clean. It's comforting.

"This was us on New Year's Eve five years ago. We splurged on tickets to the big bash at the Four Seasons."

He looks so...happy. Clean shaven, in a black suit, his smile wide as he leans in to kiss the woman in his arms.

She's...me, but not. Her blue-green eyes aren't haunted and bruised. Her smile isn't forced. Her hair is shorter. She's not skin and bones. Her red dress clings to her curves, and a blue topaz ring glitters on the hand pressed to AJ's chest. This woman is confident. She wouldn't be afraid to take this man's phone—*her husband's phone*—and look at some damn pictures.

Our fingers brush as he hands me the device. I can't control my flinch. But it's the anguish in his eyes that destroys me.

"I never gave up," he says, his voice rough and gritty, like he's trying to stop his tears before they fall. "I knew I'd find you. But this... You really don't remember me at all?"

My fingers flutter over the bandage around my head. With all my heart, I want something—anything—to come back to me. A laugh, a smell, a touch. But there's only a gaping maw where a life should be.

"I'm sorry." Will he get angry now? My shoulders curl inward, and I try to make myself as small as possible.

"No, darlin'. No. This isn't your fault. Not at all. You're alive. That's all that matters. We'll figure out the rest. No matter how long it takes, I'll stay with you. If you'll let me. There are hundreds of pictures on there. You can swipe through to see more of them."

Tears sting my eyes, unexpected and sudden. For what I've lost. For the pain etched on AJ's face. For the strange fluttering in my belly of something I ache to remember.

I look at him—*really* look. There's a softness around his eyes, lines made deeper by worry and time. But there's also love. So much of it, I can almost feel it filling the space between us.

He needs me to say something, but I can't, so I focus on the phone in my hands. The next photo is a candid one of me in a room with a dozen easels.

AJ narrates as I swipe. "You taught art classes at Austin Community College. Oil painting, beginner drawing, watercolors... All your students loved you. And my God. You're so damn talented, Grace."

Next, we're at dinner. Margaritas in front of us. Laughing again.

"That was at a steakhouse on Sixth Street. We were celebrating my birthday."

I'm working up the courage to ask him when his birthday is—and when *my* birthday is—as I swipe to the next photo.

Oh, my God.

I'm sitting on a wooden deck in a light blue dress and boots, laughing. A golden brown and gray puppy with striking blue eyes has her paws on my shoulder.

The phone falls to my lap. A single sob escapes my lips before I cover my mouth with my hand.

"Grace, do you remember her?" AJ asks. All that hope is back in his eyes. And a whole lot more. But this time, I feel it too.

"Tinker Bell?" I whisper.

"Yes, darlin'. Yes. But we started calling her Belle once the vet told us how big she was gonna be. She's almost eighty pounds now. When you...disappeared—" he swallows so hard, I can hear it "—she spent months sittin' by the door all day, every day, waitin' for you to come home."

The idea of that sweet puppy, *my* puppy, thinking I left her is too much to bear.

It doesn't even matter that I *remember* her. Only fragments. Snatches. Her bark. The way her fur felt under my fingers. Tiny moments of joy. I lose the battle with my emotions and start crying so hard, I don't know if I'll ever be able to stop.

"Fuck. I'm a dumbass. I shouldn't have told you that..." AJ balls his hands into fists on his thighs so hard his knuckles crack. "Can I hold you? Shit. You're not ready—"

But I am. I *need* him to, even if I still don't remember a thing about him. Before I find the words, he plucks the phone from my lap and swipes to another picture.

"Take a look at this one."

He's trying to distract me, and I'm so damn grateful for it. With the sleeve of the hospital robe, I swipe at my tears until the screen comes into focus. We're younger. So much so, the picture is a little grainy. But the joy on our faces is clear enough. AJ is in a black tuxedo. I'm wearing a strapless white gown and a single strand of pearls.

"That was our wedding. Almost eighteen years ago. September twenty-third. But our anniversary's the twenty-first. We wanted to get married on the first day of fall, but that was a Thursday, and the minister almost laughed us out of his office. You didn't want anything fancy, but your mama had her heart set on a big, formal shindig. I think she'd been planning it since the day you were born. So we went down to city hall on the twenty-first and had the justice of the peace marry us.

"We kept it a secret from everyone. Until I done fucked up on our ten-year anniversary. I got you a crystal picture frame with our wedding date etched on it. The twenty-first, not the twenty-third. I'd just made lieutenant. I'd faced down murderers, drug dealers, even helped the FBI with a couple of terrorism cases, but I was positive your dad was still gonna beat my ass."

The right corner of my mouth twitches slightly at his tone. Almost half a smile. But it fades too quickly. "I don't remember that either."

AJ rubs his hand over his chin, the stubble rasping against his palm. "You will, darlin'. I know you will."

HE SPENDS hours talking to me. Telling me about...us. But only thin wisps of memories flit through my mind. I can't hold onto them for more than a second before they're gone again.

I wish I could work up the courage to ask him what happened to me—why he spent the last three years looking for me—but all I can manage are the softest acknowledgements when I know he expects them.

When I saw our wedding photo, I thought I heard him say, "I do." Just a distant memory. But was it real? Or wishful thinking?

My body seems to know him. I find myself leaning toward him, wanting his arms around me. His energy—the way he moves—is familiar in a way nothing else has been since I woke up in this clinic three days ago.

But now, I'm so tired, I can barely keep my eyes open. Lourdes comes in to offer us lunch, and gasps when she sees me.

With a flick of her hand, she tries to shoo AJ out of the room. "You. Move. She needs rest."

I don't want to sleep. What if I forget him all over again by the time I wake up? "Don't go," I whisper, reaching for AJ's hand before he can get out of the nurse's way.

My words surprise him. Understandable since they surprise me too.

His fingers are warm and strong. Not soft, but not rough either as he curls them around mine. "I ain't leavin' you, Grace. I promise." He sets his shoulders and turns his gaze to Lourdes. "I can take her back to her room."

With a huff, she shakes her head. "Okay. But you will let her sleep."

The loss of his touch as he guides the wheelchair back to my little room hits me harder than I expect. I don't think anyone besides Lourdes and Dr. Reyes has touched me—at least not kindly—in a very long time.

The beige walls almost glow this time of day, and the sun kisses the roses in the garden just outside the window. Marta—another one of the nurses—has picked me a single flower every day. Five of them now. The first is losing its petals. I feel like I am too.

AJ parks the wheelchair next to the bed, then pulls back the sheet and blanket. "Is it okay if I help you?"

I've ached to know what it's like to have him hold me, but until now, wasn't sure how to ask.

"I'd...like that."

AJ leans down so I can drape my arms around his neck. He's all firm muscles and long, lean lines. The room spins, the world's worst tilt-a-whirl, but I'm not worried I'm going to fall. Not with his hands on my hips.

Too quickly, he lowers me onto the bed. But as soon as he helps me off with the thin hospital bathrobe, he freezes, his gaze fixed on the thick scars around my wrists.

Rage pours off of him in endless waves. "Fuck. *Fuck!*"

Fear steals my voice. I cower away from him, and Lourdes races into the room.

"Get out!" she snaps.

For a moment, I think he'll leave, and that terrifies me more than his anger. He even takes two steps toward the door, tears brimming in his eyes. "Grace, I'm so sorry. For yelling, for not finding you sooner, for...everything. I don't know how you'll ever forgive me. You probably shouldn't. But I'm gonna ask you anyway. Every day if I have to. Please. Let me stay."

I wish I could tell him how I got those scars. Or that it wasn't his fault. But the truth is...I don't know.

The only thing I'm sure of right now is that I need him close. He makes me feel safe.

It takes me a full minute to find my voice. A full minute of him staring at me with tears carving shining trails down his cheeks and his trembling hands balled into fists.

When I do, the single word is strong and clear.

"Stay."

CHAPTER EIGHTEEN

AJ

THE NURSE—LOURDES—AIN'T my biggest fan. Grace might have forgiven me for yelling, but Lourdes hasn't. Every time she comes to check on Grace, she mutters under her breath in Spanish. I know enough of the language to recognize a couple of curse words and *marido*—husband. The rest is a mystery.

I sit in a hard, plastic chair next to the bed, unable to pull my gaze away from my wife's face. The bruise spreads from her left temple halfway to her jaw, with a distinct waffle pattern from the sole of whoever kicked her.

On her right cheek, a scar slashes across her pale skin. It's rough. Not from a knife—at least not a good one. All the shit I've seen in my career ain't doing me any favors. My thoughts ping wildly with possibilities of what she endured the past three years.

My phone vibrates on the little table next to me, and I scramble to grab it before it disturbs Grace. She needs all the sleep she can get.

Jasper: Getting a little worried. Everything okay?

AJ: Grace is sleeping. I'm in the room with her. You can get out of here if you want. See if there's a motel nearby. Need to talk to the doc before I know when it'll be safe for her to travel.

Jasper: Do I need to come back there and pull your head out of your ass? No one goes home until Grace does.

I don't have the words to tell him what it means to have him here. I type and erase half a dozen messages before I give up and set the phone back on the table.

"Señor Stone?" Lourdes hovers in the doorway, a cup of coffee in her hands. Behind her, an orderly balances a slim, black leather recliner on a dolly. "You are tired. That is not good for Grace. Coffee or sleep."

Her stern stare warns me not to argue with her. Not that I would. She's right. I can barely keep my eyes open. I might have caught a few minutes of shuteye on the plane, but I've been up for more than thirty hours now.

"Both. Gracias." I accept the cup of strong coffee and step into the hall so the young, dark-haired orderly can wheel the recliner into the room and set it up by the bed.

The idea of sleeping next to my wife—even if I'm in a chair and she doesn't remember *us*—has my eyes burning.

Lourdes checks Grace's heart rate and temperature, then gives me a terse nod. "Rest. She needs you."

"Yes, ma'am."

The chair is heaven—despite its lack of cushion—and I'm about to drift off when Jasper's uneven footsteps echo in the hall.

"Fuckin' hell." He sets Grace's duffel bag next to me, drops into the hard plastic chair the orderly moved into the corner of the room, and rubs his hand up and down his thigh. It's got to be screaming at him. He didn't get any more sleep than I did on the flight. "She's been through it, hasn't she?"

I can't do more than nod. If I tell him about the past few hours, I'll crack into a million pieces.

Jasper nudges the duffel bag with his boot. "I thought you might want her things. Maybe somethin' in there will help jog her memory."

Fuck.

I didn't even think to bring it in from the waiting room earlier.

"Parker and Connor are goin' into town to find some food. I'm headin' back to the lobby. The doc has a couple of decent chairs out there. Better than this piece of shit, anyway." He pushes to his feet with a grunt, the corners of his eyes crinkling with pain. "Just...let me know if you need anything."

He's my twin. It shouldn't be this damn hard for me to have an honest conversation with him.

For most of our lives, we were inseparable. As kids, he was my protector, even though I'm technically five minutes older. In high school, I was captain of the football team, and he was the star kicker. We joined the State Troopers together. Applied to the Rangers together. Hell, it was only his attitude that kept him from making captain with me.

When the Cordova Cartel blew up that warehouse and ended his career, I should have been there for him. But I was in too much pain over losing Grace. I sat by his hospital bed for three fucking days, but hours after he woke up, I bolted.

"Jas...wait." I run a hand through my hair, grabbing a few of the short strands and pulling to the point of pain. "She can barely string a sentence together. It's like she's too scared to speak. And fuck. She was tied up for a long damn time."

I clock the exact moment he sees the scars around her wrists. His entire body stiffens. "We're gonna find the assholes who hurt her, AJ. And once we do, they won't live to see another sunrise."

The emotion in his voice does me in. Suddenly, I need him to know everything. "She remembers Belle. But not me. Not...

herself. We looked at pictures for almost three hours, and noth-in'. Her memory... It's just gone."

Jasper rubs the back of his neck as he leans against the door jamb. "Give it time, man. She didn't remember shit when you got here. Belle is a small step, but a good one. Maybe she just needs to be...home."

I hope to all that's holy in this world, he's right.

"When did you become the optimistic one?" I ask.

He chuckles softly. "Nah. I'm still a cynical sombitch. Most of the time."

"Fallin' in love has been good for you. Remind me to thank Emi when we get back. And apologize for bein' so much of an ass I wouldn't even come to dinner the dozen or so times she's asked."

Jasper meets my gaze, all the humor fading from his expression in a heartbeat. "AJ, the night Austin PD suspended the investigation—the night you kicked me out and stopped talkin' to me—I never should've said what I did. I'm sorry."

Forcing the lump in my throat away is harder than I expect, but Jasper ain't the only one who needs to apologize.

I reach for my brother's arm and hold on tight. "You were an ass. But you were lookin' out for me. I know you went to Harris not long after that and threatened to quit if he chained me to a desk for the rest of my life."

His cheeks take on a slight tinge and he rubs a hand over his beard. His hair is lighter than mine. A little longer. One of the few differences between us. "Ain't no thing. You're lucky he didn't do it just to spite me. Billings and McGrath heard him yellin' all the way from the break room."

"Jas, it was everything. Without the job...I might not have made it long enough to get...*here*."

He flinches, and I kick myself for being such an insensitive asshole. Losing his career almost broke him. And since I'd kicked him out of my life, I didn't know it until he needed my help protecting Emi.

That stakeout would have been *mine*—should have been mine—but I was still so fucked up over losing Grace, the chief benched me. Instead, I'm still on the job and Jasper's looking for something...*anything* he can do to feel...useful.

Before I can find the words to tell him how sorry I am for abandoning him, Grace cries out. I almost trip over my own feet trying to get to her.

"Don't...I'll be good," she whimpers. Tears gather at the corners of her shuttered lids. She's shaking, her right hand fisting the blanket like it can somehow protect her from whatever's threatening her in her dreams. Her nightmare.

"Grace?"

Fuck. Do I wake her? What if that makes things worse? She doesn't know me, but I've got to do something.

Taking a chance, I cover her hand with mine. "It's okay, darlin'. I'm here. You're safe."

Grace turns her head slightly. The tension around her eyes eases. With one final, tiny sob, she relaxes.

"Well," Jasper says from behind me, his voice so low it's practically a whisper, "if that ain't proof Grace—*your* Grace—is in there somewhere...I don't know what is. She'll come back to you, AJ. Just give her time."

Grace

The constant headache I've had since I first woke up here is starting to fade. My eyes still feel like sandpaper, and I have to blink hard for the rose garden outside to come into focus.

Something's...different. A sweet, floral scent wraps around me, and it's almost...familiar.

I turn my head.

Shit.

AJ. My husband. He's stretched out in a narrow recliner next to the bed, legs crossed at the ankles, eyes closed. Soft breaths escape his parted lips. He's asleep, I think. And holding my hand.

I jerk my arm back, then regret the motion as it makes the room tilt on its axis.

AJ sits up so quickly, he practically falls out of the chair. "I'm sorry," he says, his voice rough. He runs his fingers through his dark brown hair. A memory tries to push through, but before I can grasp it, it's gone, like a ghost that was never truly there. "You were havin' a nightmare, and I couldn't...I had to try."

I want to know if it worked—if he kept the monsters away —but fear stops me from asking.

This is ridiculous. He's my *husband*. Why am I so afraid to ask him a simple question? To touch him? To let him hold my hand?

"I brought some of your things with me." He gestures to the bed, where a colorful quilt now covers the dull beige hospital blanket. "Your mama made that for us when we got married. It's been on our bed at home ever since."

I run my fingers over the material. Each square has a different type of flower. Black-Eyed Susans, bluebonnets, sage, golden poppies, lilies, roses. It's so bright and happy—such a contrast to the drab sheets and scratchy blanket I've had for days. With the guardrail on the side of the bed down, I can almost imagine I'm somewhere else. Somewhere that might be a home. I can't quite close my still clumsy left hand around the edging, but with my right, I lift the quilt to my nose.

"Do you recognize the scent?" Leaning down, AJ rummages in a black duffel bag. When he straightens, he's holding a pearlescent glass bottle with a gold top "This isn't the one you had when you...were taken," he says, his voice dropping to a whisper. "I spray your pillow with this scent every Saturday. It's the only way I can sleep in our bed without you. I bought a new bottle last year. Damn near had a panic attack in the store before the clerk told me the company had switched from blue glass to this."

He won't meet my gaze. This man, who traveled all the way from Austin to get to me, sat with me while I slept, and held my hand through a nightmare, is breaking into pieces over a bottle of perfume.

"I almost gave up." The first tear rolls down his cheek. "So many times. Belle and the job were all that kept me going."

His pain fills the space between us until I can't *not* ask what he means.

"Gave...up?" I fumble for the remote to raise the bed, but it somehow ended up on my left side, and I can't make my fingers work the buttons.

AJ leans over and eases the small device from my hand. The brief touch seems to settle him a fraction. If I'm honest, it helps me too.

"After we graduated from college, my brother joined the State Troopers right away, but I took a month off and went to Spain with a couple of friends. You were twenty-two, doing a semester abroad, and it only took me a single date to decide I was going to marry you one day."

His blue eyes light up with the memory, and I wish I could share it with him.

"Grace, you've been my best friend for more than twenty years. My wife for eighteen of them." He's crying now, his hands balled into fists on his thighs. "And for the past three, I've started and ended every fucking day praying you'd find your way back to me."

CHAPTER NINETEEN

Grace

I REACH for AJ's hand, desperate to soothe a fraction of his pain.

It starts slowly—the light flickering in the corner of my eye, the window curtain swaying when there's no breeze. Then the entire room—the floor, the bed...*me*—lurches like I'm adrift on open water in the middle of a storm.

I'm helpless to stop it. To stop myself from falling.

Strong arms wrap around me.

AJ.

He moved so fast—like he *knew*. Now I'm cradled against his chest, my cheek pressed to the soft cotton of his Henley and the frantic beat of his heart.

"Grace!" His voice is rough. Desperate. "I've got you, darlin'. Are you okay? Lourdes! Fuck. Where is that damn nurse when I need her?"

He's trembling. Holding me like I'm so fragile, I'll shatter into pieces if he lets go.

It was just vertigo. My battered brain hasn't yet figured out how to make sense of the world around me—or so Dr. Reyes says. *I* know I'm okay. Or...as okay as one can be with a fractured skull and no memories of her life.

AJ doesn't. And he looks utterly wrecked.

I think...if I don't say something—if I *can't* say something—it might break him completely. But when I try, my throat locks and panic squeezes my chest.

Say it. Just...say it.

The first tear rolls down my cheek. AJ's fingers thread through my hair, cupping the back of my head so gently, I believe with everything I am that he'll never hurt me. It would destroy him.

"Please," he whispers. "Please don't leave me again."

"Just...dizzy." The words catch in my throat, raw and shaky. "That's all."

"You're sure?" Three years of pain deepen the blue of his eyes. "You're okay?"

"Y-yes." My heart pounds so hard he must be able to feel it, but the panic fades with each second he holds me. I ached to know what it would be like to have his arms around me. Now I do.

It's like coming home.

It doesn't matter that I can't remember what—or where—home is. This is what it feels like. It's the only thing I'm sure of.

His arms tighten around me. "You're okay," he says again, like he's trying to convince himself and not me. "I've got you, Grace. I've got you."

Closing my eyes, I let myself melt against him. For the first time since I woke up in this unfamiliar, broken world, I feel safe. Even if I don't know who I was before, maybe I can find out who I am now.

We don't move for several minutes. He sits on the floor, my legs draped over his thighs and my right hand pressed to his heart. The steady *thump* under my fingers and the slow rise and fall of his chest lull me closer and closer toward sleep.

Until I start to shiver.

"Shit. Let's get you back into bed."

AJ starts to guide my arms around his neck, but bed is the last place I want to be. "N-no," I stammer. "Not yet."

Emotion churns in his eyes, turning them the color of storm clouds over the prairie. A line deepens between his brows. "You're freezing. And you just fell. Please, Grace. Lie down and rest."

"Three d-days. In that bed. I can't..." If I were stronger, I'd tell him the tiny bed has become my prison. The place that reminds me how broken I am. It's where I woke up. Where I realized my memory—my *life*—was gone. Here, in his arms, it's safe in a way I need more than anything.

A frown curves his lips. But then he nods. "Okay. Not the bed. What about the recliner? Or...we could go back to the atrium."

We. I clutch that single word so tightly, it takes me several seconds to realize he's waiting for an answer. I wish we could stay right here, but he can't be comfortable sitting on the cold tile floor.

"Just want...you to hold me."

My words unleash something wild in his eyes. Something that looks a lot like love. I don't remember loving him, but I believe I did. Maybe...I still can one day.

AJ presses a light kiss to the top of my head. It's barely a touch, but I feel it down to my toes. For that instant, the cold, empty space where *I* used to be warms. "I can do that, darlin'. For as long as you need."

He gives the quilt a light tug, then carefully wraps it around me. Is the scent—gardenias, I think—familiar? Or do I just need it to be?

"Let's see if that poor excuse for a La-Z-Boy will fit us both."

For the first time all day, his smile isn't forced, and mine...well, it might just have found its way back from wherever it was locked away.

I DRIFT in AJ's arms. Not quite asleep, but not awake either. From time to time, he whispers something against my hair, but I can't quite make out the words. They don't matter, because the tone is clear. Reassuring. Comforting. Loving.

Until a brisk knock on the door pulls a hoarse yelp from my lips. "Shhh, darlin'. It's just the doc. You're safe."

I blink hard until I can focus on Dr. Reyes. He isn't wearing his usual warm smile. "Grace? Is your memory returning?"

"No," I say softly.

"Oh. I thought..." He gestures to the two of us crammed together in the tiny chair. Heat blooms on my cheeks until I remember it's my husband holding me.

"She got dizzy," AJ says, his back stiffening and his voice taking on a hard edge. "She *fell*."

Dr. Reyes pulls a tiny pen light from his pocket and checks my eyes. It hurts—every time—but I'm used to it by now, and manage not to flinch.

"Your pupil response is normal. That is good. You did not hit your head, did you?"

"I caught her," AJ grits out. "But if I'd been a second later..."

The doctor's gaze softens. "Dizziness, vertigo, even the amnesia are not uncommon in the early stages of recovery from a traumatic brain injury. I will run another CT scan in a few minutes to check for any additional swelling. But there is something we must discuss first."

"Unless it's life and death, get her the damn scan right now." AJ shifts his arms around me, like he's about to sit up. "Please," he adds, almost as an afterthought.

Reyes shoves his hands into the pockets of his white coat. "This will not take long, AJ, but it is important. Miguel Sandoval is coming to the clinic tomorrow around noon. If you and your *friends* are still here, I fear what his reaction will be."

I look up at my husband, confused. "Friends?"

AJ helps me turn so I can see his face. "I didn't come down here alone, darlin'. My brother, a friend of ours who used to be in the FBI, and one of my lieutenants came too. In case Sandoval made trouble."

I'm so confused. Who is this Sandoval and why is Reyes afraid of him?

"What...trouble?" The words are coming easier now. They don't fill me with as much panic—at least not with AJ.

"Miguel Sandoval is head of the Sandoval Cartel," he explains. "He controls all of Chihuahua and most of Coahuila all the way to the Texas border. And unless I'm a complete idjit, the reason this clinic has all the equipment it does, the reason it even exists, is because the good doctor here is the cartel's personal physician."

Reyes stares down at his polished black shoes. I never thought to ask why he worked here. Or why there was a clinic in the middle of nowhere.

"If Grace's scan shows no additional swelling, bleeding, or clots," the doctor says, finally meeting AJ's gaze, "you should leave first thing in the morning."

"And if it ain't safe for her to travel yet?" AJ's arms tighten around me. "You run a clinic, doc. You treat the injured. Sandoval doesn't need to know who we are."

Reyes' thin laugh isn't reassuring. "The four of you *reek* of law enforcement, *Captain* Stone, and Miguel is no fool. Treating one of the locals? That I could explain easily. But the wife of a Texas Ranger? The *missing* wife of a Texas Ranger? He would shoot me for keeping this from him. You and your friends would disappear. Miguel does not harm innocent women, so

Grace would survive, but she would be alone, and that... No. Either she is well enough to get on your fancy plane in the morning, or you will have to drive to Chihuahua and hide there until she is."

"Fuckin' hell. There ain't nothin' I want more than to take Grace home, but I won't risk hurtin' her. So you give her that scan, Reyes. And you better be damn sure of the results."

Dr. Reyes maneuvers the wheelchair next to the recliner. "I am a doctor first. Cartel second. If you trust nothing else about me, Stone, trust that."

CHAPTER TWENTY

AJ

FIVE MINUTES after I text my brother to find out where Connor and Parker are, all three of them crowd through the door of the tiny hospital room.

Parker's gaze snaps to the bed. "Is Grace okay? Where is she?"

"Ease up. The doc took her for a CT scan. We do have a problem, but right now, it ain't Grace's health. Miguel Sandoval is comin' for a look-see of his personal medical clinic tomorrow, and we gotta be long gone before he shows up."

Connor pulls out his phone. "The plane can be ready to go in four hours if you want to leave tonight."

I run a hand over my jaw, three days of stubble so thick, my beard might rival Jasper's soon.

Is that why Grace doesn't recognize me? I shaved every other day *before*.

Fuck. Focus on the problem, dumbass.

"There's not a damn thing I want more, but you should

know better than any of us that flying with a head injury ain't exactly...smart."

On the way here, Connor admitted he's still suffering from post-concussion syndrome. When he's stressed or exhausted, aphasia can make it hard for him to talk, and the migraines are no joke. Grace could have all the same side effects—and more—if we put her on a plane before she's ready.

Parker pulls a tablet from her backpack, drags the visitor's chair over to the bed, and props the device on the mattress. "Near as I can figure, Sandoval's territory goes south to Durango, northwest to Nogales, and east all the way to the Texas border. The Cordova gang takes over at the Rio Grande. Our best chance is Chihuahua. If the roads are decent, we can be there in five, maybe six hours. Everywhere else is too far away. And it wouldn't be too hard to disappear in a city that size for a day or two until Grace is able to fly."

"We'd need to find a doctor too—a good one. She can't—or won't—talk much yet. And it ain't aphasia, it's fear. Whoever had her..." I shake my head. "I think they hurt her if she talked back. And *my* Grace would've talked back."

Jasper cracks a grim smile. "She was a firecracker. Took no shit from anyone."

"There's too much at stake to just hope another couple of days will make a difference," I say as I scrub my hands over the top of my head. "Even in Chihuahua, we could end up pickin' the one doc who's loyal to Sandoval."

"AJ, have you forgotten who I work for?" Connor asks. "Or the hacker on Pritchard's payroll who helped you find me, Isabel, and Veronica? Zephyr can track down a doc we can trust. That's the one thing we don't have to worry about. Keepin' Grace comfortable during a five-hour car ride and not settin' her recovery back...that's a horse of a different color."

"Hell, even getting back to the airport is a trek." Jasper leans a hip against the wall and rubs his thigh. "If *I* had a hard time spendin' almost two hours in the car, she's—Shit."

My brother suddenly looks like the cat who ate the canary, and I turn toward the door.

Fuck.

Grace looks so small sitting in the wheelchair. Small and terrified. Her entire body trembles, and she drops her gaze to her hands, tugging at the sleeves of her robe to cover the scars around her wrists.

Dr. Reyes glares at me. "What is going on here? I told you about Miguel so you could make arrangements to leave. Not so you could ambush Grace with all these people she does not know."

I step out into the hall, pull the door shut behind me, and sidestep Reyes to drop to one knee in front of my wife. To keep myself from reaching for her—she's too scared for that right now—I rest my hands on the arms of the wheelchair.

"Darlin', I'm sorry. I didn't ask 'em all to come in here. But... they're the only people in this world—besides you—I trust. We were tryin' to figure out how to keep you safe if we can't fly home tomorrow. The guy closest to the door? That's my twin brother, Jasper. The other man is Connor Davis. He used to be an FBI agent. Now, he works for a group of...well, I don't know what they call themselves, but they help folks who don't have anywhere else to go. Then there's Parker. She's the best Ranger I ever trained, and she put her whole career on the line so I wouldn't do somethin' supremely idiotic like driving all night through cartel territory—alone—to get to you."

Grace glances up at me—just for a beat—then lowers her gaze again. "Why?"

"Why what, darlin'?"

The first tear rolls down her cheek. It's so damn hard watching her struggle for every word. What the fuck happened to her the past three years that she's this scared to speak—even to me?

"Grace, can I touch you? Please?"

I expect a nod. Or for her to pull away completely. But instead, she takes my hand. Her calloused fingers hold little strength, but still, she curls them around mine. This simple gesture shouldn't mean so much, but right now, it's everything.

There's so much I want to say, but I'm afraid to spook her. After another quick glance at the door to her room, Grace releases a slow breath. "Why would she risk her career...for me?" she asks softly.

Twenty-four hours ago, I wouldn't have had an answer for her. Hell, I would have bet money against *anyone* being willing to make an illegal border crossing to help me. But now, the words come easily. "Because the entire time she's known me, I've been too broken to care about anything—or anyone—but you. I pushed Jasper away when he needed me most. I managed to save Connor's life—but only because I had some powerful help. Those people in there? They're my family. Yours too. If you want them to be."

Dr. Reyes takes a step closer, but I wave him off. Grace's eyes shine with tears. Again, I wait for her to find her voice. To tell me to open the door or beg Reyes to get her the fuck out of here.

Her fingers tighten on mine. "Are you and Parker... together?"

I'd laugh if it weren't for the despair I find in the depths of her blue-green eyes. Keeping my gaze on hers, I bring her hand to my lips and press a gentle kiss to her palm.

"No, darlin'. There never has been—and never will be— anyone else for me but you."

Grace

Relief swells in my throat, the lump so large, for a moment, it's hard to breathe. AJ has been so focused on me since he arrived, I shouldn't have worried. But I don't *know* him. Even the small parts of him that are vaguely familiar—his scent, the way he runs his hand through his hair when he's frustrated—could be nothing more than my own desperate need to find connection.

"Grace?" Dr. Reyes hovers behind my husband, disapproval tugging at his lips. "If you are not ready, I will take you to the atrium until everyone leaves."

AJ squeezes my hand. "Say the word, and I'll kick 'em all out."

Though I'm terrified of *everything* right now, knowing AJ trusts these people—that he considers them family—provides a small measure of comfort.

"I'll...try. But..." Tugging AJ closer, I lower my voice to a whisper. "Help me stand up?"

"You won't get dizzy?" His brows furrow as his deep blue eyes search mine. "The doc said you weren't ready to walk on your own yet."

"She's not," Reyes snaps. "Grace is still my patient, and I *will* have you removed from this clinic if you put her recovery in danger."

The frustration simmering inside me—being stuck in this chair, my broken brain, my weakened body—boils over. I narrow my eyes at the doctor, and though my head aches with the effort, it's worth it to see the surprise on his face.

"Not...on my own." I turn back to AJ, a mild *zap* flipping the world upside down for a moment until I blink hard. "With... you."

The love shining in his gaze tugs on my heart. He pushes to his feet and stands toe-to-toe with the doctor. "Was her CT scan clear?"

Reyes purses his lips, then nods. "Yes. No bleeding, swelling, or clots. Marta will come in soon to remove the bandage. The incision is healing well, and I used a strong mesh over the fractured bone. As long as she is not in danger of falling, she can bathe, wash her hair...and fly. Just be sure the plane does not rise above ten thousand feet. And she should still see a neurologist as soon as possible."

The very idea of washing my hair is so exciting, I almost forget about the people waiting on the other side of the door.

Until AJ squeezes my shoulder gently. "Okay, darlin'. Let's try this. But if you get too dizzy, you tell me. Deal?"

At my nod, AJ wraps an arm around my waist and slowly lifts me out of the chair. The hallway tilts and spins for a few seconds, but then rights itself as I find my footing. My first couple of steps are little more than me sliding the hospital slippers across the polished tile, but after that, I manage something that might almost be a shuffle. It helps that AJ is supporting at least half my weight as he reaches for the door.

My stomach flips. AJ's brother and his friends will expect me to talk. To be...me. Or at least to be...*someone*. But maybe being the woman who didn't want to meet them sitting in a wheelchair—who didn't want their pity—will be enough. For now.

We stop in front of a man who looks so much like AJ, if he hadn't already told me this was his twin, I'd think I was seeing double. It's a little dizzying—or maybe that's just the vertigo again—but I blink hard until some of the subtle differences between them come into focus. He's broader than AJ. Weathered. And are those...scars high on his cheek?

"Grace, this is Jasper," AJ says. "Don't let him fool you into believing he's the older one. I got him beat by five minutes."

Jasper doesn't say anything right away. He watches me with keen eyes—not quite mirrors of his brother's, but close.

"Hi, Grace." His voice is gentle. Slower than AJ's. Like he's trying not to spook this wild, skittish thing in front of him. "Sorry if we scared you earlier. We were fixin' to be outta here before you got back. Maybe...uh...meet you one at a time later tonight."

I want to tell him it's okay. I even part my lips to try. But only a shallow breath escapes before my throat tightens and my heartbeat starts to pound hard enough, I wonder if AJ can feel it.

As if he knows I'm panicking, AJ leans down, his lips close to my ear. "You're doin' just fine, darlin'."

The other man in the room keeps his distance. He's intimidating. Tall, strong, with silver threading both his beard and his dark brown hair. Older than everyone else, with ages of pain in his eyes.

"I'm Connor Davis. I don't know if it helps any, but you didn't know me...before. This is the first time we're meetin'. AJ saved me, my fiancée Isabel, and her—*our*—kid from some pretty bad guys a few months back."

"Connor's had more CT scans than he can count," AJ says with a smile. "He thought we had at least half an hour before Reyes brought you back to the room."

"Post-concussion syndrome." Connor rubs the side of his head with a wince. "Got a permanent dent in my skull. If I start to slur my words or lose 'em completely, it ain't nothin' to worry about. I still have some aphasia from time to time."

"Hi," I manage, so softly, I'm not sure anyone but AJ can hear it. Until the corner of Connor's mouth ticks up in a half smile, and he gives me a small nod.

The blonde leans against the wall, her sharp eyes taking in everything—my various bruises, the rumpled hospital gown and robe, and AJ's arm around my waist. She toys with the end of the tight braid draped over her shoulder. "I'm Parker. I was on leave from the State Troopers when you disappeared. I'd mouthed off to my supervisor one too many times and he didn't take kindly to it. But I knew one of AJ's guys, and that first night, he asked me to take care of Belle while it was all hands on deck. She's a good dog. She'll be so happy to have you home again."

Belle.

The only solid memory I have is of my puppy.

A tear hovers in the corner of my eye, but I refuse to let it fall. What if she doesn't remember me?

"Parker applied to the Rangers a couple of months later," AJ says. "By then, I was pretty far gone. But the chief assigned me to train her. Probably the only reason I still have a job. She and her partner, Hardison, were so damn eager to learn, I *had* to teach 'em."

Everyone's watching me like they're not sure if I'm about to burst into tears, start laughing, or disappear entirely.

"Grace?" Parker pushes off the wall and shoves her hands into the pockets of her jeans. "You don't have to talk if you don't want to. We're here to keep you safe, not dish about who wore what on TV last night or the best tooth whitening cream. Unless you have a need for that sort of thing. In which case... talk to Jasper. He's the one with the hot reporter girlfriend."

That startles a sound from my throat. Not quite a laugh, but close enough, it surprises me.

My eyes flit to AJ's twin, whose narrowed gaze is trained on Parker. But somehow, I think it's all for show. Maybe it's the slight tilt of his lips. Or the twinkle rippling through his blue irises. But more than that, I *feel* it. Like a part of me *knows* him, even if I don't remember him.

"Funny," Jasper deadpans, then jerks his head at AJ. "He's rubbin' off on you. That ain't a compliment."

If her self-satisfied smirk is any indication, Parker disagrees.

The mood in the room shifts with the comfortable banter— the kind of good-natured ribbing that happens in a *family*. It eases the tight band of anxiety squeezing my ribs.

Jasper pulls out his phone, taps the screen, and shows it to me. "This is Emi. My girlfriend. She's stayin' at your house with Belle this weekend."

The woman in the photo is stunning. Dark hair and eyes, flawless skin, and a smile so wide and bright, I can believe she's an expert on tooth whitening creams. But there's warmth in her gaze too.

"Th-thank you." It's all I can force myself to say, because my legs start to shake with the effort of standing. *Shit*. I should be stronger by now. Shouldn't I? Except, I still have no idea what happened to me the past three years.

AJ tightens his arm around me and guides me to the bed. "Sit down, darlin'. We still need to talk about tomorrow, but do you want a break first? Or...some food? It's after six."

Dr. Reyes clears his throat from the doorway. "Lourdes went home to make tamales for everyone. She should be back in an hour. I can have a table set up in the atrium. If Grace feels up to it, you can all eat in there together. But after that, I must insist that she rest."

"What do you think?" AJ asks.

I tug at the sleeves of the checkered hospital robe. What I wouldn't give for actual *clothes*. A bra. Anything besides this ill-fitting gown that exposes all the bruises and scars on my lower legs. But doing something normal like having dinner at a table with my husband and his...family? That could help me remember who I am. Or at least help me not feel so very alone.

"I'd...like that."

CHAPTER TWENTY-ONE

AJ

Another one of the nurses, Marta, barges through the door of Grace's room. "Everyone out. Señora Grace needs her bandages changed."

I'm fixin' to tell her I'll turn my back and close my eyes, when Reyes clears his throat. "AJ, this would be a good time for us to go over the precautions you'll need to take on the flight tomorrow."

There's an odd edge to his voice, and something dark and dangerous churns in his brown eyes.

Leaning down, I press a gentle kiss to Grace's forehead. "You should rest until it's time for dinner."

The nurse tries to shoo me out of the way, but Grace fumbles for my hand. "AJ... You're coming back, right?"

I cup her cheek. "I promise, darlin'. I'll be just down the hall."

Marta gives me a light shove, and this time, I take the hint and back out of the room. I don't look away from Grace until the last possible moment, and a small piece of my shattered heart mends when she doesn't look away either.

Jasper, Connor, and Parker wait with the doctor in the hall. Reyes keeps his voice low as he motions for us to follow him. "I am sorry for the ruse, but Grace has done so well today, I do not wish to chance overwhelming her."

"What's this really about, doc?" Connor asks.

He takes us into a room with green tile floors and large surgical lights mounted over a metal table. It's pristine—like everything else in this clinic.

"I do not know who left Grace at the clinic's back door. Or where they found her. But once I realized she was alive, I did my best to preserve any evidence of what was done to her."

Fuck. This ain't gonna be good.

A thick padlock secures a stainless steel cabinet in the corner. "Only I have the key," he explains as he opens it and then sets a large, metal tray on the operating table. "This is everything Grace was wearing."

I can't do more than gape at the pile of silky white material stained with so much blood, I don't know how she's still alive. Before I can touch it, Parker slaps a hand against my chest and steps between me and the table. "That's evidence, boss."

"That's *my wife's* blood. Get out of my way," I growl.

Jasper sidles up next to her. "AJ, she's right. Let us handle this. Or...at least put on some goddamn gloves."

"And here," Reyes says, sliding a second tray next to the first, "is the bag she was in. Gloves are in the dispenser behind you."

The bag she was in.

This was a mistake. I should be with Grace. Not staring at her bloody clothes and a fucking burlap bag some asshole shoved her dying body into. But I can't walk away either. I promised her I'd keep her safe. This is how I do it.

Jasper hands us each a pair of gloves. Connor and Parker focus on the second tray, while my brother and I carefully lift the white material. The long, sleeveless dress looks expensive.

"No label," my brother muses. "Someone probably cut it out."

"Goddamn it!" I shout as Jasper moves the dress enough for me to see what's underneath. A pair of plain cotton panties and two lengths of white and gold braided rope. "She was *tied up*? In the fuckin' bag?"

"Sí," Reyes says softly. "Her wrists and ankles. If it helps, it did not appear that she struggled much against the ropes. The poison she was given would have caused paralysis."

Poisoned. Paralyzed. Bound and stabbed.

For the rest of my life, I'll carry the vision of my wife in this bloody dress, trapped inside a burlap bag and dumped in the middle of nowhere.

Jasper leans down to peer at the rope. "Are these...flowers?"

Pink and white petals litter the tray. A handful of stems are woven into the rope. "Yeah, but what kind?" I ask. "I don't know shit about flowers."

Connor peers over at the wilted blooms. "Doc? You got some plastic bags around here somewhere? Small ones. Like Ziplocks? And tweezers."

"Sí." In just a few seconds, he sets the bags and several pairs of forceps between the two trays.

"Bag all those petals and stems," Connor says. "I know a botanist who can probably tell us what they are."

Parker takes a step back, her sharp-eyed gaze sweeping over the trays. "Guys, this wasn't 'murder.' Not from The unsub's point of view. This was a ceremony. Hell, it could have even been some sort of demented wedding."

I can't tear my eyes away from the bloody silk. What kind of fucked up wedding ends with the bride *dying*?

God. Did someone really take Grace to be their wife? Then kill her for it?

The idea makes me want to punch a wall. Or vomit. No. Both. I swallow hard. "Explain."

She waves at the two trays. "That rope was handmade. Someone took the time to weave the flowers *into* the braids. They're fresh—or were a few days ago. And the dress..." Running a gloved finger over one of the seams, she shakes her head. "This was hand-stitched. No sewing machine."

"How can you tell?" Jasper asks.

Parker shakes her head. "You realize you're being the world's most cliche man, right? *Look*."

My brother and I lean down to focus on the stitches. "Holy shit," I mutter. "They're uneven."

"There's no tag because this wasn't bought from a store." She turns to Reyes. "I know you were focused on saving her life, but did you happen to notice how well this fit her? Was it baggy? Tight? What about the length?"

The doctor purses his lips. His eyes close for a long moment. "I had to cut it off of her. When we got her onto the table, the dress came almost to her ankles. I cannot be certain, but I believe it could have been made for her."

"You think Grace was taken for—what?—to be some lunatic's *wife*?" Nausea claws its way up my throat, and I swallow against the sour taste of bile.

"It's only a theory," Parker says. "But...it would explain all of this." She plucks a flower petal from the tray and drops it into one of the plastic bags. "Dr. Reyes—?"

"Alejandro, please."

Parker nods. "Okay, Alejandro. Did you collect any evidence from Grace's body? Fingernail scrapings? What about her hair? Has she showered since she woke up?"

For a split second, my entire world turns red. I whirl on

Parker, anger turning to fury tinged by fear. "My wife is *not* evidence!"

"Yes. She is," Parker snaps back. "She has to be. There hasn't been a single lead in almost three years. This is a gold mine. But if we go home without asking the right questions, we could miss something that keeps Grace safe."

Jasper clasps my shoulder. "She ain't wrong, AJ."

His tone—gentle, but with an edge as sharp as steel—grounds me enough to blow out a long, slow breath.

"I know. I fucking trained her. Doesn't mean I have to like it." Turning to the doctor, I cross my arms over my chest. "Well...*Alejandro?*"

He gestures to the second tray. "There is an envelope under the burlap sack with fingernail scrapings. I did not check her hair. Lourdes and Marta bathed her while she was unconscious, but I did not ask them to look for...evidence."

"Connor, bag that envelope," Parker says. "We only have another twenty minutes before dinner. Once we get back to Austin, we could lose access to all of this. Jasper, photos and video of *everything.*"

"Parker, if you think you're cutting me out of this investigation..."

She huffs. "Even if I wanted to—which I *don't*—you'd kick my ass before you'd let me. But this is your wife we're talking about. Do you really think you can be objective? About anything here?"

Again, she's right. So I stand back, hands shoved in the pockets of my jeans, watching.

Connor runs his gloved hands over the burlap sack, examining every inch of the fucking thing like it holds the answers to life, the universe, and everything. "AJ, take a look at this."

The piece of bluish plastic in his palm ain't more than an inch long and half as wide. "What the fuck is it?"

"Hell if I know. It was caught in the burlap. Get me one of those bags."

Once it's sealed, I hold it up to the light. "Looks like it broke off somethin' bigger. Tell me we ain't gonna rely on APD to analyze all this shit."

With a grim smile, Connor folds the burlap so it can be bagged as well. "Nope. I know a guy."

CHAPTER TWENTY-TWO

Grace

THE HEATER SHUDDERS to life in the corner of the room. Soon, the dark shadows will come back, but for now, the last rays of sunlight filter through the window.

Marta prattled on about my handsome husband and brother-in-law as she removed the bulky, white bandage from around my head and replaced it with a single layer of stretchy gauze. If it weren't for the thin hospital gown and bathrobe, I'd feel almost...normal.

I wish AJ had stayed. I don't want to be alone. I think...I miss him. Can you miss someone you don't remember?

The panic attack grabs me so fast and hard, I can't breathe. This bed suddenly feels like a prison with its sterile sheets and cold, metal rails. I wrestle one of them down, then lurch for the recliner.

But the floor pitches. I don't know which way is up. I can barely see, and it's only when I feel the leather under my hands that I know I'm not going to hit the ground.

Vertigo. It's just vertigo. You're safe. And tomorrow, you're going home.

Have I ever been on a plane before? What if I'm afraid of flying? Or get air sick? I touch the scar around my left wrist. What if I get to Austin and still remember nothing? Or what if I remember *everything*? What if the past three years are worse than I've imagined?

I pull the quilt up to my chest as someone knocks on the door. It's soft, tentative. Like whoever's on the other side isn't sure if I'm awake, or wants to give me time to pretend I'm not.

At first, I don't—can't—say anything. I'm curled up in the recliner, willing my heart rate to return to normal. The vertigo left me wrung out and shaky. I'm completely exhausted, but the idea of getting back into that bed makes my skin crawl.

The knock comes again. A little stronger this time.

"Grace?" Parker's steady, calm voice filters through the door, followed by a gentle creak as it opens a few inches. "Can I come in?"

"Yes," I say softly.

She steps inside, shoulders hunched, a soft smile curving her lips. Her tight braid is coming loose, though her flannel shirt is still just as crisp as ever. She looks less like a seasoned law enforcement officer and more like someone's overprotective little sister—except for the sharp glint in her eyes. I think that's all Ranger.

"I asked AJ why you were still sportin' the latest in hospital chic when he'd brought your favorite pair of pajamas. The man cursed a blue streak for so long, he ran out of air." She chuckles and tucks a loose strand of hair behind her ear. "Men. Even the best of 'em are as dense as mud sometimes."

I blink. "He...packed my clothes?" I don't know why this surprises me. AJ has been completely focused on me since he arrived this morning. The quilt. The perfume. It was already so much it never occurred to me there could be more in that duffel bag.

Parker sets the bag at the foot of the bed, pulls out a folded bundle of light blue material, and lays it next to me. She runs a gentle hand over the fabric then raises her eyes to mine. "He said these were your favorite. You can tell they've been well-loved."

A small, stunned ache grows behind my ribs. "He knows what my favorites are?"

Parker's delicate, feminine snort fits her. "He folded these like they were the most precious things in the world. I don't think there's a damn thing about you he doesn't know."

The words knock something loose in my chest. I look away, my eyes stinging, and let my fingers graze the edge of the silky material. They're soft, with a fresh, clean scent that vaguely reminds me of AJ. But there's no memory behind them.

All I have is Parker's word. And the feeling of *home* I found in AJ's arms.

As if she can sense the shift in my emotions, she clears her throat. "You want to change into them? I can help. Or...call the nurse."

I hesitate. When I moved from the bed to the recliner, the floor pitched like a boat in a hurricane. But the idea of getting out of this gown...

The thin fabric isn't much more than paper. Scratchy, sterile...anonymous. Like me, I suppose. I need something that's *mine*.

"If I stand up, I'll fall." My voice isn't much more than a whisper, and my cheeks flush hot. I hate feeling this...helpless.

"Then we'll improvise," she says with a shrug. "I promise not to make it weird."

Parker moves with quiet confidence, pulling the visitor's chair over, then sinking to her knees next to the recliner. She doesn't rush. There's no awkwardness. Like she does this every day.

"If you feel even a little dizzy, tell me, and we'll take a break. Okay?" Her blue-gray eyes search mine until I nod.

I manage to get my right leg into the pants, but she has to help me with the left. Never once does she make me feel exposed. Not even when I sway and she braces me with a gentle, yet firm hand on my shoulder.

"Have you done this before?" I ask, trying to distract myself before she has to tug the pants up to my waist.

"Helped my boss's wife into a pair of pajamas? Why, that's just another day in Texas law enforcement." She gives me a wink, and it startles a soft, choked laugh from somewhere deep inside me. Somewhere I wasn't sure I'd ever find again.

"There you are," she says quietly. "I knew you were in there somewhere."

I reach for her arm, holding on for little more than a beat. "Thank you. For this. For earlier. With Jasper and Connor. For coming so far…"

Parker's gentle smile falls away. "Grace, you don't have to thank any of us for being here. Me, Connor, Jasper…? There wasn't a damn thing AJ could've done to stop us from coming. We've got your back. Even if you don't remember what that looks like."

My throat tightens. I blink hard, trying not to give in to the tears pricking at my eyes.

Parker moves behind me, deftly undoing the ties on the scratchy hospital gown, and I clutch the thin material to my chest before it falls.

"Give me your left hand, Grace. We'll start there."

The soft material is heavy enough to hide the fact I'm not wearing a bra. And it feels like heaven against my skin, with a subtle scent—lavender and cedar and a detergent I don't remember buying. But something deep inside me relaxes a tiny bit.

After the last button is fastened, Parker takes a step back and gives me the once over. "There. Now you look more like you."

"I don't know who that is yet," I say quietly. "Me."

"You don't have to figure it out tonight." Parker reaches into the duffel bag and pulls out a pair of dark gray Keds and fuzzy pink socks. "The food should be here any minute. Want these too?"

"Hell, yes. Anything but those damn hospital slippers."

Parker snickers as she helps me with the socks. "You never know. They might be the next big fashion trend. You could regret tossing them."

"If I do, have me checked for another head injury."

She lets out a low, sultry laugh. "Grace, if you ever wonder who *you* are...? Think back to right now."

"How do you know?"

She's silent for a long moment as she helps me get my feet into the shoes. "I just do."

Her subdued tone worries me enough, I reach out and touch her shoulder. "Are you okay?"

"Don't worry about me," Parker says, her smile only a little forced. "There. You're all set."

I stare down at my arms. The sleeves cover the scars around my wrists. Parker never made me feel helpless or *less than*. If anything, I feel stronger now than I have since I woke up here.

"AJ will be back any minute," she says. "I should go wash up before dinner. But...if you need anything tonight, I'm taking first watch. Call me, and I'll hear you."

The door clicks softly shut behind her, and I'm alone. But for the first time since I woke up in this place, I think maybe...I might find *me* again one day.

CHAPTER TWENTY-THREE

AJ

"READY FOR—?" I stop just inside the door, unprepared for how much different Grace looks out of that drab hospital gown and ill-fitting bathrobe.

Curled in the recliner, dressed in her favorite pair of light blue pajamas, and without the thick, white bandage around her head, I could almost believe she's only been gone a few days—not close to three years. Except she's rail thin, dark circles swelling under her eyes, with nothing but uncertainty etched on her face.

"Thank you...for these," Grace says softly, running her fingers over the flannel. "I feel more like...who I think I'm supposed to be."

I ease a hip onto the recliner next to her. "Darlin', you're not *supposed* to be anyone but who you are right now. Give yourself some time. You'll remember."

Tears shimmer in her eyes. "What if I don't?"

I cup her unbruised cheek, and my heart squeezes as she

leans into the touch. "Then we'll start our lives over again. One new memory at a time."

"I'm sorry," Grace whispers. "For being..."

"No." I take her hands, linking our fingers and holding on tight. "You don't need to apologize, Grace. You're allowed to be scared. Angry. Frustrated. *Anything.*"

She searches my face for a long moment before one corner of her mouth ticks up in what might be a weak smile. "What about hungry?"

For the first time since I walked into this clinic almost twelve hours ago, I catch a glimpse of *my* Grace. The funny, smart, sarcastic woman I fell in love with more than twenty years ago is still in there—even if she doesn't know how to find her way out.

"Hungry is actively encouraged." I lift her left hand and press a kiss to her palm. "It's a bit of a walk down to the atrium. How about we get you into the wheelchair?"

She nods carefully. Like if she moves too quickly, the world will turn upside down. I don't know shit about vertigo, but I'm gonna have to learn.

Grace leans into me as I help her to her feet. She might not know me, but she trusts me—as much as she trusts anyone, I think. And I'm so damn grateful for every time she lets me touch her. For every look. Every hint of a smile. I will be for the rest of my life.

Her steps are a little less hesitant than earlier, but I get her into the wheelchair quickly. She's exhausted. Tomorrow is going to be a long damn day.

"Grace, say the word and we can stay right here. Dinner can come to us."

She straightens her shoulders, peering up at me from the wheelchair like I'm a complete idjit.

"I need to do this," she says. "I need to know...I can."

I ain't about to argue with her. Hell, after what she's been through, she deserves to win any fight we have for the rest of our lives. "If it gets to be too much, just tell me. I'll bring you right back here so you can rest."

Grace

I don't know how to tell AJ that "my room" is the last place I want to be. Dr. Reyes, Lourdes, and Marta have been patient and kind. I think they're good people—even if they do work for the cartel.

But in that room—in that bed—I'm no one. Out here—even stuck in this wheelchair—I feel like someone. I don't know who she is yet, but I want to find out.

My mouth starts to water once I catch the scent of the food. It's almost enough to distract me from the men's voices echoing off the tile floors.

Almost.

My heart starts to pound, and panic swells in my chest.

This is your family. There's no reason to be afraid.

If only I could convince my broken brain it doesn't need to worry.

Parker is the first one I see when AJ wheels me through the arched doorway. Her easy smile helps tamp down my nerves. "About time, AJ. We were about to send out a search party."

"And leave all this food unguarded? I taught you better than that," AJ replies, the hint of amusement in his gaze, the gentle tease, soothing me even more. He cares for these people. He trusts them. Maybe...I can too.

He parks the wheelchair in the corner of the room, helps me to my feet, and keeps his arm around my waist until we reach the table. His steady strength seeps into me—not only my limbs, but somewhere deeper. Every small gesture—every smile, every touch, every patient word—gives me hope that some day soon, I won't be this terrified, broken thing. That I'll be *me* again.

Seated with Parker on my right and AJ on my left, I risk a quick glance at Jasper and Connor across from us. Jasper loads a plate with two tamales and generous scoops of rice and beans, then sets it in front of me.

The scent hits me first. Rich and smoky. Warm. Familiar in a way I can't explain—or don't remember. Do I like tamales? Apparently I do, because my stomach growls so loudly, Connor's brows shoot up and Parker stifles a snort.

Even I smile. But it fades the moment I reach for the knife and fork. My right hand cooperates well enough, but my left...I can't quite close my fingers over the knife's handle. It slips from my weak grasp and clatters onto the plate.

I swallow a sob, my gaze pinned to the edge of the table. Five minutes ago, I felt almost...normal. But suddenly, all my broken pieces are on full display. I should be stronger by now. Better.

AJ says nothing, simply eases the fork from my hand and starts cutting the tamales into pieces. There's no fuss, no panic, no undue attention to my failings. When he finishes, he turns back to his own plate and spoons fresh crema over his beans.

"Thank you," I whisper, my throat so tight, I'm not sure he'll be able to hear me. But under the table, his hand brushes my knee for the briefest of touches.

The first bite is heaven. And when I try a piece of the masa dredged in crema, I almost moan.

As we eat, Parker asks Jasper about Emi's job and Connor shows off pictures of his step-daughter on her first college tour. AJ keeps quiet, stealing glances at me from time to time, probably checking to make sure I'm not about to topple right off the chair.

When all the plates are clean—even mine—Connor clears

his throat. "Grace, we're leavin' around ten tomorrow mornin'. It ain't too bad of a trip, but it might be a little rough on you. Almost two hours in the car, then around ninety minutes in the air. Maybe a little more since we can't fly above ten thousand feet."

Four hours. I can barely stay awake for that long yet, let alone stay upright. I must look as nervous as I feel, because AJ reaches over and links his fingers with mine. "The plane has reclining seats, darlin'. You can sleep the whole way if you want. And once we land, it's only half an hour to get home."

Home.

I've seen a dozen photos of the house on Lake Travis, but none of them feel like home. Will that change when I see it in person? Or will I still be as lost as I am now?

"Grace?" AJ leans over and cups my cheek, his hand warm and gentle against my skin. "Ain't nothing we can't handle together. I believe that. Truly. You're gonna be okay."

His words help soothe my nerves until I meet his gaze. There's real *fear* behind those steady blue eyes. Along with a man who's barely holding it together.

But he's doing it. For me.

I look around the table at the other three people I only just met. People who've already decided they'll burn down the world for me.

So I swallow hard and nod. "Okay."

On my other side, Parker clears her throat. "Can we talk about the elephant in the room?"

Connor takes a long swig from his bottle of Coke. "You mean how we keep the world from knowing Grace is alive until we want them to? That elephant?"

Parker shakes her fist in the air like she's ringing an imaginary bell. "Winner winner, chicken dinner."

CHAPTER TWENTY-FOUR

Grace

THE TENSION suddenly filling the room threatens to suffocate me. Under the table, I try to reach for AJ's hand, but he's on my left, and my fingers find only air.

He stiffens, as if he can sense my growing panic, and scoots a little closer to drape his arm around my shoulders.

Parker nods in my direction. "The minute we take Grace to Austin Memorial for that neurology consult the doc wants her to get, this stops being *our* op. APD will grab it. We'll be benched—again—while they stumble around trying to figure out who did this to her."

Who did this to her.

She says the words like I'm a puzzle they can solve. Find all the missing pieces and voila—I'll be whole again. But I'm so much more than missing pieces. And even if every one of them fits back into place, I'll never be the person I was before. I didn't deserve to wake up here with a broken brain. Or a missing life. Or with three years of horrors I may never remember.

"Seein' a neurologist won't be a problem," Connor replies.

"We can find a doc we can trust. One who'll see Grace off the books."

I wish I felt comfortable enough to ask him how. Luckily, AJ does it for me.

"Care to explain?"

After he finishes the last of his Coke, Connor runs a hand over his thick brown beard. "Pritchard. Well, or McCabe. One of them will have a contact we can trust."

I don't know these names, but the way he says them—and the way AJ, Jasper, and Parker react—gives me the courage to find my voice.

"Who's...Pritchard?"

Connor's slow smile should reassure me. It does in some ways, even if I don't understand why. There's a quiet confidence about him. I wonder how long he was in the FBI. And what he's been doing since.

"Major General Austin J. Pritchard. Retired," he says. "He used to run the Joint Special Operations Command."

"I d-don't...know wh-what that is."

"JSOC is the highest military organization in the United States. Pritchard was forced out last year after he went off book and rescued his sister and her guy from some shit down in Venezuela," Connor explains. Something dark settles in his gaze. Whatever happened...was terrible.

"A few months later, Ryker McCabe—the biggest, baddest sombitch to ever serve in the United States Special Forces— *suggested* Pritchard do somethin' with his life besides worship the ground his fiancée walks on. So he did. Started recruiting." Connor smirks. "The man done rolled up to me with the most cliché line ever." His voice changes, his Texas drawl fading, and a thick, New England accent taking over. "'We help people with nowhere else to turn.'"

"Pritchard needs to hire a PR firm," AJ mutters. "That's terrible."

Connor chuckles, the sound thin, but there's still a hint of amusement in his grim smile. "Terrible, but accurate. Pritchard's got a few of us now. Griff, who was CIA before he was injured; Zephyr, one of the best hackers in the country besides McCabe's wife; and me."

"Hey, what am I? Chopped liver?" Jasper asks. "He offered me a job two hours ago."

AJ stares at his twin for a long moment. "And you took it without even talkin' to me?"

"Five extra minutes in this world don't give you the right to talk me in—or out—of anything." Jasper scoots his chair back a few inches and crosses his arms over his chest. "And you were busy. So, yeah. I took it."

With a shake of his head, AJ mutters, "You've never even met the man."

"He chartered a plane so we could get down here without border patrol knowin' a fucking thing. That tells me all I need to know about the kind of guy he is. And the kind of work he's gonna ask me to do."

I don't understand the tension radiating from the two men. Only that they're staring one another down in some testosterone-fueled pissing contest while Connor tries to smooth things over between them.

Turning to Parker, I whisper, "What's going on?"

She blows out a breath. "It's a long story, and one you should probably hear from AJ. They've had their issues the past few years, but for most of their lives, they were tighter than two rusted lug nuts. They're just finding their way again."

"I'm tryin' to look out for you!" AJ snaps. "I failed once, and I won't let it happen again!"

Parker pushes to her feet. "Stop." Silence falls over the room, the brothers' jaws snapping shut in an instant. "Grace is tired. Hell, we've all been chewed up and spit out twice over today. We're done for tonight. We have four hours tomorrow to figure out how we're gonna keep the world from knowing she's alive until whoever took her is six feet under."

She's so certain. So absolutely confident they can keep me safe. Connor nods. AJ and Jasper share a glance, jaw muscles tightening in mirror images of one another. They believe it too.

"Six feet under...*in pieces*," AJ says.

Jasper snorts. "There won't be enough left of them to bury."

"If you're done being stereotypical over-the-top *men*?" Parker shakes her head. "Connor? Jasper? You're on clean-up duty. Then take the good doctor up on his offer of that pull out couch. AJ? Take Grace back to her room. If I see any of you before three a.m., you'll be sorry."

The men all mutter apologies and rise in unison while I stare up at Parker in awe. "That was...amazing."

She offers me a wink and a smile. "They just needed a kick in the ass. Ain't no thing. You remember what I told you earlier, okay? You need me, I'll be in the hall right outside your room. Though, I suspect AJ's gonna sleep in that recliner, so you'll be just fine."

As AJ helps me into the wheelchair, I hold onto the shred of hope I've found among family. If only I could find my memories there too.

AJ

"Remember," Alejandro says, pulling my focus away from the door to Grace's room, "headaches, double-vision, nausea, ocular phantoms, slurred speech, or worsening of the vertigo could be signs of a brain bleed." He presses a USB drive into my palm. "Here are her medical records. But if you tell anyone *where* she was treated—"

"Doc, you saved her life. That's a debt I'll never be able to repay. I'll take the secret of this place to my grave."

"We all will," Jasper adds. "You ever need a favor—*any* favor—you give us a call."

Reyes chuckles. "I have everything I need, right here."

Despite his smile, it's obvious he knows what my brother just offered him.

A way out of the cartel.

Before Jasper can say another word, the door opens.

Parker has an arm around Grace's waist, but my wife is walking mostly under her own power. Her hair is pulled back in a loose braid, a piece of thin, stretchy gauze—pink this time—fashioned into a headband to hide her stitches.

I can see the tension in her shoulders. The way her left leg trembles with each step. But she's stronger today than she was yesterday, and that's what matters.

The yoga pants practically hang off her. God, she's so thin. And a hint of fear hides in her blue-green eyes.

But her smile, shaky as it is, hits me like a punch in the gut.

I never thought I'd see it—see *her*—again, and now she's standing in front of me after all she's been through with a genuine smile on her face.

"Sorry that took so long," Parker says. "Grace really wanted to wash the blood out of her hair."

"You look beautiful, darlin'."

"I'm a walking bruise," she says softly.

Her fingers curl into the fabric of my shirt, like the long-sleeved Henley is all that's keeping her upright.

I pull her close, pressing a gentle kiss to her forehead and letting her lean against me. "But you *are* walking."

For a moment, I just breathe her in. Even the plain, industrial soap and the vague hint of antiseptic can't hide the scent of her skin. Of the woman I've loved for more than twenty years.

When it's just me—or Parker—Grace's personality is

starting to peek through. She talks more. Breathes easier. But around Jasper and Connor, she quiets. Withdraws. I haven't pushed her to understand why, though I have my suspicions.

My brother and Connor give her space, heading for the cars with Parker close behind, her stride easy. But that's all a ruse. She's always alert. Always watching. Always ready for the worst.

The people who hurt Grace are still out there, and no one's pretending they're not.

The doctor takes Grace's hands, kisses both her cheeks, and murmurs, "Vas con Dios. I will keep you in my prayers."

Grace blinks back a tear and nods. "Thank you. For... everything."

"You owe me nothing, my dear. Your husband will take care of you now. His heart is steady, and I believe it beats only for you."

She glances up at me, so many emotions flickering in her eyes. She trusts me, of that I'm certain. But she's still afraid. Still suffering from the heavy weight of not remembering the man I used to be to her.

The man I still am.

We step out into the morning light. It's too bright, and Grace flinches. I reach for the sunglasses Parker shoved into my hand earlier and slip them over her eyes. Grace releases a slow breath, her shoulders relaxing slightly.

"You okay?" I ask, supporting her weight as we shuffle slowly toward the SUV.

She stays quiet for another few steps. "I...don't know. What if I walk into that house and feel nothing? What if I *never* remember?"

I stop, turning her with her back to the sun so she can look me in the eyes. "Then we start over. We make new memories. Ones no one will *ever* get the chance to take from you."

"But...AJ...?"

"Yeah, darlin'?"

She leans into me, her entire body trembling. "We don't know who took me. Or why. What if they try again?"

I blink, seeing nothing but Grace in that bloodstained white dress, her wrists and ankles bound. Anguish, determination, and rage pulse through my veins. "Let them come, darlin'. It'll be the last damn thing they ever do."

Holding her close, I try to memorize everything about the woman she is today. Her strength. Her courage. How she feels in my arms.

We can't stay here. The longer we're out in public—even in the middle of nowhere—the more likely someone will see something they shouldn't.

Still, I can't rush her. We lost almost three years. I'll give her every second she needs now.

CHAPTER TWENTY-FIVE

Grace

THE WORLD PITCHES sideways as Parker takes a turn. I may not remember riding in a car before today, but somehow, I know she's being careful. Still, I bury my face against AJ's chest.

The SUV's tinted windows hide us from view, but if I keep my eyes open, the passing scenery triggers my vertigo over and over again. At the clinic, I was so excited to leave the broken parts of me behind. But now...I realize all that stayed in Mexico was that awful hospital gown and the fear that no one would have cared if I lived or died.

The flight wasn't terrible, at least. Well, not after the tense moment when the pilot emerged from the cockpit before takeoff and stared right at me.

Connor immediately sprang to his feet, putting himself between me and the pilot, hands balled into fists at his sides.

"If anyone asks, you flew the four of us from Austin to Chihuahua early Saturday mornin', then returned the same four of us back to Austin on Sunday. We good?"

"My instructions were to take this plane on a test flight. I haven't seen any of you. Ever."

I wanted to ask Connor how he could be so sure the pilot wouldn't tell anyone about me. But though it's getting easier to talk to AJ and Parker, and I *know* Jasper and Connor are family too, the words are so much harder with them.

"It's okay," AJ whispers against the top of my head. "We're almost home."

Home.

I wish I had even the slightest idea what to expect. My mind is like a dimly lit hallway, full of doors that won't open.

I'm so tired of trying. Of pounding on those doors until my hands ache. Yanking on knobs that won't turn. Screaming for someone—*anyone*—to find me and let me in. Or out. I can't tell which.

Parker takes another slow turn. Gravel crunches under the tires. The sharp scent of pine permeates the warm air from the heater, and I risk a quick peek through the windshield.

A lake glimmers in the distance, soft blue amid a break in the tall trees.

The butterflies in my stomach aren't fluttering anymore. They're in full battle mode. I want this to feel like home. I want it so badly, my entire body *aches* with the desperate need to find something familiar to hold onto.

The SUV rolls to a stop in front of a large, gray stone porch with a rough-hewn wooden railing surrounding it. The house looks warm. Inviting. Light glows from behind thin white curtains hanging in two big windows on either side of the door.

AJ unclips my seatbelt and somehow manages to get out of the car with me still in his arms. My legs are wobbly, but he barely lets my feet touch the ground until we're up the two short steps and at the door.

"I asked Emi to put Belle in her crate before she left," AJ

says as he pulls his keys from his pocket. "I...*we*...keep it in the mudroom off the kitchen, so she won't be able to see you right away. She's so big, darlin', she'll knock you over without meaning to. But as soon as you're on the couch, I'll get her. Okay?"

I nod.

The brief moments I *do* remember from my life all revolve around this tiny little ball of gray and brown fur and her icy blue eyes. I may feel at home in AJ's arms, but Belle is the only thing I *know* is real. The rest...it could all be an illusion.

The second AJ opens the door, I hear her. A desperate, echoing bark, so much deeper than I'd imagined.

Then another.

"Slow your roll, Belle. I'll be right there," AJ calls as he helps me over the threshold.

Inside, warm wood beams frame the ceiling. Creamy walls, rich tile floors, and a leather sofa anchoring a thick, orange and beige rug fill the space.

Did I choose all the decor? Did we do it together? Or is it all new? Replaced to ease some of the grief AJ carries with him like a second skin, even now.

It smells like him. Like the fresh, almost-spring air, along with a hint of wood smoke, cedar, and pine.

My whole body stills when Belle whines. I can barely breathe. AJ scoops me up and carries me to the couch, settling me in the corner. A large coffee table opens up to reveal thick, wool blankets, and he grabs one, then tucks it around me.

The dog whines again.

"Belle." The word claws its way from somewhere deep inside. From a part of my soul I never thought I'd find again.

It was only a whisper, but she must hear it, because she starts barking even louder.

"I'm comin'!" AJ shouts, running to the kitchen like someone just lit his ass on fire.

Hard nails scrape and scratch against the tile. Belle barrels around the corner, then skids to a stop the instant she sees me. Her thick coat gleams in the late afternoon sun. But it's her glacial blue eyes, wild with confusion—and maybe hope?—that I focus on.

Her broken, keening howl shatters my heart into pieces a second before she launches herself at me.

AJ stands back, tears glistening on his cheeks.

Belle buries her head in my lap with another mournful howl, but her tail wags so hard, her whole body shudders from the motion.

"Oh my God..." I start to cry, my arms wrapped around her torso. "Belle. Sweetie. I'm so sorry..."

My fingers tangle in her fur, raw anguish pouring out of me with each sob. The scraps of memories all tangle together. Her cold nose. Her high-pitched puppy bark. Her red collar.

She's warm. Solid. *Real.*

And she remembers me.

Her big, sloppy tongue laps at my chin, my neck, my arm. She wedges herself next to me, still whining, looking up at me after every tiny movement in case I disappear again.

"I'm here," I whisper, pulling her close. "I'm so sorry, sweetie. I didn't mean to leave you. I didn't want to go..."

Sobs big enough to pull at my stitches punctuate each word, but I could rip them all open and not care. The only thing that matters now is reassuring her that I'm never leaving again.

AJ sits on my other side, one hand on my back, the other stroking Belle's thick scruff. His voice is tight, hoarse. "She waited by the door for months. I moved her bed up there so she wouldn't have to sleep on the tile. I put one of your hoodies in it and, fuck me... She started carrying it around with her." He swipes at his cheeks with the back of his hand. "She never gave up hope, darlin'. Never."

Neither did he.

I hold her tight. She's my anchor to this place. To this *life*. I don't remember the house. Our wedding day. I don't even remember AJ yet.

But I remember love.

For this moment, it's enough to make me believe the rest will follow. Someday.

With Belle's head in my lap and AJ's arms around me, I let myself break. But for the first time since I woke up not knowing my own name, it doesn't feel like falling apart.

It feels like the start of putting myself back together.

CHAPTER TWENTY-SIX

AJ

I LEAN my elbows on the kitchen island, stretching out my back and watching my wife sleep on the couch. The house has been too quiet for the past three years. The sounds of another person existing in your private space seem so much louder when they're gone.

I tried everything to fill that silence—beer, bourbon, running, working...

Fuck.

I need to hide the murder board in my office. And shove all the photos Jasper shared with me—her dress, the ropes, the burlap bag—into some deep, dark folder on my phone Grace will never see.

But first, I have to get some food into her.

The wind scraping against the windows lends a chill to the house that's unacceptable. March in Texas is always a toss-up, but not long after we got home, it turned cold and bitter—the kind of weather that washes the color from the world and turns everything a dismal shade of gray.

I built a fire in the hearth an hour ago. Grace was so tired from all the travel, she didn't stir—still hasn't. Belle is pressed against her like a big, furry blanket. The dog hasn't left her side since we got home. It's gonna be damn near impossible to get her to go out and do her business tonight before bed. Not that I blame her.

I left the chief a message that I was taking a couple of days of personal time. But eventually, I'll have to go back to work. How the hell am I supposed to leave Grace alone and do my job when we still don't know who took her?

My phone screen lights up with a new text.

Connor: Overnighted the flower petals and that piece of plastic to Pritchard. Should know more soon.

I send him a thumbs up, then scroll through the rest of my messages from the past few hours. Two from Jasper. Four from Parker. She went to the medical supply store for a wheelchair, walker, shower chair, and grab bar for the tub so my name wouldn't be attached to the order. She also delivered four bags of groceries and several hand-written recipes.

It knocked the wind out of me. As Parker quietly set the wheelchair in the corner of the room and left the walker next to the couch, I finally realized that I was never as alone as I'd thought.

Connor. Jasper. Parker. Not to mention Isabel and Emi... I was only alone because I wanted to be. Because the one person in the world I needed most was gone.

I stare at the recipes, trying to figure out what Grace might like now. But how can *I* know when she doesn't even know herself? She used to love scrambled eggs, but according to the notes Reyes left in her medical file, she can't even be in the room with them now.

Once she fell asleep, I read through the info on the flash drive. He cataloged every bruise. Every scar. Every stitch. So many injuries that a part of me hopes she *never* remembers what happened to her.

Enchiladas. Those seem…safe. Or maybe pasta? She could eat that one-handed.

Belle starts to whine. Tension gathers in Grace's body, her fingers twitching where they rest against the dog's fur. I skirt the island and kneel in front of the couch. I have to ball my hands into fists to stop myself from pulling my wife into my arms.

"Grace?" I say, keeping my voice as even as possible.

She jerks awake with a sharp inhale, panic flashing across her face before her gaze locks on mine.

"You're home. *We're* home."

Sagging back against the cushions, Grace threads her fingers through Belle's fur. "I couldn't get out." She shudders, a single tear balancing on her lower lashes. "There was a door. But it wouldn't open."

A part of me wants nothing more than to take her in my arms and tell her it's all going to be okay. But I've interviewed enough victims in my time to know even the tiniest details in an investigation can matter.

I take her free hand between both of mine. "What kind of door? Wood? Metal?"

"Wood?" Her voice cracks with the weight of the word, and the tear tumbles down her cheek. "I don't even know if it was real."

"It's okay, darlin'. We'll figure it out. Together." She's so raw —so fragile—I don't want to push her now. Filing the information away for later, I try to steer us to more solid ground. "Are you hungry?"

"A little?"

"Parker dropped off some groceries. I think she got everything I need for a spicy bolognese sauce. Usually it takes a good three or four hours, but I found a recipe for a quick version last year. Does that sound good?"

"I don't know. Did I like it...before?"

There's that damn wobble in her voice again. I'd do anything to give her back even a fraction of the confidence she's lost. If only I could.

"You did. I used to make a big batch at least once a month. But if it doesn't work now, we'll try somethin' else."

Her gaze drifts from me to the kitchen island—and the two stools no one's used since she disappeared. "Okay."

She tries to untangle herself from the blanket and Belle's solid weight, but the dog is having none of it.

I snap my fingers. "Belle. Off."

The dog whines, but when I repeat the command, she lumbers off the couch and flops down on the rug with a very indelicate canine groan.

Grace watches, a hint of amusement in her eyes. "You taught her that?"

"I tried. Half the time she ignores me completely."

I hold out my hand to help Grace to her feet, but she shakes her head. "I...need to do this by myself." She stands slowly, her knuckles turning white as she grips the handles of the walker.

Giving her space is harder than it should be. Half a dozen steps later, her legs are shaking, but she sinks onto the stool with accomplishment shining in her eyes.

"Belle. Come." I point to a spot on the floor right next to the stool, and the dog practically races over to us. "Sit. Stay."

She's already in position before the words leave my lips, steadying Grace with her solid weight.

"Good girl."

While I prep the sauce, I talk. Nothing too serious. The windstorm that took out one of the oldest weeping willows last month. The inserts I got for the fireplaces after coming home to find Belle—and the entire house—covered in soot. And the fight Parker and Hardison had their first day as partners when he insisted Shake Shack was better than Whataburger.

Grace doesn't say much. She smiles at all the right times, but mostly, she listens and watches me.

When I set a bowl of pasta with the hearty meat sauce in front of her, she stares at it—and the fork—for a beat too long.

Fuck.

"If it doesn't smell good, we've got other options."

"No. It...does. It really does," she says and scoops up a bite of corkscrew pasta.

She manages half a serving, which is more than I'd hoped, before her grip starts to falter. I don't say anything—just slide the bowl a little closer and steady it with my free hand.

"Connor's setting things up with the hospital," I say. "We can go in through the service entrance. The tech genius he knows is sending us some sort of gadget that'll shut down any security cameras in the hallways. And no records. This ain't goin' through insurance."

"What about physical therapy?" She glances at the walker like it's her mortal enemy.

"He found someone for that too. Or Pritchard did. She'll come to the house once the neurologist gives the okay."

Grace sets her fork down and nudges the bowl away. "What if we never find out who did this to me? Am I supposed to hide here forever?"

"No." I turn the stool slowly so I can look her in the eyes. "You're gonna get your life back, darlin'. I promise."

CHAPTER TWENTY-SEVEN

Grace

With Belle pressed against me on the couch, I should feel safe. At peace. Even loved.

And part of me does. Somewhere beyond the reach of any memory—deep in my soul—I know I'm home. But until I can piece together what happened to me during the past three years, how can I trust it won't happen again? Or that this time, I won't cheat death simply because it was cold outside.

I'd hoped being home would unlock at least *some* of my memories. But so far, nothing here is familiar.

Maybe after I see more of the house, I'll feel better. I'm so tired, I haven't ventured beyond the kitchen.

But this room feels so...*lived in*. I sank into the cushions like they still held the memory of my butt—or would have if I weren't at least thirty pounds lighter than when I...left.

If I don't remember home, maybe I don't remember healing either. What if it *does* feel like this, and I'm worrying for nothing?

I glance at AJ in the kitchen. He moves with ease, sleeves

rolled up to his elbows, hair mussed from running his hands through it one too many times.

He keeps trying to fill this hollow space inside me with pieces of our lives—memories he carries like they're treasures —but they don't belong to me yet.

Exhaustion that only comes from *years* of stress and strain weigh on his face. This isn't "I've had a long day" tired. This is so much more.

Still, when he catches me watching him, his eyes soften, and he smiles at me. "Almost done. Relax. I'll be there soon."

It's too hard to keep my eyes open, and I jolt as the couch cushions shift.

"I made you some tea." AJ presses a mug into my hands, and a scent that's *almost* familiar wafts over me.

"Is that...lavender?" I ask.

"And chamomile. Honey. A splash of milk." He says the words like they should have a deeper meaning. But I don't understand until I take a sip.

My eyes close on a sigh, and I sink deeper into the cushions.

He knows how I like my tea. Even when *I* don't.

"Is it...?" He runs his fingers through his hair again, which I'm slowly starting to realize is what he does when he's in pain.

"It's perfect. Thank you." The heat of the mug anchors me, along with Belle's soft snores and AJ's scent.

"Did we spend a lot of time in this room?" I ask and take another sip.

"On Friday nights, we'd usually get takeout and watch a movie," he says, his gaze straying to the TV mounted over the fireplace. "You liked your popcorn with extra butter and a truly unhealthy amount of salt."

That pulls a laugh from somewhere deep inside me. "That's probably still true."

"On Sundays—if I wasn't workin'—we'd hit up Stonewood Coffee. Maybe wander through some of the shops on Sixth

Street. We weren't one of those couples who did *everything* together—we were both too busy for that—but we tried to make our time count. My grandfather left me and Jasper a cabin up at Lake Livingston, so when we could, we went up there for a weekend."

He's watching me so closely. Looking for any spark of recognition. Anything to convince him the wife he knew is still inside me somewhere. God, I wish I could give it to him.

My fingers start to tremble, and I set the mug on the coffee table. "I'm sorry," I whisper. "I don't remember any of it. The tea, the popcorn, Sixth Street...you. I want to. But..."

"I know." Those two words carry such a heavy weight, AJ sinks deeper into the cushions, his shoulders slumping as a muscle in his jaw tics.

"I'm hurting you." My eyes burn, tiny pinpricks of pain warning me if I start crying, I might never stop.

"No." He tugs at his hair, hard. "Yes. But that doesn't matter. You're *here*. You're *home*. The rest...even if you never remember who we were..."

His heavy sigh is so full of resignation, I wish I could reassure him. But I can't. Not yet. Even if our past is only a fraction of our story.

"We've loved each other for more than twenty years, Grace. I believe—I *know*—we can love each other again. That's enough for me."

We sit in silence for several minutes, the only light coming from the crackling fire behind the glass insert.

"Do you want to see your studio?" he asks, finally.

The question sends a bolt of panic shooting through my chest. "N-no. I... It's just..." I sink my fingers into Belle's scruff, needing something solid to hold onto. "If I go in there and nothing's familiar...it might break me."

The first tears tumble down my cheeks, and I don't even try to stop them.

AJ scoots closer. "Please, darlin'. Can I hold you?"

I practically dive for him—as much as I can dive for anything trapped by my enormous dog, a blanket, and my injuries. With his arms around me, all the noise in my head fades away. It doesn't matter that I'm broken. That I may never be the woman I was *before*. I'm alive. I'm home. I'm safe.

For tonight, that's enough.

"IT'S GETTING LATE." AJ's voice cuts through the quiet. The fire is only embers now. Dark, ominous shadows—the same ones I was so scared of down in Mexico—shimmer in the corners of the room. They're no less scary here. But at least I'm not alone. "Let's get you into bed."

He snaps his fingers, and Belle comes awake like someone just set off a firecracker. "Go do your business," AJ says and points toward the back of the house.

She looks at me, whines, and lays her head on my legs.

"Belle!" His voice is sharper this time, but she's still having none of it.

"Let me try." I stroke her ears lightly, waiting until those ice blue eyes settle on mine. "I won't leave you again, sweetie. It's okay. Go do your business. I'll wait right here until you're done."

For a moment, I don't think she believes me. Until she lumbers to her feet and pads into the kitchen. Every few steps, she looks back at us, and I give her a little nod. Finally, there's a *thump* from what I assume must be the mud room.

"Doggie door?" I ask.

"Yep. Her collar has a microchip in it. Otherwise, we'd be feedin' every raccoon, possum, and skunk in a ten-mile radius."

AJ braces his hand on the arm of the couch, barely stifling his groan as he gets to his feet, then closes the fireplace insert to quiet the last of the glowing embers. Moments later, Belle bounds back into the room, her eyes wild. As soon as she sees me, her entire body starts wriggling, her tail whipping back and forth like a windshield wiper in a monsoon.

I reach for the walker, but my left hand slips off the rubber grip and sends the metal contraption tumbling. *"Shit."*

AJ doesn't say a word. He sets the walker to rights and scoops me up from the couch like I weigh nothing at all. Probably for the best since I don't know where the bedroom is.

Belle's nails click softly on the tile floor as she pads along behind us. Photos line the walls, but I can't focus on them. The world starts spinning like one of those teacup rides at the fair. Tiny bursts of light hide everything but a hint of AJ's jawline.

I bury my cheek against his neck and pray I won't throw up.

After another few steps, he stops. "Grace? What's wrong?"

"Dizzy. Don't let go yet. Please..."

AJ sinks down, and fabric rustles under us. "Not until you tell me to."

How can he be so steady when I'm falling apart? I can hear the anguish in his voice. How very much he wants me to be *his* Grace. But I'm not. I'm not sure I'll ever be. Yet, he's still here.

After a few breaths, I risk opening my eyes, and when the vertigo doesn't immediately overwhelm me, I start to relax.

The large bed is already turned down. The warm beige walls and plush carpet tickle some long-ago memory. But it's not of this room. It's the room I was fighting to get out of in my nightmare.

"I'm...okay now," I manage. But am I? The idea of sleeping in this big bed all alone terrifies me. Plus...I can barely stand. What if they—the nameless, faceless shadows haunting my nightmares—come for me? I won't be able to get away.

AJ eases me off his lap and I sink against a mountain of pillows. "Wait here. I'll get the walker, then your pajamas."

I don't bother to tell him I can't do anything *but* wait.

Belle puts her front paws on the bed and noses my left hand. "I know, baby girl. It doesn't always do what I want these days." She whines once, then settles in a fluffy black dog bed in the corner of the room where she can see me.

AJ returns, setting the walker in front of the nightstand, and a bundle of dark peach fabric next to me. But then he backs away, his hands shoved into the pockets of his Wranglers. His gaze pings from me to the door to the bed and back again. "I... uh...I'll be on the couch in my office. It's just down the hall. If you need—"

"I don't want to be alone," I blurt out. "And..." I fumble for the pajamas. "I can't take off my bra. Or my socks."

AJ's cheeks turn bright red. "Are you sure?"

I nod, slowly.

My husband's gentle hands peel the sweater from my shoulders. He's careful not to look down as he loosens the buttons of the flannel shirt. More careful still as he draws the quilt up to my chest and moves behind me to release the catch of my bra.

His breath hitches, and for a moment, tension radiates off of him.

Shit.

He's just seen my scars. I stare down at my useless left hand cradled in my lap, fighting back tears.

The bra loosens, and he picks up the pajama top. I don't want him to see me cry—not again—so I squeeze my eyes shut until I find a tiny shred of control.

AJ helps me with everything. Each button. Each tie. He lets me lean on him until I can brace myself against the sink to brush my teeth. At least I'm steady enough to use the bathroom by myself.

I open the door to find him waiting for me in a pair of loose pants and a dark gray t-shirt. He looks so different in some ways. He carries the same strength. The same corded arms. The same lean lines and firm chest. But all traces of the Ranger have faded into the background, leaving only the *man* in front of me. Vulnerable in a way I hadn't thought possible.

AJ helps me under the covers without a word, then darts around to the other side. He flips off the light and stretches out on top of the duvet, keeping his distance. But I know he's there. A steady presence in the dark.

I stare at the ceiling, heart racing. My body aches in places I still don't understand—and don't want to.

But I'm not alone.

The gaping hole where my life *should be* isn't empty anymore. There's a single emotion there, swirling so fast, I couldn't get a handle on it at first. Not until I had AJ's arms around me.

Loneliness.

Whatever happened to me over the past three years, I know one thing for certain—I was utterly and completely alone.

Blindly, I reach for AJ. His hand closes around mine, thumb brushing my knuckles in a rhythmic pattern.

That's all it takes for me to feel...safe. To feel like maybe... this could be home.

CHAPTER TWENTY-EIGHT

AJ

IT TAKES me a second to place the soft, rhythmic sounds in the room. Belle snores at the foot of the bed. The heater kicks on with a low hum. But there's something more.

Grace's slow breathing only a few inches away.

Her fingers are still laced with mine. The pale, morning light peeks through the blinds, painting stripes on the wall above her head.

No nightmares. No midnight flinches or cries. She slept. Easily. Finally.

She might not be able to call up memories of home, but her subconscious believes she's safe here.

Carefully, I ease my hand free and sit up. Every muscle aches like I've been carrying her weight in my sleep. In some ways, I probably have.

Belle lifts her head when I slide out from under the duvet, but she doesn't give a lick about breakfast. Not when she has her best friend back. I scratch her behind the ears. "Good girl," I whisper.

Out in the kitchen, I dump some coffee beans in the grinder, then cringe at the noise. It's almost ten a.m., but Grace needs all the rest she can get.

Starting a fresh pot of coffee, I lean against the counter and stare out at the lake. It's a lighter gray this morning, the thin clouds fighting a losing battle against the sun.

The scent of the dark brew wafts over me. I drink my coffee black—no sugar, no cream—strong and scalding. Grace, though...

I open the cabinet and withdraw the tin of Cafe Vienna.

Memories of *before* hit hard and fast. Grace handing me her cup with a smug smile. Me, taking a sip, pretending to gag on it, and teasing her about drinking hot, flavored water. Her smirk as I always took a second sip...because it tasted like her. Sweet and warm.

For months after she disappeared, I made myself a cup of the weak instant coffee every morning, carrying on a one-sided version of what I once considered a silly little ritual.

Some mornings, it was everything. Others, it was the *only* thing that kept me going.

As the months gave way to years, I couldn't bring myself to keep up the tradition every day. But I always made a cup of *her* coffee on Saturdays. Every week. Without fail.

Now, I measure out the powder, add hot water, and give it a stir.

Grace always said it smelled like cinnamon and vanilla and everything good in this world. For almost three years, I thought it smelled like grief. Today...it calls up a new emotion. Hope.

When I slip back into the bedroom, Grace is still curled on her side. Her eyes are open, but unfocused. Like she's searching for something far away. She blinks when she notices me, and releases her breath on a sigh.

"I made coffee," I say softly, setting the mug on the nightstand, then taking a seat on the edge of the bed next to her.

She struggles to sit up, and I slide my arm around her shoulders to help.

The cup only wobbles a little as she lifts it to her lips. "You take yours black?"

"Yeah." I hold my breath, hoping—praying—she'll remember. But she takes a sip from her mug, smiles a little, and takes another. She doesn't know the ritual. Doesn't know it's missing.

But I do.

I don't understand why it hurts so much. She's alive. Home. In our bed. That should be enough. It *has* to be enough. Yet...

My phone buzzes on the charger, and I glance at the screen. "It's Jasper," I manage over the lump in my throat. "I'll be right back."

I don't answer until I'm halfway to the kitchen again. "Jas? Everything okay?"

"You make it through the night?" My brother's voice is about as rough as I feel. Yet, there's a gentleness to it I haven't heard in years. Not since I stopped listening.

"She slept. *We* slept."

"That's somethin'," he replies. "The doc Connor found has a break from noon to three. Go to the parking garage and find the service elevator marked E7. Parker and I will meet you there."

"She's workin' today."

"Didn't you hear? She ate some bad sushi last night. Been puking her guts out in the bathroom at the station all mornin'." Jasper chuckles. "The chief sent her home. She figures that'll buy her forty-eight hours."

"Good. Thanks, Jas. For everything. Thank Emi for watching Belle too."

"You're my brother, AJ. It don't matter how much of an ass you were. Or how long we went without talkin'. There wasn't a damn thing in this world that would've kept me from helping you and Grace. I'll see you at noon."

We hang up, and I stare at the wall for a full minute. One of our "official" wedding photos hangs right in front of me. Grace and I are hand in hand at the edge of the water on Galveston Island. She laughs as I press a kiss to her neck. Will she ever remember it like I do? Or will this forever be nothing more than a photograph to her?

As I trudge back into the bedroom, Grace sets the coffee mug on the nightstand and reaches for the walker.

I almost call out for her to wait—to let me help her—but then Belle whines.

"It's okay, sweetie. I can do this," she says, her voice stronger than it was yesterday. "But...stay close. Okay? Just in case."

Backing away slowly, I head for the kitchen. Time to see what Grace wants for breakfast.

Grace

The closet smells like cedar and dust and something soft—AJ's aftershave? It's definitely *his*. I want to remember it so badly, it aches.

I lean on the walker, fingers curled around the grips, with Belle at my side. She steadies me when I sway, her big body so solid, she won't let me fall.

The clothes are hung neatly, each shelf perfectly organized. The left side is clearly AJ's. A dozen pairs of Wranglers, pressed dress shirts, jackets, Henleys. Even a black tux.

The other side is mine.

Apparently, I like color. Dresses, soft sweaters, a leather jacket with a rip in one of the cuffs. My hangers hold jeans, blouses, and skirts in deep jewel tones and soft pastels.

The shoes on the rack don't feel like mine. But, I have no idea what my shoes *should* feel like any more than the clothes they sit under.

I lift my left hand to trail over the various fabrics and my fingers don't feel like mine either. Then again, half the time they won't do what I want, so I guess that's...normal.

A green sundress is silky soft. A pair of well-worn jeans would be perfect for dinner and a movie. I recognize a red sweater from one of the photos AJ showed me.

There's something... A flicker. A flash of purple. Laughter. Mine? I think so. AJ's voice—deep, amused, almost...teasing.

"Grace, you can't possibly wear that to the store—"

"I'm buying fifteen sets of watercolors. They'll expect me to be covered in paint."

I close my eyes, trying to chase down the memory. But it's just out of reach. Like a phantom made of nothing but smoke.

"Grace?" AJ's voice echoes through the hall. I'm about to answer, when I see it.

At the very back of the closet, hangs a plain, white dress. Long sleeves. A high neck. No adornments. Cotton. A little wrinkled. Almost...forgotten.

I try to tear my gaze away. For half a second, I do. On the shelf above it, there's a toy light saber.

It's only a Halloween costume.

But I can't breathe.

The walls close in on me. My chest constricts, a single wheeze all I can manage before my throat locks up completely. I clutch the walker, but the room tilts, sliding sideways off a cliff where no one will ever find me again.

Belle starts to whine, but it's far away now. Miles and miles and *years* from home.

A harsh, lemony scent punches through my memories. Plain wooden walls. White tile. A hand around my throat.

"Grace? Fuck. Grace!" Strong arms catch me as the gaping maw of all the things I can't—or don't want to—remember is about to swallow me whole. "It's okay. You're safe. It's me. It's AJ."

I'm frozen, but his chest at my back is warm. My entire body shakes, yet his voice is calm.

Belle barks and presses against my legs, anchoring me to AJ like she *knows* I'm about to disappear again.

My breath saws roughly over my throat. "Th-the d-d-dress... The wh-white one..."

"The costume? We were Han and Leia years ago for Halloween." He turns us just enough I can't see it anymore, but I know it's there. Waiting to take me again. "It can't hurt you, darlin'. I promise."

I twist around to bury my face in his chest. My right hand fists the front of his t-shirt. He smells like coffee and firewood and the outdoors and *home*, but bile still burns the back of my throat.

"I hate this," I choke out. "I want to remember *you*. Not... whatever *that* is."

He doesn't try to stop my tears. Only tightens his embrace, one hand cupping my neck, the other at the small of my back, holding me here—with him and Belle.

"I've got you, Grace. Always." The words—whispered against my hair—should be enough. They almost are.

Belle leans her entire body against the back of my legs, as if she's trying to press me even closer to my husband. Her cold nose nudges my left hand. For once, my fingers do what I want and stroke the top of her head.

It takes minutes to be able to breathe again. Full, shuddering breaths that don't scrape over my throat like sandpaper.

When I sag against AJ, my body no longer trapped in whatever fractured memory threatened to destroy me, he helps me out of the closet and over to the bed. I think he's going to lie down with me, but instead, he snaps his fingers. "Belle, up."

The dog hoists her big body onto the mattress and drapes herself across my lap.

"Stay," he commands, and I almost laugh. It would take a forklift to move her.

He disappears into the closet for a brief moment, emerging with the dress balled up under his arm. Without a word, he leaves the room. A door in another part of the house opens and closes. Once. Twice.

I don't need to know where he's taking it. For now, it's enough to know that it's gone.

CHAPTER TWENTY-NINE

AJ

I DIDN'T WANT to leave her. But if I go much longer without a shower, she won't want to get close to me. And having Grace in my arms is all that's keeping me together.

Plus, I'm sportin' almost a full beard, and it itches. A couple days' stubble is all I can stand.

I lift the simple, silver chain over my head and curl my fingers around her wedding ring. She always took it off for long runs, and when I found it in her jewelry box two days after she disappeared, I "borrowed" one of her necklaces so it—she— would always be with me.

She ain't ready for me to slide it back on her finger. Or maybe *I'm* the one who ain't ready. If I try and she refuses, it might break me.

I reach for my shaving kit, then tuck the ring and chain into one of the side pockets before stepping into the shower.

The hot water cascades over me, burning away some of the stress and strain. But not the memory of Grace having a panic attack over a fucking Halloween costume.

Or the vision of another white dress behind my closed lids, this one stained with her blood.

I hid the costume in the bottom drawer of my desk, then texted Parker, Jasper, and Connor asking them one question—

What do you know about cults?

It's the only thing that makes sense. But if there were major cult activity in Austin, we'd have heard about it. Especially if they made a habit of kidnapping local women.

Connor said he'd set Zephyr on some internet sleuthing. Parker can only access some of the Rangers' databases from home, but she'll do what she can. Soon, we're gonna have to read in Hardison. He's so damn quiet most of the time, I don't know him well. But Parker trusts him, and that's enough for me.

I scrub the bar of Irish Spring over my skin. I still remember the last time Grace touched me—*really* touched me—the morning she disappeared.

My dick rockets to life under my hand.

Fuck.

She ain't ready for anything more than forehead kisses and being held close, but my body doesn't know that. If I rub one out now, it'll take the edge off. I hope.

But even though the memory of our last time together is clear as day, when I close my eyes, I see her as she is now. Fighting demons she can't name. Bruised and beaten within an inch of her life. A shadow of the woman I married.

I rest my forehead against the glass wall, and let myself cry.

———

AFTER I RUN the electric razor over my face and soothe the skin with the balm Grace always loved the scent of, I cinch a towel tight around my waist. Why didn't I think to grab my bathrobe before I came in here? The last thing I want to do is make her uncomfortable. But I can't get to the closet without going through the bedroom.

She's sitting up against the headboard, Belle stretched out next to her, when I open the bathroom door.

Her unbruised cheek turns bright red as her gaze snaps to my bare chest.

Fuck.

I'm halfway to the closet when she says my name.

"AJ? Come here. Please?"

If I turn around and she looks away, I'll break right in front of her. "Let me get dressed, darlin'. I won't be more than two shakes."

"No."

No?

The duvet rustles. Grace hisses out a breath. The sound sends panic's icy fingers to squeeze my heart, and I rush over to her. "What's wrong?"

She sits on the edge of the mattress, one hand pressed to her side. "I moved a little too quickly, that's all. But...sit with me. Please."

It's not easy to keep the towel in place as I sink down next to her. Why didn't I buy those big-ass bath sheets last year?

Grace reaches up to touch my cheek. "This is how you looked in most of the pictures."

I sit up a little straighter. "There wasn't a single photo of me half naked in a towel."

She laughs—truly laughs like I haven't heard in three years. God, I've missed that sound.

"Fair point. But maybe there should have been." Turning to face me, she rests her hand over my heart. "I'm terrified of a lot of things right now, AJ. But not of seeing you. You're my husband. I may not remember getting married, going on our honeymoon, buying this house, or...*anything* from our lives together, but I know I feel safe with you."

I wrap my arms around her, pulling her against my chest and letting her hands smooth down my back.

And when her lips press to the curve of my neck—just for a single breath—a part of me I thought I'd lost forever finds its way home.

Grace

Water splashes into the tub, steam rising in slow, lazy curls, clinging to the mirror and softening the edges of my reflection.

I was so dizzy when AJ helped me to my feet, I didn't trust myself with the walker. He didn't judge. Just got the wheelchair so I wouldn't have to sit—and balance—on the closed toilet while he ran me a bath.

He drops to a knee in front of me, wearing only a pair of Wranglers, his chest still bare. He's wiry. Strong, but not bulky. I could trace his six-pack if I were brazen enough. But while I didn't lie earlier—I'm not afraid to see him or touch him—I *am* afraid of anything more. What if I kiss him and feel nothing? Or what if all I feel...is pain?

"I think I can use one of your hair clips to keep your braid out of the water." AJ lifts the long twist of hair and sets it on top of my head. But before he grabs the clip off the counter, I reach for his hand.

"Cut it for me."

He freezes. "What?"

"In all the pictures...it was shorter. And it's too heavy. It makes the headaches worse. I don't know why it's so long. If I wasn't allowed to cut it or if I didn't want to, but I want to now. I just don't trust myself with scissors."

He frowns. "Grace, I don't know shit about cutting hair. You always went to a salon downtown. What if I mess it up?"

My heart aches at the worry in his tone, and I give his fingers a quick squeeze. "It's hair. It'll grow back."

Blowing out a long, slow breath, he nods. "Okay. How short do you want it?"

"To my shoulders? Give or take?" In truth, I don't care. Anything will be better than the braid almost brushing my ass.

After a quick check of the water level in the tub, he drapes a towel over my shoulders and removes the tie holding the braid together.

It takes him almost a full minute to unwind Parker's handi-work. God, there's so much hair, I can barely see *me* once he finishes.

"I can't promise this is gonna be even," he says, his voice cracking on the last word.

"You're stalling." I meet his gaze in the mirror, hoping my smile will reassure him. It must, because the shears whisper through my locks one section at a time. With each cut, I feel lighter, until there's a pile of hair on the counter and what's left falls to just below my shoulders.

The woman staring back at me now is less of a stranger. And in her eyes? There's a tiny flicker of recognition.

"I look more like me," I say, my voice so quiet, I don't know if he can even hear it over the running water.

He gives my shoulder a gentle squeeze. "You always looked like you, darlin'."

Moving the wheelchair so it's right next to the tub, he plunges his hand through the bubbles to check the water temperature, then turns off the faucet and shifts from one foot to the other, his gaze pinned to the floor. "Can you...uh...do you need me to stay...?"

As much as I want to be strong enough to do something as simple as bathe on my own, I know I can't. Not yet.

The dizzying hum behind my eyes hasn't let up since my panic attack earlier. And I'm so tired of feeling fragile.

"I'm afraid I'll fall," I whisper.

"Then I'll stay." His tone is soft, but certain. "Whatever you need, I'm here for you, Grace. Always."

AJ unbuttons my pajama top, his eyes never leaving my face —not even when he eases the fabric from my shoulders. Gently, he guides my arms around his neck and lifts me to my feet. His warm fingers curl around the waistband of my pants, lowering them—and my panties—to the floor.

For the first time in three years, I'm naked in front of my husband.

It lasts for all of half a minute before he guides me into the tub. The water wraps around me like a warm blanket, and I let out a sigh.

AJ crouches down, but doesn't look at me. "You can reach the grab bar, right?"

"Yes. But...will you stay? Just...talk to me?"

He eases himself onto his ass, elbows resting on his knees, gaze pinned to the floor. "About what? How we met? Our friends?"

Running the washcloth slowly over my left arm, I figure out what I want to know. "Tell me about the last three years. About your life."

Slowly, he raises his head, his eyes full of grief. "I didn't have one."

Shit.

I asked too much of him. I'm searching for something else to grasp onto—a safer subject—when he continues.

"I worked. A lot. Got an apartment in town close to the station. I couldn't sleep in our bed every night without you. Belle and I...we came here on weekends, but Sunday through Thursday, we lived there."

My eyes prickle with the threat of tears, but I swallow them down. I need to know him. *Really* know him.

"You said...yesterday...that you and Jasper had issues. Why?"

His mouth flattens into something not quite a smile. "Six months in, he told me to get my ass back to work. That I had to...move on. I kicked him out of the house and didn't talk to him for almost two years after that."

"AJ! He's your twin!"

His eyes meet mine with such seriousness, I hold my breath until he speaks again.

"And you're my everything. He had no right. And he knows it."

Heat flushes over my skin. Not from the water, but from somewhere deep inside me. He loved me enough to choose me over his own brother. To hold out hope for three years that one day, I'd come home.

"You never moved on," I say softly.

"No."

A long silence stretches between us. If I had the words, I'd tell him how much I want to remember. How much I *need* to remember a love strong enough to bring us back together again. But they're lost somewhere, and I don't know how to find them.

Eventually, I lean forward and pass him the washcloth. "Do my back?"

AJ hesitates, staring at the cloth like it might burn him. But then he takes it, his fingers brushing mine. "I ran the trail every Saturday with Belle," he says, his voice soft but steady. "Where you disappeared. I thought maybe... Fuck. I don't know what I thought—especially the last few weeks. That I missed something the hundred and forty other times? That whoever took you would be stupid enough to come back? That God would drop a clue at my feet if I showed up enough. Prayed enough."

I blink hard. "AJ..."

He shakes his head, then trails the cloth over my shoulders. "It was all I had."

"What about friends?" I ask gently. "Connor? Parker?"

"I've only known Connor for a couple of months. Parker...I trained her, sure. She helped me track down the few leads we got after APD declared...you...a cold case. But we never got together outside of work."

He finally glances up, meeting my gaze. "You were the center of my life, Grace. Without you, everything just... stopped. The apartment was for sleep and work. The house was for grief. And so Belle could chase tennis balls—when I could muster the energy to throw them. All your clothes? Your studio? Hell, your hair clips and eye cream. I wouldn't get rid of anything. I couldn't. There was no world for me without you."

My voice fails me for too long, but when he dips the cloth into the water and runs it down my spine, I ask, "Why didn't you give up?"

He doesn't look away. "I wish I could say it was because I knew you were alive. Because I felt it. But...really...I'm only still here because of Belle."

Oh, God.

The dog lets out a soft whine from the hall, echoing AJ's pain. I reach for him, sloshing a little water over the edge of the tub as I wrap an arm around his shoulders.

He doesn't speak. But with one single sob, he shatters into pieces.

AJ

Fuck.

Fuck!

I try to hold myself together. Grace is still so fragile. I'm supposed to be the strong one. The one who keeps her safe.

But I fail. Again.

Another sob rips through me, jagged and loud, echoing off the tile. Grace pulls me closer, bathwater spilling over the edge of the tub and soaking my Wranglers.

I should care. I should grab a towel. I should do *anything* but sit here shaking like a rookie in his first firefight.

Her skin is so warm beneath my cheek. Her fingers move through my hair in slow, shaky strokes, and for the first time in three years, I don't feel like I'm drifting—untethered—through a storm.

"I'm sorry," I rasp, though I'm not sure which failure I'm apologizing for. Losing her? Not finding her sooner? Almost giving up? Maybe all of it.

She shakes her head softly. "You have nothing to be sorry for."

"Don't say that," I whisper. "You have no idea how many times I—" My throat closes, the words bottling up like they're scared to see daylight. I force them out anyway. "How many times I sat in the dirt—right where I found your water bottle—and tried to convince myself you were gone so my heart wouldn't tear itself in half with every beat."

Her breath hitches, but her arms stay locked around me. "You're here. *I'm* here. Nothing else matters."

Grace is crying now too. Her tears fall onto my back, tiny tremors shaking her too-thin frame.

I should comfort her. Pull myself the fuck together and be the man she needs me to be. But I don't know how.

Or how to stop myself from telling her that every week, I'd stand at the start of the trail, staring at my own shadow and wondering if the world would be better off without it.

"Belle needed me," I say, my voice cracking on the truth I've never admitted to anyone. "Without her—"

"Don't." Grace's hand cups the back of my neck, squeezing lightly. "Don't tell me you didn't fight for yourself, AJ. You did. You brought me home."

The last word escapes as a whisper. Or maybe...as a prayer.

The water on the floor has gone cold, soaking through my jeans. Hell, the water in the tub is cooling where my elbows have broken through the bubbles.

"I'm afraid if I let go, you'll disappear again."

"Then don't let go," she murmurs, lips curving against my temple. "Not yet."

We stay locked together long enough for the water on the floor to lose its chill completely. Long enough for my heartbeat to match the steady rhythm of hers. I don't know if I'm holding her or she's holding me. And it doesn't matter, as long as we're together.

CHAPTER THIRTY

AJ

I SHOULDN'T HAVE BEEN SO FUCKING honest. Or perhaps I needed to admit the truth to the person I trust most in this world. Only Grace could watch me fall apart and then put me back together with a single embrace.

Even without her memories, she's still the woman I fell in love with. Still my best friend. Still my everything.

Now, she clutches my arm as we stand in the closet. "There's too much," she says softly. "I should know what I want to wear. Shouldn't I?"

The pain in her voice stabs me through the heart. She's still so unsure. So lost, despite being right next to me.

"Maybe it's not about knowing," I offer. "Maybe it's about feeling. What *feels* right?"

Her left hand shakes as she touches first one sweater, then another, and another before settling on a purple cashmere tunic and the jeans I always thought were her favorite.

We sit on the bed together, and I draw the bathrobe off her shoulders so I can help her with her bra. Every time I see the jagged scars across her back, I want to throttle the fucker who gave them to her.

Fastening the clasp, my fingers brush right over the worst of them, and Grace shudders.

"Are they...ugly?" she asks, her voice so small, it almost fades away on the last word.

"They're a part of you, Grace. And you're beautiful." I press a kiss to the top of her shoulder where another one of them ends.

The tiny sound she makes might be a chuckle. "I'm not sure I can trust you anymore, AJ. When was the last time you had an eye exam?"

"Last month. Twenty-twenty all the way, darlin'. You need help with the rest?"

My phone lights up on the nightstand, Connor's name flashing across the screen.

Grace passes it to me. "Go ahead. I should be okay until I get to the shoes."

"Connor? Tell me you've got somethin'." I tuck the phone between my shoulder and my ear, striding out to the kitchen so I can fill Belle's water bowl.

"Nothin' concrete. Austin's fiancée, Mikayla—she's the botanist I told you about—says the flowers are oleanders."

"Oleanders?" My back hits the countertop. What are the odds...? "Grace has a tattoo of oleander flowers on her right arm. Along with the phases of the moon."

"You think there's a connection? They grow all over the goddamn state. Hell, they're native to Texas, California, Nevada, Arizona, Mexico, half of Central America... Maybe whoever wove them into the ropes did it because of the tattoo. If she meant somethin' to them, could have even been out of respect."

Rage pulses in my temples. "*Respect?* She was poisoned,

stabbed, and left for dead. What part of that says *respect* to you?"

"I was on the job for twenty years, AJ. Want to know the most important thing I learned?"

"No."

"Too bad. You're gonna hear it anyway. Ignoring a theory, no matter how batshit it sounds, is loopier than a cross-eyed cowboy."

Fuck.

He's right. My anger won't help Grace if it stops us from following a lead—any lead—that could keep her safe.

"Yeah. Okay. So the flowers are a dead end. For now."

"Did I say that? Mik's damn good at her job. She's running tests on the pollen to see if that helps her narrow down where it's from. Apparently, that's a thing. She also suggested taking a sample of Grace's hair and sending that off to a lab for analysis."

"I cut it for her this mornin'. I can pull a few strands out of the trash—"

"Fuckin' hell, AJ. You're a Ranger. You know the ends won't work. Needs to be recent growth. Down by the root." Connor's sigh carries over the connection. "Get your head on straight, idjit. Grace needs you at your best."

He's right. I'm still so damn raw from the past three days, I'm not doing anyone a lick of good. I lower my voice as I angle a gaze down the hall toward the bedroom. "Zephyr get anything on cults active in the Austin metro area?"

"Not yet. She's workin' two cases right now. I don't think she's slept in twenty-four hours. But I put in a call to my old boss at the Bureau. Maybe he'll have some resources he'll be willin' to share."

"Thanks, man. I owe you."

Connor chuckles. "We ain't nowhere close to even, AJ. What you did for Isabel and Veronica? I'll be in your debt till the end of the world. Let me know how it goes with the doctor today."

"Will do."

BELLE SITS up in the back seat of the SUV, her travel harness secured by the seatbelt. I should have known she wouldn't take kindly to Grace leaving the house without her. I got her in the crate easy enough, but the second she couldn't see Grace, she started makin' such a ruckus, I was sure she was gonna hurt herself.

Behind dark glasses, Grace's eyes are closed, and she has the door handle in a white-knuckled grip.

"I wish I could hold you, darlin'," I say, reaching over to brush her cheek with my knuckles at a stoplight. "I should've asked Jasper to drive us."

Grace leans into the touch, then grimaces. "It's not as bad as yesterday. But—" Her hand flies to her mouth. "Oh, God. Air. I need...air."

I crack the window for her, letting the biting March wind roll through the cabin. "Hang on. There's a parking lot up ahead. We can stop for a few minutes."

"No," she says through gritted teeth. "I'm...okay."

I shake my head, relieved Grace's eyes are still closed. Okay is somewhere north of the moon. She ain't even *close* to okay. The doc better have some answers for us.

In the parking garage, Parker leans against the bumper of Jasper's truck, her sharp-eyed gaze sweeping over the handful of cars. This level is reserved for the hospital staff, though I've parked down here a time or two on official business.

My brother paces the entire length of the row until he sees my SUV, then double-times it back to the truck.

Grace lets out a sigh the moment I put the car in park.

"You want the walker or the wheelchair?"

"I *want* to walk on my own," she mutters.

I cup her cheek and skate my thumb under her eye. "Soon."

"Uh, AJ?" Parker nods at the back of the SUV. "Did you get Belle an Emotional Support Animal certification in the past twelve hours?"

"She almost destroyed her crate before we got halfway to the door. Didn't know what else to do with her." I unfold the wheelchair next to the passenger door. "Maybe you can keep her calm while we go up."

Parker arches her brows. "If that's your way of saying 'stay in the van', fuck that. Jasper can take her. I'm sticking close to Grace."

My wife sways to her feet, her right hand gripping the door frame hard enough her arm shakes. The dark gray scarf hiding her blond locks comes loose and flutters to the ground.

Parker retrieves the scarf and helps Grace into the wheelchair. "Boss, if you ever retire, beauty school is a real possibility."

Grace touches her hair, her gaze pinned to her left hand resting in her lap. "I...like it," she manages.

All the color drains from Parker's cheeks. "Shit, Grace. I was being serious. It looks great." She leans closer and lowers her voice. "But next time I come to the house, I'll clean up the ends for you."

"I heard that." Once I hand Belle's leash to Jasper, I grab the handles of the wheelchair. "We're gonna be late. Parker? Lead the way."

Grace

The service elevator is quiet, but the second the doors open and we move out onto the floor, the noise is almost overwhelming. Too many people fill the halls. The scent of antiseptic reminds me of waking up in the clinic, disoriented, afraid, and alone.

I keep my head down, praying the world doesn't decide to go sideways on me.

The scarf hides my hair well enough, but even with the dark purple bruise covering my left cheek, I still look like...me.

"Sir! Your dog can't be in here." An orderly steps in our path, his voice too loud. Too on edge. My entire body tenses. I want to disappear. To hide behind AJ or Belle or even Parker so he can't hurt me.

AJ unbuttons his jacket. He clipped his Ranger star to his light blue dress shirt before we left. "We're here to see Dr. VanHorn. All of us. Including the dog."

"Ronnie, they're good." A woman waves from an open door a few feet away. "I'm Dr. VanHorn. I'm sorry I didn't meet you at the elevator. This wing is being renovated next week, and I had to get someone to flip the breaker for the MRI."

As soon as the door shuts behind us, Jasper clears his throat. "I'll keep watch. You three go with the doc."

I start to breathe a little easier when we leave Jasper behind. He's AJ's twin. Family. He's never done a single thing to hurt me. But I still have a hard time finding my voice around him.

Belle noses my hand, as if she can sense how on edge I am. I curl my fingers around her harness until the doctor leads us into an exam room where the lights are on low and the blinds drawn.

"Grace, I'm Sydney." The doctor crouches down so she can see my face, a warm smile curving her lips. She can't be much older than me—not that I remember how old that is—with a streak of bright pink in her short black hair. "Normally, I'd have a nurse, a nursing assistant, and an orderly around for a battery of tests like this, so if I'm a little flustered, that's why. But we'll get through it. Okay?"

"Can Belle stay with me?" I ask, tightening my grip on the harness. "And AJ?"

Sydney frowns. "Not the whole time."

"I ain't leavin' her alone," AJ grits out. "No fucking way."

The doctor rises, hands on her hips. "Sir—"

"No. Fucking. Way."

Parker wedges herself between my husband and Sydney. "Dr. VanHorn, how many months of funding did you just receive for your traumatic brain injury research project? Six? Or was it nine?"

With a sigh, the doctor takes a step back. "Fine. But if anyone," she glances at Belle, "*licks* the equipment or drools on me..."

"Did you hear that, AJ?" Parker elbows him in the side. "No drooling."

I HATE the sensation of the hospital gown Sydney had me change into. Even worse, it's *white*. When I first saw it, I almost begged AJ to take me home. But...I need these tests. At least that's what I keep telling myself.

The CT scan wasn't terrible. Sydney was gentle as she checked my reflexes, drew blood, and measured my grip strength.

But the MRI machine feels like a coffin. The bangs and clicks as it takes pictures of the inside of my head are deafening. Only AJ's hand on my ankle keeps me from a full-on panic attack. He hasn't left my side. Belle is in the next room, her front paws on a chair so she can see me through the window.

Every so often, she barks and whines, but Parker is trying to keep her calm.

"Only another few minutes, Grace." Sydney's voice floats through a speaker somewhere inside to the machine. "You're doing great."

I'm so exhausted. It's been more than two hours of questions, reflex assessments, scans, X-Rays, and even a set of math and word problems. I want to go *home*.

"Hold still for a count of ten. This is the last image I need."

The loud noises come from every direction. A single tear trails down my right temple. It's so bright in here, even with my eyes screwed shut. The cacophony from the machine turns into a hum so strong, it vibrates through my entire body. It goes on and on...for hours...even days...

"Your sacrifice will bring about salvation..."

The man's voice chills me straight through. My stomach twists in on itself like I haven't eaten in forever. I can't get out. Can't move. Can't breathe. My fists hit wood. It's so hot. Then freezing cold. My wrists ache. My hands. My head. Oh, God. I'm going to die in here...

"Grace!"

The bright lights fade away. My chilled skin warms where strong arms wrap around me. A wet nose presses to my calf, followed by a solid weight and wiry fur under my fingers.

"Come back to me, Grace. You're out. The scan's done."

AJ.

I open my eyes. The panic and fear etched on his face ease only slightly when his gaze locks on mine.

"You were screaming." The words are like gravel spilling from his throat. "Begging. 'Make it stop. Please. Make it stop.'"

CHAPTER THIRTY-ONE

AJ

BELLE'S soft snores rumble at the foot of the bed, her paws twitching in some happy dog dream. Chasing squirrels, probably. Or tennis balls. She loves tennis balls.

My laptop is warm against my thighs, the glow of the screen the only light in the room. I've been up and working for hours, but Grace hasn't stirred.

Hearing her broken, whimpering cries from inside the MRI machine destroyed me. She couldn't tell me why she was screaming, "Make it stop." She couldn't say much of anything beyond, "Take me home."

Jasper left his truck in the garage and drove us home so I could hold her. She clung to me, staring vacantly into the distance, not a single flicker of recognition in her eyes.

Was it a mistake to bring her to the hospital so soon? Reyes told me not to wait. That he'd done his best, but he wasn't a neurosurgeon.

I should have known she wasn't ready.

As soon as I helped her into her pajamas, she curled into a

ball under the duvet and fell asleep. I didn't even have time to get her a glass of water and one of the Xanax Dr. VanHorn prescribed for her.

I kept watch over her long after exhaustion tried to pull me under. But eventually, I wrapped my arm around her waist, buried my face in her hair, and let the nightmares come for me.

In every one, when I woke up, she was gone.

She's going on almost fourteen hours of sleep, and I've spent the past five of them searching for any and all cult activity from Austin to the US-Mexico border.

Even after so long, her face looks...hollow. Like sleep can't touch the bone-deep exhaustion that comes from constantly trying to remember who she once was. Or what was done to her.

Now on my second cup of coffee, I rest my back against the headboard and take a long, slow sip. On screen, a slideshow of the bloodstained dress Grace was found in, the burlap bag, and the white and gold rope plays on a loop. I keep hoping I'll see something—*anything*—that might help me figure out who took her. And whether they're still out there.

A ping breaks the quiet. A new email from Reyes.

AJ,

I received the toxin results from the lab this morning. Grace consumed a concentrate of oleander nectar before she was stabbed. It was strong enough that, had hypothermia not slowed her metabolism, her heart would have stopped before the blood loss killed her. I hope all is well, and that Grace's memories are returning.

Respectfully,

Alejandro Reyes

Oleander. Again.

What are the odds a woman with oleander flowers tattooed on her shoulder would be poisoned with oleander concentrate and bound by ropes woven with oleander blooms?

A soft, broken sound snaps my focus back to Grace. She twists under the blanket, breath catching in her throat. Her lips move, but no words come out—just choked sounds, her face pinched like she's bracing for a blow.

Belle raises her head. "Shhh, girl. I've got her."

Setting the laptop aside, I ease myself down and draw Grace against me. Her body fights me, caught in whatever hell she's reliving in her mind.

Her pajama top slides off her shoulder enough to expose a bit of her tattoo—the spray of oleander flowers in pink and white and red. She got it years ago, not long after our wedding, to remind her how the blossoms framed us as we said our vows.

Fuck.

I don't know what's worse—her captors taking her because of the tattoo or them discovering it and turning it into the instrument of her death as part of some sick fucking joke. Either way, they've stained something that should have been untouchable.

Her choked cries coalesce into words, repeated over and over again. "AJ...please find me."

My chest constricts. She needed me, and I wasn't there. For three goddamn years. I failed her. I won't fail her again. I can't.

Tightening my arms around her, I press my lips to her ear. "You're home. You're safe. You're loved." I repeat the mantra half a dozen times. *"You're home. You're safe. You're loved."*

Her nails dig into my skin. "I'll be good. I promise..."

Slowly, the tension starts to bleed from her muscles. Her rapid, wheezing breaths even out. She stops trembling.

Her eyes blink open, glassy and disoriented. "AJ?"

"I'm right here, darlin'. You were having a nightmare." Grace fumbles for my hand, and I link our fingers. "Can you tell me about it?"

She curls into me, pressing her face to my t-shirt. "There were men. But...I can't see them. I don't...want to see them."

The fear in my wife's voice cracks my heart into pieces. I want to pull the duvet over our heads and hide away in this room for the rest of our lives. But that won't keep her safe.

She's not just your wife. She's a victim. A witness. Treat her like one.

"Don't look at them, darlin'. Listen. Tell me what you hear. What are they sayin'?" One hand curled around her trembling fingers, I run my other over her back in long, slow circles.

"I...can't..."

"You can. You're safe. Home. With me and Belle." I keep my voice low so I don't spook her. The dog wriggles closer, flopping across Grace's legs like she's trying to anchor her in the here and now.

She shudders once, then lets out a tiny cry. "'You broke the rules. Again.'"

"What rules?"

"Not...supposed to talk. Not...Grace anymore. Can't...I can't..." Her words dissolve into weak sobs, and I rock her gently until she calms.

Not...Grace?

Did those fuckers give her a different name? Stop her from talking completely? I'm gonna cut out their tongues when I find them. See how *they* like bein' forced into silence.

After a few minutes, she lets out a sigh. Her gaze flicks to mine, then shifts to the center of my chest, right where her wedding ring hides under my t-shirt.

"I'm sorry. I *want* to remember. I really do."

"Grace, look at me. Please?" She doesn't move, so I shift enough to nudge her chin up slightly. "After the MRI yesterday —after whatever memory it triggered—you were mostly out of it. But the doc explained a little bit about retrograde amnesia.

"Your memories are in there somewhere." I press a kiss to

her forehead, and when I pull back, she doesn't look away. "They're like a ball of rubber bands—all twisted together. But what you went through, combined with the head injury, covered the ball in layers and layers of bubble wrap. Peeling them away? It's gonna take time."

A tear glistens on her cheek. "They took me, AJ. What if they do it again?"

"They won't. I swear to you, Grace. They won't."

CHAPTER THIRTY-TWO

Grace

I SINK ONTO THE COUCH, and Belle is immediately at my side. My legs feel more like wet noodles than actual functional limbs. Karen—the physical therapist who comes to the house every day at one p.m. sharp—says I'm getting stronger, but my muscles ache in ways I didn't know they could.

AJ ambles in from the hall. The first time Karen came, he stayed in the room. Just sat quietly in the corner with Belle at his side and his phone in his hand. Texting with Connor, Jasper, and Parker, I think. But for the past two days, he's retreated to his home office during our sessions. I wasn't sure I could handle being alone with someone new, but I've been okay. Even though I think Karen's secretly a sadist hiding in the form of a perky, twenty-something redhead.

Setting a glass of water on the table next to me, AJ presses a kiss to my forehead. If I weren't so tired, maybe I could have tipped my face up so his lips would have landed on mine.

Tiny cracks in the walls around my memories are starting to let flickers and shadows emerge. The brush of his hand, a little thrill going through me at the touch. A whispered, "I love you," that makes my belly flutter. My heart skipping a beat at the sound of his laugh when I say something I didn't think warranted more than a smile.

I know we were happy. I know he loved the woman I used to be. I think he even loves the woman I am now. If only I knew who she was. Until I figure that out, how can I truly love him back?

I want to. I want to love this man with all my heart.

He crouches down next to me, takes my left hand, and starts kneading the fleshy part of my palm.

"Oh, God. That's heaven. Whoever invented grip strengtheners is surely burning in hell right now."

His easy chuckle wraps around me, warm and reassuring. We're getting more comfortable with one another as the days pass. At night, we curl up together on the couch and watch a movie—comedies, mostly—with Belle at our feet.

In the mornings, he makes coffee and breakfast, though he's always a little sad after I take my first sip. I wish I knew why.

"I should start dinner," he says. "We've got fixin's for enchiladas, burgers, and a veggie pasta salad. What sounds good?"

"Enchiladas. But...?"

"Extra spicy. I know, darlin'." AJ brings my hand to his lips, and something deep in my core starts to ache.

Before I can reach for him, he heads for the kitchen, and I can only watch his ass—perfectly framed in his Wranglers—as he goes, and wonder what it would be like to kiss him.

AJ CARRIES the dishes to the sink, and I take a swig from his bottle of Shiner. I'm not steady enough on my feet to risk more than a couple of sips, but the enchiladas were a little spicier than he intended.

"You can go pick a movie," he offers. "Cleanin' up shouldn't take more than ten minutes, then I'll make the popcorn."

I wobble off the stool and reach for the walker. I can manage without it for short distances if I have something to grab onto—a counter, a chair...AJ—but I don't move from room to room without it. Not yet.

Nerves tighten in my belly. "Um...I...want to see my studio."

He stiffens and wipes his hands on a towel. "Okay. Let's go."

Softer now, I add, "I think I need to do it alone."

There's no question. No trying to talk me out of it. Just a quiet acceptance and a nod. "If you need me..."

"I know."

The walk to the end of the hall feels so much longer than it actually is. This whole side of the house is quiet. AJ's office is dark, the door open only a crack. The home gym, where Karen brings me for the first part of our therapy sessions, smells faintly of the lavender spray she uses—something about the fragrance helping calm my mind so my body can heal. Finally, I'm standing in front of my studio door, my legs burning.

A smear of paint mars the knob. He never wiped it away.

"I wouldn't get rid of anything. I couldn't. There was no world for me without you."

His tearful confession from a few days ago hasn't left my mind. He never gave up.

Did I?

More than once, I've wondered. Three years is a lifetime when your memories only span a handful of days. But the more I come to understand the depth of AJ's love for me, the more certain I am that I would have held onto some shred of hope.

I think the woman I was would have done anything to find her way back to him. The woman I am now? She will too.

Squeezing my eyes shut, I take a deep breath, curl my fingers around the knob, and open the door.

The setting sun streams through the big window, casting a

pool of golden light across the tile floor. The air smells faintly of paper, dust, and a sharp tang I think might be paint thinner.

Bold colors cover every wall. Purple, green, yellow, and blue.

Canvases are stacked in the corner, blank and ready to be filled. To the left, a large expanse of corkboard displays drawings in various stages of completion pinned in a haphazard line.

I should remember this. All of it. *Any* of it.

One of the drawings pulls at my chest. At something deep inside. A weeping willow tree done in charcoal is almost...alive. I do recognize it, but only because I can see that same tree from the deck. Yesterday afternoon, Karen brought me outside, and I sat in a chair and threw a tennis ball for Belle. The dog was so happy, I started to cry when I was too tired to continue.

Making my way to the drafting table, I set the walker aside and drop into the chair. Pencils, blending sticks, erasers, charcoals...they're all laid out neatly—though covered in a fine layer of dust. Just...waiting for me.

With a sharp puff of breath, I send the dust scattering from the sketch pad. The charcoal pencil feels right in my hand, my thumb finding a tiny groove in the wood like it knew it was there.

The first line is jagged. Slow. Shaky. The second is easier. My hand knows what to do, even if my mind has no idea what the picture will eventually be.

A curved horizon. Tall posts with lanterns strung between them. Above it all, a full moon, bright and heavy, shines over a vast empty space the pencil can't—*won't*—touch.

My hand trembles as the charcoal tumbles from my grasp. An ache builds in my chest. My heart stutters, skipping a beat, then racing to catch up.

The tears come so fast, I can't stop them from dripping onto the page, distorting the lines and sending dark streaks into that terrifying empty space in the center.

AJ

The studio door creaks, and I have to stop myself from racing down the hall. The line between sticking close and hovering is razor sharp, and I've crossed it a time or two the past few days.

Grace white-knuckles the walker as she makes her way into the living room where I've got the popcorn waiting. Even in the dim light, I can see the tiny tremors in her arms. And there ain't nothin' that can hide the red rimming her eyes.

"Fuck, Grace. What's wrong?" I throw off the blanket, and in two steps, have my arm around her waist. She melts, practically boneless, and rests her cheek against my chest.

"I'm...okay. I just... I thought I'd remember it, and I didn't." She tries for a smile, but it doesn't quite come before she gives up. "I drew something, at least. Nothing familiar. But...that's a win, right?"

I tip her chin up, searching for a way to soothe her, and find nothing but fear in her eyes. "Grace, every minute you're here is a win. But I'm worried about you, darlin'. You're not telling me somethin'."

Her lower lip wobbles for a beat. "I can't tell you what I don't know."

The admission hangs between us, and I lower my forehead to hers with a sigh. "I'm sorry if I'm pushing you too hard. I don't mean to. It's just...somethin's tryin' to break through. I can *feel* it."

"What if I don't want it to?" Her voice cracks, and a tear tumbles down her cheek. "What if whatever it is...breaks me?"

"It won't. You're the strongest person I know, Grace. Always have been, always will be."

She settles a little closer on a sigh. "Can we watch a movie now? It was hard being in there, AJ. I need to relax. With you."

Those two words mean everything right now. Wanting me close, hell, trusting me at all is a fucking miracle. "Yeah. Of course. The popcorn's salted within an inch of its life. Just how you like it."

OUTSIDE OUR BEDROOM WINDOW, the wind whips through the trees. Even in sleep, Grace's body holds onto a hint of tension. I check my phone. Midnight has come and gone, and I can't stop my thoughts from racing.

Something happened in her studio. Why wouldn't she tell me what it was?

Carefully, I ease myself out of bed, grab my phone, and make my way to the far end of the house. The door is still open, and the screen casts just enough light for me to find the switch for the lamp over the drafting table.

At first, I don't understand what I'm looking at. Dark sweeping strokes form a horizon, hills in the distance. Lights— no, lanterns—hang from tall wooden poles. Above it all, a full moon, perfectly round, against a black sky. The center of the paper is smudged, almost warped, and it takes me a full minute to realize why. Tears. She'd been crying. Over *this*.

I can't pull my gaze away from that moon.

The wind howls louder, and something bright flickers outside the big picture window, finally breaking whatever hold the drawing has on me. It's the moon shining down between the willow trees. Not full. But...a fair bit more than a sliver.

I unlock my phone and pull up a lunar calendar.

Oh, my God.

The last full moon was the night before someone dumped her body on the doctor's doorstep.

This wasn't a random drawing.

She didn't lie to me. She doesn't remember this place. But I reckon that's her mind protecting her from what happened there.

I snap a quick picture and file it away with the ones Jasper took down in Mexico. It's another clue for the board hidden in my office closet. One way or another, we're gonna find out who took her. And on that day, they'll die screaming.

CHAPTER THIRTY-THREE

AJ

I STAND AT THE COUNTER, throwing together a salad to go with the pizzas Parker ordered when she left the station. "Ugh," she says as she twists the top off a bottle of Shiner. "Delivery's running late. Still fifteen minutes out. You need help in here?"

"Nah. Go sit down. Grace is probably gettin' tired of only havin' me to talk to."

Parker scoffs, but heads for the overstuffed recliner next to the couch, kicks off her boots, and settles in. "How's the PT going?" she asks.

Lifting her left hand, Grace taps her thumb and pinky finger together. "I couldn't do that two days ago. Belle's happy I can throw a tennis ball for her now. Since I can't take her running anymore..."

The anguish in her voice breaks me. Dr. VanHorn doesn't have all her test results back yet, but she sent us a preliminary report yesterday morning.

The cartilage in Grace's right knee is almost completely gone. Her left is only marginally better.

Even though the idea of her running scared us both, when I told her we could go out together once she was stronger, she'd been excited to try. Learning something she'd once loved had been taken from her was devastating.

Belle hops off the couch and beelines for the doggie door. She's finally comfortable leaving Grace's side for short periods of time, but she still won't let me put her in her crate—even when we're only in the next room.

Parker toys with the end of her braid. "So, when you can go out in public again, what do you want to do first?"

Grace hums as she flips through several photos on the tablet in her lap, landing on one of my favorites. A selfie of the two of us at one of Austin's more unique spots—a vintage arcade in the middle of an outdoor shopping complex. "Maybe the Punch Bowl? We look so happy here. It's...*almost* familiar. I don't remember it, exactly, but sometimes when I look at this picture, I think I can hear the pinball machines."

Leaning forward, Parker nods. "Good choice. The Punch Bowl is a hoot. I sent Hardison there a couple of months ago after he said there were no good first date spots in this town. He changed his tune right quick after that."

Grace laughs, the sound lighter than I've heard in days. "I do want to go to the art supply store. I'm sure all my paints dried up a long time ago." Her smile fades as her fingers skim her cheekbone. "Much like my skin. Wherever I was, I clearly didn't have moisturizer. AJ saved *everything* of mine in the bathroom, but..." She wrinkles her nose. "I didn't know eye cream went bad."

"Oh, shit!" Parker says. "That's half the reason I came over tonight. I stopped at Niemens after work. Got you all the good stuff. But I left the bag in the car. Give me two shakes."

She tugs on her boots as I carry the salad bowl to the dining room table.

The front door opens, but the soft sound is quickly followed by a sharp crack, and a voice that sends ice flooding my veins.

"Stone! Get your lyin' ass out here!" Chief Harris bellows.

The salad bowl hits the table, and I race for the living room.

"Chief, stop!" Parker shouts. She grabs his arm as I skid around the corner, but he shakes her off and stalks over to Grace.

"Well, it truly *is* a blessed day," he says, his voice so sharp, it could cut granite. "Grace Stone, as I live and breathe."

All the color drains from Grace's cheeks. She scrambles off the couch, but her feet tangle in the throw blanket, and she stumbles. Her knee slams into the coffee table, and she crumples to the floor with a whimper.

"Grace!" I shove the chief hard enough to send him tumbling over the back of the sofa, and crouch down next to my wife.

She curls in on herself, arms over her head, her entire body shaking. "I'll be good," she whispers, the words fractured and broken. "I promise. I'll be good."

"Grace, darlin'. It's me. It's AJ. Come back now, okay?"

She doesn't hear me. She can't, wherever she is. Do I dare touch her? Every other time she's had a panic attack, I've been able to get her back with a few whispered words or my arms around her. But this feels different. *More* somehow.

"You're safe. You're home. You're loved," I murmur. She stares straight ahead, her eyes glassy, lost in a nightmare only she can wake herself from.

Fuck it.

I slide one arm behind her back, the other under her thighs, and gather her close. She's shaking, her tiny cries tearing at my soul.

"Stone, are you *tryin'* to get yourself fired?" Harris rounds the sofa, but Parker gets right in his face.

"Chief, I reckon you're two steps away from AJ beating the ever-lovin' shit out of you. Step back. Now."

"Lieutenant Elmore, you're suspended. Out of my—"

Parker's punch hits him square in the jaw.

His head whips to the side, his eyes round with shock. Before he can do more than wipe the blood from his split lip, Belle bounds into the room, teeth bared, growling at Harris like she's just met the devil.

"She'll rip your throat out, Chief," I say, keeping my voice measured and even, hoping Grace can at least take comfort in the tone if she can't make sense of my words. "And I ain't inclined to stop her."

"You owe me an explanation."

In my periphery, Parker sidles up to Belle, and I'm not sure which one of them is more lethal. "He doesn't owe you anything. Not tonight, anyway. If you actually give a shit about AJ and Grace, you'll shut your goddamn mouth, walk out that door, and keep this quiet. He'll call you in the morning. Maybe."

Harris huffs out a breath and backs away, cradling his jaw. Belle doesn't stop growling until the front door closes softly. The house stills, filling with an unnatural quiet broken only by Grace's ragged breathing.

"He's gone, darlin'. Come back to me. Please." I press my lips to her temple, rocking her gently as Belle tries to wriggle onto my lap next to her.

One of the dog's massive paws lands only a fraction of an inch from my dick. I jerk and hiss out a breath. The movement is enough to pull Grace from her trance, and her eyes flutter closed.

"AJ," she whispers. "Don't let go."

"Never."

CHAPTER THIRTY-FOUR

Grace

"No. I will *not* 'go lie down.' Or take one of those damn pills. This is *my* life you're going to be talking about, and I need to be in the room. Conscious and lucid."

In truth, I'm so tired, my bones ache. Even sitting on the couch feels like work. But under the exhaustion, there's a sharp, prickling sensation crawling over my skin.

Anger.

I've had enough of being afraid. Of not knowing. I can't control my broken brain. Or my panic attacks. But I *can* control what happens after one.

AJ sets the pill bottle next to me, along with a glass of water. "Please, darlin'. Jasper, Connor, *and* Hardison are on their way. We've gotta find out who told Harris you were here, how they found out, and who else knows so we can decide what to do about it."

"Which is why I'm staying in the room." I wrap my arm a little tighter around Belle. She snuggles close, her body still tense. "I can do this, AJ. I *need* to do this."

"Boss, stand down." Parker drapes a bag of frozen peas over her knuckles, then sinks back into the chair. "Grace knows Connor and Jasper. Hardison's...well, he's intense. But unless he's chasin' down a suspect, the man hasn't raised his voice once in the two years I've known him."

"I ain't your boss right now," AJ mutters. "Hell, by tomorrow, I reckon we'll both be out of a job. I'm sorry, Parker. I never should've let you—"

She jerks up, stalks over to AJ, and gets right in his face. "*Let* me? Now listen here, Stone. I'm a grown-ass woman, a Ranger, and Grace's friend. Yours too when you're not bein' a total and complete idjit. You didn't *let* me come with you to Mexico. You didn't *let* me call out the other day. You certainly didn't *let* me punch the chief in the face. That was my call, and I'd do it again."

The two of them glare at one another, but after a second or two, I can't see them through the tears brimming in my eyes.

Grace's friend.

I didn't know how much I needed one of those until this moment.

Before I was taken, I had friends. Not many I was close to, from what AJ said. But a few. Cristina, an English teacher at the community college. Savannah, one of the women I met at yoga. Isha, from my running club. But they don't know me anymore. Parker does.

When the doorbell rings, I yelp, blink back my tears, and shrink behind Belle. The dog lets out a low growl. Her body vibrates against me. Tension gathers in my shoulders, the muscles so tight, I feel the ache all the way to my temples.

AJ checks his phone, then snaps his fingers. "Belle, down. It's Connor."

Parker drops back into the chair next to me. "Grace, Harris is an asshole. Every Ranger who's ever served under him knows it. He had no right to barge in here like that. Screaming at you?

That was a dick move. Fucker deserved that punch. And a hell of a lot more."

"I...I wish I'd seen it." Trapped in my panic, I heard the angry voices. And somewhere deep down, I latched onto AJ's calm, soothing baritone to keep myself from disappearing completely. But the dark shadows from my nightmares were all I could see.

Parker flexes her fingers with a wince. Her knuckles are bright red and already a little swollen. "This is gonna hurt like a sombitch tomorrow. But still...totally worth it."

"Parker, I hear you went and got yourself suspended." Connor ambles in, carrying two pizza boxes.

"While you...brought pizza," she says.

"Ran into the delivery guy in the driveway. Figured we didn't need anyone else Grace didn't know comin' to the door."

I lift my gaze to Connor's and fight the almost overwhelming urge to immediately look away. I haven't seen him since we returned to Austin, but his kind smile helps me find my voice. "Th-thanks."

He nods. "Ain't nothing to it. Jasper should be here any minute. Hardison on his way?"

"If he doesn't get lost," Parker says. "I told him he had to leave his phone at home. Didn't want the chief getting to him before we did. He's a good guy, but he's not one to buck the system, y'know?"

"Well, he's about to get a crash course in rebellion. I hope he's a quick study." Connor heads for the kitchen, shaking his head the whole way.

AJ follows him. "I'll get some beer and Coke out of the garage. You think you can handle the plates?"

The men's voices fade to a dull hum. I dig my fingers into the arm of the couch, trying to steady myself, and turn to Parker. Belle shifts so her muzzle rests on my thigh. "H-Hardison d-doesn't know about m-me?"

"No. He's...kind of a boy scout. We were planning on reading him in this weekend. Until Harris showed up. Now... we've got to get ahead of this."

Guilt eats away at me. If I were braver—or if I could hold on to even the tiniest fragments of memories from the past three years—none of this would be necessary.

My breath catches in my throat as I stare down at the scars around my wrists the sweater doesn't quite hide. It's bad enough there's about to be another man in this house I don't know. I can't even find my voice reliably around Connor yet, and I trust him. But Hardison is going to take one look at my scars—at the yellowing bruise that still covers most of my cheek—and I'll have to watch his eyes fill with pity.

Parker gives my hand a quick squeeze. "Grace, I'll be right next to you the whole time."

I don't have to ask her where AJ will be. I already know. If I need it, he'll stand in front of me.

"Jasper's here," AJ says, peering out at the driveway through a crack in the drapes. "With Emi."

Emi? His girlfriend?

"Smart. She'll know how to spin this so the public is on our side." Parker accepts the fresh bottle of beer AJ offers her. "Thanks. Mine's warm as piss now thanks to Chief Yells-A-Lot."

Emi. Another person I don't know. Another person who's supposed to be family. My heart starts to beat hard enough I'm surprised Parker can't *see* it. I push the fear down, wedging it under the heavy weight of my anger.

I can do this.

The front door opens, and Jasper starts swearing the second

he steps inside. "That goddamn piece of shit don't deserve to wear the Ranger star."

"Tell me how you really feel, stud." The woman at Jasper's side is stunning. Warm brown eyes, wavy chestnut hair that falls past her shoulders, and perfect makeup. She walks with a poise I can only dream about.

The moment Emi sees me, she smiles. "Grace. God, it's so good to meet you. Jasper wasn't sure when you'd be ready for visitors, but I went shopping yesterday just in case."

Digging into her oversized purse, she pulls out a gift bag and sets it on the arm of the couch next to me. She doesn't try to touch me. Doesn't stare. Just tucks herself against Jasper's side.

I pull a piece of purple tissue paper out of the bag. "A phone?"

"AJ told Jasper he hadn't gotten you one yet. All our numbers are saved already. Even Isabel's—she's Connor's fiancée. I also loaded *a lot* of music on it. A little bit of every-thing so you can figure out what you like now."

What I like...now...

I open the box, tears pricking at my eyes. The phone's dark purple case has a big silver ring on the back, and I stare at it, confused.

Emi ducks out from under Jasper's arm and perches on the edge of the coffee table. "It's to help you hold it," she says softly. "Can I show you?"

At my nod, she eases the device from my hand, tugs on the ring, and slides her index finger through it.

"See? The case isn't slippery either. I have the same one in green." She passes it back to me, and I slide my finger through the ring, testing the weight of it in my left hand.

The screen lights up, a photo of Belle out on the deck behind the date and time.

"The passcode is AJ's birthday. It was all I could think of

since Jasper has the same one," she says, a pink tinge flushing her cheeks.

I swipe my finger up, muscle memory taking over when my brain struggles with what to do. The other night, I finally asked AJ how old he was—how old *I* was—but that also required me to ask him what year it was *now*. Not knowing even that detail was enough to send me spiraling. I know he's forty-five and I'm forty-one. My birthday is in August. But his... Panic stole everything but the month.

May.

Emi leans closer, dropping her voice so only Parker and I can possibly hear her as she rattles off the numbers. Straightening, she adds, "I kept it simple. Music, texts, photos. All the other apps are on the next screen. Don't feel like you have to use it unless you want to. We—all of us—mostly text rather than call. But you can ignore us if we get too much. Isabel, Parker, and I can be a little...chatty."

She's so casual about all of it. Like this is nothing. But it's so much more to me.

"Thank you." The words are scratchy and rough, but Emi doesn't seem to notice. I clear my throat. "How did you know I like purple?"

"You seem like a purple person. It's a strong color, but it doesn't shout, y'know?" A tiny shrug lifts her shoulders.

Before I can figure out how to respond—how to tell her what the compliment means to me—three strong knocks come from the front door.

The men all stiffen at once. Belle jumps off the couch and positions herself in front of me. AJ meets my gaze. "Hardison's here."

CHAPTER THIRTY-FIVE

AJ

THE HOUSE IS TOO FULL. Too loud, even though no one's saying a word. Belle is on high alert. Parker eases herself out of the chair and drops down next to Grace. Emi perches on the arm of the couch, close enough the two women could easily form a shield around my wife in a heartbeat.

The visual hits me hard enough to steal the air from my lungs.

They're protecting her.

Jasper and Connor lean against the wall a few feet away, but there's nothing casual about their stances.

If this wasn't Grace... If she didn't look like she was about to come apart at the seams... If we had even a single fucking lead to go on... the tension in the room would be laughable.

But it is. She does. And we don't.

Parker's right. Hardison's a boy scout. I don't think the man has broken a single goddamned rule since the day he was born. If Harris got to him already, this could be a disaster.

He knocks again.

Fuck.

I flip the lock and open the door.

Nate Hardison hunches his shoulders against the biting cold, fat drops of rain pelting the back of his leather jacket. The last time I saw him—shit, was that only a week ago?—he didn't look this rough around the edges. Then again, neither did I.

For almost three years, I've wondered about the man's past. What happened to put such constant weariness in his gaze? But he's never opened up to me—or Parker—and we haven't pressed.

"Cap." His rough voice always sounds like he's halfway to a joke he hasn't decided to tell yet. "It's Friday night. Want to tell me why my next door neighbor is probably plowing through my FoodDude order right now?"

I step back and motion for him to come in, because hell if I know how to explain the past week.

He runs a hand through his shaggy hair, dislodging a few rain drops, crosses the threshold, and scans the living room like it's a crime scene.

His eyes find Parker first. And the bag of frozen peas still draped over her knuckles. Concern tightens his lips for a beat, and then he stiffens.

The change is subtle, but we all clock it. The disbelief flickering over his sharp features. A moment of uncertainty. Followed by understanding. Or at least...acceptance.

"Hell," he says. The weight of that single word settles over all of us. "Guess I should have brought flowers."

Grace clutches the blanket on her lap so hard, her hands shake. She won't look at Hardison. She can't. Fucking hell. I knew she should have taken a Xanax. She won't even look at *me*.

Parker sits up straighter, angling her body just enough, Grace can shrink behind her. Hardison clocks that too.

His mouth quirks into a small, humorless smile. "You planning to tell me what's going on, Cap? Or do I get the fun version where I piece it together myself?"

"You'll get the version you need," I say, locking the door behind him.

"That's what I was afraid of." He glances at Parker. "So...you couldn't have waited until I was around to take Harris down a notch? Would've loved a front-row seat."

She chokes on a swallow. "Shit."

Nate hooks his thumbs into his belt with what looks—to anyone who doesn't know him—like casual ease. The rest of us know it's actually coiled anticipation. It's the stance he takes at every crime scene. The one he uses because he assumes the perp could *always* be watching.

He knew about Parker's suspension.

Fuck.

That means the chief got to him before we did. I flick my gaze to my brother for a split second. Jas ambles into the living room and takes up post next to Emi.

"Who called you?" Parker asks.

"You did," Hardison says, his sharp eyes meeting his partner's. "But less than a minute later, the chief called. Said 'Captain Clusterfuck' had gone off the rails. 'Lieutenant Loose Cannon' and her right hook were suspended until further notice. Oh, and he expects me at the station no later than eight a.m." He snorts, his brows lifting briefly. "I said I was going through a dead zone and hung up on him."

Parker's jaw drops for a beat. "You...*hung up on him?*"

"*You* decked him," Nate deadpans. "And tomorrow's Saturday. I'm off duty."

I don't have the patience for this bullshit. "We ain't here for you and Parker to play 'whose dick is bigger'," I snap.

"Nope. We're here because," he nods at Grace, "she's here. But she's supposed to be..."

"Gone." Grace's voice is so quiet, I'm not sure anyone hears it but me. Until Hardison nods.

"Yeah. Gone." He turns to me, and the boy scout facade cracks. Just a hair. Enough I catch a flicker of something—relief?—before the fracture seals itself up again.

Belle, who's been watching us this whole time, pads over to the couch and parks herself on my wife's feet. Grace reaches for her, hand shaking until her fingers tangle in the dog's wiry fur. She still won't look up. Won't lean forward to see around Parker.

Fuck.

I should be the one next to her right now. But I still don't know if we can trust the guy Harris calls 'Lieutenant Boy Scout' behind his back. Or if I'll be throwing him out of the house in the next five minutes.

Hardison's dark eyes take in everything. The wall of people around Grace. Jasper's hand on Emi's shoulder. Parker's clenched jaw. Connor blocking the door. And my unease with this whole fucking situation.

Slowly, he dips his hands into the pockets of his jacket, turns the lining inside out, and holds up his keys. "All I've got on me. My phone, star, and gun are at home. If 'Lieutenant Loose Cannon' is with you, Cap, so am I."

I hold his gaze, daring him to look away. He doesn't. Just shrugs out of his jacket and hangs it on the coat rack like he's here for a goddamn party.

"If you stay, you're gonna earn yourself a shiny new nickname too." One corner of my mouth ticks up in a grim smile. "Say goodbye to 'Lieutenant Boy Scout.'"

"I always hated that one anyway," he says. "Do I get to pick the new one? 'Lieutenant Troublemaker'? 'Lieutenant Traitor'? How about 'Lieutenant Supreme Disappointment'?"

"I think you're more of a 'Lieutenant Last Nerve'," Parker mutters. "As in 'getting on my...'"

"Works for me." Hardison returns his thumbs to his belt loops, rocking back on his heels for a moment as he assesses the mood in the room. "So...who's gonna tell me why I'm gonna get myself fired?"

CHAPTER THIRTY-SIX

Grace

GONE. I'm supposed to be...gone.

If it weren't for Parker and Belle, I'd be curled in a ball on the floor, sobbing.

For all my talk about wanting answers, the minute the front door opened, the courage I'd worked so hard to gather slipped away. I don't know Hardison. And until I can remember who took me—and why—how can I trust anyone?

AJ moves through the living room like an unstoppable force. I can't tear my gaze from the top of Belle's head, but I sense him. And how everyone else—except Parker—gets out of his way.

She doesn't leave my side until the last possible moment. Even then, she pauses to give my hand a squeeze, whispering, "You got this."

If only I believed her.

"Grace? Look at me." AJ's voice is quiet. Not soft—there's too much steel in it for that—but steady and unshakable.

The cushions next to me shift with his weight, and I force

my head up to meet his gaze. The concern etched on his face is enough to free the stranglehold fear has on my throat. "I'm... okay."

I'm not—and AJ knows it—but I can pretend for a short time.

"H-Hardison n-needs to know wh-what we know." I risk a single glance at the man Parker called a boy scout. He hasn't moved from next to the coat rack, but the way he's watching me —or maybe he's watching how AJ is with me—makes me think he's trying to get all the puzzle pieces to fit.

He sniffs the air and beelines for the kitchen. "Is there pizza? I smell pizza."

AJ watches him go, then turns to Parker. "Did he just...?"

"I'm not gonna lie to the chief's face on an empty stomach," he calls once he pulls the pizza boxes out of the oven. "And I missed dinner. From the looks of it, I'm not the only one."

Everyone starts moving and talking like we're in the world's most bizarre sitcom. Jasper gets the plates, Parker passes out napkins, and Emi brings me a bottle of Shiner with a whispered, "You look like you could use a beer."

AJ keeps his arm around me, and amid the bustling room, my mind conjures up the scent of pine. I blink, and there's a ghost of a Christmas tree in the front window. A wispy shadow of Jasper throws a wad of wrapping paper at AJ. An older woman with AJ's eyes in a truly ridiculous sweater tells the brothers to play nice.

"Grace?" AJ cups my cheek, urging me to look up at him. "*Fuck*. You're crying, darlin'. What's wrong?"

"We used to put the Christmas tree over there," I say, pointing at the window, a shaky smile curving my lips. "Your mom has a reindeer sweater that lights up..."

A hush falls over the room. AJ frames my face with his hands, searching my gaze for the woman he fell in love with.

God, I wish I could tell him I remember everything. But I can give him the same hope coursing through my veins.

"It was just...a moment. A flash. But it was *real*."

He wraps his arms around me. "You bought that sweater for Mom. Of all the things to remember..." A hoarse chuckle rumbles through his chest. "I love you, Grace. So damn much."

If we weren't in the middle of all these people, I'd kiss him. I want to. More than anything. But over his shoulder, Nate watches us. So I brush my lips to the shell of AJ's ear. "Everyone's staring."

"Let them," he grits out.

Parker clears her throat. "Boss, we've got work to do."

With a low, rumbling sigh, AJ releases me. "Fine. Someone bring us a couple of slices. Grace likes hers with extra red pepper flakes."

Jasper and Emi drag chairs in from the dining room, while Connor doles out slices. Parker sets two plates on the coffee table in front of us.

"Lieutenant Supreme Disappointment reporting for duty," Nate says, flopping into a chair next to the fireplace and shoving half a slice into his mouth at once.

I catch Parker's eye, and she huffs. "He eats like that in front of suspects too."

Nate dabs at his mouth with a paper napkin. "Keeps the blood sugar steady. Plus, the perps let their guard down when you've got marinara on your shirt."

His jokes, Parker's comebacks—they're nothing, really. But the way they spar like brother and sister gives me something solid to hold onto. My nerves don't vanish, but they ease enough, I reach for my plate.

AJ shakes his head. "Enough with the comedy routine. Your little dead zone play won't keep Harris off your back for long. We need you at the station tomorrow morning. Hell, we need you to call the chief back when we're done here and apologize. If he shitcans you too, we're all fucked."

Nate's gaze pings between AJ, Parker, and Connor, before landing on me. "Can do. What do I know? More importantly, what *don't* I know?"

"You don't know shit," Connor says.

"Yeah, that isn't gonna fly." Leaning forward so he can grab his bottle of Coke off the coffee table, he nods at Parker. "She's been acting squirrely all week. Harris might have bought the 'food poisoning' story, but I didn't. Maybe I don't 'officially' know anything, but here? Now? I want the whole truth. Not some FBI-level intelligence briefing with black bars all over the damn place."

Silence fills the room, broken only by the pounding in my head that's been nearly constant since my panic attack.

"Cap," Hardison says, "you can't give me a shovel and not tell me how deep to dig the grave."

With a heavy sigh, AJ drapes his arm around my shoulders and presses a gentle kiss to my temple. "Fine. Last Friday night—"

"Hold up." Jasper straightens in his chair, eyes narrowed on Nate. "Ground rules first. Rule number one: until the chief spells somethin' out for you, you don't know shit. Rule number two: nothing you hear tonight leaves this room. Got it?"

Nate glances in my direction. The urge to cower behind AJ rears up, but I swallow hard and force it away. If I'm going to get my life back, I can't shrink into a quivering ball of panic every time a man so much as looks at me.

"Got it. But there's one more. Rule number three," Nate says. "If it comes down to protecting my job or protecting Grace, my job can go fuck itself."

Parker chokes on a sip of her beer. "You sure about that?"

Nate huffs. "Listen, Lieutenant Loose Cannon, I didn't drive all the way across town on a Friday night after a ten-hour shift because I was worried about my pension. Yes. I'm sure." He picks up his slice of pizza and takes another massive bite.

AJ gives him a terse nod. "Then I'll try this again. Last Friday night, I got a call from a doctor down in Mexico."

AJ

"Nothing?" Hardison asks, brows hidden somewhere in his shaggy mess of hair. "Not being taken? Not escaping?"

Anger prickles along my spine. "She didn't *escape*. The unsub left her for dead."

"Doesn't change the original question."

I clench my hand around my bottle of beer until my knuckles ache. "For fuck's sake—"

"Nothing," Grace says softly. "I have...flashes." She stares at the plate in her lap, unable—or unwilling—to make eye contact with Hardison. And while her voice isn't loud, it's mostly steady. "A wooden door. A man's voice. Being some-where...all alone."

Nate leans forward, elbows on his knees. "What about before? Your life with AJ. Going out for that last run."

"None of it." She finally lifts her head, and her gaze finds mine, tears lending a subtle shimmer to her eyes. "Everything I know about my life came from AJ. Without him, I wouldn't even know my own name."

She's so damn strong. If we weren't in the middle of a clus-terfuck the size of Hell's half acre, I'd beg her to let me kiss her.

So many emotions play across her face—fear, determina-tion, gratitude...and love. She may not remember loving me, but I think—I hope—she's close to falling all over again.

Hardison runs his hand over his jaw with a frown. "Got it. So what's the *official* story then?"

I don't want to tear my focus from Grace, but this might be the only way to protect her, so I glance over at Hardison. "Everyone knows I run the trail on Saturdays. When I got to her last known location, she was just...there. Barefoot, disoriented, wearing a white dress with her blood all over it."

"And Harris is supposed to believe you didn't call 911 because...?" The skepticism in Nate's tone sets me off all over again, but Parker clears her throat.

"Because he's an overprotective sonofabitch who'd just found his missing wife after almost three fucking years, dumbass. She was scared, didn't know who he was, let alone who *she* was, and could barely string a sentence together. He got her into the car and called me."

"You? Not his brother. Or Connor. You. How did *you* land so high on his 'call in case of emergency' list?"

"Because unlike *you*, I've actually asked him about Grace before," she snaps.

Nate flinches, his shoulders curling inward for a beat before he meets my stare. "I didn't want to open up old wounds."

"Enough. Both of you. I called Parker because Grace needed another woman there. Because she'd know what to do when I didn't. Be able to handle things I...couldn't."

The story we're telling now might be a complete fabrication, but what I just said about Parker? That's the God's honest truth. I'll never be able to repay her for what she's done for Grace—what she's done for me. I always knew she was a good Ranger. One of the best. But watching her with Grace... protecting her, caring for her, standing guard like she was born for it—the realization cuts deeper than I expect. She stopped being just one of my lieutenants down in Mexico. She's family now.

And if I want to keep it together, I can't even look at her. Not when gratitude and relief are so close to breaking me wide open. Not when I need every ounce of control to keep our ducks in a row—and make sure none of them turn out to be crazed pigeons in disguise.

"Got it," Nate says, his tone even. "Keeping things simple. Less for Grace to trip up on when Harris does his best impression of a pressure cooker without a release valve."

I grit my teeth hard enough to feel it all the way in my temples. If the chief so much as raises his voice at Grace, I don't know how I'll stop myself from beating the ever-loving shit out of him.

Nate nods, a faraway look in his dark eyes. "It's a good, clean story. And after you brought her back here, you called a doctor you could trust. Decided to keep things quiet until she got her strength back."

"That's the truth," Parker says. "Just not the whole of it."

Connor leans forward in his chair, his cold stare locked on Nate. "I got a spare burner phone in my truck for you. If Harris even *hints* that he don't believe Grace's story, you call. If you find out how he knew Grace was here, you call. If he's comin' after *any* of us—"

"I'll call."

CHAPTER THIRTY-SEVEN

Grace

THE FRONT DOOR locks with a dull *click*, and the house is once again quiet. Peaceful.

Ours.

AJ braces his palms on the doorframe, his forehead resting against the dark, polished wood. A heavy sigh heaves his shoulders.

"Are you okay?" I ask.

"Yeah. Just tired, darlin'." He straightens, rounds the couch, and kneels in front of me. His fingers skim along my jaw. "You were amazing tonight."

My lips curve into a small smile. Finding my voice in front of Nate Hardison—a man I'd never met—was a huge step toward reclaiming my life. But it was the memory of Christmas in this house with AJ that truly made up for losing my grip on reality when Harris screamed at me.

"Let me load the dishwasher and then we can turn in. It's been a day, and tomorrow's gonna be hard on both of us."

I nod, and the room takes on a soft focus, like someone dragged a blending stick over all the clean lines and edges.

"Grace?" Concern lends a roughness to AJ's voice. I blink hard, and everything sharpens once more. "What just happened?"

"Sorry," I say with a little chuckle. "I spaced out for a second. Go. I'll be fine here with Belle." The dog snores at my feet. I tug the blanket off the back of the couch and snuggle under its warm weight as he heads for the kitchen.

In truth, I'm a little dizzy. Not from exhaustion, but from the sharp burst of pain after Harris's tirade sent me tumbling off the couch. My head hit the floor before I could catch myself. Heat and a dull ache had bloomed over the still-tender bruise, but then the gruff, angry voices from my nightmares sent me into a panic so deep, nothing else mattered.

I tick off the symptoms Dr. Reyes told me to look out for. Nausea? No. Light sensitivity? No. Neck pain? No. Memory loss...I stifle a laugh. I've got that in spades. But it's getting *better*, not worse.

If the constant thrum hasn't faded by morning, I'll say something. But for now, AJ has enough to worry about.

As my husband moves about the kitchen, I close my eyes. A memory slips between my fingers, warm as the sun and smelling of cinnamon.

I'm leaning against the counter, only wearing one of AJ's t-shirts, rumpled from sleep, while he ladles pancake batter onto a griddle. I can almost feel the heat of the pan, taste the syrup, and feel the velvet of his lips against my neck.

Basking in the warmth of the memory, I'm unprepared when icy fingers crawl over my skin. Harsh, lemony soap. A windowless room. Only a bed and a desk and...a book.

Leather. Something burned into the cover. I can't see it. I don't *want* to see it. Not tonight. Not ever again.

My chest tightens. I shove the room and everything in it

back into the dark where they belong, and focus on those delicious pancakes—and the equally delicious man who was making them.

———

WE MOVE through the motions of bedtime, through the rituals we've developed since I came home. AJ helps me take off my bra and steadies me so I can put on my pajama pants. I could probably do it on my own now, but when AJ's hands mold to my waist and I stare up into his blue eyes, the full force of his love hits me in a way I desperately need.

All the new skincare products Parker bought me are lined up on the bathroom counter. By the time I finish applying the ones marked "nighttime," AJ has changed clothes and is turning down the bed.

Crossing the room, I lose focus for a second, dizziness hitting me like a slap, and I stumble.

Shit.

I catch myself quickly, and when AJ turns, I'm mostly steady again. He offers me his hand, and my heart skips a beat. He's been my rock for a week now. Held me as I've cried. Tied my shoes. Cut my hair. And he's done it all like it's the most natural thing in the world to him.

In the middle of the chaos tonight, I knew I was finally ready to kiss him—really kiss him. Not a casual brush of my lips to his neck or the press of his to my forehead, but the kind of kiss a husband and wife *should* share. The kind I know we used to share, even if I don't remember them.

Placing my fingers over his, I let him help me the last few steps to the bed, then drape my arms around his neck.

His hand lifts to my cheek, warm fingers sliding into my hair.

My breath catches, but I don't pull back. I lean into his

palm, tilting my face toward him, drinking in the rough heat of his skin against mine.

His thumb brushes my jaw, slowly, deliberately, and I press closer, closing my eyes for a heartbeat before daring to open them again. He's watching me, searching for hesitation. There isn't any.

I curl one hand around the nape of his neck, holding on like he's the only steady thing in the room. My chest grazes his, the whisper of contact sending a shiver through me. With a soft sigh, I press my forehead to his and let the last of my fear slip away.

When I finally close my eyes and lift my mouth a fraction closer, I know he'll understand. I'm ready.

The first touch of his mouth to mine is gentle. Brief. Light. But even so, I find something I've been missing since I woke up in that lonely clinic more than a week ago.

A piece of myself.

I lean in, chasing his lips so he can't pull away. Our kiss deepens, and I taste his sigh, minty from his toothpaste. Heat crackles between us, embers waiting to explode into flame.

I want more. More of his solid weight against me. More of his skin under my fingers. More of the sound of his breath catching as my fingers curl around the back of his neck.

Behind my closed lids is another kiss from a lifetime ago. Another bedroom. Smaller. But the same quilt. The same scent —AJ's aftershave mixed with my perfume. The same steady, bone-deep certainty that we belong to one another. That we always will.

Too soon, AJ pulls back, his forehead resting against mine. "God, Grace. I want you," he manages, his voice ragged. His arousal strains against my stomach, hard and hot. My core aches, though fear prickles along the back of my neck.

I want him. All of him. But...what if...I can't? What if whoever took me stole not only my memories, but *this* too?

AJ shakes his head softly. "It's too soon."

He's trying to convince himself as much—if not more—than me. I swallow my disappointment, knowing he's right.

"Tonight...the memory of us all being together at Christmas..." I press a light kiss to his lips. "In those few seconds, I remembered loving you."

He pulls me against him even tighter and takes a deep, shuddering breath. Then another. It takes me too long to realize he's fighting back tears.

I curl my fingers in his soft t-shirt, and they catch on a chain around his neck. "AJ?"

For a long moment, he doesn't move. But eventually, his arms loosen, and he takes a step back.

Slowly, almost reverently, he pulls a silver chain out from under the dark blue tee, his hand fisted around whatever's hanging from it.

"This... I found it a couple of days after you were taken. I couldn't put it back where it belonged, but I couldn't let it go either."

He unfurls his fingers, and I freeze. The silver band with a delicate filigree is a smaller version of the one on his ring finger.

My wedding ring.

"Two hearts...to one?" The tears fall hard and fast. Our vows. I remember a piece of our vows.

"Yes, darlin'. Yes." His voice wavers, and he pulls the chain over his head, opens the clasp, and lets the ring fall into his palm.

I lift my left hand, fingers shaking. He cradles my palm and slides the ring back where it belongs.

"You're home, Grace. You're really home."

CHAPTER THIRTY-EIGHT

AJ

THE COFFEEMAKER HISSES, filling the kitchen with the rich, dark scent I depend on to get me going in the mornings.

After I put the ring back on Grace's finger last night, I watched her sleep for an hour, memorizing everything about her. All the things I'd forgotten and all the things that have changed.

Her lips still form a perfect bow. But the scar across her cheek pulls tight against the pillow. Her fingers are still calloused, but after rediscovering her favorite body lotion, her skin has started to glow again.

The electric kettle beeps, and I pull the tin of Cafe Vienna from the cabinet. It's still early, but the chief ain't a patient man. If I don't call him soon, he'll either break down my door, have me arrested, or go to the press. Hell, he might do all three out of spite.

Emi made a few calls last night. If any of the three major news outlets in the city get any info on Grace, she'll know before the story airs. We hope.

Grace shuffles into the kitchen wearing one of my sweat-shirts over her pajamas. The sleeves are so long, only the tips of her fingers peek out from the cuffs. Her brows are pinched together, a faint crease between them.

"What's wrong?" I ask. "Did you sleep okay?"

She rubs the back of her neck with a frown. "I think so. I'm just a little...fuzzy. It's early. I'll be fine after some coffee."

The faint tightness in her shoulders, the way she blinks a beat longer than normal, the rasp to her voice... Is it stress? Or do I need to worry?

I study her for a moment, until she stares pointedly at her empty mug. "You gonna make that for me, handsome? Or leave me to face the day uncaffeinated."

Her grin dispels any lingering concern, and I reach for the kettle. Cinnamon and chocolate fill the space between us as the hot water hits the instant coffee powder. I give the mixture a slow stir, then set the spoon in the sink.

Without a word, she wraps her hands around the mug and takes a sip. Her eyelids flutter. I'm about to turn away—unsure how much longer I can go without our little ritual—when she pauses with the cup halfway to her lips.

Her head tilts, and after a beat, she sets the mug in front of me.

The simple gesture hits me so hard, I can't breathe.

I take the cup, my hands trembling enough I'm scared I'll drop it. The first sip is enough to undo me.

Grace's brow furrows. "You don't like sweet coffee. I don't understand why I did that. It just felt...like I was supposed to."

"You were," I manage. "It...it was a thing." From her frown, she's not satisfied with my answer, so I fake a grimace, like I used to. "Still tastes like flavored water."

Something flickers across her face. Confusion, but also the faintest smile. "No. It tastes like cinnamon and vanilla and everything good in this world."

My chest aches. I take a second sip—like I always did—and pass it back to her. "It tastes like you."

She curls into my chest, her left hand over my heart. I feel the weight of her ring—or rather the lack of it around my neck. But then I cover her hand with mine and remember. The white gold band is back where it belongs.

———

Parker meets my gaze in the rear view mirror. "Harris didn't scream at you?"

"Nope. Didn't give him much chance. Just told him we'd come in at ten and we were bringin' you with us." In the back seat, I hold Grace close. She stares straight ahead behind the dark glasses. Until Parker takes a left at the next light. Then her breath hitches and she curls against me. "Darlin'?"

"I'll be fine. Turns are still...hard. Don't worry."

I snort and press a kiss to her hair. "You might as well expect a flea not to bite." Turning my attention back to Parker, I ask, "Did you talk to Hardison?"

"As if he'd risk that." Parker slows and pulls into the station's back lot. "He's been at the station since oh-dark-thirty. Zephyr sent him a little somethin' to install on the chief's computer. She's gonna go hunting around in there and see if there's anything we need to know."

I offer Grace my hand to help her out of the SUV. She grips the door handle, hesitates for half a second, and stands on her own. But after eyeing the uneven pavement, she lets me wrap an arm around her waist for the short walk into the station.

Harris waits at the back door, a steaming mug of coffee in his hand. He's trying to look relaxed, but the moment he sees Parker, his shoulders tense up. His free hand rubs the dark bruise on his jaw.

I have to clench my teeth so I don't smile.

"This ain't doggie daycare," he says, voice rough. Behind him, Hardison's eyebrow twitches.

Dammit. The man better work on his poker face right quick.

"Belle won't leave Grace's side." I fix my stare on the chief's busted lip. "If she hadn't been outside when you showed up last night, we wouldn't be havin' this conversation. You'd be missin' half your face, and I'd be scramblin' to bury the body."

"Is that a *threat*, Stone?" Harris's lip curls into a sneer.

"Nope. Just the God's honest truth." I give Belle a glance. Her ears are back, teeth bared, but she's not growling. Not yet.

Harris shakes his head. "I should suspend you right now."

"Do it. See if I give a fuck."

The dare hangs between us for so long, I think he might actually do it. But eventually, he jerks his thumb over his shoulder. "Elmore. Interrogation Room One. Stone. My office. Hardison? Take Mrs. Stone—"

"No." I tighten my arm around Grace. "She doesn't leave my side."

"Mine either," Parker adds.

Harris sputters, but Hardison clears his throat. "Chief, unless you're planning on arresting them...let it go. We can get what we need in a group interroga—*interview*."

Damn. Nate might have some decent acting chops after all.

Harris leads us down the hall to the smallest, darkest interview room in the whole goddamn building. Asshole.

I help Grace into the hard metal chair, then take a seat next to her. Belle sits on her other side, fully alert, while Parker leans against the wall by the door.

"Your wife has *supposedly* been missing for—" Harris checks the file on the table "—two years, eleven months, and somewhere between three and ten days. Care to explain her miraculous reappearance?"

As I lay out the details, sticking to the story we rehearsed the previous night, Grace keeps her gaze pinned to a spot on the table in front of her.

Fuck.

She wasn't ready for this. None of us were.

I rest my hand on her thigh, and she laces her fingers with mine.

"Convenient. No witnesses. Just like when she disappeared," Harris says. "I don't believe for a goddamn second that she can't remember *anything*."

Grace lifts her head, her fingers so tight on mine, one of my knuckles cracks from the pressure. "Believe what you want," she says, her voice soft but mostly steady. "It's the truth. AJ had to tell me my own name. My *entire life* is...blank until that morning. Until AJ was holding me in the back of a car and everything hurt."

Harris nods at her right hand where it rests on the table. At the thick scar visible around her wrist. "You were tied up. Probably for a long time. Stabbed. With a head injury. And you just...let a strange man you didn't know put you in the back of a car?"

"I..." Grace shifts her gaze to mine, and a hint of a smile curves her lips. "Yes. Clearly some part of me knew I could trust him."

The chief scribbles something across the page only Hardison can see. The change in Nate's expression is subtle. A brief tightening around his eyes. A tic in his jaw until he gets himself under control.

"Captain Stone," he says, a smug edge to his voice that better be a fucking act, "did it ever occur to you that by bringing your wife anywhere but the hospital, you've compromised any evidence she may have had on her person at the time she *reappeared*?"

Parker unzips her backpack and withdraws an evidence bag. "Here's the dress she was wearing. Sealed, signed, and dated by me and Stone. Her nails were clean. I'm not a fuckin' rookie, *partner*. And you know it."

"I don't care if this was signed by the goddamn Pope," Harris sputters. "You still broke chain of custody."

My eyes narrow on the man who stopped us from going to the cabin the day Grace disappeared. I dedicated a corner of my crime board to the theory that he'd ordered those stakeouts on purpose. But I never found a single shred of proof. He's an asshole, but he's clean.

I lean forward, letting Harris see the full force of my anger. "And I'd do it again. We're *done* answering questions, Chief. It's your turn. How'd you know she was back? Because I sure as shit didn't tell you, and neither did Parker."

Harris shifts in his chair like he's not sure I should be privy to that information. But after a long moment, he meets my gaze. "Marvin told me."

"Marvin?" He could've claimed a psychic pigeon whispered in his ear and I'd have been less surprised. "How the fuck did *he* know?"

"He was worried when you called out this week." Harris shrugs. "You know how he is."

"If you mean a busybody with a hero complex," Parker mutters, "yeah. We know."

Harris ignores her. "He stopped by your place night before last with a bottle of whiskey. He reckoned the anniversary of Grace's disappearance was weighin' on you, and saw you with a blonde who looked a lot like your missing wife. Figured you'd finally broke."

"And he waited an entire *day* to call you?" I ask. "That dog don't hunt, Chief."

Harris closes the file in front of him. "Put yourself in his shoes, Stone. Would you tell me if you thought Elmore was losin' her grip on reality? He only confided in me when you didn't answer his call yesterday."

Fuck.

I pull out my phone and check the history.

Missed Call From: Marvin Kinkaid, 1:07 p.m.

Grace's physical therapy starts at one. By that time, I would have been on the treadmill, trying to outrun my demons. The ones who keep whispering in my ear that her captors are still out there. Just waiting for the right time to finish what they started.

CHAPTER THIRTY-NINE

Grace

AJ's FEET hit the treadmill, strong and steady, as I open the door to my studio.

Yesterday's trip to the station left me exhausted and shaky, so, between naps, I spent that afternoon swiping through photos from our life together. And today, the headache I've had since Friday night finally lifted.

Twice during the night, I woke in a cold sweat, gasping for air. The first time I managed to stay quiet enough AJ didn't hear me. But the second...I couldn't stop crying. His arms were around me in seconds, his voice in my ear steady and calm.

"You're home. You're safe. You're loved."

When I finally caught my breath, he'd begged me to talk to him. To share even one tiny detail from the nightmare. But the images were too slippery. Too jagged and terrifying for me to hold onto. So I'd buried my face against his bare chest and let the warmth of his skin banish the ice from my veins.

Through the window, the lake shines in the thin winter

sunlight. Belle stands on the deck, barking at a Canada goose nesting in one of the large flower pots at the edge of the lawn.

"That's right, sweetie. Keep your distance. Wouldn't want you getting attacked again."

Again.

The image before me shimmers, and suddenly I'm looking at Belle as a puppy, racing toward that same pot, with another goose sitting on top of a clutch of eggs in the late March sun.

My throat clogs with tears. These tiny memories, mere moments amid the years—the *decades*—missing from my life give me hope that one day, I'll be something more than a shadow of who I'm supposed to be.

I blink, and my huge, loyal dog is back, running from one end of the deck to the other, but never once venturing onto the lawn.

Turning my focus to the drafting table, my eyes land on the haunting image I drew days ago. It sucks all the oxygen from the air. That big, empty space in the center terrifies me.

I can't be in here with *that*. And the walls are too bright. Too loud. Too...unfamiliar. The room doesn't feel like mine anymore. It belongs to someone else. Someone I fear I'll never know.

But the need to draw is like an itch under my skin. My fingers ache to hold a pencil. To give shape to all these brief, dark flashes I've been shoving down under the few fragments of happy memories I've found with AJ and Belle.

They won't stay buried forever. Worse, they'll claw and poke and scratch until they finally slice me open. Then they'll laugh as I bleed.

"...a hundred small cuts before the end..."

The man's voice is so clear, I whirl around and almost topple over. My heart hammers against my ribs. I'm alone. The only sound breaking the silence is the steady thump of AJ's feet hitting the treadmill. Even Belle's stopped barking.

Scooping up my sketchpad, pencil, eraser, and blending sticks, I retreat back to the living room.

The couch is safer. The cushions welcome me, and I tuck my legs to the side so I can balance the sketch pad on my thighs. Belle trots into the room, bringing a whiff of fresh air with her.

"Come here, sweetie." I pat the spot next to me. She has to try three times before she finds just the right position, but finally settles with an undignified groan.

With her at my side, I can be braver. At least that's what I tell myself as I touch the tip of the pencil to the pad.

Lines and curves stretch across the page without much thought. An oval. Too wide, too thick. Rough shapes that defy explanation. I add texture. Depth. Blend from dark to light. An arm? No. Horns?

The harder I try, the more the images blur, almost melting into one another. It's all too much. Too...*wrong*.

Turning the page, I try again. Another fragment claws its way free. This one a rectangle, shaded until the weight of it presses against my chest. A book? My nails dig into the eraser as I drag a white scar through the center.

More lines. Pages and pages. So many, I have to stop and shake the blood back into my fingers.

Words whisper in the background, but I can't—I *won't*—hear them. I scratch the pencil across the page so hard, it tears.

One more. I'll try one more. Because right now, the image in my head is so clear, it might as well be hanging in front of me.

My heartbeat thrums in my temples. My stomach twists, bile burning my tongue, and for a second, I worry I'm about to throw up all over the couch. But I swallow hard and flip to a fresh page.

Two tall beams, thick and rough, with a bowed line between them. String? A cable? A chain? I can't tell. But the lantern dangling from whatever it is? That I'm sure of.

The metal housing takes shape first. The coil at the top. Three loops. Wound from left to right, top to bottom. Six glass panes. Shading reveals the bevel at the edges. The wick is too tall. The flame is too bright. It hurts my eyes, but I don't stop. It's almost right. Almost done. On the base, there's a symbol. I can't see it. Can't commit it to the page.

My hand spasms, and the pencil tumbles from my fingers. "*Shit.*"

AJ clears his throat. I yelp, and the sketchbook hits the floor.

"God, I'm sorry, darlin'. I didn't mean..." He stands a few feet away, his face sweaty and flushed, with a towel looped around his neck. "That drawin' was pretty clear. Mind if I take a look?"

"I don't want to remember," I whisper.

His eyes soften. His voice does too. "I know. But tomorrow, the world's gonna find out you're alive. After that..."

"The people who took me could try again." I lean down, pick up the sketchpad, and clutch it to my chest.

Belle whines when AJ snaps his fingers, but after a beat, she settles on the floor in front of me so he can take her spot.

I set the book in my lap, swallow hard, and trace one edge of the lantern with my fingertip.

"I see it when I close my eyes sometimes. I don't know why."

He frowns, his gaze shifting from the lantern to me. "How does it make you feel?"

My chest stutters with each ragged breath. "Alone. Afraid." A single sob catches in my throat, turning into a hiccup when I can't hold it in. "Cold. It was so bright it hurt. Or...maybe...*I* hurt. I don't know."

I can't look away from the glowing flame. And despite the warmth of the room, I'm shivering. I want to curl into him more than anything in the world. Let him wrap his arms around me and chase all the nightmares away. But that won't keep us safe. I need to tell him as much as I can. Before I can't tell him anything.

"I'm not supposed to move. Not supposed to speak. If I do... he'll be angry." My voice is getting smaller and smaller. I'm losing myself. Soon, there won't be anything of *Grace* left. Maybe she's already gone. I pull my knees up to my chest and start rocking back and forth. "I need you. In the dark where the light hurts. I need you."

"I'm here, Grace. I'm here." He pulls me against him, rocking with me until the light fades away.

CHAPTER FORTY

AJ

GRACE'S ROCKING SLOWS, her breath hitching less and less with every beat of my heart. She clings to me like I'm the only thing holding her together.

I press my lips to her hair. God, if I could, I'd rip these horrible memories from her, drag them out to the center of the lake, and drown them.

But I can't.

I wasn't there.

I couldn't stop her from being taken.

Couldn't find her.

Couldn't save her.

And the truth of it grinds me down until there's nothing left but guilt and rage.

"I've got you, darlin'," I murmur, though I have no idea why she'd trust me. "I won't fail you again. Please believe me. If it's the last fucking thing I do, I'll keep you safe."

After one final shudder, she lifts her head. Her blue-gray eyes are bloodshot, tears clinging to her lashes.

"Again?" Her fingers tremble slightly as they skim along my jaw. "You didn't fail me, AJ. I may not remember how I was taken, but I *know* it wasn't your fault."

Her words cut deep, despite how desperately she's trying to reassure me. I want to believe her. I do. But my entire goddamn purpose in this life is to protect her, and she was taken anyway.

I press my lips to her forehead. "Come on. You need to relax. I'll draw you a bath."

"I'll be fine—"

"Please?" The single word escapes on a whisper. Can she hear the desperation in it? Does she see how close I am to breaking?

With a sigh, she eases back, sets the sketchbook on the coffee table, and nods.

I get to my feet and hold out my hand. The total and complete trust she gives me as I lead her into the bedroom threatens to snap my last shred of sanity. "It's gonna take a few minutes for me to fill the tub. Why don't you lie down until everything's ready."

Leaving her curled up in bed with Belle, I close myself in the bathroom. Hot water cascades from the faucet as I light candles and find her favorite bubble bath—the one with lavender and shea butter.

Despite the calming scent filling the room, my mind races. She drew that lantern with such precise detail, Zephyr might be able to identify it. Maybe find out who purchased it. Where it was shipped.

For days now, I've spent every minute I've had alone researching cults in Texas and Mexico. My desk is covered with Post-It notes—hidden by the leather blotter Grace bought me for Christmas five years ago.

But I haven't found any suspected of kidnapping women off the street—or trails. No other body dumps in the middle of nowhere. No white dresses or braided ropes. And *none* with a fondness for oleander.

I'm more worked up than ever by the time I turn off the faucet. But I force a deep breath and pray Grace doesn't notice.

"All ready for you, darlin'."

She lets me help her off with her pajamas, then sinks into the steaming water with a sigh. "This is heaven. Thank you." The look in her eyes cuts me in two. Trust. Gratitude. Love. All so much more than I deserve.

I step out before I drown in my own guilt. In the living room, I pick up the sketchbook. The lantern stares back at me with its clean lines and glowing wick.

"It was so bright it hurt. Or maybe...I hurt."

I snap a quick picture, close the book so it can't cause her any more pain, then retreat to my office.

My shirt is plastered to my skin, my hair damp and sticking up in all directions, but I don't care.

Connor answers the video call almost immediately. "You look like five miles of bad road, man. What's wrong?"

"Can you conference in Zephyr? Hell, maybe Pritchard too. I've got somethin' potentially...traceable."

"I'm out rakin' leaves. Give me five minutes, and I'll call you back." The screen goes black before I can respond.

I'd call him an asshole, but this ain't a conversation we should be havin' in public. Sinking back in my chair, I hiss out a breath as my damp shirt chills my skin.

He's better than his word, and less than ninety seconds later, my tablet screen lights up with an incoming call.

The video splits in two, Connor on the left, and a woman with teal hair, a silver barb through her eyebrow, and vivid green eyes on the right.

"AJ, this is Zephyr," Connor says. "Pritchard's in the middle of somethin', but we'll fill him in when we're done. What do you have that's so important you called me lookin' like *that*?"

I hold up my phone. "Grace drew this. It's a lantern. The other day, she sketched a whole-ass scene with half a dozen poles and lanterns hangin' between them. But there wasn't any detail to it. This one..."

Zephyr narrows her eyes and swipes a lock of teal hair behind her ear. "Send me that picture. I'll run a reverse image search on the whole thing, but if that comes up empty, I'll work the individual components. The glass, the base, the handle..."

"How long until you get somethin'? The news conference is tomorrow—"

"It takes as long as it takes, AJ. Even if it's pre-fab, I'll still have to check regional suppliers and specialty importers. If it's not, I'll scrape the survivalist forums, look for design specs. I could have something in an hour, or it could take me two days."

Fuck.

Zephyr's voice softens. "I get it. Really, I do. And I'm damn good at my job. With as much detail as Grace put into that image, I'll find something. And if it's not enough to go on, I'll call in reinforcements."

"She means McCabe's wife," Connor says before I can ask. "The two of them together could topple governments."

"You're assuming we haven't already." Zephyr flashes a quick smile. "AJ, I'm sending you a link to a secure file share. Drop the photo in there. The one Grace drew the other day too. Vague doesn't mean useless. I'll be in touch as soon as I find anything."

Her side of the call goes dark, but Connor studies me for a long moment. "There's more goin' on than just a new lead. What is it?"

"Not now. Grace...I don't want to leave her alone for too long. I'll see you tomorrow at the news conference."

I end the call before I'm tempted to confess all my failures in harsh detail. Because if I did that, I might never find the strength to go back to my wife and beg her to forgive me.

CHAPTER FORTY-ONE

AJ

Steam billows out ahead of me as I yank the bathroom door open, the towel knotted low on my hips. No amount of hot water could wash away the ache in my chest.

The room still smelled of lavender when Grace emerged ten minutes ago. I'd asked her if she needed help getting dressed, but she'd just looked me up and down, brows lifted.

"You help me now, and I'll end up needing another bath. Or... maybe I'd just have to join you in the shower."

Since our kiss the other night, I've wondered about the next step. About when she'd be ready for more. But having her break in my arms this morning changed everything.

I know she doesn't blame me, but that ain't gonna stop me from blaming myself for the rest of my life.

She sits cross-legged on the little bench in the closet, wrapped in one of my old, flannel shirts, her damp hair curling against her shoulders. Waiting. For me.

"Didn't mean to take so long," I say, my voice rougher than I intend. "Just needed...to get my head on straight."

She studies me like she can see every thought—every emotion—I'm trying to bury. "I just need *you,* AJ. Straight, crooked, or ass-backwards, I don't care."

I scrub a hand over my face, then force myself to meet her gaze. "Grace...the lantern. God—you needed me then, and I wasn't there."

"Stop." She rises, sways for a breath, then crosses to me. The shirt hits her mid-thigh, exposing one of the deep, jagged scars running almost to her knee. She's still so thin. Still unsteady. But so much stronger than she knows.

"You keep saying you should've protected me. But...you did. I don't need my memories to know that. You're the reason I didn't give up. The reason I'm still alive. The reason I'm here now."

My chest tightens. She's staring up at me like I hung the moon. But she's wrong. "Grace—"

She takes my hand and presses it to her chest. Her heart beats steadily against my palm. "Feel that. Feel *me.*"

Draping her arm around my neck, she pulls me down to seal her lips to mine.

Her taste is sunlight and spring time and fresh mint. My dick throbs, and under the old flannel, I feel her nipples harden to tight buds against my chest.

The towel I'm wearing like armor keeps us apart when we should be coming together. But it's too soon. She's not ready.

Her other hand slides down my back to my ass.

Fuck. Fuuuuck.

"Grace, are you sure? Don't do this because I'm an idjit who can't find his way—"

She silences me with another kiss. Her tongue traces the seam of my lips, and I open for her. Three years fade away in an instant as my wife presses closer, her hips grinding against me.

Pulling back a fraction of an inch, she whispers, "I'm doing this because I'm strong enough to choose you. Because even without all my memories, I know I want you, Aaron."

The air leaves my lungs.

Aaron.

I never told her what AJ stood for. I couldn't. It was something sacred I thought we'd never have again. But she remembered. Somewhere deep down, she remembered.

"Then I'm yours, darlin'," I manage. "Always."

Hooking my hands behind her thighs, I lift her so she can wrap her legs around my waist, then carry her to the bed.

We sink down together. Her fingers comb through my damp hair as I press kisses along her jaw. The scent of her arousal is sweeter than honey, and fuck if I don't want to bury my face between her thighs right now and taste her.

But this ain't about me.

"What are you ready for, darlin'?"

She slides her hands over my chest, tracing the curves of my pecs, down my abs, all the way to the towel knotted at my waist.

I catch her wrist before she can tug it loose. "Grace." My voice is so raw, it hurts. "Are you sure you want this?"

Tears shimmer in her eyes. "I want...to see you. To touch you. I want you to touch me."

Behind the need, behind all that strength, there's still a hint of fear.

"You can touch all you want. But I'm gonna keep askin'. Enough you're gonna yank that towel off just so you can smother me with it."

Her lips twitch, the smile giving way to a nervous giggle before she sobers. "I'd never smother you, AJ. You're the reason I remember what it feels like to breathe."

The knot in my chest loosens a fraction. I shift her off my lap so we can lie down side-by-side, leaving enough space between us for her to make the next move.

"I'm yours, Grace. In whatever way you want."

She releases the knot on the towel, and her gaze slides down my body, all the way to my dick. Wriggling closer, she presses her lips to mine. There's no hesitation. No fear. Only the two of us together.

Her hands explore my torso, sketching tentative patterns over my ribs while she trails kisses down to my shoulder.

A drop of precum leaks from my tip. The scent mixes with her arousal, and she stills.

"Grace..." I reach for the towel, ready to cover myself in a heartbeat. "We can stop."

With a small, steady smile, she lets her fingers brush my shaft. "I know we can. Maybe that's why I don't want to. Touch me. Please."

I kiss her forehead, the tip of her nose, then pause a breath away from her lips. "Here?"

"Yes."

I linger there, my tongue dancing with hers, until she cups my ass and gives it a squeeze.

My hand shakes as I smooth it down her spine, all the way to the hem of my shirt she's wearing. "What about here?"

She shudders, but it's not from nerves. "Yes."

Undoing the buttons is pure torture. I pause after each one, my gaze finding hers, checking for any sign she's pushing herself too far, too fast, too soon.

But every time, I see only desire in her eyes.

I help her sit up, ease the flannel from her shoulders, and drink in the sight of her.

I've seen her every day. Helped her in and out of the bath, washed her hair, fastened her bra. But every time, I tried to keep things...light. Quick. Gentle.

"You're so damn beautiful," I manage over the lump in my throat. "And I've missed you. God, I've missed you."

A tear slips down her cheek. "You don't have to miss me anymore, AJ. I found my way home."

With a choked sob, I wrap her in my arms, hold her there, memorizing this moment. Every inch of her pressed against me is a vow. She's still here. Still choosing to fight. Still choosing... me.

The guilt, the grief, and the pain I've carried for three years melts against the warmth of her skin, and I find something I thought I'd lost for good.

Hope.

CHAPTER FORTY-TWO

Grace

AJ's LIPS, tongue, and teeth explore from the shell of my ear, down my neck, and across the hollow of my throat. My body is on fire. Tiny sparks race along my spine. Every part of me aches for him—my heart most of all.

We're close enough for the heat of him to warm my skin, but with his hands braced on the headboard, he's barely touching me.

"Please," I whisper. "I need more."

I wrap my fingers around his wrist and guide his hand to my breast.

"Grace." Need roughens his voice, the word ragged in the quiet of the room. "Are you sure?"

"Yes. I need...*you*, Aaron."

He stiffens, his gaze snapping to mine. Wonder, grief, and hope flicker across his face in a heartbeat.

The first time I called him Aaron, he almost came undone. I'm not sure how I even knew what AJ stood for. But I know what it means to him.

Everything.

"I never told you... I couldn't. It had to be...yours." Tears deepen the blue of his eyes. He blinks them away, then dips his head to press a light kiss to my nipple.

My core trembles, and I arch my back, silently begging him for more.

AJ parts his lips, and—*oh, God*—scores his teeth over the tight nub. I moan, the sensation shooting all the way to my clit.

"More?" he asks, whisper-soft against my breast.

He's so careful with me. Gentle. Tender. In his arms, nothing can hurt me. Not even my own fears.

I hook my leg around his, tugging him closer. "More."

Easing me onto my back, AJ stares down at me like I'm the most precious thing in the world. In this moment, I'm not broken. Not scared. Not alone.

His hard length presses to my hip. The scent of him—of his need—stirs a faint memory.

I blink, and it's not early afternoon anymore. It's morning. The summer sun streams through the window. AJ—younger than he is now, without the lingering grief in his gaze—struggles to kick off his boots, his hands tangled in my hair.

A kiss to the underside of my breast brings me back to the here and now. He moves lower, skimming the top of my panties with his lips. "God, Grace. You smell like heaven."

His hand slides up my thigh, over the deepest of the scars on my legs.

My wrists ache. Pain tugs at my shoulders, so sharp and fast, all the air leaves my lungs.

AJ notices. He *always* notices.

"Hey." His hand stills on my hip and he sits up. "Talk to me, darlin'."

I can't answer right away. Static hisses inside my head, so loud I can feel it all the way down to my toes. My throat tightens. Memories press against the edges of my mind, dark shadows I can't see—can't name.

AJ's lips are moving, but I can't hear his voice. A furrow deepens between his brows. I focus on his eyes. On the pure, never-ending love reflected there. The static starts to fade.

"Grace. We don't have to do this. Not now. Not *ever*."

The safety he gives me—the resolute promise that if I said no, he'd live the rest of his life without sex just so I'd feel safe—sends my fears retreating to the deep, dark place they hide until my nightmares set them free.

"AJ...I d-don't remember... If they... What if they...hurt me... like *that*?"

He touches his forehead to mine, his breath unsteady. "Then I'll kill them. Slowly."

His words shouldn't be romantic. They shouldn't fill me with relief. But they do.

A chill settles over my skin. I want this. I want *him*. But most of all, I want to be *me* again.

"I'm scared."

"I know." He pulls the duvet over us, and settles me against his chest. "You're allowed to be scared, Grace. You're allowed to feel whatever you need to feel, whenever you need to feel it. There ain't no timeline for healing. Even bones take a while to mend. Scared don't mean broken."

Tears blur my vision. "How do you always know what to say?"

He chuckles and rubs slow circles over my lower back. "Darlin', I *never* know what to say." His thumb traces the edge of my jaw. Slow and steady. "Except this. I love you, Grace. There ain't nothin' I wouldn't do for you. If you need to stop—any time, for any reason—we stop. You have all the control, Grace. *All* of it."

My shoulders loosen at the absolute conviction in his voice. That slow, steady tone that makes him such a good Ranger, my protector, and my best friend. The fear doesn't fade completely, but desire shoves it aside. I want this. I want *him*.

I hold his gaze, my voice clear, strong, and sure. "Take off my panties."

A shudder runs through AJ's body. In his eyes, I see relief, restraint, and fierce tenderness. After a blink, there's something more.

A vow.

He'll never hurt me. Never leave me. Never pity me. He'll just...love me.

I kiss him. And when I truly let him in, it's not desire that drives me—it's trust.

Hooking his fingers in the light blue cotton, AJ slides the panties down my hips with a reverence I think—I *know*—isn't new. It's who he is at his very core.

He doesn't take. He offers. Every touch is a question, and he waits for my body to answer.

A single kiss grazes the top of my mound, just above the glistening dark blond curls. "Okay?"

"Yes," I breathe. "Touch me, Aaron."

Lower. Another press of his lips. This time, over my clit.

I reach down, cup the back of his neck, and guide his mouth where I'm desperate for it to be.

He looks up, a silent question in his eyes.

I'm not afraid. Not with AJ. My husband. My protector. The man I'm falling in love with all over again.

"Taste me."

AJ settles between my legs, his hands resting lightly on my inner thighs. The first swipe of his tongue through my folds is like coming home. With the second, I come undone. My whimper turns into a moan as he finds a slow, easy rhythm.

My core tightens. Every muscle strains. My heels scrape at the mattress. I curl my fingers in the sheets, desperate to hold on. I want to savor the pleasure AJ's giving me.

But even after three years, my husband knows my body. And within minutes, I'm hurtling toward the edge.

"Aaron, please..." I beg. "I need...to come."

AJ sucks hard on my clit, and I fly so high, I may never come down.

I'M SHAKING. Not from fear. From something bigger. Something I don't want to name, but think...maybe...could be hope.

Held in AJ's arms, his face buried in my hair, I'm safe. I'm loved.

His chest heaves with the overwhelming emotions we both feel, as over and over again, he whispers, "You're here. You came back to me."

CHAPTER FORTY-THREE

AJ

Grace's voice cuts down the hall. "Dammit!"

I jolt upright in my chair. She's fine. I *know* she's fine. But the frustration in her tone rips through my chest like shrapnel.

"Try again. You unclipped four clothespins Friday. Today, I want six." Karen—part cheerleader, part drill sergeant—has worked wonders during Grace's physical therapy sessions.

Another week, and she won't need me to fasten her bra or tie her shoes anymore.

I want her to have that independence. God, I want it for her more than anything. But I'd be lying if I said I won't miss those moments that have kept us tethered so tightly together since she came home.

"That's five," Karen says with pride. "One more, and you can stop. *Two* more, and we'll go out on the deck so you can throw the tennis ball for Belle."

The dog barks, and I chuckle as I close my office door. Karen is *very* good at her job.

The video call comes in almost as soon as I open my laptop.

Zephyr's face takes up the left half of the screen, with my brother and Parker sharing the other side.

"No Connor?" Jasper asks.

"He's meetin' with Hardison. The head of major crimes at APD is hollarin' about bringing Grace in for an 'interview,'" I grit out.

Jas snorts. "Interview my ass. It'd be an interrogation."

"Oh, they won't push too hard," Zephyr says with a hint of a smile. "Captain Keller has a whopper of a gambling problem. AJ, I'm sending you a bit of *leverage*. Should you need it."

"Hot damn." Jasper shakes his head. "Where were you when I was on the job?"

Something dark flickers in Zephyr's gaze. "Nowhere...good." *Fuck.*

She runs a hand through her teal locks and the darkness fades. "I'm coming up empty on the lantern. I've tried everything. Proportions, the angle of beveling on the glass, the twist of the handle, down to the seams on the base. It's not mass market. No match in any catalog online."

I slump back in the chair. "So, it's custom."

"Possibly." Zephyr shrugs. "Or antique. The glasswork has an old-world vibe. Could be hand cut. I'm still digging. Nothing on the dress either. What I wouldn't give for a closer look at it. Or actual measurements."

"Harris was already madder than a long-tailed cat in a room full of rocking chairs," Parker says. "Turnin' in the dress was the only card we could play to keep AJ on the job."

"You think you can trace it?" I ask. A small spark of hope flares to life amid all the shit raining down on us from every direction.

"No idea. But whoever made it might have used a commercial pattern. If they did—and the pattern's proportions are online *and* the perp used a credit card—well...that would only leave about a thousand retailers to hack into."

"How long would that take? We're running out of time. The news conference is in four hours."

"A fair bit longer than that." Zephyr lifts the biggest teacup I've ever seen and takes a long sip. "But I could write an algorithm to handle the hacking while I caught some shuteye. Pritchard's got to stop assigning me two cases at once. Or find some way to clone me."

I rub the back of my neck, my gaze locked on the crime board I pulled out for this conversation. Grace's drawing is pinned to the top left corner, with the photo of the blood-stained white dress just below it.

"And nothin' on the oleander?" It's our last lead. Hell, at this point, it's our *only* lead.

"I haven't heard from Mikayla yet today. She's been working on the pollen. It's definitely from somewhere between the twenty-fifth and thirty-fifth northern parallels. But that's as far as she's been able to narrow things down."

Zephyr brings up a map of the United States and Mexico, with a band of teal—not unlike the shade of her hair—stretching across half the land mass.

"Well, that ain't much help. Grace could've been anywhere from California to Georgia to Monterrey, Mexico." Slumping back in my chair, I scrub my hands over my face.

"Not quite that far of a range. At least not when she was stabbed," Zephyr says. The color band fades away, replaced by large ovals of blue, some overlapping, some completely isolated. "These are the only places it could have been cold enough for hypothermia to set in. She could have been held anywhere. But they tried to kill her somewhere cold. I'm betting east Texas, New Mexico, or within two hours of the US-Mexico border."

Parker cuts in, her voice sharp. "Has Grace remembered anythin' else? Even the smallest detail could make the difference."

My gut twists. I drop my hands. "No. Nothin' new. Or… nothin' she's been willin' to share with me."

Jasper's lips flatten, and he gives a small shake of his head. "AJ, have you even told her we think she was taken by a cult?"

Silence stretches for too long. Zephyr holds the tea cup like a shield. Parker looks like she's about to lose her shit on me, and Jas… The disappointment in his gaze is clear as day.

"I haven't brought it up."

"Are you fucking kidding me?" Parker snaps. "Let me guess. She's too fragile? You don't want to cause her any pain?"

"Somethin' like that," I mutter.

I've never seen Parker this mad. Her steely gray stare bores right through me. Thank fuck she's still at home or Chief Harris and I might be sportin' twin bruises.

"Let me guess. You haven't told Grace about the oleander connection either." Her eyes roll skyward at my silence. "Dammit, AJ. You're the walking embodiment of every bad decision a man can make in the name of 'protecting' a woman. She ain't a porcelain doll. Stop treating her like one."

Her words cut deep, and shame crawls up the back of my neck. "She's been through so much—"

"Exactly," Parker says, the fire in her voice cooling by degrees. "And she survived. Hell, she's done a fair bit more than that. Did you know she joined our group chat on Saturday night?"

I give Parker the side-eye. "What group chat?"

"Men," she mutters. "The one with Emi, Isabel, and me. When Emi set up Grace's phone, she added her. Your wife is a hell of a lot stronger than you're giving her credit for. And she's gettin' a little more of herself back every day."

Fuck.

Dropping my head into my hands with a groan, I wonder when I became such a goddamn hypocrite. For all my talk about how strong *Grace* is, I've been the weak one. Terrified of pushing too hard. Of breaking her when she's only just put herself back together.

"Scared don't mean broken."

"Aaron," Jasper says softly. "Grace does need protectin'. Just not from herself."

I drag in a breath, steadying my voice. "You're right." The admission is bitter on my tongue. But it's necessary. "I'll tell her. Before the press conference. If she remembers anything else, I'll let all y'all know."

The call ends, and the silence in my office is deafening. Through the wall, I catch Grace's soft laugh, the sound light. Happy. At peace.

I hope what I have to do next doesn't shatter that peace into dust.

CHAPTER FORTY-FOUR

Grace

I STOP HALFWAY down the hall, breathing through a sudden sharp stab of pain in my temple. My legs feel like rubber bands stretched too tight, and every step from the front door—where I said goodbye to Karen—to here has been a battle.

"Your brain is rewiring itself, Grace. That ain't an easy thing to do. Give it time."

While I know Karen's right, I want to be able to trust my own body again. In the early hours of the morning, I dreamed of running. The sun kissing my skin, the breeze cooling my cheeks. Running is—*was*—freedom and joy and strength.

But I think it was also something I did just for me. Now what do I have? Drawing only brings up dark images I don't understand. Cooking? AJ says I never much cared for it. And even if I wanted to try it—see if I like it as part of my *new* life— my body isn't up to it yet. There's an old guitar in AJ's office. I almost laugh. Like my fingers would cooperate enough for *that*.

What do I have that's *mine*?

I need a minute before I take another step, so I lean against the wall, pull out my phone, and launch the group chat.

Grace: Do you think if I asked him to, AJ would arrest Karen's stash of clothespins? I'm pretty sure they're trying to kill me.

Three dots trail across the bottom of the screen next to Parker's photo. But they vanish a second later.

Did I go too far? Joking about inanimate objects trying to kill me less than two weeks after I was poisoned, stabbed, and left for dead in the middle of nowhere?

The bubbles come back, then stop again. And again.

Yep. I went too far.

Shit.

My eyes prick with tears. The group chat was mine. Or…I thought it could be. Mine and Parker's and Emi's and Isabel's. Emi's probably busy preparing for the news conference. Isabel's at work. But still…

A tiny buzz almost startles me enough to drop the damn thing. The relief at seeing Parker's *haha* reaction is so over-whelming, a single tear *plops* onto the screen.

Sliding the phone back into the pocket of my yoga pants, I grit my teeth and straighten. If AJ's done with his call, I'll try to convince him to join me for a bath. And this time, maybe he won't just help me wash my hair.

My steps are slower than I'd like, but mostly steady. Picturing AJ naked helps.

The door is cracked, so I don't bother knocking and push it open.

AJ's back is to me, his shoulders tense, his hands on his hips, staring at a large bulletin board propped up on the credenza by the window.

Every inch of it is covered. Note cards, newspaper clippings, torn pieces of paper. Messy, but methodical at the same time. My gaze sharpens on one of the headlines.

APD Suspends Grace Stone Kidnapping Investigation

I take a step closer. The notes...they're all in AJ's handwriting. A map of Austin covers the bottom right corner, circles and arrows pointing to Lady Bird Lake. Above it, there's a photo of a water bottle next to a cell phone with a cracked screen.

My chest tightens. Dozens of notes are pinned one over another. He did this—all of this—trying to find me.

"AJ?" I whisper.

He doesn't hear me. He's too focused on the board. I take another step closer, my hand braced on the wall for balance.

Shit.

In the top left corner, he's pinned a photo of the lantern I drew the other day. And the picture under it...

I swallow a sob. The dress I was found in. Crimson covers it, so much I don't understand how I'm standing here. I knew about it. Dr. Reyes described it to me. But when Parker gave it to Chief Harris, it was all sealed up in an evidence bag.

In the next breath, snowflakes sting my cheeks. It's dark. I'm so cold. My stomach cramps. There's a bitter taste in my mouth. My arms. Why can't I move my arms?

I blink hard, shoving the memory away. But my gaze lands on a notecard slanted over the pictures. Three words stand out in AJ's messy scrawl. *Oleander? Full Moon?*

I can't breathe.

Does he think my kidnapping had something to do with my tattoo? No. He would have told me.

My legs wobble, and I know if I don't sit down, I'll fall.

I stumble over to his desk, but stop before I reach the chair. He's pushed the leather blotter aside, and a sea of Post-It notes fans out around his laptop.

Cult?

The dress? Made just for her?

Oleander flowers woven into the ropes.

Why the lanterns? Symbolic?

Full moon the day she disappeared. And the day she was dumped.

The world tilts and blurs, swaying enough I lose my balance. I can't catch myself in time. The dark wood chair skids across the floor. I'm falling. Flailing. My knees hit the tile.

"Fuck! Grace!" AJ shouts, catching me an instant before my head slams into his desk.

"AJ." My voice is too thin. Filled with so much pain, I can't look him in the eyes. "What...what is all this? A cult? You think...I was taken by a cult?"

He keeps one arm around me, bracing the other on his desk. "I should have—"

"Don't." The word cuts deep, and I'm not sure who it hurts more. "All of this... Oleander? Full moons? You're talking about my tattoo."

"No." After a beat, he releases a slow breath and his shoulders slump. "Maybe."

Tears blur my vision. I blink hard to force them away. "You didn't think this was something I might need—or want—to know?"

Guilt churns in his eyes, settles deep into the lines around his mouth. "Grace—"

"No!" I shove against his chest hard enough he releases me, and my ass hits the floor. "You've been doin' all this behind my back? I was in here with you yesterday and didn't see any of this. You've been hiding it this whole time?"

A vein in his temple throbs. He scrubs a hand over his jaw, the only sounds in the room his stubble rasping against his palm and my ragged breathing. There's no denial. No apology either.

I press a shaking hand to my chest, trying to hold myself together. "I can't remember most of my life, AJ. The only thing I've been sure of since I first felt your arms around me...was you. But you've been keeping secrets from me. Do you have any idea what that feels like?"

AJ staggers to his feet, rights the chair, and sets it next to me. He offers me his hand, but I won't take it. I may feel like I'm on a tilt-a-whirl, but I'm determined to do this on my own.

My right knee buckles the first time I put any weight on it, but I don't give up. After three tries, I make it into the chair, my chest heaving from the effort.

Leaning his hip against the desk, AJ shoves his hands into his pockets, his shoulders hunched.

"I didn't tell you because... Fuck. I didn't want to make anythin' worse," he admits. His voice is rough, the edges of it frayed and thin. So unlike his usual warm, reassuring tone. "You've been fightin' so damn hard to get through every day, Grace. To stand. To talk. To play with Belle. And I—" He shakes his head. "I couldn't bury you under the weight of all this. Not when you're already carryin' so much."

"You don't get to decide that for me," I whisper.

"I know." His gaze lowers to mine. "Every time I thought about tellin' you, I'd remember how you looked that first morning in Mexico. You were so *lost*, darlin'. But then you started findin' yourself bit by bit. You came back to me. I couldn't risk losin' you again."

My chest aches, a battle between fury and something softer —something I can't quite name—raging in my heart. "So you kept it all hidden."

"I did," he says quietly. "And I'm sorry. I'm so damn sorry, Grace. But I swear to you, I wasn't tryin' to shut you out. I've been workin' to piece it together, to make sense of it, so I could give you answers instead of just...all these fucking questions."

My eyes drift to the board again. The photos. The scribbled notes. The careful lines of string connecting one horror to another. Some of the clippings are curled at the edges. Faded. A few crumpled and smoothed out again.

He's been doing this for three years. All the days and nights I was lost, he was here. Fighting for me the only way he could.

The sharp edges of my anger dull a little. I spin my wedding ring around on my finger. It's still loose, but the weight of it grounds me. "You never stopped looking."

His eyes close, and a shudder runs through him. "Never. Not for one goddamn second, Grace."

The tears I've been fighting spill over, hot and fast. And for the first time since I woke up in that hospital bed, I don't feel like a ghost of someone who vanished. I feel...seen. Wanted. Remembered.

AJ doesn't move right away. Like he's afraid if he does, he'll break some spell and I'll run—okay, shuffle—from the room. But eventually, he offers me his hand again. This time, I take it.

He guides me over to his leather couch, his arm tight around my waist. We sink down together. One of his knees cracks, and the sound is so achingly *normal* that I almost laugh.

"Can I hold you?" he asks.

I hesitate. Just for a second. But then I lean into him, pressing my cheek to his chest. His arms close around me, strong and steady, the scent of leather and soap wrapping me up like a blanket.

I take an easy breath. Then another.

AJ rests his chin against the top of my head. "I should've told you, Grace. You deserve better than secrets. Better than me stumblin' around, tryin' to protect you the wrong damn way."

"I stumble enough for the both of us," I say, and the single moment of lightness helps heal a little of what fractured between us. "But...AJ, we *work* because we're honest with one another."

He sucks in a breath. "Fuckin' hell. You said almost the same thing to me the mornin' you disappeared."

"I did? Was I mad at you then, too?" After a beat, I twist

enough to look up at him, my eyes wide. "AJ, were we...*fighting* that morning?"

His hold tightens, the kind of squeeze that says he's hanging on as much for himself as for me. There's so much pain in his gaze, my heart aches for him.

"I was an idjit. We were supposed to go up to the cabin that Friday night, but Harris pulled rank and ordered me and Jasper to stake out a couple of strip malls all weekend. I...texted you. And when you called me back, I didn't pick up."

"AJ!"

He stares up at the ceiling, and a single tear glistens on his cheek. "I should've refused. But I was so close to gettin' promoted to captain, I didn't think I had a choice." A harsh laugh shakes his body, but there's no joy in the sound. "Would you believe right about the time you started your run, Harris handed me that promotion? I called you. But..." Another tear joins the first. "If I'd just said no, we'd have been up at Lake Livingston that whole weekend, and none of this would have happened."

"Aaron." I cup his cheek, urging him to look at me. His eyes are bloodshot, ringed with guilt and exhaustion, but steady on me. "You can't change the past. I might not remember that day, but I *do* know even when we were fighting, we loved each other."

AJ rests his forehead against mine. It's such a simple gesture, but intimate in a way I can't explain.

"We did make up that mornin'."

Something about the way he says the words triggers a memory.

AJ standing in the doorway of our bedroom, fixing his tie with a smile. "*...make-up sex is pretty damn hot.*"

Heat blooms in my cheeks. If I felt steadier—if we didn't have that damn press conference in a few hours—I'd take him into the bedroom and suggest he recreate that reconciliation.

But when I do finally work up the courage to take him inside me, we can't have all these secrets still hovering between us.

I brush my fingers along his cheek, drying the last of his tears. "I think it's time you told me everything."

AJ PUSHES to his feet and starts to pace. The shift in his demeanor is so abrupt, it catches me off guard. Until I realize he can't do this as my husband. He has to be Captain Stone.

"Reyes sent samples of your blood and stomach contents to a lab in Chihuahua. They came back a few days ago. You were poisoned with concentrated oleander nectar mixed into grape juice. More than enough to kill you. But you were also hypothermic, and his theory is that the cold saved your life. It slowed your digestion, your heartbeat, even the swelling in your brain after the skull fracture. It bought you time." He scrubs a shaky hand over his face. "Barely."

My stomach twists in on itself, a sour burn coating my tongue. My throat tightens, and I fight not to gag.

"Drink!"

A man's voice. Angry. Rough. I don't want to listen.

I shove the memory down hard, balling my hands into fists and squeezing until I'm here again, bright red crescents throbbing on my palms.

AJ's gaze narrows on me. "Grace? What is it? You're remembering something."

I don't want to answer. Especially not now. Not when I'm about to stand up in front of cameras and reporters and let the world—including whoever took me—see that I'm still alive.

But I asked him to be honest. I owe him the same. "Just...a voice. Someone telling me to drink. And a bitter taste in my mouth. I don't know what it was, or when it happened. Or if it's even a real memory."

He crouches down in front of me. "What else? Did you hear other people? Were you hot? Or cold? Sitting? Standing?"

"I...I don't know." A headache starts at the base of my skull and tightens around my head like a fist. My stomach roils. A sob threatens to break through, but I swallow it down. "Please, AJ. Don't ask me to remember more. Not right now. If I have another panic attack, there's no way I'll be able to stand up in front of the cameras and the reporters and prove to everyone—*especially* the assholes who took me—that I survived."

He exhales slowly, his gaze softening. He's not Captain Stone right now, he's AJ. My husband. "Okay. Do you want to take a break?"

"No. I can hear the facts. I want to. I...*need* to."

With a nod, the Ranger in him takes over. Pushing to his feet, he clears his throat and pulls a picture from under his laptop. "These are the ropes you were bound with when Reyes found you. Someone *made* these, Grace. By hand. They wove oleander flowers all through them. We're tryin' to narrow down where they came from. Pritchard's fiancée is a botanist, but oleander grows damn near everywhere."

The white and gold braided cord is almost...pretty. Or would be if not for the scars around my wrists.

"The dress you were wearing was custom," AJ says, his voice softer now. "We can't be sure, but it might have been made specifically for whatever twisted ritual they put you through."

Silk whispers over my skin. Clings to my breasts. Brushes the top of my feet.

AJ cracks his knuckles, the sharp sound pulling me back from the abyss. "The first drawing you did? The moon was full. It was so fucking *big*, I thought...maybe it meant something. So I checked the lunar calendar. Reyes found you the morning after the full moon." He swallows hard, his Adam's apple bobbing over the collar of his Henley. "When you disappeared, I was out on the trail that first night until dawn. I remember how bright the moon was. But I never gave it a second thought until yesterday. You were taken on the full moon. It's got to mean something."

I close my eyes. Lanterns glow above me, swinging in the frigid air. Shadows sway on all sides. I can't feel my cheeks. Or my lips. My hands… I shiver. Why can't I move my arms?

Raw agony slices through my side, and all the air leaves my lungs.

"Grace. Come back to me." AJ's gentle tone soothes the pain. His arms wrap around me, and I find the strength to shove the memory into a tiny box and shut the lid with a bang.

I expect to find a sea of worry in his gaze. But when I open my eyes, I see only love.

"There you are, darlin'. You can relax now. That's the whole of it. Everythin' we know for sure. Everythin' we're still tryin' to piece together."

I turn to the bulletin board. I thought all the notes and clippings and scribbles were just horrors to be feared. And in some ways, they are. But they're more than that.

They're love. Desperate, raw love.

And knowing that gives me the strength to face them.

CHAPTER FORTY-FIVE

AJ

I PULL the duvet up to Grace's shoulders, lean down, and press a kiss to her forehead. She agreed to rest when I promised her I'd not only help her wash her hair before the press conference, but I'd do it naked.

I'd worried hearing the evidence we'd gathered would break her. But it might have made her even stronger.

Slipping out of the bedroom, I unlock my phone. Connor picks up on the first ring.

"What happened with Hardison?" I ask as I close myself back in my office.

"Harris was fixin' to hand the case back over to APD," Connor says. "But when Hardison came in this mornin', he was going on about how badly they done fucked up last time and how the Rangers were gonna show 'em how it was done."

Worry prickles along my spine. "I ain't about to argue with him about APD's shoddy police work, but does Hardison have any idea *why* he changed his tune?"

"Nope. And Zephyr hasn't found anything on his computer. But with all the angles she's workin', can't say I'm surprised."

A ball of ice settles in my gut. "This don't feel right. Harris handed the case to APD—and shut me out—less than forty-eight hours after Grace was taken. Why would he be so territorial now?"

"That's the million-dollar question," Connor says. "Outside of the twenty minutes he spent with me, Hardison's been stuck to Harris like glue all day. He's got good instincts, AJ. Almost as good as Parker's. If there's somethin' to find, he won't stop until he digs it up."

With a sigh, I sink into my chair. "You'll be there? At the press conference?"

"What the hell kind of question is that? Of course I'll be there. Are you okay?"

I stare at the crime board leaning against the wall. "I... hadn't told Grace about the oleander poison. Or...anything, really. Until an hour ago."

"Shit," Connor mutters. "I'd read you the riot act for keepin' all that from her, but it sounds like you're beating yourself up enough already. How'd she take it?"

"Better than I would have." I run a hand through my hair, tugging hard enough a few strands come loose in my fingers. "But...fuck, man. After tonight, the whole world's gonna know she's alive. How long until they come for her again?"

He doesn't answer right away. That ain't good.

"I can pack a bag. Take her up to the cabin. It's got a decent security system." My voice, already rough around the edges, cracks. The last time I went to our grandfather's cabin on Lake Livingston, it was to save Jasper and Emi from a mess of cartel hitmen. If I'd been even two minutes later, they'd both be dead.

"No. You can't make Grace leave her home. Not when she's still findin' her way back. Plus, you'd be all alone up there."

"Even here, it's half a mile to the nearest neighbor. I've got security cameras at the front and back doors, but—"

"That ain't enough," Connor says, his voice calm and steady. "But I've been workin' on a solution."

"You... What kind of solution?" The man's already done so much for us. He claims we'll never be square. But helping to save him and his family was my fucking job. This? It's a hell of a lot more.

"I called Graham."

It takes me a second to place the name. "Your brother's guy?"

"Yeah. He's part of Ryker McCabe's K&R team in Seattle. Their logistics specialist—a former Navy SEAL—is married to the woman who runs Emerald City Security."

"Is that name supposed to mean somethin' to me?"

He chuckles. "It might if you watched the news once in a while. Emerald City is *the* name in security. Ain't no one better. Their systems have helped put a stop to a couple of high-profile crime rings in San Francisco, Denver, and Chicago. But they don't do home installs. Unless you happen to be family."

"I ain't family."

His laugh turns into a snort. "For fuck's sake, AJ. How can you still think that? If it weren't for you, I'd be dead. Isabel and Veronica too. They're sendin' a team of installers out on a red-eye tonight. They'll be at the house by ten tomorrow."

The knots turning my shoulders to granite don't unravel completely, but they loosen a fraction. "Connor—"

"And tonight, Jasper, Parker, and I have you covered. You and Grace won't be alone. Not for one damn second."

"I can't lose her again," I manage through the overwhelming wave of relief threatening to carry me away.

"You won't. Grace'll have a wall around her everywhere, AJ. One with teeth. Anyone tries to get to her, they'll have to go through us. *All* of us."

Grace

My nap was nothing but a never-ending series of nightmares. If only I could remember what they were beyond dark shadows and people chanting words I couldn't understand.

I was so exhausted when I woke up, I couldn't even muster the energy to ask AJ to join me in the bath.

Now, I sit on the edge of the bed, staring at the closet like it could swallow me whole at any moment. I know the clothes are mine. Some of them even feel...almost familiar. But they all belong to the woman I used to be.

Emi pops out, a deep green sweater in her hands. "This one will bring out the color of your eyes and soften the bruising a bit." She studies my face. The dark purple covering my cheek and temple has started to fade into a sickly yellow. "It's strong, but not flashy. It says survivor, not victim."

She lays the sweater in my lap, and I run my fingers over the soft knit I can't remember buying. "I don't want to pretend everything's fine. It isn't."

"You don't have to, hon." She crouches in front of me and takes my hands. "The bruises speak for themselves. What we're doing here is making sure people see *you*. Not just the damage."

I want to ask her how she can be so sure there *is* a me under all the damage, but she pulls a shopping bag from her over-sized purse and dangles it in front of me. "I went to the beauty supply store and got you everything you'll need for makeup."

"You..." My throat tightens, and I just stare at the bag. First the phone, with all that music, the group chat—where messages fly by at a dizzying speed, and whenever I say something, the heart emojis and replies come almost immediately—and now this?

"I don't... You hardly know me. Why would you—?"

Emi's eyes soften. She sets the bag down and takes a seat next to me on the bed. "Because you deserve to have choices again, Grace. When you're ready, I'll go with you to the store. Help you pick out anything you think you might want that isn't in here. But since the world can't know you're alive for another two hours, this...well...it'll get you started." She grins and squeezes my hand. "You're tougher than you think, funny as hell, and Parker's already adopted you as her sister. That's enough for me to know we're going to be great friends."

The heavy weight I've been carrying on my shoulders all day lifts a fraction. I'm not brave enough to hug Emi, so I run my thumb over the sweater again, grounding myself in its texture.

"Come on," she says, rising and holding out her hand. "Let's get you into this and start on the makeup."

I let her help me up, then trade the fuzzy pink sweater for the one she picked out. "See?" Emi angles me toward the mirror. The green makes my eyes look sharper. More alert. Alive. "This is the one. Strong, not flashy."

Once I take a seat at the vanity, she arranges tubes, bottles, and brushes all in a row. "We'll keep it simple. A touch of concealer, some powder, and a hint of color on your lips. No eye makeup. Nothing heavy. But, if you decide you want to go all out for a date or just...'because' some time, you call me and I'll come show you what to do with all the rest of this."

Her steady hands move with confidence. Gentle dabs here and there, soft brush strokes. Warmth blooms in my cheeks as she evens out the harsh edges of the bruise.

"In all the pictures from...*before*...I didn't have much makeup on," I whisper.

"And we're not changing that. What we want most is for the cameras to see your eyes. To see the woman you are now."

When she's finished, I almost don't recognize myself. The

scar on my cheek is still there—it always will be—but it doesn't catch the light like it did before. The bruise isn't gone, but it's softer now.

Emi smooths my hair, tugging a few strands into place over the butterfly bandages on my scalp, then crouches so we're eye level in the mirror. "Grace, people are going to want to see two things today—that you're human, and you're still standing. You don't need to smile. Or be funny. Or look perfect. You don't need to hide the strength you have, or fake strength you don't. You just need to breathe. And if it gets to be too much, lean on AJ. Or look for me and Parker. I'll be in the first row, and she'll be standing in the back. Okay?"

The bruise throbs under the thin veil of concealer, the sweater doesn't completely cover the scars around my wrists, and panic still threatens to turn my stomach inside out. But Emi's words put a tiny crack in the wall of fear I've been hiding behind for over a week now. Just wide enough for a hint of light to slip through.

I nod softly. "Okay."

I SMOOTH my palms over the dark green sweater for the tenth time in as many minutes. After Emi left, the exhaustion tried to pull me under again. Two cups of Cafe Vienna were enough for me to feel moderately human, but the caffeine also left me with a stomach full of angry hornets. God, I hope I don't throw up all over the microphones.

The doorbell sends my heart rate into the stratosphere, though Belle's tail is wagging as she trots in from the kitchen.

"Parker," AJ says, his voice subdued as he lets her in. The look she gives him could freeze Hell itself until he adds, "I told her. Everything."

Well, I'm definitely filing *that* away for the group chat. If I survive the next couple of hours.

"Good." She crouches down to greet Belle, scratching her behind the ears and cooing, "Hey, pretty girl. Got something for you and your mama. Let's go show her what it is, okay?"

Belle barks, running over to me with her tongue hanging half out of her mouth.

Parker sets a box in my lap before dropping into the chair next to me. "Go ahead. Open it."

"Please tell me you didn't stop at the beauty counter again. Emi came over earlier with a whole bag of makeup, and I'm still trying to figure out when to use all the stuff you bought me last week!"

She grins. "I'll write up a cheat sheet. I really should have done that for you on Friday, but...then I went and decked the chief, got myself suspended, all hell broke loose..." With a soft shake of her head, she meets my gaze. "What's in there should make tonight a little easier on you."

"Is it tequila? A 'get out of this press conference free' card? Or a whole boatload of Xanax?" I lift the lid, and pull out a sleek, black leather dog harness with a long, sturdy handle. "Oh, my God."

"It's a mobility support harness," Parker explains, scooting to the edge of the chair. "It distributes weight across Belle's body, so you can lean on the handle without hurting her. I figured...it might let you ditch the walker."

I curl my fingers around the soft leather, testing the weight of it. Belle sniffs the straps with an inquisitive little *ruff*, like she knows it's for her.

All those angry hornets settle a bit. Not gone, but muted. Like Parker's gift soothed them.

"You—" My voice breaks, and I swallow hard before trying again. "How did you even know something like this existed?"

She shrugs, the movement casual, but there's something in

her eyes I can't read. "You don't go anywhere without Belle, and this way, you won't have to try to manage her *and* the walker. I started the paperwork to get her registered as a proper service dog, but until we jump through all those hoops, places that don't usually allow dogs should understand she's not with you just for shits and giggles."

"Will you...um...help me with the buckles?"

"I gotcha, babe." She drops to her knees, adjusting and fastening the various straps until they lie flat against Belle's sleek fur. "Try it out."

Parker helps me to my feet, and Belle moves immediately to my right side. As if she *knows* my left hand is the weak one. As soon as I grip the handle, I feel steadier. The world doesn't tilt quite so much under me.

We try a few hesitant steps. When my knee buckles, Belle is there to support me. I let the handle take part of my weight, and after a moment, when I haven't crumpled to the ground, I try again until I've completed a whole circuit of the living room.

I wrap my arms around Parker. "Thank you."

"That's what friends do," she says softly.

CHAPTER FORTY-SIX

Grace

AJ KEEPS his arm locked around my waist as we move down the Ranger station's wide hallway, Belle steady at my side and Jasper right behind us.

I only had a single bout of vertigo on the way over here, and being able to navigate the world without the walker is freeing in a way I couldn't have imagined even two hours ago.

The clothes Emi picked for me, the hint of makeup, and Parker's hug as she told me she'd be in my eyeline as soon as I step up to the podium all remind me I'm not walking into this as a ghost of the woman I used to be, but as someone who survived.

Still, my pulse hasn't gotten the memo. It hammers harder with every step. And AJ, at my side, is strung tighter than a fiddle.

Chief Harris waits at the end of the hall, arms crossed, chest puffed out. Nate leans against the wall behind him. His posture screams boredom, but even though I only met him a few days ago, I can tell it's all an act.

"Stone," Harris says, his tone clipped, but not unkind. "Before we walk out there, you should know—this case is stayin' here. APD's sorry excuse for a missin' person's unit ain't gettin' their hands on it. Marvin's right. They fucked it up when Grace was taken. I'm not lettin' them do it again."

AJ stiffens, and he pulls me even closer. "Marvin's idea, huh?" He keeps his voice steady, but anger simmers just under the surface of his skin.

The chief's eyes narrow. "Marvin's been coverin' your caseload for over a week, Stone. He's good people."

"Maybe he is, Chief, but Grace is *my* wife. And I don't want him anywhere near her case. Understood?"

The chief's mouth flattens, and for a beat he looks like he's about to bite AJ's head clean off.

"You don't get to pick who works what case, Stone. That's my call. But"—his gaze lands on me, then shifts back to AJ—"I hear you. Loud and clear."

Nate pushes off the wall and clears his throat. "Chief, Captain Vern with APD is here."

I glance over my shoulder. An older man in dress blues strides down the hall like he owns the place. "Harris, you and I are gonna have words when the cameras are all gone. This is APD's case. Always has been."

"You had your shot three years ago," Harris snaps. "You pissed it down the drain. You don't get to do it again."

The APD captain turns his glare on me, and I suck in a sharp breath. "Mrs. Stone, we need you to come in—"

"No." AJ's voice is practically a snarl. "You don't get to touch her. She's been through enough. APD gets to stand behind her while she faces the press, but that's as close as you get to her ever again."

Nate makes a show of checking his watch. "Press is waiting. Save the pissing contest for later."

The chief, his jaw tight and hands balled into fists, leads the way. Nate only a step behind him. The APD captain and Jasper bring up the rear. AJ's twin keeps *accidentally* bumping into the guy, and I think the captain just called him a cretin under his breath.

We stop in front of a set of double doors. "Wait here," Harris orders. He and Captain Vern march through the doors first. For the brief moment they're open, the loud buzz from the reporters sends my heart into my throat.

AJ's arm tightens, as if he knows I'm close to unraveling. Jasper cracks one of the doors open so we can hear what's going on.

"Almost three years ago, Grace Stone, the wife of Captain AJ Stone, disappeared while running on the Butler trail by Lady Bird Lake. Austin PD and the Department of Public Safety investigated the case for months, but no trace of Mrs. Stone was ever found. Until nine days ago."

"That's our cue," AJ murmurs softly, and Nate holds the door open for us.

With Belle and my husband at my side, I manage to shuffle up the two steps and onto a raised platform without tripping. Half a dozen microphones line the podium. The constant click of camera shutters is almost overwhelming. Bright lights glare overhead. My headache returns with a sudden vengeance, and I sway until AJ steadies me.

Chief Harris and Captain Vern move off to one side of the platform, while Nate stands on the other, close to the double doors.

For a moment, I search the crowd, seeking out the handful of people—besides AJ—who can anchor me if I panic. Emi's right up front, her press badge hanging from a lanyard around her neck.

Connor and Isabel are in the fourth row, and Jasper ambles down the center aisle to take a seat next to them. In the very back, I find Parker, who gives me a little nod of encouragement.

AJ clears his throat. "When Grace disappeared, I started runnin' the Butler trail every weekend. Never really knew why, 'cept it was the only thing that let me feel close to her. A week ago Saturday, when I got to the spot where her water bottle and phone were found, she was standin' there. Disoriented, barefoot, wearin' a white dress stained with her blood. And she had no memory of me, her life, or even her name."

Half a dozen reporters shout questions at once. I flinch, curling closer to AJ. Belle's low growl rumbles against my leg.

"My wife's been through hell," he snaps. "Show her some goddamn respect."

The shouts fade to dull whispers, and AJ nods. "I'm fixin' to tell you the rest, and then Grace'll take a few questions."

AJ sticks to the fabricated story. The truth that's not the truth, but not entirely a lie either.

After he tells the reporters that only small fragments of my memories have returned, he presses a kiss to the top of my head. "We waited to come forward until Grace was strong enough to take questions and face a room full of people she doesn't know. Don't make her regret showin' up here today."

AJ takes a step back, but I can still feel the heat of him behind me. Still smell his aftershave. Still feel his hand brush mine.

Belle stands up, pressing against my legs, and letting me lean on her through her harness.

"Grace?" Emi's polished, confident voice carries over the din in the room. "Emmylou Marsh with Channel Five News. Can you tell us how you're feeling today?"

My throat tightens, but we rehearsed this, and I grab onto the lifeline she offers me. "Tired. A little...overwhelmed. But grateful. To be here. To be alive. To be back home with my husband who never stopped looking for me."

Emi's gentle smile gives me a tiny boost of confidence.

A couple of seats over, another woman rises to her feet.

"Natalie Rosa from News Network Now. What's the first thing you remember after being found?"

I glance down at Belle, then at AJ. This...wasn't one of the questions we practiced. But...

"AJ's arms around me. How safe he made me feel, even though I didn't kn-know who he was."

Murmured voices ripple through the room. The anxiety squeezing my chest tightens a notch. I'm so exposed up here. The shutters don't stop clicking, and half a dozen red lights glow where video cameras are trained directly on me.

"Do you remember your family? Your friends?" a man shouts from a few rows back.

I swallow hard, my throat dry as sand. "N-no. Not yet. Moments, here and there, from years ago. But nothing more."

Before I can even take a breath, another voice cuts in. "Where were you held? Were there others?"

The questions pile on top of one another.

"Was it a trafficking ring?"

"Why wasn't there a ransom demand?"

"Can you describe your injuries?"

"How did you escape?"

"Do you think your captors are still out there?"

Flash bulbs erupt. Voices overlap until they turn into a crashing wave, threatening to pull me under. Belle whines, nosing my thigh and pawing at the floor.

AJ steps forward, one hand braced on the podium, the other curling around my waist. "One question at a time or this is *over*."

Silence descends so quickly, it's disorienting. Until a younger man in the back stands. "Captain Stone, Mrs. Stone. With respect, this is all a little too neat and tidy. She vanishes, no clues for almost three years, then magically reappears in the exact same spot? You honestly expect us to believe that?"

"It...it's the truth," I say, my voice cracking on the last word. "I don't know how I got there. Or why...when..."

The questions hit harder and faster with every passing second.

"Were you drugged?"

"Why were you wearing a white dress?"

"Were you raped?"

My grip on Belle's harness tightens until my fingers go numb. I can't breathe—

"Enough!" AJ snarls and pulls me flush to his side. His glare finds the man who called our story too neat and tidy. "My wife ain't a fuckin' piñata you can bash with a stick until all the answers fall out. You want to speculate? Write a novel."

Nate takes a step forward. Then another. Slowly. Deliberately. If I hadn't met him the other day, I'd cower under his icy stare. He leans in, close to the microphones. "Cool it with the conspiracy theories. If one of you vultures has the next Pulitzer in your notebook, get out and go publish the damn thing. Otherwise, settle down."

"One more question," AJ says, his voice measured, barely restrained control wrapped in a fragile shield that could snap at any moment. "Then we're done here."

Mercifully, Emi rises, her voice anchoring me as much as AJ's strength, Belle's harness in my hand, and Parker's encouraging nod. "Grace, is there one thing you'd like the people watching today to know?"

AJ, Connor, and Parker fought about this question for an hour. Whether it was worth the risk. Whether the people who took me would hear it as a challenge. In the end, I told them I *had* to answer it if I wanted my life back.

Swallowing hard, I lean into AJ, then take a deep breath. My pulse steadies. I can do this.

"That I survived. That surviving matters. Even though I

came back different. Even though I came back broken. It still matters. *I* matter."

The room goes completely and utterly silent. And for the first time since the press conference began, I don't feel like I'm about to shatter. I feel like I'm starting to put myself back together.

AJ squeezes my waist, drawing me against his chest. His lips brush my temple, steady and grounding, and Belle leans harder into my leg, her warm weight reminding me I'm not alone. The flashes and whispers fade into background noise as AJ guides me toward the double doors, every step both terrifying and freeing.

At the podium, Nate clears his throat and sweeps his gaze over the crowd. "Mrs. Stone is done for today. You have more questions, you direct them to me. But keep in mind, this is an active investigation, not a late-night true crime special. You take one step outta line and your press credentials won't be worth the paper they're printed on."

The doors shut behind us, and the muffled voices of the reporters fade away.

"You did great, darlin'." In the empty hallway, AJ slides his fingers into my hair, cupping the back of my head and slanting his lips over mine.

The promise in his kiss seeps into every part of me. I'm home. I'm safe. I'm loved.

CHAPTER FORTY-SEVEN

Grace

OUTSIDE, the wind whips through the trees, leaving them as battered as I feel. For the past eighteen hours, my face has been splashed across all of Austin's television screens. But instead of a photograph, it's *me*. Walking—sort of—talking, and daring the people who took me to try again.

They know the poison and the blade and the skull fracture didn't kill me now.

Will they try to finish the job?

My stomach twists into a knot, and the edges of my vision pulse as the headache creeps in.

For hours, a team of installers has been in and out of the house, wiring every room like it's Fort Knox—panic buttons tucked into corners, cameras with three-hundred-and-sixty-degree views, tech so advanced it makes me dizzy.

AJ calls it peace of mind. A "shield around our slice of the world." But it's not. It's proof I'm not safe. And he knows it.

"Ma'am? Sorry to bug you, but I need to get into that corner to mount a motion sensor."

Lucas stands by the kitchen island, a clipboard tucked under one arm. He's six-four and built like a linebacker, but his grin takes the edge off the sheer size of him. When he first walked in the door, I wanted to bolt to the bedroom, bury myself under the covers, and pretend all these people were part of a bad dream.

But then he'd offered me a warm smile. "Don't worry, ma'am. I read the manual twice. But it's more fun to ignore it and see where that gets me."

The corner of my mouth twitched. "So...we're in good hands?"

"Best you'll find," he'd deadpanned, and for a second, I felt almost normal bantering with a stranger in the middle of my foyer.

Now, he moves around my house with ease. He feels...safe. Like he knows when to be quiet, when to make a joke, and when to be serious about the dangers this system will protect us from.

I take my sketchbook and pencil with me as I shuffle from my favorite spot on the couch to one of the less comfortable chairs on either side of the fireplace. I haven't been able to spend more than a couple of minutes at a time in my studio. It still feels...*wrong*. So whenever I have the focus to put the pencil to the page, I've been drawing in the living room.

The acrid tang of burnt metal curls from the soldering iron. The scent twists my stomach, dragging me unwillingly to another place. Another time.

Sun kisses my cheeks. My tank is soaked with sweat, but the gentle breeze helps keep me from overheating. The barely there thud of my running shoes on the pavement, strength in my legs, my watch beeping as I pass eight miles.

Lightning hits me square in the chest.

My muscles spasm.

Can't...breathe.

The clear, blue sky fades to gray. Everything's blurry. Dark. I hurt. Why do I hurt?

"Grace?" A man—his voice familiar, but too bright and out of place for the dark in my head—calls my name, but I can't find the strength to respond. "Yo, AJ! Get in here!"

AJ. He'll find me. He'll save me. He always does.

I'm moving. Being lifted. Being taken.

No. Not there. Don't let them put you in there!

I thrash against arms holding me too tightly. Whimper. Beg. "Let me go. Please!"

"You're home. You're safe. You're loved." AJ's voice cuts through the fog, and a cold, wet nose swipes over my cheek. "Come back now, darlin'."

Belle whines, nudges me again. My fingers sink into her wiry fur. She's tense. Shaking. Or is that me?

"AJ—" My voice cracks. I can't make my lungs work.

"Breathe, Grace. Just breathe," he croons.

The room comes back into focus by degrees. The thick rug under my fingers. The warm wood beams overhead. The fire crackling in the hearth. The leather sofa with the thick beige blanket. Belle, her bright eyes locked on me.

Lucas is halfway to the back door. "I'll...uh...check how Lindsay's doing outside. Give you a few minutes."

AJ shifts, pulling me into his lap. "Talk to me."

I *know* I can't keep banishing all my painful memories somewhere they can't hurt me. But that doesn't mean I'm strong enough to face them. "Not yet."

"Grace—"

"Tell me something real," I whisper. "I need something real to hold onto."

AJ takes my left hand, his fingers resting on my wedding ring. "This is real."

"More. Please..." I beg.

He drops his forehead to mine. "*You're* real. *We're* real."

I cling to him, still shaking, my cheek pressed to his chest, right over his heart. "I remembered running. That day."

As if he can sense how close I am to breaking again, AJ presses a gentle kiss to the top of my head. "Our first Thanksgiving in this house, we hosted everyone. But Jas and I caught a case and didn't wrap it up until early that mornin'. So you had to put the turkey in the oven. You'd never made one before. We'd always gone over to Mom's house." He chuckles, and the sound is enough to soothe my raw nerves. "You had no idea the turkey neck and giblets were stuffed inside the bird. Wrapped in wax paper. I came home to a house that reeked of smoke to find you and my mom half drunk on mimosas with at least a dozen Chinese takeout containers on the table. It was one of the best Thanksgivings ever."

God, I wish I could call up *that* memory. "I want to meet your mom."

"She spends most of her time goin' on cruises with her travel group. Can you imagine? Ten women, all between seventy and eighty-five, with enough Queen of the Seas points built up, they ain't gotta spend a cent most of the time. She's cruisin' around Cape Horn in Africa right about now, but she'll be back to port in two weeks. You'll meet her then."

Comforted by AJ's story, I let him help me up onto the couch. He settles next to me, his arm around my shoulders.

"My watch read a little over eight miles. I felt so good, AJ. Strong. Like I could have run forever. But then...something hit me."

I touch my ribs. Just under my breasts. "Here. Then I was on the ground. I couldn't move. I think...it might have been a taser."

He asks me question after question, his voice calm, smooth, measured. Did I see their faces? Hear their voices? Did they have a car? A truck? A van? What happened after they tased me?

But I can't give him any answers. "That's all I know," I whisper.

"It's okay, darlin'. You faced it. You let yourself remember." He rubs gentle circles over my thigh. "What triggered you? Any idea?"

God, I'm so tired. If I could, I'd crawl back into bed and sleep for a week. But the installers won't be done for another few hours. "I think...the soldering iron."

AJ nods. "How about you move into your studio for a while. They finished in that room an hour ago."

A hard knot clogs my throat. "I...can't."

He tilts his head, studying me. "Why not?"

"Because it doesn't feel like mine." The words escape before I can stop them. "I walk in there, and I don't recognize any of it. The walls are too bright. And all the sketches and paintings—I know they're *my* sketches and paintings—but it's like someone else made them. It...hurts."

Belle nudges my knee, and AJ drapes his hand over mine, his fingers resting on my wedding ring. The contact should be enough for me to shake the hollow, haunting echo I feel every time I look at my own art. But it isn't.

"My office, then," he says, scooping up my sketchbook, pencil, eraser, and blending stick. "Unlike Lucas, *I* ain't gonna learn this system without readin' the fuckin' manual."

CHAPTER FORTY-EIGHT

AJ

Stone,

Your "leave" is starting to look more like retirement. Never thought Marvin would turn out to be more reliable than you. Be back at your desk on Monday or I'm giving it—and your star—to him.

-Chief Harris

I stare at the email, grinding my teeth so hard, my jaw cracks. Of course, Harris would threaten to give *Marvin* my job. Never mind that the Department of Public Safety don't work that way, he'd do it out of spite.

The idea of leaving Grace alone—unprotected—when we're still no closer to finding out who took her sits like a lead weight in my gut.

I type and delete half a dozen replies ranging from "I'll be at the station at eight a.m. Monday" to "With all due respect, chief, retirement suits me just fine" before my phone buzzes, Parker's name flashing across the screen.

For half a second, I think about ignoring it. She hasn't quite forgiven me for hiding our theories from Grace. But Parker put her career in jeopardy for us. She can be angry at me for the rest of my life, and I'll still consider her family.

"Parker. You findin' ways to keep outta trouble?"

She snorts. "So far today, I've washed, dried, *and* folded my laundry, scrubbed the baseboards, and bought one of those damn mini-blind dusters. If I don't find some trouble soon, I might need to try my hand at a sourdough starter. Or worse. I'll give myself bangs."

Laughing feels...like the return of a long-lost friend.

Jas and I used to prank the new recruits—and even the other lieutenants—on the regular. But once Grace disappeared...I stopped laughing completely.

"Did Harris give you any idea when he'd lift your suspension?"

"Nope. And he ain't paying me for it either."

"Fuck." This is all my fault. *I* should have been the one to deck the chief. Not her. "Look...if you need...if things get tight..." I've stared down gunmen high on PCP, joined SWAT on more than a dozen raids, but offering a friend money? That's a whole other level of hard. "I can float you some cash."

Parker's utterly silent for several seconds. Finally, she huffs. "AJ, if you think you're gonna pay me for doin' the right thing, you're half a bubble off plumb."

That frees another laugh, this one a little shaky, but just as real. "Fair enough. For now."

"I actually called to give you a heads up on somethin'," she says. Her tone softens. "Isabel, Emi, and I usually get together on Wednesdays. Movies, junk food, maybe some pampering. We're gonna ask Grace to join us tonight."

Every muscle in my body goes tight. The lump in my throat makes it hard to breathe. "No. She's not—"

"Ready? For fuck's sake, AJ. Look in the damn mirror. *You're* the one who ain't ready. Grace held her own at the press conference. You said she was even jokin' around with Lucas by the time he left yesterday—after havin' a damn panic attack. She can handle this. And it's at Isabel's. She and Connor have the exact same security setup you do."

"We don't have any new leads..." The words sound feeble, even to my ears. And hell, it *is* possible whoever took her is so off the grid, they have no idea she's alive.

But from the minute I found her down in Mexico, we've been...together. In the same house. The same space. How the fuck am I supposed to cope with her being halfway across town?

"Look, if it helps, I won't touch a drop of alcohol tonight, and I'll be armed. I'll even text you every hour if it'll make you feel better." After a beat, Parker's voice softens. "She needs this. Hell, *you* need this. You've been glued to her side for almost two weeks. She's gonna drown if she can't breathe without you watching her."

Fuck.

She's right.

The mere *thought* of Grace leaving the house without me is enough to make my chest ache. But our home isn't a prison. And if I make it one, how am I any better than the assholes who took her? She needs her own friends. Her own *life*. One that fits the woman she is now.

"If you're even two minutes late textin' me..."

"You'll be over here faster than a duck on a June bug. Got it, boss. I'll text her as soon as I hang up. Assuming she says yes, you want to drop her off, or should I plan on pickin' her up? We usually start at six thirty, end around eleven or so."

A ghost of an idea hovers in the back of my mind. "I'll drop her off. But I need you to promise me all y'all won't leave Connor and Isabel's. Not for anything."

"Wild horses and rabid dogs couldn't drag us off Isabel's couch. It's too damn soft," she says, and I can hear the smile in her voice. "Don't worry, AJ. I got her. Promise."

When the call ends, I start my own group chat. I add Connor and Jasper, but before I can figure out what to say, scroll through my contacts until I find Hardison's name and add him too.

AJ: I need a favor. It involves paint and some heavy lifting, but pays in pizza and beer. If you're in, be at my place at 7:30.

Grace

I sink deeper into the couch with a mug of tea, the scent of chamomile and lavender as soothing as Belle snoring at my side. Karen took it easy on me today, which means she's got something truly sadistic in mind for tomorrow.

If she tries to combine the clothespins with some sort of balance exercise...I might cry. But for now, I'll relish in the victory of having had enough stamina to throw the tennis ball for Belle more than a dozen times—with my left hand—before my grip strength faded into nothing.

I *should* pick up my sketchbook and try to coax some of my memories free, but it's so quiet and peaceful right now. Yesterday's winds gave way to a clear blue sky, and AJ's outside raking leaves, leaving me a few minutes to just...be.

Did I have this where I was? These little moments of quiet? Belle's breath tickles my palm. I smell fresh pine. And... carrots?

Don't fight it. Let yourself remember.

"She's kind of like you," an older man says. His face is lined, but there's a wary kindness in his brown eyes. "If she could, she'd run away from here and never look back. Go ahead and give her a treat."

I stare down at my hand. At the piece of carrot clutched in my fingers. The horse stamps her foot, and I yelp.

Panic threatens to drown me, but Belle noses her way under my arm until her head rests in my lap.

I'm home. And though my heart is pounding hard enough I can feel it in my ears, I know one more thing about the place I was held.

There were horses.

THE HEADACHE THROBS in my temples. I should get more tea, but when I tried to get up a few minutes ago, the room tilted sideways, and I almost toppled over. So, I pick up my phone and scroll through all the playlists Emi made for me. Music will be a good distraction.

I'm about to try "Late 90s Rock," when a new message comes in to the group chat.

Parker: Girls' night. Isabel's place. 6:30. Grace, you in?

My heart leaps into my throat. Leave the house? Alone? Without AJ?

My hands start to shake. I don't remember going to restaurants, shopping...*living*. I'm sure I used to do all those things, but now...?

Grace: You know I can't drive, right? Then there's the matter of my slightly overprotective husband. Y'all would have more fun without him standing in the corner of the room all night.

Three sets of chat bubbles dance across the bottom of the screen.

Emi: We have queso. And tequila. Fun is a given.

Isabel: Popcorn too. With extra butter.

Parker: Don't hate me, but I already cleared it with AJ. He was a bit twitchy, but I got him to agree to drop you off and not hover outside Isabel's house all night. There may have been threats involved.

Grace: Wait. You called him first?

Parker: I had to, babe. AJ doesn't do well with surprises. He would have gone full growly caveman. It would have been a whole thing.

Isabel: She isn't wrong.

Emi: He does that thing with his jaw. Jasper does too, but with AJ...it's twice as intimidating.

Grace: You're all sure you want me there tonight? I don't exactly remember how to have fun.

Emi: Yes. Absolutely. And don't worry. We'll remind you.

CHAPTER FORTY-NINE

Grace

AJ TURNS onto a quiet street lined with tidy lawns and colorfully painted mailboxes. The first spring flowers are starting to bloom in window boxes and garden beds.

If I had to guess, Connor and Isabel are probably on a first-name basis with all their neighbors.

My husband is tense, his knuckles pure white where he grips the steering wheel.

"I can be back here in twenty-seven minutes. Twenty-four if I use the siren," he says, his voice gritty and strained.

The idea of him flipping on the siren to pick me up from girls' night is so absurd, it eases a tiny fraction of my nerves.

He pulls into the driveway, cuts the engine, and my heart rate skyrockets. Until I spot the cameras. They're tucked into the eaves. Over the garage. Watching the front steps. Just like home.

The tight knot in my chest loosens. Not completely, but enough for me to breathe.

"Your panic button will alert me, Connor, Jasper, Hardison,

Parker, Connor's former boss at the FBI, Zephyr, and Pritchard out in Connecticut if anything happens. I'll pick you up at eleven."

He doesn't ask me if I'm sure. Doesn't tell me he'll drive me home right now if I want him to. Probably good, because I'm equal parts excited and terrified.

AJ gets out of the SUV and comes around to open my door. My knees wobble as I get to my feet, but Belle is at my side seconds later. With her harness in my hand, I feel almost steady. In control.

"Grace." AJ rests his hand at the small of my back, presses his lips to my forehead for a long moment, and then straightens. "Have fun, darlin'."

Fun.

I don't remember fun. But if anyone can help with that, it's Parker, Emi, and Isabel.

Belle helps me make it up the three short steps without losing my balance, and the front door bursts open before I can reach for the doorbell.

Parker—dressed in yoga pants and a baggy sweatshirt—ushers me inside, waves to AJ, and then shuts the door. As soon as she's double-checked the locks, she pulls me in for a gentle, one-armed hug and whispers, "If this gets to be too much, let me know."

The house smells like spicy queso, and my stomach growls. "As long as there's food, I'll be okay."

At least...I'll try to be.

"I...hope it's okay that I brought Belle." I cling to her harness like it's a security blanket. It is, in a way. Not only do I have a panic button in my pocket, but there's a second one hidden under the top strap of the harness.

"Hon, she's welcome any time," Isabel says, coming in from the kitchen with a bowl of chips and a warm smile. "Connor and I have been talking about getting a dog once Veronica goes off to college in the fall. Empty nest and all."

She bustles about for a moment, setting the chips on the table, giving Belle a scratch behind the ears, and helping me off with my coat before hanging it on a rack by the door.

"Okay, Grace," she says, "since this is your first official girls' night, we have two questions for you."

I must not hide the quick stab of panic in my chest, because her eyes widen. "Oh, shit. Don't worry, hon. They're easy and there are no wrong answers, okay?" At my slow nod, she continues. "First question. Are you a hugger? Or are fist bumps more your jam?"

"Fist bumps?" Memory is such an odd thing. I remember how to brush my teeth, work the television remote, and use the microwave. But sometimes, the most basic phrases confuse me.

Isabel's dark eyes turn serious. "This is a judgment-free zone, Grace. Unless you don't like queso. Then...well... Oh, who am I kidding? We'll just make you something else."

I lean on Belle, my legs shaking. "I'm...a hugger. I think."

"Oh, good." She wraps me in a gentle embrace, giving me a light squeeze before she lets go. "I'm sorry we didn't get to meet after the press conference. But AJ had you out of there quicker than small town gossip."

Emi comes in from the kitchen, wiping her hands on a dish towel. With no makeup, no heels, and her hair in a low ponytail, she almost looks like a different person. Except for her eyes. And her smile. "Second question. How do you like your margaritas? Frozen or on the rocks?"

"I...I don't know." My voice falters. I should have *some* idea. Shouldn't I?

Emi's hug lasts longer. Almost like she knows that simple question is threatening to send me over the edge. "Then I'll make you one of each so you can decide," she says softly as she draws me toward a couch that looks like it could swallow a person whole.

Parker takes my arm for the last few steps, helping me sink into the cushions while Belle settles at my feet.

"The three of us have been gettin' together for a couple of months," she says over the sound of the cocktail shaker rattling from the kitchen. "When Jasper got hurt—shit, a little over a year ago now—he and AJ weren't on speaking terms. But AJ asked me to check on Jas when he was in the hospital, and it was so damn obvious the two of them needed an intervention, I kept trying to make it happen. I met Emi not long after she and Jasper got together."

"And Isabel?" Despite joining the group chat and starting to get to know these women, I never asked how they knew each other.

"Hardison and I were on the night shift protecting Isabel and her daughter after Veronica stumbled onto a drug ring while reporting for her school newspaper. Veronica's at her bestie's house tonight. You'll meet her soon. She's a good kid. Eighteen. Full of sass, smart as fuck, and twice as stubborn."

"Drinks are served!" Emi calls, practically waltzing in from the kitchen with a tray of glasses rimmed with salt. "Parker, the virgin one is on the right."

Isabel follows and presses a warm bowl into my hands. Steam rises from the surface, carrying the delicious scent of melted cheese and peppers.

"Careful, it's not for the faint of heart. But that's where the margaritas come in," Isabel says with a little chuckle.

"Spicy is...pretty much all I can eat," I admit, scooping up some of the cheesy goodness with a tortilla chip. Heat blooms across my tongue, sharp and comforting at the same time. "Oh my God. Okay, I might never leave."

"See? I knew the queso would hook her," Emi says as she

sinks down next to me. "It's my grandma's recipe. She said it was how she convinced my grandpa to marry her. Works every time." The women all laugh, and I surprise myself by joining in.

Isabel clinks her glass lightly against mine. "You're safe here, Grace. We've got cameras, locks, and enough carbs to keep us fortified for weeks. All you have to do is relax. And hopefully have some fun."

Relax. Have some fun. But one word sticks in my heart. Hope. I hope my memories return. I hope these new friendships can help. I hope one day, I don't feel so broken.

As Emi, Isabel, and Parker argue over what movie we should watch tonight, I take a bite of queso and smile as another broken piece of my life begins to mend.

AJ

I'm unloading all the shit I picked up at the local DIY Warehouse when Jasper pulls in next to me.

Sliding out from behind the wheel, his lips tighten in a brief flash of pain before he leans in and snags a six-pack of Shiner. "Paint, drop cloths, lumber? Should I be worried?"

"You see any duct tape or shovels? We ain't buryin' a body. Put the beer in the fridge and help me get this stuff inside."

He ambles off, his gait uneven, muttering something about my lack of polite conversation skills.

Connor shows up, toolbox in hand, as Jasper hauls the last two paint cans down the hall. "I thought you said there'd be pizza. I don't smell pepperoni."

"You've gotta earn it," I shoot back. Then, because I probably shouldn't piss him off when we only have four hours to get all this shit done, I add, "It's on the way. Grab a beer."

Before I can shut the door, a dark blue sedan pulls up. "Goddamn. He actually came."

Hardison stares at the house like it's about to bite him. For a full minute, he doesn't move from behind the wheel. But eventually, he notices me leaning against the door jamb.

I slide my gaze from him to my watch and back again. That gets him moving. He gets out, shoulders hunched and hands jammed in his jacket pockets.

"You call this 'on time'?" I ask.

He shrugs one shoulder, his gaze darting back to his car for a beat. "Figured you added me to that thread by mistake. But, I decided showing up and getting the door slammed in my face was better than a write-up for insubordination."

Well, fuck.

The vulnerability in his voice is so out of character, if it weren't for his body language, I'd think he was playing me.

"No mistake. You already got your hands dirty by installing that trojan on Harris's computer. Paint is the perfect companion to clandestine operations. Get your ass inside. There's beer. Pizza's on the way."

He eyes me for another few seconds, then heads into the house. Tossing a quick glance over his shoulder, he adds, "Painting isn't messy if you do it right."

"Gonna give us all lessons?" I ask, flipping the lock behind me.

In the kitchen, Hardison accepts a beer from Connor. "Maybe. But if your plans involve ladders or power tools, there better be breadsticks to go with that pizza."

"So...gonna tell us all why we're here?" Connor asks.

I jerk my head for the three men to follow me down the hall, and open the door to Grace's studio.

Every wall is a different color. Purple, blue, green, and orange around the big picture window looking out over the lake. Paintings in various stages of completion rest on easels, and a bulletin board spans the purple wall with old pencil drawings tacked one over another.

The memory hits hard. Grace perched on a stool, a brush in one hand and a palette in the other. The painting of the weeping willow tree is only half done. She was supposed to finish it after the marathon. But it's sat there for three years, yet I could never put it away.

"AJ?" Jasper says, his hand on my shoulder.

"This used to be Grace's sanctuary," I manage. "But she won't come in here now. Says it doesn't feel like hers. So we're strippin' it. Everything goes in the garage, but it's gotta be organized and labeled so she can find it again if she changes her mind."

A long moment of silence fills the room. Connor nods. Jasper takes a deep pull on his beer, then starts rolling up his sleeves. Hardison shakes his head and mutters, "I knew I should've stayed home." But he shrugs out of his jacket anyway. "We're gonna need a hell of a lot of primer."

AN HOUR LATER, Grace's studio is more construction zone than zen oasis. Connor keeps swearing at his tablet—and the spreadsheet where he's recording every item as it goes into a box or a bin or on a shelf in the garage.

A dozen canvases are still stacked in the hallway, and we've ripped three drop cloths already. But save for a few streaks of purple left on the west wall, the primer's mostly done.

Jasper's up on the ladder, muttering about the cobwebs clinging to the overhead light while Hardison—the only one of us not covered in primer and sweat and pizza grease—dips an angled brush into the can of "Dove White" paint and starts in on the south wall. He's put away five slices of pizza and two beers, but even so, hasn't stopped working for more than five minutes at a time.

"Y'know," he says at last, glancing over at me, "most guys, when left alone for a night, sit on the couch in their boxers and watch bad action movies."

"Guess I'm not most guys." I swipe a rag over Grace's drafting table, the only piece of furniture staying in the room, and hope to all that's holy in this world I'm not making a mistake doing this.

"There are worse ways to spend an evening," he says, dragging another perfect streak across the wall. "If I'd walked in here to find the room filled with IKEA boxes, I'd have bolted."

The ladder rattles as Jasper barks out a laugh. "Fuckin' A. Don't give him any ideas or next week, we'll all be elbow deep in cardboard and Allen wrenches."

"Shut up and keep workin'," I mutter, but I can't help smiling.

Hardison shakes his head and keeps on painting. Jasper fights with yet another cobweb, and Connor hefts the last of the canvases to carry it out to the garage.

I'd forgotten—or maybe I never knew—what it was like to have people who showed up for you. Not colleagues. Not acquaintances. Friends. Real ones.

But I know now. And I sure as shit ain't gonna forget again.

CHAPTER FIFTY

Grace

"And there's Mr. Overprotective now," Parker says. "Want to bet he's been pacing for at least the past ten minutes?"

I laugh, and my stomach muscles ache from the motion. Clearly I haven't laughed this much in a very long time. "I'd lay odds he's been standing there since we left Isabel's."

AJ's at my door before she even puts the car in park, helping me up, then letting Belle out of the back seat.

"Uh...thanks for bringing Grace home," he says. "I know it's a long way, but I—"

"Ain't no nevermind." Parker stifles a yawn. "It's not like I've gotta get up early for work in the morning. Don't forget, we're talkin' to Zephyr at noon."

"Parker?" AJ asks before she can roll up her window. "You sure you're okay to drive home?"

She lifts a travel mug from her cup holder. "Isabel made me coffee so strong it could double as rocket fuel. I'm good, boss. Oh, and Grace? Next week, you're pickin' the movie."

The idea of another night with friends—and the lingering

buzz from two margaritas—has me practically floating all the way into the house.

But as soon as AJ locks the door and removes Belle's harness, his shoulders tense. He runs a hand through his hair, his body nothing but coiled tension and nerves.

The headache that hasn't truly faded in days comes back with a vengeance. "AJ, what's wrong?"

"I've got somethin' to show you." My heart rate spikes, my mouth going dry until he holds out his hand. "It's nothin' bad. At least...I hope not."

I lay my fingers over his palm, and he brushes a kiss to my wedding ring before wrapping his arm around my waist and guiding me down the hall to my studio door. It's been closed for days. I thought...maybe it'd stay closed forever.

"No," I whisper. "Please, AJ. I had such a great time tonight. I can't go in there right now."

"Trust me, darlin'."

God help me, I do. So much that I nod while preparing myself for the warm glow of the evening to fade in an instant.

But when he opens the door, the studio...isn't the studio anymore. Every wall has been painted white. The drafting table and chair still hold their space in front of the window, but the drawings I left half-finished three years ago are gone. The paintings that the *other* me did—before the scars and the loneliness and the pain stole her away—no longer rest in easels all over the room.

Blank canvases are stacked neatly in the far corner, but the rest of the room is bare. Just...waiting. Like me.

"You shouldn't have to live with choices you didn't make, darlin'." His voice drops to a whisper, and he touches his wedding ring. "Any of 'em. Really."

I shuffle forward, alone, until I reach the drafting table. A circle of paint swatches—there must be fifty of them—is fanned out like a rainbow.

"You can pick whatever you want. Colors. Furniture. Fabrics. The room is yours now."

The words crack something loose inside of me. Warmth and light and freedom and *joy*.

AJ didn't just repaint a room. Or banish some clutter. He's making it clear I don't have to be the woman I was before. I don't have to find her or *become* her to matter. To be loved.

I can be someone new. I can be the woman I am *now*.

"AJ..." His name escapes on a whisper. So quiet, yet still so loud in the blank slate of the room.

He shifts his weight, one hand rubbing the back of his neck as he stares at the floor. "If you hate it, we'll put it all back. Everything's in the garage, labeled and organized and—"

"Hate it?" In two wobbly steps, I'm in front of him, my arms winding around his waist. "I... You did all this in four hours?"

"Not alone." The corner of his mouth twitches into a weak grin. "Jas, Connor, Hardison. They helped."

Tears give the room—*my* room—a gentle glow. "I don't have words for what this means to me."

AJ nods in the direction of the drafting table. "You can always start with a color."

I turn, still leaning against him, and brush the swatches— the endless possibilities—until I land on a purple so pale, it can't be more than a drop of tint in an ocean of white.

"This one."

AJ

Did Grace understand? That when I told her she shouldn't have to live with choices she didn't make, I wasn't just talkin' about this room?

I love her with all my heart. The woman she was before *and* the woman she is now. But I'll hand her a clean slate a thousand times over, even if that means she fills it with a life without me in it. Her freedom—her chance to be whoever she wants or needs to be—matters more than anything.

The light turns her dark blond hair a hundred shades of gold. She's so fucking beautiful, and I hope she knows that every life I've ever imagined has her in it.

Grace turns her gaze to me, steady and sure. Her fingers tremble as she rests them over my heart. "You keep doing this, AJ. Giving me back pieces of myself I thought were lost forever."

"Not givin' them back, darlin'. I'm just reminding you they're yours to claim. On *your* terms."

Her breath catches, eyes shining. For a moment, I think she's about to cry. But then she wraps her free arm around my neck, pulls herself up, and kisses me.

There's nothing careful or tentative about the way she seals her mouth to mine. This is desire. Need. Passion. This is Grace finally letting herself *want*.

Pulling Grace closer, I slide one hand up her spine, the other resting just above her ass. She steals the breath from my lungs, but what the hell do I need air for anyway when I have her in my arms?

She's here. Alive. Stronger than she's ever been. Every stroke of her tongue, every tiny moan, every shift of her hips tells me she's choosing this.

She's choosing *me*.

When Grace finally breaks off the kiss, she peers up at me, breathless. Completely unafraid. "It's been days since you... since we almost..."

Brushing my thumb across her cheek, I catch a single tear that slips free. "I didn't want to push you, darlin'." My chest is too tight. My heart pounds like it wants to escape right into her hands. I'm not surprised. It's hers, after all. "We have time.

There's no need to do anythin' unless—or until—you're sure you're ready."

Her lips part, eyes searching mine, and then she fists her hands in my shirt, holding on as if her life depends on it. "Of all the choices I've made and don't remember, there's one I'm sure of. *You*, Aaron. It's always been you."

I gather her in my arms, crushing her against me. Because if I don't hold on tight, I'll come apart. My mouth finds hers, and I take my time. Each kiss is a slow, reverent promise I'll spend my whole damn life keeping.

Coming up for air, I trail my lips along her jaw and down to the hollow of her throat. "I love you, Grace. I loved the woman you were. But I love the woman you are now even more."

Every touch, every taste of her skin, every tiny moan pulls me deeper. And then she hooks her fingers in my belt loops and tugs me toward the door.

I follow, stumbling along with my dick so hard, each step is pure torture. I ache to carry her to the bed, lay her down gently, and hold her so close, she'll never doubt a single damn thing ever again. But this ain't about what I want. It never was. Never will be.

Grace isn't mine to claim. I'm hers.

She deserves the chance to choose this—to choose *me*—without the weight of anything that came before. And I'll walk through Hell barefoot and burning to prove it to her.

We reach the bed, and for a moment, she stops, shoulders so tense, it's like she's holdin' up the whole damn world. I'm about to tell her I'll carry the weight when she guides my hands to the hem of her sweatshirt.

"Are you sure, darlin'?" The words escape, dry as dust and twice as broken, and she ain't the only one breathin' hard.

Her lips press together, part, and a breath catches in her throat. "I'm scared," she whispers. "I don't remember how *not* to be. But when I look at you—when you touch me—I know."

Tears shimmer in her eyes, but she doesn't let them fall. "You'll never hurt me."

I can't speak. I don't have the words to tell her how strong she is. Or what her trust means to me. Slowly, I tug off her sweatshirt, then toss it away. Her nipples are hard points under her pink lace bra, and I dip my head to capture one between my lips.

Goosebumps cover her shoulders and race down her back under my palm. She melts against me, her arms winding around my neck as I curl my fingers into the waistband of her yoga pants.

"If you need me to stop—"

She silences me with a searing kiss. Shoving the offending material to the floor, I drop to my knees in front of her lace-covered mound. God, her scent is enough to undo me. I could come right here, with my zipper threatening to do permanent damage, and not care a lick.

Grace eases herself down onto the bed, legs spread, and I press my nose to the lace. The gentle pressure coaxes a moan from her lips.

Her thighs tremble, but not from nerves. From arousal.

"AJ... I need you. Naked." Her soft words carry so much emotion. She's still scared—maybe she always will be—but underneath, her fierce determination to survive, to fight, to claim the life *she* wants is so damn strong.

I get to my feet, strip off my paint-splattered flannel, and work my jeans and briefs over my erection with a wince.

Grace lets her gaze trail up and down my body, until it settles on my dick. Her eyes go glassy for a beat, but then she licks her lips and scoots back on the bed. "Come here. I want to touch you."

When I stretch out next to her, the dark shadows that have haunted her gaze for the past two weeks finally start to fade away.

She presses her lips to my collarbone, trailing kisses across my chest and up my neck. Her teeth score the shell of my ear as she skims her fingers over my aching shaft.

"*Fuuuuuck.*"

I'm not gonna last if she keeps touching me like this, but I won't stop her. Not when she's just finding her footing.

Moving lower, she swirls her tongue over my nipple. *My God.* The sensation shoots straight to my dick. Her hand slides along my length to the precum beading on my crown. Her breath stutters.

I try to sit up, to tell her we can stop, but before I can get the words out, she lifts her fingers to her lips and tastes me.

It's the sexiest damn thing I've ever seen.

And then she kisses me.

The world could burn down around us, and I wouldn't care. There's nothing rushed about her movements. Every brush of her fingers across my skin is a question, and my body's answer is always the same.

I'm here. I'm yours.

"Take off my bra," she whispers. "I don't want anything between us."

My hands ain't steady, but I manage to undo the hooks as she wriggles out of her panties.

Her focus lands on the scar from the blade, slashing across her skin like an angry bolt of lightning. Her shoulders hunch, and I nudge her chin up, meeting her gaze.

"You're so damn beautiful, Grace. I don't know what I did to get lucky enough for you to choose me once, let alone twice."

I lean in for another kiss, cupping her breast and skating my thumb over the hard point of her nipple. My other hand slides down her back to her ass. "Still okay?" I whisper against her lips.

"No." She slides her fingers into my hair, a small smile curving her lips. "Because you're not inside me."

Easing her onto her back, I brace one arm on the head-board and position myself between her thighs. "Well, I reckon we could fix that."

With my other hand, I guide myself to her entrance. My eyes don't leave hers as I slide my crown past her lower lips. She's so damn tight, I have to ease myself in by inches. After every one, I stop, kiss her until she's breathless, then nestle myself deeper.

She's shaking by the time my hips are flush against her. "I'll go slow, darlin'."

Grace nods, then lifts her hand to my cheek. "Just to start. I'm not fragile, AJ. I want this. I want you. *All* of you."

There ain't nothin' in this world I won't give her.

My first thrusts are gentle. Letting her get used to me. To my weight pressing her against the mattress. But when her muscles start to tremble, and a moan spills from her lips, I risk sliding deeper. Harder.

Grace arches her back, and a flush blooms over her skin. "Touch me, AJ," she whimpers.

Fuck me.

I find her clit with my thumb, circling the tiny nub, teasing, trying to draw her pleasure out as long as I can. But between her desperate cries and tight channel, my own release is barreling down on me like a bullet.

"Aaron...I'm...."

Grace's eyelids flutter. Her muscles seize, heels digging into the mattress as she flies apart. Her channel throbs around me, and with one final thrust, I let myself soar with her.

WE CLING TO ONE ANOTHER, our legs tangled under the sheets, her breath warm against my chest. I should get up. Turn the lights off. Give the security system one last check. But then I'd have to let her go, and I can't. Not yet.

Not when I can feel the world shifting around us. Like all the jagged pieces of my life finally fit together—with Grace at the center.

Her fingers trace slow patterns over my skin, then still. "Aaron?"

"Yeah, darlin'?"

She lifts her head just enough to meet my gaze. Strength and vulnerability battle in her blue-green eyes. "I love you."

The words gut me. Break me open and put me back together in the same heartbeat. My eyes sting, and I crush her tighter against me, my voice ragged when it finally comes. "I love you, Grace. More than anything. Always."

She lets out a shaky breath, burying her face against my neck as her tears dampen my skin. We're both crying. Both healing. Together.

CHAPTER FIFTY-ONE

Grace

I WAKE up with the taste of metal in my mouth. It isn't real. A ghost of a memory. Electricity from the taser that let someone I still can't see steal me away.

For a moment, I can't move. Can't breathe. I'm on the ground at the side of the trail, every nerve ending on fire, staring up at the sky.

But then AJ shifts next to me, his breath tickling my neck.

I'm home. I'm safe. I'm loved.

And a little sore. But only because last night, I found a piece of myself I feared I'd lost forever.

The soft smile curving my lips banishes the last of the nightmare. For now—for these few minutes at the break of dawn—I'm at peace.

If only it would last. In a few hours, we're supposed to talk to Zephyr, the tech genius Connor works with. And I'll have to tell her everything I can remember. AJ will want me to go deeper. To dive deeper into my memories—maybe deep enough to trigger another panic attack.

I decided days ago that I wouldn't keep shoving the dark fragments of my memory away. I have to face what happened to me. If only it were that simple.

Belle sits up in her plush doggie bed, staring at me like I should know what to do.

Shit.

I do.

My legs tremble, and the world lurches so quickly, I grab the edge of the nightstand before I fall on top of AJ. The throbbing in my head is deep and dull, almost like the headaches I had my first few days in Mexico.

The floor ripples, like I'm walking on water, but I manage one step. Then two. Belle pads over to me, pressing herself against my legs to steady me.

She stays by my side all the way to the living room, where I scoop up my sketchpad and the little pouch with my pencils, erasers, and blending sticks, then wobble down the hall to my studio.

The empty, white walls stare back at me. I can't believe AJ did all this. The room still smells vaguely like paint—latex, not oil—and lavender spray cleaner. Even the window is sparkling and clear. The lake glitters, a million tiny diamonds scattered over the surface, and I open the sketchbook to a blank page.

My thumb finds the familiar groove in the pencil, and I draw a faint line. Then another.

Shit.

The lantern. Again.

How many times do I need to draw the damn thing before my broken brain lets me move on? Why can't I see faces? Landmarks? Or even the writing on the cover of that old book?

I try to tear the page free with my left hand, but it slips from my traitorous fingers. The sketchbook tilts, and so does my perspective.

I can't draw the rest of the image fast enough. The sides

slant upward, narrowing to a point, like it's hanging above me. My chest tightens with each line and curve I couldn't remember until now.

There's something there. On the base. Something...new. A mark carved into the metal.

I trace the image with the edge of the pencil. The unbroken circle mirrors the moon high above the lantern. And cutting across it? Is that...a leaf? It's long, with narrow edges that look almost...sharp. It's not from an oak or maple tree. Maybe a rhododendron? Or...

Shit.

My pulse won't settle. This is too important. I hug the sketchbook to my chest and push up from the chair. I wish Belle had stayed with me. But I heard AJ get up somewhere between the etched glass panes and the base of the lantern, and she went in search of food.

The floor doesn't tilt sideways, thank God, so I risk a few wobbly steps toward the door. So far, so good.

The low hiss of the coffee maker carries down the hall, along with the rich scent of his dark brew. The faint clink of mugs has become the sound of home.

Shirtless, wearing only a pair of loose pajama pants, my husband stares out the kitchen window with Belle at his side, her tail thumping.

She notices me first, barks, and runs over to her bowl. "In a minute—" AJ's whole face softens. "Mornin', darlin'."

If I don't sit down, I'm afraid I'll pitch over, so I ease myself into a chair and flip the sketchbook open. My hand shakes as I slide it toward him. "I...think this means something."

He peers over my shoulder, bracing his hand next to mine so the heat of his skin seeps into my back. "Is that symbol on the bottom?"

"Yes. It's unique, right? The leaf...you don't think it could be...?" I glance up at him.

The muscles in his jaw shift, slow and deliberate. "If it's not, I'll eat my Ranger star."

I'd laugh if he weren't one hundred percent serious. "I don't know why I couldn't see it before."

AJ presses a kiss to the top of my head. "Because you weren't ready. Remember what Dr. VanHorn said? That your memories were covered in layers and layers of bubble wrap? Maybe you had to feel safe before you could peel that bubble wrap away."

He covers my hand with his. Strong and steady and reassuring. Safe.

There's one thing I'm sure of. You, Aaron. It's always been you.

I sit on AJ's office couch, staring at the bulletin board filled with every clue, every article, every scribbled note he'd hoped would bring him one step closer to me—the shrine he built to my memory.

On the desk, the video call waits for Parker, Connor, and Zephyr to join. I cup the mug of tea in both hands, take a sip, and settle closer to AJ.

"Zephyr's a little intense," he says. "But I think you'll like her."

The left side of the screen flickers to life. Zephyr's teal hair falls over one eye, and in her right hand, she holds a ceramic mug half the size of her head.

Her dark purple lips form an *O*, and her eyes widen. "Grace. Hi. I'm Zephyr."

AJ's arm tightens around me. But I'm not scared. Not yet, anyway.

"Um...hi."

I wish I could find the words to thank her for all she's doing.

To thank *everyone*. But instead, I settle a little closer to AJ and fiddle with the hem of my sweater.

Parker joins next, a yawn hidden behind her hand. "Sorry," she says. "Didn't get home until after midnight because *someone* needed more time to finish his 'grand romantic gesture' while Grace and I were at girls' night."

"Well, *that's* a story I need to hear one of these days," Zephyr says.

Connor is the last to join, his arms folded, against a backdrop of a bookcase filled with photos.

"Zephyr, we've got somethin' new on the lantern," AJ says. "There's a symbol on the bottom. Sendin' you a picture of it now."

She taps her keyboard a few times, narrows her eyes, and frowns at the screen. Her eyebrow piercing winks in the overhead light. "Well, if that's a leaf, it shouldn't take me long to figure out—"

"Oleander," I say, my voice steady. "It's an oleander leaf. I... looked it up."

Zephyr cracks a smile. "Good work, Grace. I'll feed the image into my web crawlers and see what they spit out. Every little detail helps."

"Tell her the rest," AJ says, his voice low and smooth in my ear.

I take a sip of tea, my throat suddenly dry, and swallow hard. "There were horses. Or...one horse, at least. The room I keep seeing...it was all wood. Not painted. Or stained. Sealed maybe."

She takes it all down. Everything I've remembered. The book with words my mind won't let me see, the lanterns hung all around the big gaping *nothingness* I'm terrified to remember, and the taser.

I taste metal again. Sharp and sudden. My breath stutters.

The laptop screen blurs. Everything's dim. Dark gray and black and stifling hot.

"I've destroyed the watch and tossed her phone. I'll burn the rest later. We should go. Now."

"Grace?" AJ squeezes my forearm. I stare down at my wrist, at the thick scar I don't remember getting, and a spot of blood wells on my skin.

But after a blink, it's gone.

"M-my watch. They took my running watch. I think...they cut it off me." I tighten my hands around the mug of tea and inhale deeply. Lavender and chamomile. A touch of honey.

I'm home. With AJ. Nothing can hurt me here.

"I can see the blood. And...maybe...a zip tie." A sob threatens to escape, but I force it down so I can tell them the rest. "It was a white van. Kind of beaten up. But everything else is fuzzy. Like...I was there but not at the same time."

No one says a word for several seconds. Zephyr's gaze is soft, but her voice roughens. "They drugged you."

At my side, AJ's so tense, I'm surprised I don't hear his muscles snapping one by one.

"There has to be more." It's getting harder to keep my tears at bay. "I want to remember. Even if it hurts. Even if I'm not ready."

"That's why we're here," Zephyr says. "And I've got an update from Mik that might help."

CHAPTER FIFTY-TWO

AJ

"GRACE WAS DEFINITELY *in east Texas or within a hundred miles of the Texas-Mexico border. The oleander flowers woven into the ropes had pollen signatures that aren't found much north of Odessa or south of Laredo. Mik's still working with the dirt she was able to pull from the ropes and the burlap bag.*"

If I don't stop pacing, I'm gonna wear a hole in the tile in front of the bulletin board. Zephyr sent me a fresh map, marked up with the rough borders from Mikayla's tests.

My phone screen lights up with a new message.

Zephyr: One of my contacts just confirmed we'll have fresh imaging of the area Mik identified by tomorrow night. We're still talking several thousand square miles, but it's a start.

I stagger back until my ass hits the edge of my desk.

AJ: You wrangled a military flyover in under an hour? It takes me longer to get a brisket plate on a Friday night.

Zephyr: I am very good at my job. And...you're welcome.

I chuckle, but before I can reply with a proper thank you,

Belle noses her way into my office, dragging her leash behind her.

She drops the braided nylon at my feet, looks up at me, and whines.

Fuck.

She's been restless the past few days, pacing circles around the house whenever she's not at Grace's side. I crouch down and start scratching her behind the ears. "I know, girl. Two weeks without a run and you're goin' a little stir crazy, huh?"

The second she hears "run" she perks up. Her tail whips from side-to-side faster than greased lightning, and she's practically vibrating.

I don't want to leave Grace alone. Especially not to go do what used to be *her* thing. I always hated running—until it was the only way I could feel close to her.

But Belle has so much pent-up energy, if we don't get out of the house, she's gonna start eating my shoes again. Or worse. She'll start in on the furniture.

I leave the leash right where it is—if I pick it up, there's no going back—and head out to the living room. Grace is curled up on the couch, a blanket tucked around her shoulders. She's staring at the street view image of the spot I found her phone and water bottle, brows furrowed and frustration pouring off of her.

"There's...nothing," she says with a huff. "I can *feel* the taser. See the sky above me. But after that...nothing."

I sink down next to her, take the tablet, and set it on the coffee table. "Bubble wrap, remember? Layers of it. It's gonna take time, darlin'."

With a sigh, she winds her arms around my waist and snuggles against my chest. "I know. Doesn't mean I have to like it."

"That it don't." Belle trots over, her icy gaze laying the guilt on thicker than molasses in June. "I'm thinkin' you need a distraction."

"Oh?" Grace peers up at me, a smile tugging at her lips. "What did you have in mind?"

My dick aches at the raw need in her voice, but then Belle lays her head on my thigh.

Fuck.

"Belle's fixin' to climb the walls. We could take her to the dog park for a bit. But after that...I'm open to suggestions."

Her entire body stills. It's too soon. I never should've suggested it. But before I can take it back, a flicker of excitement—fragile, like it could wink out at any moment—shines in her eyes.

"She'd really like that. I think...I would too."

———

"Go get it, girl!" Belle bolts after the tennis ball, so quick she's nothing but a gray and brown blur.

"I wish I could throw it half that far," Grace says, watching our dog having the time of her life. "With either hand."

Wrapped in her thick wool coat, she tips her face up, eyes closed, and lets the sun warm her cheeks.

"You're gettin' stronger every day. You see that, right?" I scoop up the ball Belle drops at my feet and hurl it again, farther this time, all the way to the very edge of the off-leash dog park.

Grace shakes her head softly. The corners of her eyes crinkle for a beat. "All I see are those damn clothespins."

My heart aches at the pain in her voice. "Darlin', two weeks ago, you couldn't make it more than a couple of steps without the walker."

Her gaze finds mine, the sunlight turning her blue-green eyes a deeper hue. "Two weeks ago, I didn't know my own name."

I swallow hard, fighting the emotion clogging my throat.

"And now you're sittin' here in the sun, givin' me grief about my throwing arm."

That earns me the faintest flicker of a smile. "It's a little weak. For a guy who hangs the moon for me."

I give her a wink as Belle drops the ball again, then nudges my knee with her nose. "Hangin' and throwin' are two different muscle groups. I'll have to start cross training."

Grace's smile falters. Her fingers curl tighter around the sleeves of her coat, knuckles pale. "I haven't remembered anything new in days. About...my life. About...us. What if I never do?"

I drop to one knee in front of her, take her left hand, and run my thumb over her wedding ring. Dirt and grass grind into my Wranglers, but I don't give a damn. "Then I'll tell you. One story at a time, startin' with the night we met. How you looked at me like I wasn't worth a second of your time, and I knew right then, I'd never get enough of you."

Her breath catches. Tears shimmer in her eyes.

"I'll remember for both of us, Grace. And I'll keep tellin' those stories until they stick. Until they feel like yours again. And if they never do..." I shake my head, fiercely certain. "It won't matter. You're mine, memories or not. Always."

Her lips part like she might argue, but Belle bounds back, panting, and shoves her slobbery tennis ball against Grace's boot.

Slowly—carefully—Grace scoops it up and tosses the ball seven or eight feet. Belle takes off like it's the best throw in the history of throws.

I can't help my grin. "See? Belle don't give a damn about distance. She just wants you in the game."

Grace lets out a soft laugh, and I wish this moment could stretch on forever.

Pushing to my feet, I sweep my gaze around the park— habit after more than twenty years on the job. A corgi tries to keep pace with a German Shepherd in the west corner. Teenagers—three of 'em—hover by the fence line smoking. Two puppies chase each others' tails while a young couple looks on.

No one's payin' a lick of attention to us. But I'm no fool. Every time we leave the house, we take a chance she'll be recognized. Could be as simple as a curious local, as annoying as a bottom-feeding reporter looking for a payday, or as ominous as one of the bastards who put those marks on her skin.

But for now, my only worry is how long it's gonna take to tire Belle out.

She drops the ball at my feet six more times before sprawling in the grass, tongue hanging out, the happiest damn thing on four legs.

I pull the leash out of my jacket pocket. "Time to go home, girl."

Belle lifts her head, but then her hackles raise and a growl tears from her throat—low and rumbling.

I scan the park just in time to see a flash of black fur barreling across the grass, headed right for us. The dog is fucking huge. Ears pinned back. Tail rigid.

"Fuck!" I jump in front of Grace, but Belle's already braced for battle. Her lips curl back over her teeth, and she starts barking and snarling, ready to snap.

The mastiff hits her like a freight train, rolling her with a loud snarl. I dive, fingers closing on its collar, yanking with all my strength.

Belle snarls again, snapping at the other dog, and Grace's scream slices through the air.

"Get...behind...the bench!" I shout.

For half a second, I think I've got him under control—then the bastard bucks like a bull, slamming me shoulder-first into the ground. Pain rockets down my arm.

I shove myself up, heart pounding. The black dog stands its

ground, growling and snapping its teeth at Belle, both dogs vibrating with fury. Neither gives an inch.

Grace stumbles around the bench, clutching the back of it, pale and swaying, her eyes wide with terror.

Grace

I'm going to be sick. The pounding in my skull, the bile clawing at my throat, the sight of Belle—my sweet, Belle—being tossed around like she's a rag doll.

She snarls and barks, a furious wall of muscle and fur and teeth, throwing herself between me and the monster trying to tear her apart. AJ has his hands locked on the mastiff's collar, but the beast already drove him to the ground once.

Seeing him hit the hard-packed dirt—the man who's carried me, who's held me together since the moment we met for the second time—shatters something deep inside me. I can't breathe, and I'm barely keeping myself upright against the bench.

The mastiff lunges again. AJ goes down hard, his entire body jolting, and a scream tears from my throat.

Shouts explode all around us. People. *Men*. Too many of them. Boots pounding.

"Grab the hose!"

"Got an extra leash here!"

My chest seizes, and when I try to crouch down behind the bench, my knee gives out. The ground pitches, and I stumble, catching my heel on the edge of the cement.

Air whooshes from my lungs as my shoulder smashes into the wood slats. The grass and the bench and the people and the sky all blur together. My ears ring with barks and snarls and shouts, the chaos pinning me down, paralyzing me.

A hand appears in front of me. Thick fingers. Pale skin. The cuff of a dark sweatshirt.

"Here," a man says softly. "Let me help you."

I blink up at him. A hoodie shadows part of his face. Hazel eyes catch the sunlight. Something stirs in the back of my mind. Familiar, but not. Fear skitters over my skin.

Before I can speak, his hand closes around mine, helping me up with surprising care. His grip steadies me when my knees buckle, and for a heartbeat, I'm caught. Trapped between gratitude and cold, primal fear.

Out of the corner of my eye, I see two men race toward the dogs with huge, stainless steel bowls, water sloshing over the sides.

"You okay?" the man asks. He's polite. Concerned.

I can't find AJ. He's lost in the middle of the shouts and the barks. Where's Belle? I need to find Belle!

"Ma'am? I need to know you're all right."

I nod. My throat won't work. I don't know him. The way his eyes search mine makes my stomach turn. Like he's waiting for me to look down. To cower.

Belle's snarl shatters the moment, dragging my focus back to the fray.

"Call animal control!" AJ roars, fury roughening his voice.

"We've got more water!" another man yells.

A sharp, piercing whistle slices through the air. It's so strident, it stabs straight into my skull. Belle whines, then shakes her head.

The mastiff bolts. One second it's snarling, and the next, it's gone. Nothing but a streak of black muscle clearing the chain link fence like it's only an inch tall.

Belle bounds over to me, hackles still high. AJ staggers after her, his movements stiff, like he isn't quite sure nothing's broken. Relief nearly sends me to my knees.

"I think she's okay, darlin'. Are you?" His eyes dart to Belle, then back to me.

I look around, careful not to move my head too quickly. The man in the hoodie is gone. "Y-yes. I... Check Belle. Please."

AJ runs his hands all over her from ears to tail. She doesn't whine or flinch, and by the time he's done, she's almost calm. "No blood. No bites. But we can take her to the emergency vet. Just to be sure."

I nod, still trembling.

"Stay here with Belle for a minute." His voice is steady, but I hear the steel in it. The barely contained fury and frustration. "I'll call this in when we get home. Need witness statements if we're gonna track down that bastard's owner."

From his wallet, he pulls a handful of his business cards, then moves stiffly through the thinning crowd, pressing cards into hands, thanking two men who stepped in, then returning to my side.

"Let's get out of here," he says, wrapping an arm around my waist before he snags Belle's harness from the bench and guides us both back to the SUV. He limps a little, his jaw tight.

"You sure you're okay?" he asks after starting the engine.

"Just a little vertigo," I say softly. "I'm more worried about you."

His hand finds mine across the console, rough and warm, his knuckles scraped raw. "We'll get her checked, then I'll let you fuss over me. Deal?"

I squeeze his fingers, but the image of the mastiff's eyes, wild and angry, won't let me go.

CHAPTER FIFTY-THREE

Grace

STEAM CURLS up from the water, fogging the edges of the mirror. The scents of lavender and shea butter soothe my raw nerves, but I won't be able to settle until I know AJ's okay.

Dinner feels like hours ago. He'd cooked, of course, moving around the kitchen with that stubborn set to his jaw, pretending his bruises weren't bothering him. That everything was fine. Just like he had at the emergency vet when they'd checked Belle over from nose to tail. She was okay—thank God —but AJ...that's a different matter entirely.

He'd suggested I take a bath. Even started the water and added my favorite bubbles. But he's still fully dressed—lighting candles, each movement stiff and forced—while I brace myself against the counter in nothing but my robe.

If he thinks I'm going to let him hide his pain from me, he's a damn fool. I'm done letting him shoulder everything for the both of us.

"AJ, stop." I wrap my fingers around his wrist, tugging gently. "Get undressed. You're joining me tonight."

The soft glow from the candles highlights the dark shadows beneath his eyes.

"I'm fine," he mutters. "I should go...start laundry."

"Laundry can wait." I tighten my grip, my free hand resting over his heart. "You can't."

His gaze flickers to mine, defensive for a beat, but then softening. If he weren't holding himself like he was made of glass, I might relent. But it's *my* turn to take care of him for a change.

"AJ." I close what little distance is left between us. "You got tossed around out there tryin' to protect me and Belle. Don't tell me it doesn't hurt."

His sigh pulls at something deep in my chest. "Darlin', you've been through enough today. I know I said you could fuss over me, but I'd rather you relax."

"I want to. I love you, remember?"

"I remember how stubborn you've always been," he murmurs, his lips curving into a crooked, weary smile. "You shouldn't worry about not findin' yourself again, Grace. In so many ways, you already have."

He slides his fingers into my hair, dips his head, and brushes his lips to mine. "I'd be a damn fool to fight you over this. Any chance I get to be naked with you...I'm gonna take it."

I step back, pleased when my legs seem to hold me up just fine, and reach for the buttons on his flannel shirt. "I'll get 'em," he says.

"No." With a quick glance at the water level in the tub, I blow out a breath. "I can do this. I *need* to do this. To prove I can."

My fingers slip off the buttons several times, but I manage, stopping only once when I reach the bruised patch of skin blooming along his ribs. He doesn't flinch, but the way his chest shudders says more than any words could convey.

When the shirt slides off his shoulders, I swallow hard. He

fought Hell itself for me and Belle—in the form of a growling, angry mastiff—and I love him even more for it.

"Grace..." His voice stutters, like he's about to argue with me again, but I just point to the tub.

"Get in."

With a gravelly chuckle, he shucks his jeans and briefs, then steps into the steaming water.

Shit.

The bruise covering his right ass cheek is twice as dark as the one on his ribs.

Draping my robe over the towel rack, I take the hand he offers and let him help me into the tub. The bathwater laps against the porcelain as we lower ourselves down. I straddle AJ, my knees braced on either side of him. The position draws a grunt from his lips, and I freeze.

"You okay?"

"Fine," he says, wincing briefly. "Water's hotter than I thought."

"Liar." My hands skim over his chest, down the ridges of muscle I'm learning again for the first time, until they stop just shy of one of the bruises.

"Grace—"

"Don't," I whisper. "Don't tell me it's nothing. It's a miracle that dog didn't take a bite out of you."

"He tried. But my jacket stopped him well enough." AJ shows me his right arm. Purple dots his skin in a distinctive bite pattern, but there aren't any punctures. "You and Belle are safe. That's all that matters to me. Bruises fade. You should know that." He gently traces my left cheekbone with a single knuckle, finding the edge of the bruise that stole my memory away. It's almost gone now, no more than a bit of sickly yellow I can hide with some of the concealer Emi bought for me.

I huff. "You should have gone to urgent care."

His lips purse, a hint of frustration in the set of his

unbruised shoulder. "Makin' us dinner was a much better use of time. We would've been there for hours, only to be sent home with my arm in a sling and a bottle of ibuprofen."

I can practically *see* the waiting room at Austin Memorial. Hear sirens from approaching ambulances. The clatter of gurneys rolling by one after another.

My chest tightens, and the edges of the room blur.

The memory hits hard and fast. The knock at the door. Another Ranger, a friend, I think, his hazel eyes soft as he tells me there's been an accident. That AJ's been hurt. That he's here to take me to the hospital. In case...

I grip the edges of the tub. "You...you crashed. It was a high-speed chase, and it went bad. I didn't know...for hours, I didn't know..." My throat locks up, the words sticking like glue. "When they finally let me see you, your arm was in a sling. Broken ribs? Your collarbone?"

"Fuck," AJ growls, the curse rumbling through his chest. He steadies me, his hand firm and warm on the back of my neck. "Of all the things to remember..."

Tears sting my eyes. "Someone came to the house. To get me. To take me to the hospital. He—he wouldn't let me drive."

AJ's jaw tightens, something sharp flashing in his eyes. "Marvin," he says. "The fucker who told the chief you were... back. He probably volunteered so he wouldn't have to work the scene." His voice softens, and his hand slides lower, coming to rest at the small of my back. "But he got you there. That's what mattered."

I shift closer, wrapping my legs around his waist, trapping the bubbles between us. My fingers comb through his hair in a desperate attempt to reassure myself it was years ago. That he's here with me now. Bruised, but safe.

"I remember what it felt like, AJ. Almost losing you."

His thumb brushes my cheek, catching a tear before it can fall. "You didn't lose me then. You won't lose me now."

Something in me breaks open. I seal my lips to his, needing the taste of him to ground me. In the quiet of the bath, all that matters is the heat of his mouth, the steady thrum of his heartbeat against my breast, and the way he whispers my name.

It's a promise of everything we once were. Everything we are now. Everything we'll become.

The water starts to cool, but we're still tangled together, his hard length pressing against my ass.

"Let's take this to the bed," he murmurs, rolling one of my nipples between fingers starting to prune.

I nod, and though I'm worried about hurting him, I need him inside me. If only to prove to myself that he's alive. He's whole. He's mine.

CHAPTER FIFTY-FOUR

AJ

ZEPHYR'S EMAIL comes through not long after lunch. Hours of flyover footage stitched together into a seamless slow sweep of east Texas. I check the run time. Five hours? I don't know what the fuck we expect to learn from it, but I carry my laptop into the living room to start my search.

Grace is curled up on the couch with her sketchbook braced on the arm, tapping her pencil against the spiral binding. The sight punches the breath from my chest. For so long, I thought I'd never have this again. But we're here. After everything we've clawed back from the dark, I'll never take this for granted.

"Hey." I sink down next to her and set the laptop on the coffee table. "This is the longest shot in the history of long shots, but in case I'm wrong, I could use another set of eyes."

"And you want...mine?" She sets the pencil down, the furrow between her brows deepening. It's been there since we woke up this morning, and I'm starting to worry.

"Always." Leaning in, I press a kiss to her forehead, hoping to soothe whatever's bothering her. "The plane was flyin' at thirty thousand feet, so even if the bastards have a neon sign flashin' 'Cult Marks the Spot' we won't see it. But you're an artist. You notice things other people don't."

She gives me the side eye. "You just want someone else to be as bored as you are, don't you?"

I flash her a quick grin. "Maybe. Or maybe I just want to spend as much time with you as I can before Monday."

The brief spark of humor in her eyes fades. "I wish you could stay home with me a little longer."

"Me too, darlin'." I wrap my arms around her, and she tucks her head under my chin. "Jas and Connor will be around whenever I can't be. You won't be alone. Not until we know the bastards who took you are six feet under."

She nods against me, but doesn't relax. "Don't tell her, but I'm a little sad the chief lifted Parker's suspension. She'd be more fun to hang out with."

"She'll be lucky if he doesn't make her ride a desk for the next...forever," I mutter. "And she's too good for that."

I should tell the chief to go fuck himself. But while we're comfortable, we ain't made of money. And what the hell else am I supposed to do? Being a Ranger is all I've ever wanted. Despite my asshole of a boss, I love the job, and I'm good at it.

We don't move for several minutes, just soaking up each other's warmth. But eventually, Grace sighs. "If you're gonna force me to watch this boring-ass footage, at least throw it up on the television and make us some popcorn?"

I chuckle. "I think you mean 'make us a bowl of salted butter with a side of popped corn.'"

Her smile lights up my entire world. "Well, duh."

Every day, a little more of her sass shines through. The woman I fell in love with ain't gone. She's comin' back one joke, one memory, one kiss at a time.

Once the popcorn's ready, I set the bowl in her lap, kick off my shoes, and press play. Thousands of trees turn into a green blur beneath the AWAC's camera. Pine, oak, and willow. Dense, tall, and endless.

After ten minutes, Grace stifles a yawn. "Well, I know what to put on if I can't sleep at night."

I bring up the menu and double the speed. Within a few minutes, the trees give way to prairie, and I slow things down again. Grace leans forward, her eyes fixed on the screen.

"Darlin'? Do you recognize this area?" I pause the video, watching her carefully.

"No. But there's something..." She presses the heels of her hands to her eyes for a long moment. "I could see...for miles, I think. Nothing but grass, barely any trees..."

In the next moment, her entire body goes rigid. "Can't stop running. Another few miles... I'll find *someone*. They'll call AJ..."

Fuck.

She's trapped in her memories. Do I try to pull her out? Or see where this goes?

"It's cold. God, it's so cold I can't feel my face. How much farther? It's been hours." She's shivering now, her arms wrapped around herself so tightly. Every so often, she swipes at her face. "It's too dark. *Shit!*"

The anguish in her voice tears a piece of my soul into shreds. I grab her hands, holding on tight. Grace struggles, and my fingers slip down to her wrists, right over her scars. She jerks away, cradling her hands to her chest.

"Grace! It's me. It's AJ."

Her eyelids flutter, and tears tumble down her cheeks. "I tried to escape once. I ran for miles," she swallows a sob. "It was so dark and cold. Everything hurt. They...caught me. God. Dragged me back. Tied my wrists...to a...a *horse!*" Her voice breaks, her entire body shuddering with each sob.

"Fuck me," I mutter. "Grace, I will find them, and I'll drag them by their *balls* until they're beggin' for me to put an end to 'em."

She won't look at me. Her gaze is still fixed on the screen.

I shut the laptop, severing the connection to the TV. "That's enough for today."

Her eyes are glassy, and I'm not sure she can see or hear me. I scoot closer, snap my fingers, and Belle—who'd fallen asleep in front of the hearth, jerks her head up. In seconds, she's crawling into Grace's lap.

"Oh, God." With a shudder, Grace wraps her arms around the dog and buries her face in Belle's thick fur. "How could anyone be so cruel?" she sobs.

I don't have an answer for her, so I do my best to hold them both until Grace's tremors fade away.

I KNOCK on Grace's studio door. She closed herself in here hours ago, while I kept scanning the footage as the popcorn went soggy next to me. I can't get her question out of my head.

"How could anyone be so cruel?"

Her scars are so deep, so thick, she must have been dragged behind that goddamned horse for hours. For what?

"Come on in," she calls. Thank fuck her voice doesn't sound as shaky as it did earlier.

She sits cross-legged in the chair, sun on her face, looking... *almost* at peace. Her sketchbook is open on the drafting table, with the beginnings of a vague, male face on the page.

"Who's that?" I ask, rubbing gentle circles over her upper back.

Grace sighs. "The man who gave me...these." She holds out her hands, and the sun turns the thick scars almost silver. "I can only see his eyes. The rest...I'm just guessing at."

I ease the pencil from her clenched fingers and set it on the drafting table. "Then take a break for today."

"I can't. They're still...out there, AJ. What if I stop right before I remember their names? Or why they took me? Or—"

Her left hand spasms on the page, smudging the curve of the asshole's jaw.

"Shit!"

I take her hand, my thumb skating over her wedding ring. "You're still healing, Grace. Workin' yourself into exhaustion ain't gonna help. Why don't you rest for a bit?"

"I'm not tired. Or...not sleepy, anyway," she says, a hint of defiance in her voice.

If I let her keep spiraling, she'll still be digging for memories when the clock hits midnight.

"Okay." I brush my thumb over her knuckles, then bring them to my lips. "If you don't feel like resting...how about you let me take you out instead?"

Her brows lift, surprise flickering across her face. "Out?"

"A date," I clarify with another kiss, this one to her palm. "You remember that picture from the Punch Bowl? You told Parker it looked like fun. I reckon we could both use some fun."

She hesitates, chewing on her lip. "That's...so public. What if—"

"I've got you." I keep my voice even. Calm. "I'll be carrying, and there will be plenty of people around. Anyone after you would be a damn fool to try somethin' there. Even if they did... they ain't gonna get to you without going through me. And I'm an ornery sombitch when I want to be."

She laughs, though there's still a hint of fear in her eyes.

"If we go now, it won't be too crowded. Just enough noise and people and *life* to remind us what a normal Friday night feels like."

"Normal," she echoes, testing the word. Then, finally, she smiles. "I think I'd like normal."

CHAPTER FIFTY-FIVE

AJ

THE DOMAIN HUMS softly when we arrive. It's early enough we can take our time, window shop and talk and laugh without a press of people all around us. Grace keeps a firm grip on Belle's mobility harness with her right hand, her left tucked in the crook of my elbow.

My sport coat does its job, hiding the SIG at my waist, but I went out of my way to pull the tie Grace bought me for Christmas five years ago—dark purple shot through with silver so it catches the light, almost like alligator skin—out of the back of the closet.

She spent twenty minutes—twenty long minutes—deciding what to wear. And then she walked out of the closet in that off-the-shoulder peach sweater, those ripped jeans, and soft brown boots. And damn if I didn't forget how to breathe.

Not because of the clothes, though they're perfect. But because she chose them. She's choosing this. Choosing us.

Every damn day she braves something new—something that scares her—to reclaim another piece of her life.

"Maybe on Sunday, you'll let me take you to Stonewood Coffee?" I ask as we drift toward a shop window filled with glittering jewelry.

Her gaze lands on a ring—three center diamonds, all different shapes, with smaller jewels on the sides that look almost like stepping stones.

"Were diamonds ever my thing?" she asks, a flicker of curiosity in her eyes.

I'm already working out whether I'll have time at lunch on Monday to get back down here for that ring for our anniversary. And if I should call the store from the restaurant and beg them to hold it for me.

"You wouldn't let me buy you one when I proposed. Said it was silly to spend all that money on a ring when we were just startin' out. But I got you a pair of diamond studs for your thirtieth birthday. You wore them almost every day. They're in your jewelry box."

Grace reaches up and touches her left ear. "I didn't even know my ears were pierced."

She turns from the window, and there's the barest flicker of a wince.

"What is it?" I ask, tipping her chin up gently.

"Just a little headache. Nothing serious. Come on. I'm getting hungry."

Her smile's a little weak, and my gut twists. "You're sure?"

"Yes, Captain Overprotective. I'm fine." She tucks her hand back into the crook of my arm and rests her head on my shoulder for a beat. "Food first. Then I want to see the arcade. I think I used to be pretty good at Skee-Ball."

"You beat my ass every time," I say and press a kiss to the top of her head. "Okay. We'll find a place to eat. But if the headache gets worse, you'll tell me?"

Grace lifts her head, her gaze meeting mine. "I will. I promise."

Fuck. I'm wound so tight, I'm seein' danger everywhere. She's allowed to have a goddamn headache without me sweeping her into my arms and rushing her home.

At a little Italian place, their covered patio strung in golden lights, Grace studies the menu like it's a test she might fail. "What if...it's like the eggs?" she says, her voice small and quiet.

"Then we'll switch plates and you can have my fettuccine. Or we can ask for a to-go box, stop at a taco truck on the way home, and order the spiciest thing on the menu."

Her eyes soften, and she reaches across the table to take my hand. "How do you always know the right thing to say?"

"I don't. But there ain't nothin' I wouldn't do for you, Grace. Even burn off all my taste buds—permanently."

She laughs, her fingers tight on mine. "You are a damn fool, AJ Stone."

I wink at her. "But I'm *your* damn fool."

Over pasta and wine, she starts to relax—even tries a bite of my fettuccine.

"What do you think? That's got to be the least spicy thing you've had since comin' home. Any good?"

She dips her fork into the bowl a second time with a small smile. "Maybe."

A drop of Alfredo sauce lingers at the corner of her mouth, and I lean forward to swipe it away with my thumb. Her cheeks flush bright pink, but she doesn't look away.

For a moment, my world narrows to her laugh, the feel of her skin, and the love reflected in her eyes.

Until someone just behind me gasps, and a woman's voice cuts through the air. "Oh, my God. You're *her*. You're Greta? Gloria? Grace! Grace Stone!"

Conversations fall silent all around us. Chairs scrape over the tile floor. A guy with greasy hair darts around one of the tables, his phone pointed right at my wife.

Grace's fork clatters to the plate. All the color fades from her cheeks. "AJ?"

I'm on my feet in an instant, my chair shoved back hard enough to rattle the table behind us. Putting myself squarely between her and half a dozen gawkers, I narrow my eyes at the men and women turning our night of fun into their own personal true crime documentary.

"Back. Off," I grit out, keeping my voice low but doing nothing to hide the warning in my tone.

"Grace! How are you feeling?" a woman calls out. "Have you remembered—"

"Ma'am, I suggest you walk away. Right now. And if all y'all don't stop pointin' your goddamned phones at my wife's face, I'm gonna forget the manners my mama worked so hard to teach me."

The woman stumbles, bumping into the next table. "I—I'm sorry. I didn't mean... I just..." Her cheeks flame, but there's fear in her eyes as she backs away.

More than one person is still filming though, preserving every second of Grace's fear for the whole of the fucking internet to see. My fists ache with how hard I'm fighting *not* to punch someone.

Grace's hand brushes my arm. She's pale, her eyes brimming with tears, but she ain't panicking. She needs me to stay calm. At her side. Not spendin' a night in lockup for assault and destruction of property.

I drag in a breath, yank my wallet from my back pocket, and dig out one of my business cards. Our server, a young woman who's probably still in college, is frozen next to our table, her tray tucked against her chest like a shield.

"I'm a captain with the Texas Rangers," I say, fighting to keep my voice steady as I pass her the card. "I'll call you once we're in the car and settle the bill, okay?"

She nods and darts back to the kitchen.

I wrap an arm around Grace's shoulders, shielding her as best I can while Belle, hackles raised, growls softly.

Every few steps, I glance behind us, and when the last of the gawkers disappears, guide Grace over to a bench. "Sit down for a minute, darlin'. Ain't no one watchin' anymore."

Belle lays her head on Grace's thigh, an eighty-pound anchor in a storm.

"Well, that was...fun." Her voice is raspy. Thin. "I was really lookin' forward to Skee-Ball."

I lower myself down next to her, gritting my teeth when the bruise on my ass sends pain shooting up my back. "I'll clear out the whole damn place if you want me to. In the name of public safety."

Her laugh soothes a fraction of my anger. "You will do no such thing. This...what just happened..." She presses her hand to her chest. "It's going to happen again. I wasn't prepared. Next time...maybe I will be."

"Grace, you ain't giving yourself near enough credit. You didn't run. You didn't hide. Hell, you kept me from losing my shit. That's what courage looks like. I'm so damn proud of you, darlin'."

Her lips part on a shaky exhale. I skim my knuckles along her cheek, and she leans into the touch.

"I love you," I whisper. "More and more every damn day."

She settles closer to me, with Belle pressed to our shins. Under the warmth of the outdoor heaters, it feels like this moment could go on forever.

"Stone?"

The familiar voice grates along my spine. Marvin hustles across the promenade, his shirt rumpled and that God-awful belt buckle flashing like a beacon in the overhead lights.

Grace tenses, her fingers digging into my thigh.

"Marvin," I say, unable to keep the ice from my tone. "You remember Grace."

He offers her his hand with an easy smile. "Ma'am. Good to see you out and about."

Belle growls, and Marvin takes a quick step back. "Whoa there, girl. Stone, you sure that dog should be out in public?"

"She's got more manners than you," I snap and push to my feet. I've got a good four inches on Marvin, and I'm gonna use it. "Sendin' the chief to our house like that? What the fuck were you playin' at?"

Marvin shoves his hands into his pockets. "I didn't mean for things to blow up the way they did. You called out with no explanation. I was worried. Thought the chief should check in with you."

My jaw tightens. "Check in? He barreled through the door screamin'. At *my wife*."

His gaze drops, shoulders slumping as his focus slides to Grace. "AJ. Ma'am, I'm truly sorry about that. I hope you can forgive me."

Grace doesn't say a word, and I can feel the tension coiling in her limbs.

"Get the fuck out of here, Marvin. We might have to work together, but I ain't gotta forgive you any time soon."

Marvin holds up his hands. "You're right. I'll...see you at the station on Monday." He tips his Stetson. "Ma'am. You have a good night now."

He ambles back across the promenade, and I turn back to Grace. "Darlin', let's go home."

CHAPTER FIFTY-SIX

Grace

THE RICH SCENTS of butter and pancake batter pull me into the kitchen. Yesterday's headache—along with the halos that plagued me as I drew page after page of senseless shapes and cold, uncaring eyes—have fled with a good night's sleep. And though I'm scared how I'll handle AJ going back to work tomorrow, that's a worry for later.

AJ's at the stove, barefoot, and humming softly. The man can't carry a tune in a bucket, but it's the most relaxed sound I've heard from him since I came home.

Bracing myself against the counter, I let my gaze drift to his ass. "Need a hand?"

AJ glances over his shoulder, and his slow, almost boyish grin sends warmth flooding my core. "You offerin' to flip? Or just taste test?"

"I can work the ladle." I edge closer, breaking a piece off one of the pancakes on the plate beside him. "But, quality control is important too."

"Oh, is it? How am I doin', then?" He swats my hip lightly

with the spatula, laughter spilling out of him, softening the lines around his eyes. For a moment, he looks like the man I sometimes see in my dreams. The AJ from before. Younger. Unburdened. Without an ocean of sadness in his eyes.

"Fair to middlin'."

Lightning cuts across the sky, followed by a loud crack of thunder. Rain lashes against the windows. The kind of fat drops that sound like they're about to crack the glass at any second.

My hand stills on the bowl. The warm, beige walls of the kitchen fade into the palest wood. The floor is cold against my bare feet. They take my shoes now. Every night. So I won't run again.

As if I could. They took that from me too.

I press my forehead to the window pane, watching sheets of rain blur the world outside. It hits so hard, I can *feel* it.

Is it raining where you are, AJ? Are we caught in the same storm?

I feel him sometimes. Or...I think I do. But it could be nothing more than the last shreds of hope fading away.

The damp seeps into my bones. And locked in this tiny room—this *cell*—I can do nothing but cling to the scraps of my former life that come to me in my dreams.

Like one of our first dates. Mini-golfing on a Sunday afternoon. Until a storm rolled in. Running through a downpour, my hand clasped in his. We were soaked by the time we reached his truck, breathless with laughter, our clothes plastered to our bodies.

He'd kissed me, and I'd tasted the rain on his lips. That was the moment I knew what forever felt like.

Quiet, hopeless tears soak into my simple, white dress. But still, I pray we're both seeing the same rain.

Warmth seeps back into my body by degrees. I blink,

suddenly home again. In our kitchen with AJ watching me, a frown curving his lips.

Only then do I realize I'm crying here too.

"Grace?" He keeps his voice soft and steady. Soothing.

I touch my cheek, then stare at my wet fingers. My chest doesn't tighten with panic. I'm not afraid. But an echo of the bone-deep loneliness remains. I press my hands to the granite counter and blow out a breath.

"I'm okay."

He doesn't believe me. I can see it in his eyes. So I wrap my arms around his waist and lay my head against his chest. "I remembered something," I say softly. "It was raining. Wherever I was. I was so lonely, AJ. All the time. And I wished...I hoped... that you were watching the rain too."

AJ's chest heaves. He presses a kiss to the top of my head. He doesn't question me. Just sets the spatula aside, turns off the burner, and holds me.

The rain keeps battering the window, even as the lightning and thunder fade away, but I don't care. I'm not alone anymore.

THE STORM RETREATS SLOWLY, a last burst of darkness before the start of spring.

We painted one wall of my studio yesterday. Well, AJ did. I still get tired so easily. The whisper of pale purple provides a hint of calm, while still giving the room a light, airy feel. Maybe next weekend, we'll do another one.

The steady patter of rain against the roof carries me into a sketch I haven't been able to get out of my head since breakfast. On the page, a window takes shape—small, narrow, sealed shut. No latch. No air. I shade the lines darker. So dark, the paper nearly tears.

For the first time, I can see the rest of the room with a clarity that takes my breath away. The bare wood floor. The narrow bed with its single pillow and thin blanket. Next to that useless, inescapable window, a rough-hewn desk that gave me splinters.

Nothing of any comfort. No plant on the sill. No closet. No color. Only two small bins—one with several clean white dresses and folded cotton panties, and the other serving as a laundry hamper.

On the facing page, I start again, and this time the window fills the entire space.

I add the horizon. Low hills fold gently into one another. They would have been calming if they hadn't stood between me and freedom. A squat building in the distance. Gray and flat, with a winding road leading up to it. But I don't remember what it was for.

Closer now, tension gathers in my shoulders as first one pole, then another, then another loom over an area my pencil doesn't want to touch. But I can't run from these memories anymore. Facing them is the only way I get my life back.

Still, I add the lanterns first. Six of them. They're not lit—when I close my eyes, the image behind my lids is mostly gray. Dawn, perhaps. Or dusk.

The door behind me creaks open.

"Grace?"

AJ slips into the room, two bottles of Shiner dangling from his hand. He's still *mostly* relaxed, his shoulders loose, his mouth free of the tight line it's held so often the past week. But this morning's ease is starting to fade.

"You want some company?" His gaze searches mine, and I see the question in his eyes.

How can I make up for three years of aching loneliness?

I want to tell him he can't. Nothing can. But he's here now, and that's enough.

My smile comes easily now. Finally. Even knowing I'm

about to draw something that terrifies me, I can still find it—as long as he's with me. "I'd love some."

He sets one of the bottles in front of me, but doesn't stare at my sketchbook. Doesn't ask to see it. Just settles into the chair in the corner with his phone in one hand and the beer in the other, his long legs stretched out.

His presence fills the quiet in a way I can't explain. I used to yearn for something as simple as having him in the same room. The same house. The same...life. Now that I have it again, I'll do *anything* to keep it. Even draw the one thing that's scared me most since I started to remember.

I touch the pencil to the page. Right in the center of the empty space. If I want to make it through this, I have to jump in with both feet.

Fear coils in my belly, sharp and sour on my tongue. I don't remember what happened there. But *something* did.

The scar at my side aches.

Four lines. A rectangle. Then, a base underneath. A platform. No. An altar. Flowers all around it. Pink and red and white. Oleanders. Even the memory of the scent sickens me.

The voice is so clear, I almost drop the pencil.

"...the bright light to banish all darkness and bring about the Glorious One's return..."

My throat tightens, but I keep adding more shading, turning the page darker and darker.

AJ's hand covers mine. He crouches beside me without a word. He doesn't ask about the drawing. Doesn't ask if I'm okay. He just...stays.

For several minutes, neither of us move. It's enough to simply *be*. To feel the warmth of his skin, smell his aftershave, hear his soft, steady breaths.

But we can't stay like this forever. Not when I finally understand why everything under the lanterns terrifies me.

"It's an altar," I say, my voice barely stronger than a whisper. "That's where they tried to kill me."

CHAPTER FIFTY-SEVEN

AJ

"I CAN DO THIS." Grace glares at me, a hundred and twenty-five pounds of grit and fire, and I back off.

"Okay. I'll open the wine."

Her steps are mostly steady. She doesn't reach for the wall once as she carries plates, two at a time, into the dining room. Pride swells in my chest—along with worry about her pushing too hard, too soon.

By the time I pull the roast out of the oven, and Connor's fussin' with vegetables like he's auditioning for Texas's next Top Chef, the table looks like it's set for Christmas.

Grace sinks down in her chair with a sigh, her left hand trembling slightly, but the smile on her face lights up the room.

Dinner starts off with laughter and the kind of gentle ribbing you only find in the closest of families. Parker laughing at the amount of butter Belle stole off the counter before I caught her. Emi's shock at how much hot sauce Grace put on her mashed potatoes. Connor reminding his step-kid, Veronica, not to feed Belle green beans under the table. Grace even joins in the teasing when Emi tells everyone that Jasper used to think kale was some sort of "fancy parsley."

"They're *nothing* alike. I can't remember if I even like the stuff, but I *know* I'd never mistake it for parsley," she says. "We need to find you a Veggie 101 class."

Everyone laughs, and the knot I've carried in my chest for more than two weeks now fades away.

But the quiet doesn't last. Connor's phone buzzes, and he checks the screen. Isabel tenses. Veronica looks to her mom. "If he can check his phone..." she says.

"He's working, V. You know they're tryin' to find out who took Grace. This is important." Isabel gives her daughter's arm a squeeze, and Veronica stabs another green bean with a sigh.

Connor slips the phone back into his pocket. "Zephyr found at least four cults whose 'holy' texts use the phrase 'the Glorious One.' But none of them have ties to Texas. There's one in California, another in Montana, and two overseas."

"Oleanders are popular in California." I rest my hand on Grace's thigh under the table. "But that's a long way from where Grace turned up in Mexico. No other hits on the phrase?"

"Hundreds. Most in worship songs. It has ties to Buddhism, Vaishnavism, and a handful of other religions, but according to Zephyr, none of them would use it the way Grace remembers it."

Grace's knife hits her plate a little too loudly. Her left hand trembles, and she clutches it to her chest like she's trying to hold herself together. "I'm not wrong. About the wording," she whispers, then forces her voice a little louder. "I can hear him— the man who locked edde in that tiny room. I can't see him, but his voice..." Her breath hitches. "He was talking about *me*. I'm the one who was going to 'banish all darkness and bring about the Glorious One's return.' That's why they..." Her gaze darts to Veronica, then back down to her plate. "Why they did what they did."

Isabel takes her daughter's hand. "V, if you want to go watch television, you can. Or use AJ's office and call Mitzi."

"I can handle this, Mom. Promise." The young woman turns to Grace, her eyes sharp, but steady. "You can say it. I heard Connor talking the other day. They tried to kill you. I'm sorry. That blows."

Grace blinks at her, then lets out a sound that might be a laugh. "Yeah. It really does."

The look Connor gives his stepdaughter is nothing short of awe. But then his brows furrow. "Lil' bit, we've talked about your eavesdropping."

She shrugs, completely unapologetic. "Hey, I can't help it if you leave your office door open."

Parker snorts, nearly choking on her wine. "Please. That's how AJ ended up with a whole damn posse on the flight down to Mexico. The man can't whisper to save his life, and won't shut a door in a dust storm."

I'm fixin' to tell her I wasn't about to put Reyes on hold after he told me my wife was alive, when Hardison leans back in his chair, arms crossed, and one eyebrow disappearing under his shaggy black locks.

"If AJ was running his mouth loud enough for the whole damn station to hear, *why* am I lying to the chief again? And why wasn't I right there with you, Lieutenant Loose Cannon?"

Parker rolls her eyes at him. "Because you dumped all your paperwork on me and cut out early that night. You were probably face down in a brisket plate by the time the call came in."

Hardison doesn't miss a beat. "Right. You were drowning in forms, I was drowning in BBQ sauce."

Connor cuts in, his voice putting an end to the brief moment of levity. "If the two of you are done? This still ain't addin' up. How does a cult keep themselves hidden for three fuckin' years?" He leans in, forearms braced on the table. "Cults don't survive without fresh blood. They need to recruit, have some sort of income stream to keep the lights on. If there's nothin' to find, either they've got help coverin' their tracks—"

Parker says what Connor won't. "Or their recruits—their victims—are hidden so deep, no one's gonna find them."

Grace's breath stutters in her chest. "They hid me. For three years."

The words gut me. The whole room feels it. No one makes a sound for several long moments. Even Veronica stares down at her plate, poking her mashed potatoes with her fork.

Hardison leans back in his chair. "No one's *that* off the grid. Grace, when you see that room—the wood one—is there electricity?"

She frowns, her eyelids fluttering closed. "I...think so. The lanterns burned oil, but...yes. The room had a light."

"Then somebody's paying a bill," Hardison says. "The power company doesn't care if you're a plumber or the second coming of God. If there's electricity, there's paperwork. Receipts. We find those, we find a name."

Veronica's sharp brown eyes narrow on Hardison. "But if you don't know where the cult is, how do you find the paperwork? No one's gonna sign up for a credit card with the name 'Glorious One, Cult Leader.'"

"That's Zephyr's job," Nate replies. "But you're not wrong, V. We just gotta hope someone—somewhere—got sloppy."

Grace grips the edge of the table, her knuckles white. "What if they weren't? Sloppy."

"Then," Nate says, his voice flat, "someone's cleaning up after them. Which means we've got to find the janitor."

Grace

Nate and Parker trade jabs as they clear the table. And while Connor washes the dishes and Veronica dries them, I bring Isabel and Emi to see my studio.

"It's so empty now," I say, still in awe that AJ—along with the rest of the guys—did all this for me.

Emi skims her fingers along the newly painted wall. "I knew you were a purple person."

"I wish I remembered *anything* about decorating." I lean against the drafting table, suddenly a little shaky. "AJ said he and I picked out all the furniture in this house together. So I must have had an eye for it. But now..." Tucking a lock of hair behind my ear, I sigh. "I can't just pick something off a website. I need to *touch* it. *Feel* it. But after Friday night..."

"Hon," Emi says, draping an arm around my shoulders, "If you need to go *anywhere*, Jasper and Connor will take you. With those two at your side, no one would dare bother you."

The women close ranks around me, and the three of us stare out the darkened window at the lake. "God, I feel like such an ass for suggestin' this, but if you gave an interview," Emi says, "it might send some of the vultures back to their nests."

"Emi!" Isabel takes a step back, her eyes narrowing. "You can't be serious."

"It'd be a softball piece. I promise. No hard questions. No questions at all that you don't approve ahead of time. Hell, if AJ wants to vet them too, that's fine. But people love a tragedy turned love story. That's partly why they're so fascinated by you now." Emi rests her hand on my arm, warmth in her brown eyes. "Give them a glimpse into your life—maybe a bit of physical therapy, throwing the tennis ball for Belle, along with a little white lie that you haven't remembered anything about the last three years—and they might back off a bit. Talk to AJ. See what he thinks."

"Coffee's on," Jasper calls from down the hall.

We drift back to the living room, the clink of dishes fading as the scent of AJ's dark brew replaces that of his—supposedly—famous roast and buttery mashed potatoes.

Parker presses a mug of tea into my hands, her quiet way of reminding me not to push too far, too fast. The warmth steadies me even as the dinner conversation churns like broken glass in my chest.

AJ takes his usual seat next to me, with Belle lying at our feet. His first sip of coffee seems to steady him as he links his fingers with mine. "You'll have Connor or Jasper—or both—with you at all times," he says. "But...please, darlin'. Don't leave the house. The security system can't protect you outside these walls."

My heart rate kicks up, and I pull away from my husband. "No." I tighten my grip on the mug and work to steady my voice. "I was locked away for three years, AJ. I can't—I *won't*—be kept hidden again. Not even in my own home. Not when I'm finally getting my life back."

His eyes flash, protective fury warring with something softer. But I don't let myself look away. I need him to understand.

Parker breaks the tension, easing down beside me on the sofa, her shoulder brushing mine. "Grace is right," she says gently. "Hiding isn't the same as keeping her safe. We need a plan, not a prison."

From his seat by the fire, Connor leans forward. "The plan is to watch Grace's back. If she's here, Jasper or I will be with her." He turns his gaze to me. "If you want to go out—for anything—we'll go. But you'll have both of us with you. That sound fair?"

I nod. "I don't even know if I'll *want* to go anywhere. I just need to be able to decide that for myself."

"We got your back, Grace," Jasper says. "Any creep playin' at bein' an amateur reporter is gonna regret it."

Nate clears his throat. He's so quiet, sometimes I almost forget he's in the room. "Speaking of creeps... Marvin's been acting twitchy as hell lately."

"He used to be a halfway decent guy," Jasper says. "Until he broke chain of custody on a piece of evidence against the cartel four years ago. After that, he turned into a whiny piece of—"

Connor clears his throat, then cuts his gaze to Veronica.

"You *do* realize I'm eighteen now, right?" V says.

"Marvin's an ass," AJ grits out. "But twitchy? That's new."

"Trust me. I've got a PhD in twitchy. Marvin's hiding something. He took half a dozen calls on Friday—outside." Nate shoves his hair out of his eyes and drains the last of his coffee. "When I left, the dude looked like country music's top ten, personified."

"What the hell does that mean?" Parker asks.

"Standing on the corner after his wife left him for his best friend and took the dog, his truck, and his Stetson?" With a small shake of his head, Nate gives his partner the side-eye. "I thought you were born here."

"I was. Country's a hell of a lot more than *that*." She snorts, but even their banter can't quell the unease turning my stomach into a twisted knot.

The way he looked at me on Friday night made my skin crawl. But maybe my fear being filmed for the whole world to see moments before was what set me off.

I lift my mug to my lips, letting the honeyed warmth seep into my bones, and focus on the family I have around me. Parker and Nate are still arguing about the virtues of country music. Jasper, Emi, and Connor are talking baseball stats and spring training games. And Veronica sits on the floor, her back against her mom's legs, stroking Belle's side while the dog snores loudly.

AJ drapes his arm around my shoulders. "I won't let anything happen to you again, darlin'. On my life, we'll keep you safe."

I turn to him, cup his cheek, and brush a soft kiss to his lips. "I know."

CHAPTER FIFTY-EIGHT

AJ

I STOP outside the station door. The last time I crossed the threshold, Grace was nothing but a ghost I couldn't stop chasing. Now she's back in my arms at night. Sharing her coffee with me in the morning. Laughing, *healing*. And somehow, that makes the ground under me shake harder than when she was gone.

Losing her once damn near killed us both. I won't lose her again. I can't.

Parker joins me, her hands shoved in her jacket pockets. "You fixin' to stand out here all day? Or are we doing this?" she asks.

"We're doing this. Not much choice, I reckon."

I hold the door open for her, my jaw clenched. Feels like I'm walking into a fight I ain't ready for, though I don't know why.

The scuffed linoleum floors, the mix of burnt coffee, sweat, and gun oil hanging in the air, the low hum of conversation punctuated by ringing phones...it's all the same. I'm the one who's different.

Harris is waiting for me—for us. "Lieutenant Elmore, you're on desk duty until I say otherwise. Stone? My office. Now."

"Mornin' to you too, Chief," I mutter, too low for him to hear, as Parker stalks over to her desk.

He's already back in his chair when I shut the door, his cheeks red and splotchy. "The lab came up empty on the dress. Marvin was spinnin' his wheels all week tryin' to find out how your wife got to the trail. Your story's fishier than week-old gas station sushi, and I ain't buyin' it. Bring Grace in so Marvin and I can question her."

"No." I cross my arms and widen my stance. "She's not a suspect. She's a victim. A goddamn *survivor*. And she's already told you everything she knows. And I recall you promisin' me you wouldn't let Marvin anywhere *near* her."

His cheeks get redder, and he sputters, "Th-that ain't a request, Stone."

"Two weeks ago, we thought harassing victims was a *bad* thing. We change our policy while I was out?"

I don't wait for him to answer. "You want to drag her in here, sit her in an interrogation room, and grill her like she's done somethin' wrong? Try to get her to break? She won't. She's tougher than anyone in this fucking building. But she's tryin' to heal. And I'll be damned if I let you interrupt that process because *Marvin* can't track down a clue to save his life."

Harris's jaw flexes, but he doesn't fire back right away. For a second—maybe two—I almost think he's gonna agree with me.

"You think *everything* is about her," he snaps. "It ain't. It's about a case with no leads, no evidence, and a whole goddamn town breathin' down my neck. You don't get to pick and choose what parts of her story are useful. That's *my* job. She can heal *and* answer my questions. Stop lettin' your personal life interfere with the job."

I drop my voice, forcing control I don't feel into my tone.

"She ain't steppin' one foot into this station unless *she* wants to. You try and force her? You'll have to go through me."

Harris slams his hand down on his desk. "Get out of my office, Stone. Before I forget how much rope I've already given you."

Shoving at the door, I stalk out, my pulse hammering so hard, I can feel it in my temples.

The bullpen quiets as I cut through, my fellow Rangers watching me with everything from respect to pity. I have my office in sight when Marvin swoops in like a goddamn vulture, his signature smirk plastered across his smug face.

"Guessin' that didn't go so well," he drawls. "Can't blame you, though. If I had a woman like Grace, I wouldn't want her put through the wringer. You're doin' the right thing—keeping her close. Protecting what's yours."

The way he says the words—like Grace is a possession or some prize to be hoarded—rubs me raw.

"Get out of my sight, Marvin. Or Parker won't be the only one with a suspension on her record." I clench my right hand into a fist, raising it just enough he gets the hint and double-times it back to his desk.

I slam the door and put my back to it. How the hell am I supposed to protect and serve the people of Texas when all I can think about is Grace and the assholes who tried to use her as a human sacrifice?

Fuck.

Shedding my jacket, I force a couple of deep breaths. For almost twenty years, this was all I wanted to do with my life. Move up through the ranks, eventually replace Harris when he retires, and have a chance to do some real good. Now...I'm not so sure.

By the time lunch rolls around, my eyes are burning from all the paperwork Harris sent my way the past two weeks. Jasper's been texting every hour—thank God—or I'd have called Grace a dozen times by now, and probably gotten my ass handed to me for it.

But the second I'm outside the station, I reach for my phone.

She picks up on the second ring. "AJ." The gentle warmth in her voice raises a lump in my throat. God, I needed to hear her say my name.

"Just checkin' in. Jas said everything was fine, but..."

"It is. Connor's in the kitchen making jalapeño poppers, and Jasper's trying to teach me how to play poker. Apparently, I used to be good at it?"

"You were a card shark, darlin'. Couple times a month, we'd host poker night, and you almost always came out on top."

"Well, that explains why he's already lost twenty dollars," she says.

That pulls a laugh out of me, though it's rough around the edges. "If he's got a single cent left by the end of the week, maybe we can have folks over on Saturday."

"I'd like that." A door closes softly, and she sighs. "It's strange being here without you. The only memories I have of this house...are with you."

Her words tear through me, ripping open a wound I'm not sure how to heal. She should have those memories. God, she should. Weeknights with friends, lazy mornings with Belle, quiet moments that belong only to her.

"You deserve to make our home yours in every way, Grace. With me *and* without me. Just..." I swallow hard, desperate to soften the rough edge to my voice. "Don't ask me to like the idea of you bein' there all alone."

"I won't." Her voice trembles. "And I'm not ready for that either. I don't know if I'll ever be."

Damn if I don't want to floor it all the way back to the lake, wrap her in my arms, and tell her she'll never be alone again. But even if I could, that's not what she needs.

"You will be, darlin'. Once the bastards who took you are gone, you'll find your footing again. I promise."

"I hope so." A hint of warmth returns to her tone, along with an undercurrent of longing. "I'm glad you called."

"Me too. I like hearin' your voice."

We linger for a little longer before I let her go with a promise that I'll come home safe.

Twenty minutes later, I slide into a booth at a run-down diner a few blocks from the train station—the kind where the servers don't care who you are or what your business is, as long as you tip well.

Parker has jammed herself in the corner, a plate of greasy fries untouched in front of her as she sucks down half a milkshake in under a minute.

Hardison sits across from her, looking on in shock. "And you're chasing that with grease. This isn't how superheroes get origin stories, y'know."

"Sure it is," Parker deadpans. "Mere mortals would have died of brain freeze by now."

Despite the jokes flying between the two of them, obvious rage simmers just under Parker's skin. "How long is the chief keeping you chained to your desk?"

She drags a fry through a mountain of ketchup. "Until I've 'learned my lesson.' He says it's 'for my own good.' It's bullshit. I rearranged his jaw, and he's never gonna let me forget it."

"He can't keep you caged forever. You're too good at your job," I say and signal the server to bring me a cup of coffee.

Parker snorts. "Wanna bet?" Another quarter of the milkshake disappears in under five seconds. "I punched him. And I'd do it again in a heartbeat to protect Grace. But my career's fucked. Once we find the assholes who took her, I'm out."

"No," I say, a little too loudly, startling the server enough, a splash of coffee hits the table before she can set my mug down. Once she rushes off, I narrow my eyes at Parker. "I'm not losing you because the chief's a fucking asshole. If you go, I'm out too."

Hardison flops back against the cracked vinyl booth. "So the two of you are just gonna abandon me to suffer Harris's mood swings alone? A sad sack just weeping into all the paperwork I can't dump on Parker's desk anymore?"

"No one's leaving." I give the coffee a sniff. Motor oil would probably be healthier. "Not while Grace is still in danger. Zephyr's still workin' the cult angle. I think the three of us should go back to the beginning. We know *why* the cult targeted Grace. What we don't know is how. There have to be hundreds of women in Texas with oleander tattoos."

"But there can't be very many who also have a full moon inked on their arm," Parker says.

"You aren't seriously suggesting we call every tattoo parlor in Texas, are you?" Hardison asks. "Unlike my favorite MMA fighter, Lieutenant Loose Cannon, and Captain AWOL—aka Captain Clusterfuck—I have a full case load. I'm holding shit together with duct tape and caffeine."

"I'll be sure to put that on your promotion paperwork," I say, suddenly so tired, I try a sip of the sludge this place passes off as coffee.

Parker finally abandons her milkshake long enough to level a gaze at both of us. "Can we stop with the one-liners and try to figure out who put a target on Grace's back in the first place?"

I glance at my watch. "If we don't get back to the station, Harris is gonna have all our asses in the same damn sling. Hardison, you've gotta stay on the chief's good side. Work your cases and keep an eye on Marvin. He's rubbin' me the wrong way and I don't know why. Parker? Look for any unsolved kidnapping cases where the victims had tattoos. Especially flowers or full moons."

"What does that leave for you, Cap?" Hardison asks.

"I'm gonna talk to everyone who was in Grace's life three years ago. And hope to God she remembers *something* that might help."

Standing, I throw a twenty on the table, and Parker slides out of the booth after me. Hardison gets to his feet, glances at the remains of the milkshake, and makes the sign of the cross. "Rest in peace, double-chocolate with extra whip. Your sacrifice won't be forgotten."

CHAPTER FIFTY-NINE

AJ

IT FEELS like I've been gone a month. How the hell am I supposed to do this—walk out the door and trust that my wife will still be here when I come home? It don't matter that Jasper and Connor will protect her with their lives. Or that our house is a fucking fortress after Emerald City Security got done with it. She should've been safe running the Butler trail too.

Parker simmered like a pressure cooker all day chained to her desk. Hardison was still there when I left, half a dozen files in front of him, and one eye on the chief's office.

Jasper looks up from one of the living room chairs as I shut the door, his phone cradled in his hand. "Connor just left," he says as he rises, wincing slightly. "Grace is in the kitchen. I'll give you two some space. Emi's off tonight, so we're gonna grab some takeout and hunker down at home. Call if you need me."

"Jas." I grab his arm, holding on until he meets my gaze. "Thanks for bein' here. For everything."

"Ain't no nevermind."

"It is. You're puttin' your life on hold—"

His eyes turn stormy, and he stands up a little straighter. "Maybe. But if you hadn't come through when you did, I wouldn't have a life at all. Neither would Emi. You and Grace are family. There ain't a damn thing I wouldn't do to keep you both safe."

I nod, not trusting my voice, and watch him walk out the door.

The scents of garlic, butter, and poblano waft in from the kitchen. I hang my Stetson and sport coat on the rack, then follow my nose to find my wife standing at the stove, a wooden spoon in her hand, staring at a steaming pot like it might explode on her at any moment.

"Grace? Darlin', you didn't have to cook."

Her cheeks are flushed pink, and she grins. "I wanted to. Connor had to do all the chopping, though. It's not burned. Yet."

I drink in the sight of her. Alive. Happy. Home. For three years, I never thought I'd have this again. Crossing the kitchen, I wrap my arm around her waist and kiss her. She melts against me, and what started out soft and tender turns deeper. The rest of the world blurs, and the constant noise in my head—all the worries over her safety, her happiness, her health—fades away.

When I pull back, my voice is rough. "Best thing I've seen all day."

She laughs. "Well, you haven't tasted it yet."

"I wasn't talkin' about the food, darlin'. I was talkin' about that smile," I say, skimming my thumb over her lips. "But it does smell damn good in here."

The pasta with poblano cream sauce is delicious. But sitting at the counter with Grace at my side is perfection.

"You never much cared for cookin' before," I say, scooping up another forkful of rigatoni. "But your cinnamon rolls were the stuff of legends. I can't bake to save my life."

"Any idea where the recipe is?" Grace picks up her water

glass, but her hand starts to shake, rattling the ice against the sides. *"Shit."*

Worry punches me in the chest hard enough, I have to force myself to breathe. "What's wrong?" Freeing the glass from her trembling fingers, I take her hand in both of mine.

She shakes her head softly. "I...I don't know. I spent a couple of hours drawing today. Maybe I just overdid it."

Her skin is cool, almost clammy, but she *was* just holding a glass of ice water. "I think we should call Dr. VanHorn. Right now."

"I feel fine, AJ. No headache, no vertigo. I managed ten clothespins today *and* balanced on my left leg for a full thirty seconds. If this doesn't pass in an hour, then we'll call. But for now, can we just enjoy the rest of our dinner?"

I search her gaze, caught between my own fear and her need to be trusted with her own well-being. She's not dismissing the tremor. She's asking for time to decide if it's serious.

"Okay." I nod, my jaw tight. "But if it's not better by the time I finish the dishes—"

"I'll call the doctor myself." Grace twists her hand in mine, linking our fingers and squeezing gently. "Now, tell me about your day."

Grace

AJ stabs a fat piece of pasta and twirls it through the creamy sauce. "Harris is throwin' his weight around. If he lets Parker off desk duty before summer, it'll be a fuckin' miracle. She's the best of us, and he's got her doin' paperwork all day. Hardison's miserable handlin' a full case load without his partner. And

Marvin keeps tryin' to be 'supportive,' but after the shit he pulled with the chief, I ain't buyin' it."

I frown and pick up my glass again. This time, my hand is steady. At my side, AJ blows out a breath, and his shoulders start to lose some of their tension.

"You outrank him, right?" I ask.

"Yeah. He's been tryin' for his captain's badge since before you went missin'. But his close rate is half of what mine is. He ain't a bad guy. Just...lazy."

I finish the last of my pasta and push my bowl away. A shadow flickers in the back of my mind. Something I've forgotten but *know* is important. Before I can grab hold of it, it's gone again.

"Zephyr can only find a handful of images that resemble the symbol you drew, and none of them lead anywhere. A headstone in New Mexico, a chalk doodle in a parking lot in Dallas, and an occult shop in Louisiana—but the leaf in their logo is sage, not oleander." He wipes his lips with his napkin, turns to me, and takes both of my hands in his. "I keep comin' back to how they picked you in the first place. They had to be watching you. Waiting until you were alone to grab you."

A chill settles over me, sharp enough to drown out the warmth of the food in my belly and his hands on mine.

"Austin PD...they were fixated on the trafficking angle. You were just in the wrong place at the wrong time. Far as I know, they never considered that someone wanted *you* specifically."

AJ pauses, indecision in his eyes. His jaw works for a moment before he lets out a heavy breath. "I made some calls today. Your old yoga studio, the community college security center, even Stonewood Coffee. But after three years...folks remembered you, but couldn't tell me shit about anyone hoverin' when they shouldn't've."

The lines around his mouth tighten, and he shifts on the

stool like he can't get comfortable. "Some of your friends might know more. If you reached out…"

I twist my napkin in my lap, my palms damp. "I want to. I do, AJ. I want to know who I was, what I liked, what we talked about. But…what if they expect me to be the old Grace—the woman they remember. They'll want to pick up where we left off.

"Or worse—they won't want to pick up at all. What if all they see are my scars?"

My voice wavers, and I press a hand to my chest, trying to keep the fear from splitting me open. "I was so lonely. I don't think they let me talk to anyone. Or let anyone talk to me. For three years, I wasn't *living*. I was barely existing. While my friends from before…they've moved on. They've laughed and worked and read books and watched movies and gone to concerts and—"

"Darlin', stop." AJ kisses me, but not even his touch can convince me everything will be okay. Not this time. "You've been hangin' out with Parker, Emi, and Isabel. You hold your own with us guys too. You might not see it, but I do. You've found yourself these last two weeks. And the woman you are now? She's funny and smart and brave and strong and beautiful. All you have to do is look at the group chat you have with the girls to see it. Parker says you blow it up as much as the rest of them."

"Parker, Isabel, Emi…they only know *this* Grace," I say, my voice wavering. "My friends from before…"

AJ slides off his stool and takes me in his arms. "They'll get to know this Grace too. And if for any reason, they don't want to put in the work? That's their loss. Because you're a hell of a woman, darlin'. Don't you ever forget that."

CHAPTER SIXTY

Grace

I'M on my second cup of tea, but the lavender and chamomile haven't been able to soothe my nerves.

Connor's in the living room, chatting with Zephyr about the power grid and solar panels. While I sit at my drafting table, trying yet again to draw the images swirling around in my messed-up head.

For a moment, I think I've got it. An arm. Held high in the air. Another lower. Holding onto something? But then the arms turn into horns. The curve of the man's back bends the wrong way.

I press even harder with the pencil, as if pressure can force the image to make sense. But soon, it's nothing but a smear of charcoal and graphite.

"*Shit,*" I mutter. Next to me, Belle lifts her head with a deep, inquisitive sound. "I'm okay, sweetie. Just...frustrated."

I set the pencil back in the bag and scrub my hands over my face. It's not the sketch that's troubling me. Or...not *only* the sketch. It's the thought that I should be doing more.

AJ's working himself into exhaustion. Connor's giving up time with his family to babysit me. Parker might lose her entire career.

And I'm hiding here, trying to trap ghosts of my memories on page after page of my sketchbook.

Karen will be here in an hour. After that, Jasper promised to stop by so he and Connor could take me to the art supply store. I've burned through five pencils and an entire sketchbook since I've been home. If I don't go shopping soon, I'll be drawing on napkins with ball point pens.

My phone mocks me from the edge of the drafting table. AJ thinks one of my friends might be able to tell me if there was someone following me three years ago. Or anyone who made me uncomfortable.

I laid awake for several hours last night, wondering what I might say if any of them answered. But I couldn't come up with anything beyond, "Hi. It's Grace."

Before I lose my nerve completely, I send a message to the group chat.

Grace: I'm thinking about calling Isha, one of my old friends from my running club. But what if it's weird?

Parker: It will be. But that doesn't mean it won't be good, too. Girls' night was a little weird for you at first, right?

I love how blunt and honest she is.

Grace: Maybe a little.

Emi: Just be you, hon. People who really care about you will meet you where you are.

Isabel: And if she doesn't, we'll be here when you're done.

My throat is tight and raw. For more than two weeks now, I've hidden in this house, supported by AJ's complete devotion, Parker's gentle encouragement, and Karen's never-ending obsession with clothespins.

They'd all let me lean on them when I couldn't stand on my own. Maybe they're right. Maybe I can do this.

I find Isha's name in my contacts—AJ must have dug it up since this isn't my old number—and hit call before I can talk myself out of it.

"Hello?" Her voice is gentle, but unfamiliar.

"Isha? It's...uh...Grace," I say softly.

She sucks in a sharp inhale. "Oh, God. Grace. I saw the press conference. I've thought about calling every day, but you just looked so...scared, and I didn't know what to say or if you'd want visitors or if you remembered me at all..."

Her words sting, even though I understand. "I...wasn't ready for a while. And I don't remember much of anything. AJ had to tell me your name and how I knew you. But...I'm trying."

Silence fills the air between us. It's not empty. Not even awkward. Just...*there*. Like we both *want* to talk, but don't know what to say.

Isha's the one to finally break it. "You sound...different. Not bad. Just...different."

"I am. I think. I don't know how, though. I barely remember running—except for that last day. And...I...can't anymore. My knees...something happened to them. *Shit*. This was probably a mistake—"

"No," Isha says quickly. "Wait. Running wasn't why we were friends. It's just how we met. I tore my ACL a couple of months after I joined. You brought me cinnamon rolls for *weeks*. I gained five pounds from those damn rolls, but they were *so* worth it." She laughs, and the sound is so warm, so rich and *relieved*, I relax a little.

"AJ keeps talking about them too. I don't suppose I ever shared the recipe?"

"No. You said it was your secret weapon for all potlucks and holidays."

"Well, that sounds like me. I think."

"Grace, we can...start over. Heck, we'll start a new club. Former runners who can't anymore. We'll talk about physical therapy and what we're supposed to do with the industrial-sized box of running fuel that's still in the back of our pantries and oh my God how nice is it to be able to sleep in on the weekends rather than get up at the ass-crack of dawn to run twenty miles."

I stifle a snort. "Well, I don't remember all those early mornings, but I did find the box of running fuel today. I counted. Fifty-three packets of the stuff. It doesn't really taste like chocolate chip cookie dough, does it?"

"God, no. Not unless that cookie dough was made by a demented mosquito."

Maybe reconnecting won't be this terrible, awkward thing I've been dreading. At least not with Isha. We could still run out of things to talk about in five minutes, but she isn't treating me like I'm broken.

I stare at the strange, messy sketch I can't seem to finish. The question slips out before I can stop it. "Isha? Do you remember if I ever mentioned anyone...watching me? When we got together, was there anyone...creepy hanging around?"

She's quiet for several seconds. Shit. This was too much, too soon. She probably thinks it's the only reason I called. She wouldn't be wrong. If AJ hadn't asked, I would have put this off for weeks.

But eventually, her voice softens. "Once. We were at the Taco Shack, eating on their outdoor patio, and this old truck kept driving around the parking lot. It would slow down whenever it got close to us. That was...early March, I think. A month before you disappeared. The windows were tinted, so we couldn't see anyone inside. The fifth or sixth time it passed us, I flipped the driver off, and they left."

My stomach twists itself into a knot. Proof? No. But it's something. "Oh. Th-thank you. I...I still don't know who took me. Or why, and I just...*shit*. This isn't what I wanted to talk about...why I wanted to call, but—"

"Grace...it's okay," she says, her gentle tone holding back the tears threatening to spill down my cheeks. "Whatever you need, I'm here."

The words break me, and I have to mute the call to let out a single, rough sob. Belle jumps up, nudges my arm, and waits for me to tangle my fingers in her wiry fur.

After a shaky breath, I tap the unmute button. "I should go. M-my physical therapist should be here soon. But this is my new number. Maybe...we can talk again in a few days?"

"I'd like that," Isha says softly. "A lot."

We say our goodbyes, and I set the phone down before wrapping my arms around Belle and sobbing into her neck. For what I've lost, but also what I've found. A little more of *me*.

CHAPTER SIXTY-ONE

Grace

BELLE MARCHES PROUDLY through the automatic doors, her steady warmth grounding me against the fluorescent lights and overwhelming size of the artist supply store.

I curl my fingers around the leather handle of her harness, hoping the dull ache behind my eyes is nothing more than a side effect of the tears I cried after talking to Isha. Learning at least a small spark of our friendship survived left me shaken in a way I wasn't prepared for. Halfway through physical therapy, I had a vague memory of the two of us crossing the finish line of some race together. It shocked me so much, I lost my balance and jammed my shoulder against the wall of our home gym.

Karen made me promise to rest this afternoon. I will. In an hour. Because I *need* this. I need to know I can do something as normal as go to a store. Even if I do have two of the three most overprotective men in the world with me.

"You'll be able to see me the whole time," Jasper says. "But I won't stick too close."

Connor stays near the front windows, casually browsing a

display of framing supplies. But his gaze sweeps the parking lot every few seconds.

I wander down the watercolor aisle first, my fingers brushing over metal tins of cobalt and crimson and verdant green before curling around a long-handled brush.

"Water will always seek out the dry parts of the paper. It flows. Don't be scared if what shows up on the canvas isn't what you had in your head. Sometimes, beauty comes from the unexpected."

The sudden vision of a classroom full of students, easels arranged in a semi-circle, all watching me teach is so shocking, I almost drop the brush in my hand. I don't remember painting. Don't remember how. But maybe tomorrow, I'll try.

The oils are achingly familiar. But something about them makes my heart beat too quickly, and the ache drumming against my left temple sharpens. There's a memory here too. An important one.

A woman a few feet away glances over at me, elbows the teenager next to her, and starts whispering in the girl's ear. Belle stands up a little taller, the fur along her back bristling slightly.

"Shhh, sweetie. It's okay," I murmur, even though it's not. I don't have to hear to know what they're saying to one another.

It's her. She's the one who disappeared. Who came back. What's she doing here?

Jasper moves into their line of sight as the teen pulls out her phone. "Ma'am. Mind if I step in here? My sister-in-law is tryin' to do some shopping."

They rush to the end of the aisle, and the mother—a little too loudly—tells her daughter to put her phone away.

"You doin' okay?" Jasper asks, his voice quiet and gentle.

"Yes." I force my fingers to unclench, then rub at the tight knot in my chest. "I think so. I...need to find the sketch pads."

He offers me his arm, and though I want to do this on my own, the store is too busy. Too full of people. Jasper is safe. And while he can't stop people from gawking—or whispering—he'll at least make sure no one gets too close.

We find the drawing aisle, and I pick out a handful of graphite pencils, some new charcoals, and three different sketch pads. I almost go back to the watercolors, but my head is pounding. I'm ready to be home, curled up on the couch with Belle and a cup of tea.

At the register, I realize I didn't think to ask AJ about my wallet. My credit cards. Driver's license. Does he have them? Or was I carrying them when I disappeared?

The cashier rings everything up, and Jasper waves his phone over the card reader before I can say a word. It shouldn't sting. He's family. I'll pay him back. I must have a bank account. Somewhere. But my cheeks catch fire and I stare down at the floor as the cashier passes him the bag.

"Hang on," Connor says when we meet him at the doors. "I want a clear line of sight to the car."

I almost laugh at his grave tone. We're at a busy little shopping complex. No one's going to try to grab me here. But he's giving up his day to keep me safe, so I adjust my grip on Belle's harness and wait for a handful of cars in the parking lot to clear.

The sun is blinding—it's one of those days where spring is fighting hard to chase the last vestiges of winter away. I fumble for the sunglasses in my coat pocket, and round the hood of Connor's truck to the passenger side.

The cloying scent hits me first. A sickeningly sweet mix of almond, honey, and vanilla. Nausea crawls up my throat. A bouquet of white and pink flowers is stuck through the door handle.

The whole world tilts sideways, carrying me with it. I'm so cold. Lying on my back, my arms pulled tight over my head. Snowflakes sting my cheeks. The lanterns swing in the wind, burning bright above me.

My muscles cramp, the pain so intense, it steals my breath.

Voices. All around me. They're singing. Or chanting. But the words don't make any sense.

"Please—"

The plea spills from my lips. My shoulder hits cold metal, and I'm falling. Somewhere close, Belle whines, but I can't see her. Can't get to her. My knees give out.

I can *feel* the poison stealing my life away. My heart beat slows. A knife glints in my periphery. This is it. This is when Prophet kills me.

CHAPTER SIXTY-TWO

AJ

I RUB MY EYES, the case file in front of me blurring. A dead body found only a few blocks from the warehouse on Grand where Jasper almost lost his life last year.

My phone buzzes next to me. Before I can even say hello, Jasper's voice bursts from the speaker.

"AJ, Grace collapsed. We were gettin' her some art supplies, and when we left the store, we found a bouquet of fuckin' oleander flowers on Connor's truck. It shook her somethin' fierce. She's dizzy and she ain't...*here*. I think she's trapped in her memories. We're headed to Austin Memorial. Connor called VanHorn, and she's gonna meet us there."

"Fuck! Jas...put her on. Please. Just for a minute. Let me try to get her back." I shove my chair so hard it hits the credenza behind me.

"Go ahead," he says, his voice far away now.

"Grace? Darlin', listen to me. You're gonna be okay. You're home. You're safe. You're loved."

"Not...your Nova," she whimpers. "Prophet..."

"*Goddammit*. Listen to me, Grace. You ain't back there. You're in Austin. With Jas and Connor. I'm comin' for you, darlin'. You're home. You're safe. You're loved!"

Her sob cuts through me, sharper than any blade ever could.

"Jas!"

"I'm here," he says.

"Keep tryin' to get through to her. And for fuck's sake, take down every word she says."

"Will do. We're pullin' up now." The call cuts off.

I burst through the door of my office and into the bullpen. "Parker!"

Whatever she hears in my voice must be enough, because she's out of her chair in a heartbeat, keys and phone in her hand.

"Grace collapsed. Austin Memorial."

She shoots Hardison a look across the desk, then turns for the door.

The chief barrels out of his office. "What the hell do you think you're doing, Lieutenant? You have paperwork. *Weeks* of it."

"You want to fire me? Fire me," she snaps. "Grace is hurt and I'm takin' AJ to the hospital so he doesn't drive himself right into the side of a bus. I reckon that's a mite bit more important than any paperwork."

"I can drive him." Marvin steps in front of us, and Parker almost runs right into him. "All of my reports are already on Elmore's desk. I'm free."

Anger prickles along the back of my neck. He's too calm. Too damn polished. Like it don't even matter that Grace is hurt.

Parker doesn't miss a beat. Just sidesteps him with a glare that could split concrete. "You want to help? File your own damn reports. Assumin' you know how."

Harris grabs her arm before she reaches the door. "If you

ain't at that desk first thing tomorrow, you're done here. Understand?"

"Oh, I hear you. But if you make me choose between my job and her life, I know which one I'm pickin'. Spoiler alert—it doesn't come with health insurance."

THE ELEVATOR DOORS whisper open on the fourth floor. Connor leans against the nurses' station, hands balled into fists at his sides, but straightens the moment he sees us.

"Jasper's got Belle in Room four forty-four. Grace is with VanHorn gettin' a CT scan. AJ, go on back. Parker, I need you on with Zephyr. She's got questions and I think you might be better at answerin' them."

I push through the double doors, scanning the bright orange placards until I find the right room. Inside, Jasper holds Belle's harness with both hands, and I can't tell who's growling louder.

"Belle!" I snap my fingers. "Sit."

She tosses her head at me, defiant, until I repeat the command then drop down to one knee so I'm at her level. "She'll be okay, girl. She has to be."

The dog whines, then leans her entire body against me. I wrap my arms around her, and, for a moment, let myself break.

Jasper's hand comes down on my shoulder. One quick squeeze and I pull myself back together.

"She was mostly coherent by the time we got her upstairs," he says, his voice rough. "But before...she was goin' on about a Prophet. I wrote down everythin' I could remember."

He shows me his phone.

Prophet, please

Hurts

Can't do this

Not yet...I'm not ready...

The next moon...

Not...your Nova...

I run a hand through my hair, pulling hard on the strands. "You send all this to Zephyr?"

"Yeah. It ain't gonna help much, though. Unless she can find somethin' about 'your Nova.' Or 'Prophet.' But when you can talk to Grace, maybe she'll remember more."

Maybe. Or maybe her battered mind will shield her from whatever horrible memory those goddamn flowers triggered.

The scent of antiseptic is too thick in the air. The hospital bed too empty. The room too quiet. It feels like hours pass, but my watch says it's only been twenty minutes when the door opens and Dr. VanHorn wheels Grace back into the room.

Fuck. She looks so frail. Eyes glassy, mouth slack, and her hands shake as she fidgets with the hospital gown.

"Captain Stone." Dr. VanHorn's voice is calm—too calm as she rolls the chair right next to the bed and pulls back the sheet. "Grace's vitals are stable, but I'd like to keep her overnight for observation."

"No. I want to go home." Grace tries to stand, but her left knee buckles and she collapses back into the wheelchair. "*Shit.*"

"Darlin'," I drape her arm around my shoulders and help her to the bed, "you collapsed."

She gives me a look that might as well say, *"I know. I was there."*

The doctor slides a small tablet from the pocket of her coat. "Grace's CT scan worries me. There's a small bone fragment lodged in her temporal lobe that wasn't there when I saw her two weeks ago." She taps the screen, then points to a white slash amid a sea of dark gray. "Scar tissue has started forming around it. Left unchecked, it could lead to increased pressure in her brain."

Pressure. In her brain.

My throat goes dry. "And that means…?"

"Surgery." Her voice is gentle, but the word lands like a hammer. "Soon. Within the week if possible. Right now, her intracranial pressure is only slightly elevated. But if it continues to rise, the risks increase. Seizures, partial paralysis, even the loss of speech."

Grace jerks in my arms, a sharp inhale catching in her throat. I curl around her, pulling her against me like I can shield her from all the potential horrors the doctor just called out in harsh detail. "And if you take it out—she'll be okay?"

Dr. VanHorn shakes her head. "*I* can't take it out. Neurosurgery *is* my field, but I was in a car crash last year that left me with minor nerve damage in my dominant hand. But I can tell you that any brain surgery carries serious risks—bleeding, infection, stroke. Because of the fragment's location, I'd be especially worried about language and memory side effects. Aphasia. Cognitive changes. Short and long term memory loss."

Grace's hands ball into fists in her lap. She trembles once, then shudders like the weight of the words is too much to bear. "The last time someone cut into my head, I lost everything— even my name. I won't—I can't—go through that again."

I cup her face, desperate to anchor her, to anchor myself. "Look at me, darlin'." When her eyes finally lift to mine, fear swimming in their depths, I swallow hard past the fire in my chest. "We'll find the best neurosurgeon in the country. You hear me? You're not losing yourself. Not this time."

Dr. VanHorn's gaze flicks from me to Grace, then softens. "If it were my wife, Captain Stone, there are three or four surgeons I'd call. I'll get you their names. Grace, I know you want to go home—and I actually agree, that's the best place for you right now. But I need you here for the next couple of hours so I can track your intracranial pressure. If it stays stable, I'll discharge you. If it doesn't, you'll be admitted. No arguments."

Grace presses her lips together, her hand tightening on mine. "Two hours. I can't stay here any longer than that. Please."

I kiss her knuckles, holding on, hoping she'll understand that I'm on her side. Always. Forever. "Two hours, darlin'. Then you, me, and Belle...we're either walkin' out of here together, or sleepin' here tonight. All of us."

CHAPTER SIXTY-THREE

Grace

I FOLLOW the rich scent of coffee down the hall to the kitchen. AJ leans against the counter, staring out the window with two mugs lined up side by side.

"You're up early," he says, his voice low and controlled in the quiet of the kitchen.

"I never sleep well when you're on a stakeout."

The memory brings tears to my eyes. If I have the surgery—even if I don't—I could lose the few fragments of our life together I have. Our whispered "I love yous." AJ standing at the stove, pouring so much butter over our popcorn, it practically *dripped* with the stuff. The look on his face the first time I called him Aaron.

"Did you sleep?" I ask, shuffling over to him and wrapping my arms around his waist from behind.

"Didn't want to." He shrugs, like spending the night watching me breathe is just what he does now.

Nightmares woke me more than once. Memories of the ceremony that almost killed me slowly piecing themselves together. Each time, I found him sitting up, his back against the headboard, and his gaze fixed on me.

Dark circles smudge AJ's eyes, but he pours the hot water into my mug, gives it a stir, and passes it to me. Tenderness softens his expression, the deep, all-consuming *love* we've found for the second time so very obvious in his gaze.

Steam curls between us, and I lose myself in the ritual—the familiar comfort of sharing my coffee with him—before I find the courage to speak again.

"I think I know when it happened. When the piece of bone...when it broke off."

His jaw tenses, teeth grinding together for a beat. "When?"

I force myself to meet his eyes. "The night the chief came. I fell, and...I think my head hit the floor."

He slams his coffee cup down on the counter, and the handle snaps off in his hand. "Christ, Grace. That was two weeks ago! Why the hell didn't you say anything?"

His sudden anger, along with the complete destruction of his favorite mug, is so unlike him, it takes me a moment to muster enough composure to reply. But after a breath, my own frustration rises to the surface.

"Oh, I don't know. Maybe because I was busy having a panic attack? Then we had to figure out how to keep me from being dragged in front of the cameras, or into an interrogation room before I was ready?"

My voice rises higher and sharper than I intend, but a part of me doesn't care. "You picked me up off the floor, AJ. *I* remember that. Do you?

"I also remember your brother and Emi were here. Connor. Parker. Then Nate showed up.

"I could barely find my voice in front of Jasper, let alone a man I'd never met before! What did you expect me to do? Wave my hands in the middle of all that and say, 'I've got a little bit of a headache'?"

AJ stares at me, eyes blazing, knuckles white around the broken handle of the mug. "But it wasn't just a headache, was it? The tremor in your hand on Monday night? The dizziness last week? The vertigo?"

I'd roll my eyes if they weren't so dry and swollen from crying myself to sleep. "I've had those symptoms since I woke up in the clinic in Mexico. Was there some magical way I was supposed to be able to tell what was new and what was just... normal for me now? I wasn't hiding things from you, AJ. I didn't know. Not for sure."

He finally lets go of the broken piece of the mug, spreading his palms flat on the counter and blowing out a breath. "You still should have said something the second you suspected you were getting worse."

"Worse? AJ, look at me." He doesn't, and I take a step closer. "Really look at me. Please."

He lifts his head, and the raw anguish in his eyes hits me harder than a punch.

"I'm standing. On my own. I made it in here from the bedroom *on my own*. I've started to remember something new almost every day. I can leave the house now. I managed *ten* clothespins yesterday and put on my own damn bra. What part of that says 'worse' to you?"

His mouth opens, then shuts again. After a beat, he looks me square in the eyes. "The part where you faint in a parking lot."

I cross my arms tight over my chest, trying to hold myself together. "Is that what you think happened? I didn't *faint*. I had a panic attack. Because some asshole who *must* be connected to the men who took me left a bouquet of oleanders on Connor's truck. Because I remembered some of what they did to me that last day. But you never even asked me about *that*."

He jerks back like I just shoved him. Dragging his hands over his face, he shudders, and all the fight bleeds out of him in seconds. "Fuck. You're right, Grace. I should've asked. It guts me every goddamn time you remember even a fraction of the hell you went through. But that's on me. *You're* the one who survived it. Who's still survivin' it. You've had the weight of the fuckin' world on your shoulders since you came back, and all I've done this mornin' is add to it."

I drop my arms, my anger fading into something softer. "AJ, the only reason I've been brave enough to remember...is you. Because I know you love me. That you'll keep loving me no matter what they did to me."

He swallows hard, staring at me like I've just given him the whole damn world.

Taking one final step, I wrap my arms around him and tuck my head under his chin, pressing my cheek to his chest so I can hear the steady beat of his heart. "I love you, Aaron. I'll love you for the rest of my life. But those oleanders..." I squeeze my eyes shut against the tears threatening to spill over. "Someone followed us to that art store. Watched us. Got past Connor and Jasper to send me a message. They ain't done with me. And that scares me more than anything."

Not long after I finish my coffee—and AJ has gotten a fresh mug for himself—a nurse shows up with a portable ultrasound machine. It takes her all of ninety seconds to declare my intracranial pressure "within normal limits" and remind us she'll be back at six to check again.

"I got the names from VanHorn," AJ says, leaning against the door of my studio while I stare at a blank page, pencil in hand. "The neurosurgeons she recommended. Zephyr vetted them for me. Dr. Ellicott out of Chicago has the best rep. VanHorn says she can work it out so he can do the surgery here. At Austin Memorial. But he's only available this Saturday."

The tip of my pencil wobbles over the paper. A faint gray dot turns into a messy line, the start of something I have no idea how to finish.

"It's so...soon." My voice is steadier than I expect, but when my hands start to shake, I drop the pencil and press them against my thighs. I can't look at AJ. I don't want him to see how scared I am. "What if...what if I wake up and everything's...*gone?*"

"Grace..."

"I know I can't put it off forever. But he—this *Prophet*—won't stop until he's killed me." I finally turn, and the look on my husband's face would reassure me if not for those damn flowers. "If I lose the few memories I have, I can't protect myself."

AJ pushes off the door frame, closing the distance between us in three strides. His hand curls around the back of my neck, steady and sure.

"You ain't losin' shit, Grace. Not as long as you let them cut that thing out of you. And this *Prophet* sure as hell ain't gonna get his hands on you again. I'll burn this whole goddamn city to the ground before I let that happen. Jasper, Connor, Parker, Nate—hell, I'll even take Marvin's help if I have to—will be standin' guard the whole damn time. During the surgery. For as long as you have to stay in the hospital. And when you come home again. You will be protected. Period. End of story. You hear me?"

I nod, and though I'm still terrified, I know he's right. The only chance I have to truly get my life back depends on this surgery. If I can get through that, I can get through anything.

CHAPTER SIXTY-FOUR

AJ

THE FIRE POPS and cracks behind the glass insert, and Grace tucks herself tighter against my side. She's been cold all day, and even wrapped in a blanket with Belle curled up at her feet, her hands are pale and clammy.

Physically, she's stable. For now. But damn if I don't want to surround her in bubble wrap to keep her that way. If she falls— or if the bone fragment moves—it could be debilitating.

I can't lose her. I won't survive it a second time.

Zephyr leans closer to her webcam, face lit by the blue glow of the monitors around her. "I pulled everything I could from a two-mile radius around the art supply store," she says. "The best angle I found was from a pawn shop on the corner."

The screen splits, and a grainy video reveals a man in a dark hoodie and jeans, sunglasses hiding his eyes, carrying a tightly wrapped bouquet of white and pink oleander flowers.

"He gets off a bus a block over, hangs at the edge of the parking lot for a few minutes, then double-times it to Connor's truck when a couple of cars block your view from the store's front windows."

"That's it?" Parker's hushed tone doesn't hide her frustration. But, she's sittin' less than twenty feet from Harris's office pretending to go through receipts for the fucking motor pool. I'm amazed she hasn't imploded already.

"He waits to make sure Grace sees the flowers before he takes off. But he's no fool. Never picks his head up, never removes the hood, never takes off the sunglasses. I can tell you he's five-foot-nine, close to two hundred pounds, but that's it."

"Fuckin' hell," Jasper mutters from the armchair next to us. "Here I was thinkin' we'd be going after yahoos chanting in the woods by candlelight. Not whatever black-ops rejects these sombitches are."

Connor takes himself off mute and clears his throat. "Mikayla got the flowers this morning, but she doesn't think they're gonna tell us anything. Oleanders bloom in late spring and summer. These were likely from a hothouse somewhere."

"It was the smell," Grace says softly. She's twisting the corner of the blanket hard enough, I'm surprised it's still in one piece. "That's why I panicked. He—everyone called him Prophet—held this...ceremony on the full moon. That's what I've been drawing. The lanterns. The altar. It's where I..." Her voice cracks, so tiny it sounds like she's about to disappear.

Sliding my palm over hers, I give her hand a gentle squeeze. "You're safe, darlin'. No one's gonna hurt you here."

She nods, though I'm not sure she believes me. Still, she lifts her gaze to the orange light on my laptop. "It's where I was supposed to die. He poisoned me first. I don't know how I know that, but I do. Then tied me down on that altar under the lanterns. The flowers...they were everywhere. All around me. In my hair. In the ropes. I couldn't breathe, the scent was so thick. And people were...chanting. Or singing. But I can't remember the words. I just know it hurt. God, I hurt everywhere."

She presses her hands to her chest, her breath stuttering, shallow enough I'm worried she's about to hyperventilate.

"Grace, look at me." I nudge her chin up. The fear in her blue-green eyes does me in. "Stay here, darlin'. Tell us the rest, but stay here. There's no poison. No flowers. No ropes. There's just Belle and me and home."

The dog jumps up onto the couch and stretches across our legs until she can slide her head under Grace's hands.

"I...wasn't Grace there. I was Nova." Tears spill down her cheeks. "He took my *name* from me, AJ. He took *everything*. All so he could have his ceremony. So he could tie me down and stab me."

"Can you describe him?" Parker asks.

Grace swallows a sob. "No. I...knew I was panicking. I could hear Jasper. Then AJ. I held on to your voices because I was so scared. I didn't want to remember what it felt like to die. God. I should've been braver—"

"No. Fuck, darlin'. You've been fightin' monsters every day for three years. I don't know a single person who's braver. Who could fight harder. And look around you. There are some pretty damn brave people in this room." The words escape harsher than I intend, but I don't soften my tone. "This is more than we've had yet, and it's all because of you."

"Hey, don't forget the two cowards at the station," Hardison says. "While you're over there facing down nightmares every day on the regular, Parker and I are armed with keyboards, coffee that could strip paint, and a pact that if Harris yells too loud, we run."

Grace hides a snort behind her hand. "God, Nate. You're making my panic attacks sound like a weekly staff meeting."

"Don't encourage him," Parker says. "Or he'll put them on

an *actual* calendar. Color-coded, categorized, and everything. It'll be a literal work of art."

I'm about to remind the two of them that this is serious—that in three days, my wife is having fucking brain surgery—when Grace sits up a little straighter at my side. "Parker, you're brilliant."

"Tell that to the chief," she mutters. "He thinks my *talents* are best spent on fuel efficiency calculations and auditing the motor pool's yearly maintenance bills. But...go on..."

Grace turns to me. Her unsteady fingers comb through Belle's fur. "The board in your office... You'd pieced together a timeline of my day. At least...until my phone stopped moving. I went to my classroom. That's where I started my run?"

"Yeah, darlin'. I found your car in the lot. It's...been in the garage ever since."

Her breath catches in her throat. "I went to meet a student. He turned in a painting. His final project, I think. I can't quite see it. I remember thinking it was beautiful in an eerie sort of way. But I didn't understand what I was looking at. I think it was a painting...of the ceremony. Of...*me*."

Fuck.

Parker whistles softly. "We need to find that painting. And whoever turned it in."

ZEPHYR TAKES down everything Grace has remembered so far. A man calling himself *Prophet*. Forcing Grace to give up her name and become *Nova*. Men dressing in dark gray pants and lighter gray shirts. The lanterns, hammered metal with thick, faceted glass and an oleander leaf etched on the bottom. How cold it was the night Prophet tried to kill her. Snowflakes falling and stinging her cheeks. The poison working its way through her veins. A painting so beautiful, she couldn't look away.

I don't want her to relive any of it. But she's proven, time and time again, that she might panic, she might stumble, she might even fall, but she won't break. She won't back down. She'll survive.

And she'll give me hell when I deserve it. Like now.

"AJ, I won't spend every minute until my surgery locked away in this house. If those paintings are still somewhere at the school, I'm the one who has the best chance of finding them." A hint of color tinges her cheeks. "If we go now, we'll be back before the nurse gets here at six. Parker and Nate can meet us there. If it turns out I'm wrong, fine. At least I'll know I tried. That I didn't just sit here waiting for the inevitable."

I let out a rough breath. She's flushed, alive with purpose for the first time since the art store, and I can't—I won't—smother her. Not with surgery hanging over our heads like an axe about to fall.

"All right, darlin'. We'll go." I tuck a lock of hair behind her right ear, and let my thumb linger at the curve of her jaw. "But the second you so much as sway on your feet, we're done. No arguments. You're worth more to me than answers ever could be."

Belle trots over to us, the mobility harness held carefully between her teeth. *Fuck*. She knows what I'm just startin' to figure out. Grace needs to be an active member of this team. And I have to let her.

CHAPTER SIXTY-FIVE

Grace

THE PARKING LOT is mostly empty when we arrive. "Wednesdays were always early days," AJ says, his hand at the small of my back as we make our way to the art building.

I don't remember my car. Or coming here day after day. But the rain slicked leaves are vaguely familiar. They have a scent I used to savor. Fresh and green and teeming with possibilities.

Parker tells AJ to watch our backs, then replaces him on my left side. She doesn't push. Doesn't try to give me a pep talk. She just...is. And that's enough to keep me moving forward.

"You doin' okay?" she finally asks. There's no pity in her voice. Just a hint of concern. Along with a quiet resignation that makes me think she's asked this question before. Another person. Another time. Someone she cared for.

"Not really," I admit, the honesty shocking even to me. I tuck my left hand into the pocket of my jeans. "I can't stop thinking about the surgery. About what I could lose."

Parker angles her shoulder just enough it brushes mine. The contact grounds me. "You won't lose anything, hon. And

I'll be there the whole time. Before, during, and after. You want chick flicks? Queso? Popcorn? I'll bring 'em by the truckload."

"What if I can't stand up without falling over?" I ask, my voice not much above a whisper.

"Then I'll have AJ bring your favorite pajamas, and I'll perform my civic duty once again. Just don't ask me to braid your hair this time. It's too short now." She cracks a smile, then winks at me. "But once you've healed up, I still need to even out those ends for you."

The knot in my chest had been getting tighter and tighter since Dr. VanHorn told us about the bone fragment. But with just a few words from Parker, it fades away.

Behind us, Nate gives a low whistle. "You two are walking like you're about to storm the castle. Which, for the record, is not in my contract. I was promised a short field trip with minimal cult activity and maximum climate control."

I glance back at him, his lanky frame an odd mix of sharp angles and slouching curves. He looks more like a student lost on his first day than an armed escort into the land of my night-mares. Yet, his eyes never stop moving, sweeping from side to side, and pausing on every car, at every voice—no matter how far away.

"Don't worry," I say. "If anything goes wrong, you can distract them with your perfectly organized calendar and Park-er's motor pool audits."

"Finally, someone recognizes my true calling," Nate dead-pans. "Weaponized spreadsheets."

Parker snorts, the corners of her mouth quirking briefly before she touches the butt of her gun. Like she needs to reas-sure herself it's still there.

Belle trots along at my side, and after a moment, I realize I'm smiling. I'm still terrified of Saturday's surgery. Still abso-lutely positive the cult will find a way to get to me. To finish what they started. But right now, I'm walking under my own power, surrounded by my husband, the first real friend I made as the person I am now, and her partner, who slips jokes into the conversation so easily, I forget to panic—and start to laugh.

I'm not broken. I'm the closest to whole I've been in three years. And I won't stop fighting until I get there.

AJ UNLOCKS the door to what used to be my classroom, but Parker steps over the threshold before I can move. She scans the room, her gaze seeking out any shadows hiding in dark corners. After a moment, she nods, then turns to AJ. "Hang back a little. Grace needs to do this on her own."

His eyes lock on me, searching, quietly asking if this is truly what I want.

"I've got this." I force a tight, brief smile. His hand brushes mine, warm but fleeting, before he steps back into the hall.

Parker nods at the easels arranged in three distinct rows facing the whiteboard. A vague memory flashes behind my eyelids. I always had my students in a semi-circle so no one felt *watched* as they worked.

The scents of turpentine and oils are mostly hidden by bleach and cheap air freshener. It's almost...lemony. And it turns my stomach.

Canvases line the wall, all bright and eager—landscapes and bowls of fruit and flowers.

After three years, if any of my former students' pieces *are* still here, they won't be out in the open. I tighten my grip on Belle's harness—not to help me walk, but to keep me calm. She nudges my thigh with a little inquisitive grunt.

Nate's voice drifts in from the hall. "How much you want to bet campus security is already on their way? We look like a heist crew, and Cap's got resting murder face."

I almost laugh. Nate isn't wrong.

The cabinets far in the back look like they haven't been used in years. Dusty and forgotten behind stacks of chairs, collapsed easels, and folded drop cloths.

My body remembers what my mind doesn't, and I sink down to my knees in front of one where the door isn't quite true.

The lock sticks, but my fingers know what to do. Lift, jiggle, twist. It pops open, and I take a deep breath.

There are only three canvases inside. The first is an idyllic landscape at sunset. Good use of color and shading, though mostly unoriginal. The signature looks almost like "Shelby."

Next, a weeping willow tree with a picnic spread out underneath it. This one's rough. Almost forced.

My heartbeat quickens, and I scrub my damp palms over my thighs. If the painting I remember is here, I'm about to see it for the first time in three years. About to see...*myself* in its darkness.

I'm shaking now, and almost topple over as I slide it out of the cabinet. I could stop. Tell AJ I want to go home. But that won't keep me safe. So I take a deep breath and turn the painting around.

The night sky consumes the top of the canvas. Tiny stars dot the midnight blue expanse, with a glowing moon in the corner, hauntingly full. A crowd of people gather along the fringes, some with their hands pressed together in prayer, others on their knees.

I have to force my gaze to the center. Tears prick at my eyes. The woman has her arms raised to the sky, facing the moon. She wears a white dress, and her long, blond hair is held in place by a crown of pink, white, and red flowers.

Parker is suddenly kneeling next to me, her fingers squeezing my arm. "Grace. Breathe. I've got you."

I blink up at her. The painting lies on the floor in front of me. No longer in my hands. I touch my fingers to my cheek and find it soaked with tears.

"Well, son of a bitch," Nate says, peering over my shoulder. "I think we just found ourselves a cult member."

AJ shoves one of the stacks of chairs away and angles the canvas to get a better look at the bottom corner. "J.N." He pulls out his phone and starts flipping through his Notes app like it holds all the secrets of the universe. "Goddammit. We had him. And we let him go."

"Who?" Parker asks. She has her arm around my shoulders now, and I lean against her. Seeing my death depicted as something almost *beautiful* has shaken me in ways I can't explain. I don't even know that I can speak.

"Joshua Nichols," AJ mutters. "He emailed Grace a few days before she disappeared and asked if he could turn in his final project that Saturday. She said no—because we were goin' up to the cabin. But when Harris ordered us on that stakeout, Grace agreed to meet him. Kid had a rock solid alibi. Went from here directly to his bachelor party and was at a bar with half a dozen of his friends until closing."

Nate tucks the canvas under his arm. "Well, I think we've done our part to introduce Grace to new experiences today. This concludes Breaking and Entering for Beginners. Let's get out of here before this turns into Evading Rent-A-Cops 101."

AJ helps me to my feet, and with his arm around my waist and Belle at my side, we make it to his SUV seconds before a campus security vehicle pulls up to the curb.

I lean against Belle in the back seat, and a wave of dizziness threatens to send me pitching right over. But I don't think the bone shard in my head is the cause.

This is the closest I've been to remembering Prophet's face, and I'm terrified of what will happen when I do.

CHAPTER SIXTY-SIX

AJ

Joshua Nichols is a fucking ghost.

A single call to one of Grace's friends in the admissions office got me a copy of his transcripts. In addition to Introduction to Oil Painting, he took 3D Printing Fundamentals, something called Advanced Additive Manufacturing, Renewable Energy Systems 101, Sustainable Agriculture, and two quarters of Metal Shop.

Useful shit for someone playing survivalist for the rest of their lives.

But there's nothing else. No leases in his name. No vehicle registration. Hell, not even a driver's license, birth certificate, or social security number. It's like the kid just *appeared* one day, signed up for classes, then vanished fifteen months later—the same day Grace did.

Someone purposely scrubbed all traces of him from the system.

I drag my hands over my face, stubble scratching against my

palms, but doing nothing to quell the itch under my skin. The one that says this kid is the key to finding out who took her.

Grace has a vague memory of him turning in his painting. She even managed to sketch him last night. I stare at it until my eyes burn. He looks like the stereotypical white, Texas twenty-one year old. Broad shouldered, fit, with dark eyes and short-cropped dark hair.

Austin PD finally got a hold of him two full weeks after Grace disappeared. But he'd moved to some podunk town in Iowa—or so he'd claimed. His alibi checked out, so they never pushed for more than a phone interview.

Fucking idjits. If all of Joshua's so-called friends *and* the bar owner who claimed he spent the entire afternoon and evening celebrating his bachelor party aren't cult members, I'll eat my Stetson.

I push to my feet and head for the break room—and yet another cup of coffee so bitter, it's probably eating a hole in my stomach—only to find Marvin pulling a container of yogurt out of the fridge. I almost turn right around, but without another hit of caffeine, I'll fall asleep and drool all over Joshua's transcripts.

"AJ? You got a minute?" Marvin asks.

I pin my gaze to my mug as I pour. "Nope."

"Please, man. I fucked up, and it's been eatin' at me somethin' fierce." The shame in his voice is such a change from his usual cockiness, that I set the cup down and glance over at him. "I thought I was lookin' out for you. I know how hard you took it when McGrath and Billings were killed last year. But I didn't say a damn thing then, and I've been regrettin' it ever since."

A sharp pang of grief spears my chest. A drug ring murdered two of my lieutenants a few months ago to get to Isabel's daughter, Veronica. The young woman had evidence that could have sent the dealers to jail for the rest of their lives. If they'd lived. Connor and I made that a non-issue.

"They were good men." I lift my mug in a vague salute toward the remembrance wall at the far end of the bullpen.

"Two of our finest," Marvin agrees. "Listen...goin' to Harris like I did...it was out of line. I didn't mean for all that shit to land on Grace like that. She's been through enough."

He takes a step closer, and his tone softens even more. "Look, it's gotta be tough, man. You get her back and then find out she's gotta have fuckin' *brain* surgery? What do you need? Is there anythin' I can do to help? Run interference with Harris? Take shifts at the hospital? Start a meal train?"

For a long moment, I don't have an answer for him. If it weren't for his CIs—and Harris's unwavering confidence in a man too lazy to go out on his own stakeouts—we would've been up at the cabin that weekend. I've never forgiven him for that. Even if he couldn't have known what would happen.

The cult would have come for her anyway. But maybe...I'd have been there to stop them.

"We're good, Marvin. But...thanks." I sidestep him, but he grabs my arm.

"You stickin' by her through all this... Most men would've cut and run. That kind of love is worth fightin' for, Stone. Don't ever stop."

TALKING with Marvin leaves me off balance and desperate to get home to Grace. But when I told Harris that I'd be takin' tomorrow and all next week off, he almost fired me on the spot.

"If we weren't so damn understaffed already, I'd cut you both loose faster than greased lightning. But knowin' you—and Elmore— you'd keep showin' up anyway. Probably find some fuckin' medical leave law that says I can't fire you while your wife's under the knife."

So Parker and I are stuck here until the chief walks out

the door. At least Hardison is still on Harris's good side. We need *someone* who can come and go without constant scrutiny. He's gonna pay the bar owner who alibied Joshua Nichols a visit.

Unable to focus on much else, I shut myself in my office and call Zephyr.

The video call connects in seconds. "Tell me you've got *somethin'* on Joshua Nichols, Nova, Prophets, or any large players in the power market." I take a sip of coffee, grimace, and set the mug aside. Battery acid would be healthier.

"AJ, I'm working half a dozen different angles all at once. I don't get out of this chair unless it's for tea, sleep, or sex, and there's been precious little sex lately."

"Fuck, Zephyr. I...I'm sorry." A flush crawls up the back of my neck. If I've learned one thing about the woman in the past two weeks, it's that she ain't gonna sugar coat a thing. Not for me or anyone else.

"I'm buying a walking pad this weekend. At least then I won't be sitting on my ass twelve hours a day."

The screen splits, and Zephyr overlays a map with half a dozen green dots. "Grace was taken three years ago. And I'd bet my *considerable* skills, the cult didn't pop into existence because some kid saw her tattoo. So I've been going through the past ten years of bulk solar panel purchases."

"Ten years?" I rub the back of my neck. "Fuck, Zephyr. You think they've been operatin' that long?"

"Minimum," she says. "Cults don't sprout up overnight. Neither do cartels for that matter. It takes years to amass enough infrastructure, move people off the grid, and ensure their loyalty. Or their compliance. Solar panels are just *one* fingerprint. They couldn't exactly get these delivered with free overnight shipping, so I dug into industrial distributors...down to the freight logs."

Zephyr highlights one of the green dots. West Texas.

Another deep in East Texas. One in New Mexico. Oklahoma. With each possible location, my gut tightens even more.

"More than a dozen bulk purchases in the last decade don't align with businesses or legit co-ops. No schools, no ranches, no solar farms. Just pallets of panels disappearing into nowhere."

"Fuck," I mutter. "And no idea if any of them could be theirs?"

On screen, Zephyr leans back, cracking her neck from side to side. "I can narrow it down a little based on locations that were cold enough to induce hypothermia the night Grace was dumped. But that still leaves me with at least seven leads to chase down. I'm cross-referencing with shell companies that also made secondary orders. Bulk fertilizer, water filtration systems, razor wire..."

"We gotta get closer. Grace's surgery—"

"I'm working as fast as I can. But...there's something else we've got to talk about. Remember that broken piece of plastic that was found in the burlap bag with Grace's body?"

I sit up straighter, frustration raising the hairs on the back of my neck. "Fucking hell. I do now. Why is this the first you're mentioning it?"

"It ended up in the bag with the ropes and the oleander flowers. Mikayla thought it was just some random piece of plastic and set it aside. But when Pritchard picked her up from her lab yesterday, he took one look at it and knew exactly what it was."

"Well, spit it out." My chest is already tight, and I force myself to breathe.

"It's part of a firing pin. PLA filament, 3D printed. No serial number."

"Ghost guns. *Christ.*" I rake a hand through my hair. "That's cartel shit. The Cordova Cartel has been flooding the black market with ghost guns for the past five years now. Both here *and* in Mexico. Untraceable. Hell, when Jas got blown up, he was lookin' for evidence the cartel was storin' the raw materials in a warehouse down on Grand."

I shouldn't finish the sludge in my cup, but it gives me a beat before I have to give voice to my rage. "So the bastards who stole Grace from her life, who put her through three goddamn years of hell, are in bed with the cartel that almost killed my brother. The one I've been chasin' for near my entire career."

Zephyr's expression doesn't change. But her voice carries a sharp edge. "Whoever this Prophet is, he's smart. Which means finding him just got a hell of a lot harder."

"It means more than that." I force the lump in my throat away. "It means Grace ain't safe anywhere. Not at our home, not in the hospital. Not even in my fuckin' arms."

Zephyr leans forward, understanding in her eyes. "Then we'll have to find them before they find her."

"For fuck's sake, how?" I'm actively shaking, rage and fear churning in my gut so violently, I worry I'm about to be sick. "This ain't a cult livin' off the land and singing about the damn 'Glorious One' around a campfire every night. These bastards have firepower, and they ain't gonna be afraid to use it. Every step—every *single* move—we make from here on out just got a hell of a lot more dangerous. For all of us, but *especially* for Grace."

"AJ… In the past two days, we've learned more than in the whole of the last two weeks. Knowledge is power, and we're gonna ace whatever test gets thrown at us next. Go home. Be with Grace. As soon as I find *anything*, I'll call."

I lean back in my chair and close my eyes. One way or another, I'm gonna burn this cult—and the whole goddamn cartel—to the ground.

CHAPTER SIXTY-SEVEN

Grace

"I'll be fine." With Belle curled up next to me on the couch, a fire in the hearth, and blankets piled all around me, I might as well be covered in bubble wrap. Since we missed girls' night with our impromptu field trip to my old classroom—and I have no idea if I'll even remember Parker, Emi, and Isabel this time next week—after we met with Dr. Ellicott this morning, I told AJ I needed time alone with them tonight.

He tried to dissuade me. He's convinced Prophet is working with the Cordova Cartel. If he's right, I'm not safe anywhere. Not even here, with a security system that rivals that of Fort Knox and enough fire power to burn down half of Austin.

But he also won't deny me something this important. So, we compromised. The guys will hang out around the fire pit in the backyard until it gets too cold, then move their poker game into the heated garage while we hunker down in the fortress.

Emi and Jasper are the first to arrive. Emi carries a tote bag that looks like it could fit a week's worth of groceries, and sets a little potted plant next to me on the side table. "I figured flowers were a no-go, but this little guy can come with you to the hospital," she says before heading straight for the kitchen.

Isabel and Connor are only five minutes behind. This time, it's Connor who hefts a giant bag while Isabel digs a pair of fuzzy purple socks out of her purse and drops them in my lap. "For after surgery. They have those little gripper dots on them and they're super warm. Veronica loved hers after she got out of the hospital."

Finally, Parker strides through the door like a woman on a mission. "All right, ladies. I brought the popcorn. What ridiculously funny and unrealistic movie are we watching tonight?"

I didn't realize how much I needed this until all three women descend on the living room. Emi spreads a blanket over the coffee table and lays out bottles of nail polish, a stack of eye masks, and a bag of neon-pink marshmallows.

"Girls' night emergency kit," she says with a smile. "The queso and a couple of enchilada plates from Taco Aranda are in the oven warming up."

My laugh surprises me. I wasn't sure I had it in me today. "Exactly what kind of emergency requires marshmallows *that* bright?"

"Every kind," Isabel says. "Tonight, we eat until we regret all of our life choices. Or none of them. It could really go either way."

Belle hops off the couch and settles at my feet. Almost as if she knows tonight isn't about her. Parker sinks down in the vacated space beside me. She's quiet for a minute, scanning the room, listening to the hum of the guys' voices from the back deck. Until she nudges my shoulder with hers. "You're not alone, Grace. Not tonight. Not Saturday. Not ever."

The words break me. Crack my heart open until all my worries and tears spill out in silent sobs.

Parker wraps me in her arms, her hand gently cradling the back of my head. Emi slides her hip onto the arm of the couch on my other side. Isabel crouches in front of me. And these women, who've become my closest friends, hold me until I can breathe again.

"I'm scared," I whisper. "What if I wake up and I don't remember AJ? Or any of you?"

"That's not going to happen," Emi says when she and Isabel extricate themselves from the group hug. "But you know what we'd do if—worst case—it did? We'd just make new memories. We're not going anywhere, Grace. You're one of us now. There's no leaving the friend group. Not allowed."

Isabel's dark eyes meet mine. "I know we don't have years and years of inside jokes or whispered secrets or outrageous escapades. But we'll still be here to fill in every blank until you're absolutely sick of us."

Parker slides her arm from my shoulders and swipes a tear from her cheek. "I—" Her voice is so raw, so utterly wrecked, that we all turn to her. "I watched my mom lose pieces of herself every day. Hardest thing I've ever lived through. But...it taught me something important."

I draw her against me, and she releases a shaky breath.

"Love doesn't *need* memories. Love finds its way, even when the brain doesn't cooperate."

Her words hang in the air for several seconds before she reaches for my hand and gives it a gentle squeeze. "AJ would burn down the world for you, Grace. Then walk through the flames without a second thought to bring you back to him. And he'd do it again and again and again."

A fresh wave of tears spills down my cheeks. She's right. I know she's right because even when I didn't know who *I* was, when I had no idea if anyone had *ever* loved me, something deep inside me trusted AJ—*knew* AJ.

We found one another. Twice. If we have to, we'll do it again.

"Of all the choices I've made and don't remember, there's one I'm sure of. You, Aaron. It's always been you."

Emi passes tissues to everyone. "Crying is allowed tonight, Grace. But only if you let me paint your toes while you do it." She shakes a bottle of glittery purple polish that looks like it came from a mermaid's treasure chest.

"You did *not* have that color at home, did you?" I say, laughing through the last few tears.

"I plead the fifth." She pulls a small spa pillow out of her bag and sets it on the coffee table. "Foot, please."

Isabel opens a bottle of wine, pours three glasses, then hesitates. "Grace?"

"The doctor said I could have one drink tonight and one cup of coffee tomorrow. Then it's nothing but decaffeinated tea and water."

"Well, then it's a good thing I splurged on the expensive bottle," she says.

Parker, still quiet, disappears down the hall to AJ's office for a minute, then returns with a stack of index cards and a handful of colorful pens. She waits until Emi finishes with the first coat of polish, then passes each of us a card and a pen.

"Last serious task of the night," she says. "We all write down a memory with Grace. Doesn't have to be important or big. Just...real. Grace, you can pick a memory with one of us, with AJ, with Belle, or alone."

"You realize you're making me break the rules, right?" I ask as more tears threaten. "Emi can't write and paint my toes at the same time, and I'm gonna cry again."

Parker shrugs. "Sorry, not sorry."

For a few minutes, no one speaks. I stare at my blank card, wondering how I pick from all the happy memories I've made since coming home. There are so many.

Eventually, I settle on the one that surprised me the most.

> *You all welcomed me to girls' night with hugs, a*
> *bowl of queso, and margaritas. And I remembered how*
> *to laugh again.*

Parker, Emi, and Isabel slide their cards into my hand. I cradle them carefully, because though they're nothing but paper, they hold the weight of solid gold.

The first one is Isabel's.

> *I remember how hard you laughed when Belle*
> *tried to lick the empty bowl of queso and got a poblano*
> *stuck to her tongue.*

Emi's is next.

> *I remember your smile when you told me you liked*
> *purple. Right then, I knew you'd found a piece of your-*
> *self again.*

Parker's is the most serious, her handwriting neat and precise.

> *You became my family the first time you trusted me*
> *with your fears. I'll never forget that moment. Or any*
> *of the ones after.*

I clutch the cards to my chest, unable to speak. No matter what happens on Saturday, I'll survive. I'll remember.

Because my friends—my family—won't accept any other outcome.

Emi starts in on my toes again. Isabel offers me a marshmallow so bright, it can probably be seen from space, and Parker gives my hand a squeeze.

I'm still nervous about the surgery. Still terrified Prophet will find me. But I'm not alone. And if the worst happens...I know I'll never be forgotten.

CHAPTER SIXTY-EIGHT

AJ

GRACE SNUGGLES CLOSER, cheek pressed against my chest, her hair a tangle under my chin. I don't dare move. Not when everything we've worked so hard to reclaim could be ripped away from us tomorrow.

I trace patterns along her shoulder blade. God, her skin is so soft. Delicate. The scars under my fingers remind me of what she's endured. How much she's already lost. Three goddamn years. Three years of smiles. Of laughter. Of freedom.

Yet somehow, she fought her way back. To me. To herself.

I press my lips to the crown of her head, breathing her in like I can memorize the shape of her soul. She smells like gardenia and graphite and jasmine—like home. My home.

What if I never wake up like this again? To the weight of her body pressed against mine. To the way her heartbeat stutters when she dreams. To the quiet sighs she makes when she finally succumbs to sleep.

I squeeze my eyes shut, fear clawing its way up my throat. I want to believe I'm strong enough to carry her through this storm. But I'm not. I lost her once. If I lose her again, I won't survive.

Grace's lashes flutter, and I brush my thumb along her temple. "Mornin', darlin'. You want me to bring you some coffee? Or should we stay in bed for a while?"

"Mmm. Bed. Then coffee. Then more bed."

I chuckle, but the sound is rough as I wrap my arms around her. If it were up to me, we'd stay here forever. Avoiding the world and pretending nothing—and no one—would ever tear us apart again.

But as soon as we get up, I know that's not an option. Her hands shake, and she braces herself against the wall every few steps.

Still, she insists on helping with breakfast. And even though she burns the first two slices of bacon, I declare them the best I've ever had.

After the dishes are done, Belle drops her leash at my feet, her tail wagging like she just *knows* today's a day the women of this house can have anything they want.

Then again, how is that different from any other day? Grace could ask me for the moon and I'd find a way to lasso it out of the night sky.

I kneel in front of Belle, running my hand over the top of her head. "Not today, girl. Your mama needs to rest."

"AJ..." Grace wobbles to her feet from her spot on the couch. "It's warm outside. I want to feel the sun on my cheeks. And walk our dog. Together."

She takes it slow, refusing the walker but hanging onto my arm. Belle runs circles around us, dropping the tennis ball at my feet time and time again as we wander down to the edge of the lake and then back up to the house.

The promise of spring is in the air. And for a short time, the world doesn't feel like it's on fire.

"Our girl ain't gonna know what to do if you have to stay in the hospital for a few days," I say, keeping my tone light. Even teasing. "She'll probably go on a hunger strike."

Grace shifts closer, resting her head on my shoulder. "She loves you too, AJ."

I nod and press a kiss to the top of her head. Grace isn't wrong. Belle does love me. But she looks for Grace when the house gets too quiet. She sits at Grace's side in the studio, ready to defend her against anything—even her own memories. She sleeps with her nose tucked against Grace's foot. Like if they aren't touchin', Grace will just...disappear. Again.

The truth hits, harder and faster than any bullet. I'm not afraid of Grace being in the hospital for a few days. I'm fucking terrified she won't come home at all.

CHAPTER SIXTY-NINE

Grace

WRAPPED in blankets on the couch, my sketchpad balanced on my thighs, I try to draw AJ. He's in the kitchen making my favorite meal—extra spicy enchiladas—and he looks so serious.

I manage his hair. His forehead. His dark brows. His eyes. But then my hand starts to shake. What ends up on the page looks nothing like the man I love.

AJ brings me a cup of tea, presses a kiss to my forehead, and stares down at my half-finished attempt.

"I'm better at this when..." My throat tightens, trapping the words in my chest.

When my brain isn't breaking in real time. When I'm not hours away from someone cutting into my skull. When I'm not terrified I'm about to lose everything.

He eases himself down, and takes the sketchbook. His big hand dwarfs the pencil. With a frown, his tongue trapped between his teeth, he starts to sketch. Quick, simple lines, his gaze flicking up to my face once. Twice.

In just a couple of minutes, he turns the pad around.

Two stick figures. One with long hair. Both with huge, lopsided grins.

The laugh starts deep in my belly, and before I know it, I can barely breathe with the force of it. "That's...awful."

"Everyone's a critic," he murmurs. "This is true genius."

My laugh crumbles into a sob before I can stop it. I cover my face with my hands, my whole body shaking as I finally let go of all the fear I've been holding in for so long.

AJ wraps his arms around me, tugging me to his chest, holding on like he'll never let go. "I've got you, darlin'." His voice is rough and steady, but breaks on the last word. "No matter what happens tomorrow, I've got you."

I want to believe him. God, I want to.

But tomorrow feels like a cliff, and I'm standing at the edge.

ALTHOUGH IT'S UNUSUALLY warm for late March, AJ builds a fire after dinner. He says it'll help me sleep tonight, but that's not the reason. He needed something to do with his hands besides hold me.

Curled up on the couch, Belle wedged between us like a furry chaperone, we try to watch a movie. But neither one of us pays much attention to the screen, and finally, he turns it off completely.

"I'm scared," I whisper to break the oppressive silence filling the space between us. "More than I've ever been. Even more than...when I knew I was about to die."

AJ's hand finds mine. The calluses I don't remember getting have finally faded, and his fingers are rough in comparison. Solid. Real.

"Me too." The words are so raw, so ragged, they hit like knives, stripping away the last of my resolve to stay strong.

I blink against the sting in my eyes. "If I don't remember...or if I don't wake up at all—"

"Don't." His grip tightens. "Don't you dare."

Tears spill anyway, carving hot trails down my cheeks. "I have to say it. I need you to know—Aaron, you're the reason I'm still here. You're why I fought when it would've been easier to give up. Why I've remembered anything at all. Why...I have to do this even though it could be the end of... *me.*"

His shoulders heave with one deep, shuddering breath. Hauling me into his lap—right over Belle—he touches his forehead to mine. "Grace, you listen now. If there's one thing I know —one thing I'd bet my life on—it's that you're gonna wake up. You're gonna come back to me. Again. And we're gonna live the rest of our lives knowin' that we can survive *anything* else this world throws at us."

I bury my face in AJ's neck, ugly, rough, loud sobs tearing out of me. He rocks me, whispers reassurances into my hair, and presses his lips to my temple like he can anchor me to this world by sheer will alone.

When I have no more tears to cry, I raise my head. His eyes are wet too. I cup his cheek, and he leans into my touch. "If... *shit.* I don't want our last memories of each other to be of fear."

His gaze churns, the blue depths of his eyes darkening. "Then give me this instead."

And he kisses me.

Slowly. Achingly. Reverently.

It's a promise. A reminder of everything we've fought for. Everything we can't lose.

When we finally break apart, I'm breathless. AJ carries me to the bedroom and lays me down, stretching out next to me and flicking open the buttons of my flannel shirt one at a time.

There's no rush, no desperation. When he's shed his clothes and I'm left in just my bra and panties, I start to kiss him. His jaw. His neck. His collarbone. The hollow of his throat. Down his chest. Across his abs.

I commit every line, every ridge, every muscle to memory, praying it's not all for nothing. As I reach his erection, I realize the truth. Even if I don't wake up tomorrow—or if I do, but everything is somehow...gone again—this night, this day, this love we have...it's everything.

We are everything.

I press a kiss to his crown, tasting him. Salty. Strong. Mine.

"Grace, I need to be inside you," he whispers. "Please. Let me make love to you."

I turn on my side, letting him unhook my bra and slide my panties down my hips. His arm wraps around my waist from behind, and I fit my back against his chest. Why does this position feel so right?

AJ guides his length to my channel, and God, he fills me so completely. "This was always your favorite," he murmurs and skims his lips over the shell of my ear. "How you liked me best. You always said it made you feel—"

"Cherished," I whisper.

I remember now. The truth of it clogs my throat, but I don't cry. I'm so lost in AJ. In this moment that's only for the two of us.

AJ starts to move his hips, and I meet him thrust for thrust.

Sensations build. He plays with my nipples, pinching and rolling them between his fingers. His teeth score the curve of my neck. I reach back and grab his ass, digging into the firm muscle and pulling him even harder against me.

His hand drifts lower. Over my mound. Down to my clit. He finds his rhythm, swirling his finger around the tight, aching nub as I arch my back and moan.

"Aaron...please..."

"I love you, Grace. Always," he says.

And with one last thrust, we fly over the edge together.

AJ's ARMS ARE A FORTRESS, holding me long after we've come down from our highs and Belle sprawls across our feet. When the nightmares come, his arms tighten, and he whispers the mantra that always brings me back from the edge of panic.

"You're home. You're safe. You're loved."

At some point in the night, I wake up to find him sitting against the headboard, his eyes open, watching me in the dim light from the hall.

"You're not sleeping," I slur, my voice rough.

His thumb brushes over my knuckles. "Didn't want to miss a second of time with you, darlin'."

I swallow my tears. He's carrying so much fear for the both of us, I can't add to it. Not now. Not this close to...the unknown. Instead, I prop myself up on an elbow, kiss him, and whisper, "Stay with me."

"I will. Every minute. Every heartbeat. Forever."

Sleep drags me under again, but this time I dream of him, not the dark shadows that want to swallow me whole.

Morning comes too quickly. My stomach is hollow, but even if I were allowed to eat, I couldn't. I'm too nauseous.

The hospital is too bright. The antiseptic smell too strong. The gown too rough. AJ never leaves my side. Not even as they wheel me toward pre-op.

At the double doors, he signals for the nurses to wait. We're on a schedule, and they try to rush him, but he fixes them with his hard, unyielding stare and practically growls, "You can give us two minutes."

They back off then. But not too far.

"I'm not ready," I whisper, fighting for each word.

AJ bends down so his lips brush my ear. "You don't have to be ready, darlin'. You just have to be you. Stubborn, brave, smart, kind, you. That's enough."

The nurses try to move in again, saying something about anesthesia, but I don't care. My whole world is right next to me.

"I'll be here when you wake up," he promises. "No matter what. The first thing you'll see when you open your eyes is me. I love you."

Tears blur his face, but I blink them back. I want one last clear view of him. One last memory. "I love you, Aaron. Always."

CHAPTER SEVENTY

AJ

THE DOUBLE DOORS SWING SHUT, and she's on the wrong side. Or maybe I am.

My chest feels like it's about to cave in. I don't move. I can't. My knuckles crack with how hard I'm clenching my fists. Hell, my entire body is shaking. I shouldn't have let her go. But this is the only chance she has of remaining...whole. At least as whole as she is now.

Every one of my instincts screams at me.

"Protect her!"

But this is the one battle she has to fight on her own.

Jasper squeezes my shoulder. Emi, Connor, Isabel, and Parker are only steps behind me, an immovable wall against anything that might come for her here. Hardison mutters something about coffee and distractions.

I close my eyes and pray like I've never prayed before.

"Please Grace. Please come back to me."

EACH TICK of the clock above the nurses' station might as well be a nail driving deep into my skull.

Four hours and seven minutes. The doctor said it could take up to six hours—assuming no complications.

Jasper paces, his muscles coiled like he's some caged animal ready to strike. Connor sits in the chair across from me, his gaze fixed on a stain in the middle of the scuffed linoleum. Emi and Isabel take shifts visiting the cafeteria, bringing back coffee and snacks no one eats.

Parker and Hardison are bent over their phones, pretending to focus on some stupid game, but every few minutes, one of them has to remind the other to take a turn.

They're not fooling anyone.

Connor runs a hand through his dark hair and blows out a breath. "AJ, this is shitty timing, but—"

"Whatever you're gonna say...save it. I ain't interested." I slump back in the hard plastic chair, wondering if every hospital in the world shops at the same supply store.

"The oleanders on Jasper's truck." Connor leans forward, elbows on his knees. "Either the cult or the cartel is watching us. Watching *her*. Hell, could be both of them for all we know. She's never gonna be safe until we take the bastards down."

"The doctors are *drillin' a hole in her skull*," I grit out. "I want these bastards six feet under. In pieces. But I ain't doin' a damn thing about that until Grace wakes up."

For several long moments, no one speaks. The harsh antiseptic is practically choking me. I'd give anything to be home right now. Curled up on the couch with Grace in my arms, the scent of her gardenia and jasmine perfume filling my nose.

"You've got a plan," Parker says, abandoning her phone and moving into the chair next to Connor. "What is it?"

The former FBI agent glances over at me, and eventually, I nod. "Spit it out. You're gonna tell me whether I want to hear it or not."

"What if we get Zephyr to alter her hospital records? Double down by leaking a story to the media—through Emi—that her surgery was so successful, she's being discharged early. Sent home. Give the bad guys a target they can't resist."

My gut clenches. "You want to use *my wife* as bait?"

"No." He shakes his head, the word sharp. "The opposite. Use *us*. If Jasper shaves the beard, he could easily pass for you behind the wheel of your SUV. I know Parker ain't leavin' this hospital for anything, but I've got an old FBI buddy who's about Grace's build. Slap a blond wig on her, along with a pair of dark glasses and a bandage? No one would suspect a thing.

"You, Parker, Hardison...you stay with Grace. Bring in a couple of your Ranger buddies if you want a stronger wall. I'll run point from the edge of your subdivision."

Jasper drags a hand down his jaw. "Gonna take me a month to grow this back. Emi's gonna hate it. But...it could work."

"Tomorrow's the full moon," Hardison says, his gaze locked on Connor. "They don't have the luxury of waiting. Any move they make is gonna be soon. And if they're that desperate...they could be that gullible too."

Parker frowns, her eyes unfocused like she's running the play in her head. "Good. Let them be gullible. We'll use it. But Grace is off the board. No one touches her. Not now. Not ever. I'll put an end to anyone who tries."

I turn and look at Parker—really look at her. She's all sharp edges and shadows. She inserted herself into my life when I had nothing. All because I asked her to keep an eye on Jasper after he got blown up and lost everything that mattered to him—including me. But she's never let me in. Not really.

Grace though...she slipped past every one of Parker's defenses. Hearing that determination—that steel—in her voice now, I breathe a little easier for the first time all fucking day.

Grace doesn't just have me in her corner. She's got all of us.

Every single one of us is willing to bleed—to die—for her.

I glance back up at the clock. Four hours, nineteen minutes.

"It's a good plan," I say, the words bitter on my tongue. "Connor, get Zephyr looped in. But make sure she knows... We ain't doin' a damn thing until Grace is awake. I need her to open her eyes. To feel me squeeze her hand. I need that."

Fuck.

I scrub a hand down my face before meeting Connor's eyes.

"*Grace* needs that before anyone leaves this hospital."

One by one, our *family* nods.

And we wait.

CHAPTER SEVENTY-ONE

AJ

Five hours and twenty-three minutes pass before the double doors finally swing open.

Dr. Ellicott, dressed in green scrubs with a flowered cap covering her black hair, steps through the double doors and scans the waiting room.

"Mr. Stone?"

I'm on my feet before the words leave her lips. Connor, Isabel, Jasper, Emi, Hardison, and Parker form a wall at my back.

"Grace did very well," she says with a weary smile. Her voice is calm and professional, the kind of tone meant to anchor panicked family members in the middle of a storm.

My knees threaten to buckle. "She's okay? She'll *be* okay?"

"She's stable. The fragment was lodged in her left temporal lobe, only a couple of millimeters from her skull. There was some scar tissue starting to form around it, but we excised that as well." Dr. Ellicott holds my gaze, as if she's making sure her words are penetrating the haze of my worry.

Are they? I have no idea. I latched onto the word "stable." After that...it's all noise.

"No complications?" Parker steps forward, right at my elbow, her entire body rigid.

"There was a small amount of bleeding, but we controlled it easily. That's not uncommon. Slight swelling, but again, nothing more than we expect. She'll be in the neuro ICU overnight so we can monitor her closely, but if everything looks good in the morning, she can transfer down to the regular neuro floor."

I grab onto Jasper's arm, unsure I'll be able to stay standing much longer otherwise. "How long until she wakes up?"

"She's still under anesthesia," the doctor says. "But we'll start easing her off soon. She should be awake in the next couple of hours. I will warn you that she'll be groggy and possibly nauseous. Headaches are normal as well. Given the location of the surgery, we'll be watching for any speech and memory issues, but I don't anticipate any permanent deficits."

The relief almost takes me to my knees. If it weren't for Jasper's support, I'd be on the floor.

"I'll have a nurse come get you in half an hour. Until Grace is fully awake and we can assess her condition, only one person at a time, please."

I manage a nod. After five and a half hours of hell, I can survive another thirty minutes.

The doctor slips back through the double doors, and everyone closes ranks around me. Parker holds onto Isabel, tears in both women's eyes. Emi dabs at her cheeks with a tissue and leans against Jasper. Connor sinks into the chair and drops his head into his hands. Hardison stays on the fringes, but I don't think his eyes are completely dry either.

We made it through the first hurdle. The one that Grace had to jump alone. The rest...we'll figure out together.

THE ICU IS MOSTLY QUIET, a low hum of machines punctuated with the beeping of heart rate monitors. The nurse pulls back a curtain, and there she is.

Grace looks so small against the white sheets. An IV is taped to the back of her hand, and wires seem to protrude from almost everywhere. Her blond hair fans across the pillow, a bandage covering part of her temple. It's so much smaller than the one she had in Mexico.

Hopefully that means her recovery will be easier. Grace has already carried more than anyone should ever have to. She's breathing. That should be enough. But, God help me, I need it to be easier this time. *She* needs it to be easier this time.

"She's still waking up," the nurse says, her voice barely above a whisper. "You can hold her hand, but try to let her rest as long as you can, okay? I'll come check on her every ten or fifteen minutes. But if you need me, you can always press the call button."

I drop into the chair beside the bed, and gather her fingers in mine. "I'm here, darlin'. The doctor says you're gonna be okay."

A hint of pressure against my palm answers me. It's so weak, I think maybe I imagined it. Until it happens again. "Just rest. I'm not goin' anywhere."

It takes another twenty minutes before her eyelids flutter. My heart skips a beat, then thuds against my ribs so hard, I suck in a sharp breath. Slowly, her lids part. I only catch a glimpse of her blue-green irises before they close, but she tries again. I'm not sure she can focus, but then relief eases the tiny lines bracing her mouth.

Her lips part, but what slips out is nothing more than a jumble of syllables that don't fit together. With a frown, she tries again, but it's no better, and a tear slips down her cheek.

My chest caves in, like someone kicked me hard enough to break my sternum. I want to jump up and scream for the nurse, but...we knew this was a possibility. Don't mean either of us were prepared for it, though.

"It's okay, Grace. This...it's all normal," I manage, my voice barely steady, then reach for the call button.

Nothin' about this is normal. I don't care what the doctor says. My wife went through those doors able to walk and talk and love. Now...I don't know if she can do any of those things. For all I know, she doesn't even remember me. Without her words, how can I tell?

Fear claws at my throat. Rage at the complete unfairness of all of this burns through me. What if this doesn't get better? She's been through so much already—clawed her way back from hell, pieced herself together again from nothin'—and now this?

Fuck.

Words or no words, she's still Grace. Still mine. And I'll spend the rest of my life—every breath, every touch, every heartbeat—showing her I'll never stop loving her. She could lose every word she's ever known, and she'll still have me. Always.

The door opens with a whisper, and the nurse steps in with a serene smile. "You doin' all right, hon?"

"She can't—" My voice breaks. "She...she tried to talk, but it's just...sounds. She can't...can't get the words out."

Grace blinks back her tears, and another weak mumble escapes her lips.

The nurse pats Grace's shoulder lightly, her gaze softening. "That's okay, hon. It's common. Really. Especially after the type of surgery you had. I'll page the doctor, though. She'll come talk you through what's happening, okay?"

The sharp edge of my panic eases just enough for me to

take a breath. I scoot closer, lifting Grace's hand gently and pressing her fingers to my chest, right over my heart.

"I love you, darlin'. Always. Words or no words, it don't matter. You hear me?"

Her tears haven't stopped, but she curls her fingers against my shirt. She's here. She's alive. And she knows how much I love her. For now...that's enough. It has to be enough.

Grace

The fog pressing against my skull won't clear. But AJ holds my hand to his chest, and the steady beat of his heart under my palm is my anchor in this storm.

If I had the strength, I'd try to speak again. But I'm so tired. A little dizzy. And a lot scared. I want to tell him I remember. Not our lives before. But the past two weeks. Or...at least the important bits.

Belle.

Spending nights curled up on the couch watching movies with popcorn so salty and buttery, it was like heaven in a bowl.

Sharing my coffee with him.

Making love last night, his arm around my waist and his lips pressed to my ear.

But I can't.

So I close my eyes until there's a soft knock at the door. Dr. Ellicott steps inside. "Grace? Nurse Robin says you're experiencing some aphasia."

Does she expect me to say something? In my head, I'm screaming, "*Yes. Nothing I try to say comes out sounding like actual words!*"

The doctor skirts the bed, comes around to the other side,

and takes my hand. "Can you understand me, Grace? If so, squeeze once."

I do, and she nods, her lips curving into a hint of a smile. "That's good. Now, follow my finger with just your eyes."

This is harder. But I manage without the room spinning out of control. "Excellent. The bone fragment was in your left temporal lobe. That's the language center of the brain. When we removed it, we had to excise a very small amount of healthy tissue in addition to the adhesions and scar tissue that had started to form around it."

"Why can't she speak?" AJ asks. He's in full Ranger mode. Protective. Demanding. Unwilling to put up with any bullshit. If I had the strength, I'd smile. Some things never change.

The doctor takes a small pen light from her pocket and checks my pupils. A tiny whimper escapes my lips, the pain shooting straight through my skull like a blade.

"Think of it like road work," she says, apparently satisfied now that she's blinded me. "We just ripped up a section of the highway and didn't put up any detour signs. So Grace's brain has to figure out a whole new route from here to home. That takes a little time."

"How much time?" he demands.

Despite the halos currently turning everything around me blurry, I can sense AJ's eyes on me. The laser focus he always seems to have where I'm concerned is grounding in a way I desperately need right now.

"I can't say for sure, but things usually even out within two or three days. We'll watch for any swelling, any worsening headaches, and any changes in Grace's pupillary response. Trust me, Mr. Stone, your wife is right where she needs to be. And she's doing just fine."

I want to say something. *Anything* to tell the doctor this isn't "just fine." I'm so damn tired. I just want AJ to hold me. But I can't ask him to. Even if I could, I'm covered in wires and sensors and too weak to move.

"I'll have a speech therapist come by in the morning. Until then, rest, Grace. This is the worst of it. It gets better from here."

After a moment, I hear the click of the door, and let my eyes drift closed.

AJ squeezes my hand. "You're safe, darlin'. I'm not goin' anywhere. I'll be here all night."

Safe. I hold onto that one word. It's my lifeline. The only thing that matters. I'm safe, and AJ won't leave me. Even if I can't speak, he'll do it for me until I can.

THE NEXT TIME I open my eyes, the room is quieter. Someone dimmed the lights, but the steady hum of the monitors hasn't faded. AJ still has a hold of my hand. Tightly enough, it feels like if he lets go, my entire world might unravel.

I squeeze his fingers, and his head snaps up. His eyes—red-rimmed and raw—soften the second he focuses on me.

"Hey, darlin'," he whispers. "You with me?"

I try. God, I try so hard. The word in my head is as clear as glass. *Yes.*

But when I open my mouth, it tangles and collapses on my tongue, escaping in a garbled mess that sounds more like "smythiea" than anything else.

AJ doesn't flinch. Just leans closer, his thumb tracing patterns over my knuckles. "It's okay, Grace. You'll get there."

Bitter frustration coats my tongue, cementing it to the roof of my mouth. Tears prick at my eyes. I want to tell him I love him. I *need* to. He has to know I'm still...me.

With my free hand, I point at him, my fingers trembling, then rest my palm over my heart.

"A...ayjun..." The sound warps, fades. My chest aches with the weight of all the things I can't say.

"Shhh." His hand cups my cheek, and the warmth helps steady me. "You don't need the words, Grace. I know what you're trying to say."

That's not enough. I open my mouth to try again, but he presses his finger to my lips.

"I love you? Is that what you're tryin' to say?"

I nod, amazed at how he always seems to be able to read my mind when I need it most.

"I don't need to hear it to feel it." His voice breaks, just a little. "And I love you. So much, there are times I can't breathe from the weight of it."

His words wrap around me, warm and steady, cutting through a fraction of my fear. I'm still terrified, but I know—deep down—we'll be okay.

He catches one of my tears before it can fall. "You'll get your words back. I promise."

CHAPTER SEVENTY-TWO

AJ

PARKER SNEAKS into the room a little after five p.m., silently slipping through the door, little more than a shadow to anyone watching. She goes straight to Grace's side, crouches down, and takes her hand.

"Hey there, hon." Her voice is soft. Light. But I catch the crack in it. She smiles, then lowers her head for a moment and brushes away a tear before Grace can see it. When she looks up again, her tone is steadier. "Me and AJ—we've got you. We ain't goin' anywhere until you do. Got it? You're not alone. Not now. Not ever."

The way she grips Grace's hand makes the promise feel solid. Heavy. Real.

I clear my throat, shifting closer to the bed. It's time to let Grace in on the plan. She might not be able to talk, but she's clearly *here*. And Emi's goin' on the air in an hour.

Grace's hand curls in mine. Her eyes are still a little glassy, like she can't quite focus, but the sound she makes—not a word, but definitely a question—tells me she knows there's *something* in the works.

"Darlin', we need to tell you somethin'."

Her brows knit. She squeezes my fingers hard, and my gut twists.

Fuck.

Parker slides a hip onto the very edge of the bed, and leans close. "Grace, we came up with a plan. A way to keep you safe. But me and AJ...we're stayin' right here with you. Can AJ tell you what it is?"

Grace tries to nod, but almost immediately winces.

"Wait. I've got an idea." Parker digs into her bag and comes up with Grace's sketchbook. She flips to a blank page and helps Grace curl her fingers around a pencil. "Language...it ain't always what people think. Try writin' something."

For a long moment, I don't think anyone in the room even breathes. Grace's hand shakes, but she manages two words.

"What plan?"

The sheer joy of being able to communicate with my wife almost does me in. Until Parker smacks my arm and hisses, "She asked you a question. Answer the woman."

"Sorry, darlin'. Connor thinks there's a way to draw attention away from the hospital. Maybe get Prophet and his cartel buddies a little desperate. Emi's gonna help us. On the six o'clock news, she'll do a little human interest story piece about you needing surgery for an injury sustained before you were found. She'll report that it was successful and you've been discharged. That you're home. Jasper..." I chuckle, because I *know* my brother ain't happy about this next bit. "Jasper's shavin' his beard. He'll drive my car back to the house with one of Connor's former FBI buddies passin' as you."

Grace frowns, but only gets two letters down before the pencil slips from her grasp. Parker's right there to pick it back up again.

Eventually, she scratches out, "*Too dangerous.*"

I soften my tone, my hand resting on her forearm. I need to keep touching her. To reassure her she's not alone. Or maybe... to reassure myself. "Hardison will be here with us. And I called the chief. He's sending a couple of other Rangers in street clothes to the hospital. The full moon is the day after tomorrow. They've got to be gettin' desperate."

Grace's throat works, her lips purse and press together before a strangled sound escapes. Eventually, she steadies the sketchbook and writes, "*Belle?*"

"She's at Emi's," I reassure her. "You know she spoils that dog rotten." I brush my thumb over Grace's wrist, feeling the rapid beat of her heart. "She's safe, darlin'. Just like you."

Grace stares at the page, then at me. God, I'd give anything to ease the glassy, shell-shocked look in her eyes. But despite the exhaustion, despite her brain betraying her, despite the hole in her goddamn skull, she's still fighting.

I squeeze her hand again. "We don't move forward unless you agree. Emi can go on in half an hour, or she can pull the segment and we keep all hands on deck here."

Her pencil scratches one last time. "*You. Parker. Don't leave.*"

I dip my head, pressing her hand to my lips. "I promise. We're staying right here."

Grace

The television hums above the bed, a low drone I can't quite tune out. AJ found the news channel earlier and left it on mute, saying it would help keep me distracted until Emi's segment came on. I'm not sure if it's working or just making things worse.

Parker fiddles with the remote, tapping it until the volume rises enough for me to hear the anchor.

"And now, with an update on the Grace Stone kidnapping case, Emmylou Marsh," the man says.

The camera pans to Emi, poised, perfect makeup, hands folded in front of her. She painted her nails dark red just the other day. Right after she did my toes.

"Grace Stone miraculously reappeared on the Butler trail a little over two weeks ago with no memory of her life. Her injuries required brain surgery, and she underwent that surgery this morning at Austin Memorial. But I'm pleased to report that Ms. Stone has been released and will be recovering at home with her family."

God, I wish that were true. I'd do anything to get out of this hospital. Even out of this bed.

Footage of me—or at least someone who looks like me—appears on screen. Jasper, who really can double for AJ without his beard, thanks to his dark glasses and Stetson, wheels the other me through the hospital's front doors. The woman smiles faintly, a scarf pulled low over her face and a bandage covering her left eye.

Emi's voice plays over the clip, crisp and confident. "I have a short statement from the family. 'After everything Grace has survived, she deserves peace. We're grateful to the surgical team, and to everyone who worked so hard for so long to bring her home. What she needs now is privacy and time to heal.'"

The camera returns focus to Emi, and she smiles, her eyes shimmering. "Good for her. Back to you, Jim."

My chest tightens with the effort of merely breathing. *Shit.* Panic edges closer, until I fumble for Parker's hand. I want to know who this other *me* is. If she's good enough at her job to defend herself if the cult comes for her. If they even told her what Prophet did to me.

"Write it down, hon. Don't worry about talkin' yet. That'll

come back to you soon." She slides the sketchpad onto my thighs.

"Worried. Jas. Fake me."

I blink hard, trying to clear the fuzz at the edges of my vision. It's been hours, and I still feel like I'm walking through quicksand. Or...thinking through quicksand. Can you think through quicksand?

Shit. I can't focus. All I want to do is sleep. But I need to hear Parker's answer first.

Parker leans closer, her blond brows pinching together. "Grace, you're okay. Promise. Jas and a whole team are headin' to your house right now. AJ's just outside talkin' to Connor, who's posted up at the entrance to your subdivision. And Hardison's chatting up the nurses down the hall."

She sounds so confident. And one thing I've learned about Parker the past few weeks? She doesn't sugarcoat anything.

I want to tell her I'm grateful. That I trust her. But I'm so tired, I just keep hold of her hand until I drift off to sleep.

CHAPTER SEVENTY-THREE

Grace

THEY WHEEL me into a new room—smaller, quieter, but with a wide window that lets in a gray wash of Austin sky. The constant hum of machines has faded, and there are fewer wires to manage and navigate. A kind nurse comes to help me to the bathroom. My entire body is heavy, my head wrapped in a dull, constant ache. If I nod, the entire world wobbles, the vertigo threatening to come back with a vengeance, so I keep the sketchpad close, like a lifeline.

AJ dozes in the hard plastic chair. He's been right next to my bed—in both rooms—all night. Parker's curled up in the corner under the window, a blanket tugged up to her waist. They're both still here. Both still wearing yesterday's clothes.

The speech therapist comes and works with me for almost an hour. Simple sounds. Vowels. My name. AJ's. She says it's all about waking my brain back up. Letting it remember how to form words. I try—God, I try. But the words don't come. Only broken echoes of them. By the time she leaves, I'm wrung out.

"You did great, darlin'," AJ says, as if he knows how much I hate this forced silence.

I lift a shaky hand, point to my temple, and wince.

"Do I need to get the nurse?" AJ's entire body stiffens, his voice laced with panic.

I frown, shaking my head softly. A tiny moan slips out before I can stop it.

He grips the call button anyway, thumb ready. I cover his hand with mine, hold for a beat, then lift it so I can swirl my finger in the air. I'm just dizzy, and my sketchbook is too far away for me to reach easily.

In the corner of the room, Parker sits up straight, her gaze narrowing on my hand. "I've got an idea. AJ, Isabel's coming by with a little something for Grace. Go meet her in the waiting room." She cracks a smile. "And bring me some coffee when you come back, will ya'?"

AJ doesn't move. A low rumble in his chest could almost be a growl. I don't like the idea of him leaving anymore than he does, but I'm safe with Parker. And he won't be far. I squeeze his hand, trying to let him know it's okay.

As soon as the door clicks shut behind him, Parker takes a seat in the chair. "You need another way to communicate if you don't feel like writing." She slides the table stretching across the foot of the bed closer so my sketchbook and pencil are within my reach. "Or if this somehow ends up too far away again."

I reach for the sketchbook, but the pencil rolls off the table and lands somewhere in the tangle of blankets.

Shit.

For three years, no one heard me. No one talked to me—at least with any kindness—but I still *had* a voice, even if I chose not to use it. Now...this is so much harder.

Parker holds up her right hand, fingers curled into a loose fist, thumb pointed up. "This is A." Then she straightens her fingers and angles her thumb across her palm. "And this is B."

It takes a couple of seconds for the fog swirling around in my brain to clear, but once it does, I copy her first letter.

A.

Her fierce grin holds so much pride, my cheeks flush with heat. "There you go. Okay. We're gonna go through the whole alphabet, but also a couple of important words. Like yes...and no."

A flicker of hope stirs in my chest. I grab the pencil, and scratch out, *"Need to tell AJ—"*

"You want to skip to the good stuff first?"

I nod, and she laughs. "That's the Grace I know. All right." She points to herself. "I."

Once I've copied her, she closes both hands into loose approximations of the letter A, and crosses them over her chest. "Love."

This is a little harder with the IV still taped to my hand, but I manage.

"You." She points to me, I point to her, and for a moment, I feel like I've just climbed a mountain.

"You need one more. Remember A?" she asks.

I show her, and she nods. "Good. Now stick out your pinky finger, hold your thumb across your other fingers, and draw a J."

After I struggle through the gesture, her eyes light up, glassy with emotion, but her grin doesn't falter. "That's his name. You just said AJ."

Tears spill, hot against my cheeks. Parker leans closer, carefully wraps one arm around me, and gives me a gentle squeeze.

"You're still here, Grace. You're still you. In a couple of days, all this silence will fade into a memory. But until it does, we've got you. Always."

She's only just pulled back when AJ returns, two cups of coffee in hand, and a small paper bag dangling from his wrist.

Parker practically sashays around the bed, takes one of the

cups, and heads for the door. "I'll be back in a few minutes. I'm betting AJ forgot that I like sugar in my coffee."

AJ starts to protest, but Parker cuts him off. "Grace has something to tell you."

She leaves, and I point to myself, cross my arms over my chest, and point to him. Then...I sign his name.

"I love you, AJ."

The bag hits the floor. He barely manages to set his coffee down before folding me into his embrace. "I love you too, darlin'. Always and forever."

AJ

I tried to send Parker home for a couple of hours. As expected, she refused. Isabel dropped off a change of clothes for her—along with a tin of decaf instant Cafe Vienna for Grace—and she's making use of a shower in one of the empty rooms on this floor.

When she's done, I'll do the same. Hardison is patrolling the halls, doing laps around the neuro floor like he's training for the world's slowest, scariest marathon. One with a strict "arrest anyone who even blinks suspiciously" rule.

Grace fell asleep less than twenty minutes after we shared a cup of her decaf. The normalcy of that single act almost did me in. Nothing about where we are is normal. Especially not this overwhelming, almost oppressive silence. But knowing she's still in there—that she's still *her*—lets me relax a degree or two.

Until a soft knock at the door puts me on high alert.

Parker would quietly slip back inside like she'd been there the whole time. Hardison would barge in with a running commentary about how the vending machine coffee is a crime against humanity. And the rest of our little family is either at our house, preparing for Armageddon, or holed up at Isabel's under lockdown.

Before I can check to see who it is, Marvin ambles into the room. He's dressed head to toe in black, from his jeans to his long-sleeved button down to his sport coat. No star clipped to his shirt. No double belt. He's still wearing that goddamn ugly-as-sin rodeo buckle though, and he grabs it like it's connected right to his dick.

"Afternoon," he says, a little too loudly.

Grace stirs in her sleep, her legs restless under the blankets, and I push to my feet, shielding her from his view.

"What the fuck are you doin' here?" I demand.

His brows lift, creasing deep lines in his forehead. "Harris sent me. He figured you could use a little extra backup."

Goddammit. I *knew* telling Harris about our attempt to draw out the cartel was a mistake. But he called last night, warning me APD was pushing hard to talk to Grace. I told him the story was a smokescreen, that she wasn't going anywhere for days. Figured he'd keep that to himself. Fucker.

I narrow my eyes at Marvin. "The chief didn't say anything to me about 'backup.'"

Marvin shrugs and flashes me an easy smile. "He probably didn't want to bother you."

I straighten my shoulders, hiding the wince at the pain in my back from too many hours in the hard plastic visitor's chair. "Yet you did?"

"Better to intrude for a minute than have Hardison tackle me in the hall."

Grace stirs again, a soft sigh slipping from her lips. Marvin takes a step to the side, his eyes flicking to her, then back to me.

I force myself to relax. I might hate the man, but another set of eyes on Grace—or on the hallways and stairwells, at least—won't hurt.

"Appreciate it. But keep a low profile. No need to draw attention to this room—or the neuro floor."

Marvin nods. "Understood. I just thought...if you needed to step out for food, coffee, a shower...I'll be around."

A small bit of tension eases from my shoulders. Better Marvin than someone Grace doesn't know.

"Around. But not in here. She needs rest, and visitors ain't gonna help that."

Marvin's mouth ticks at the corner, like he wants to argue, but then he nods. "Fair enough. I'll stay close. You just call me if you need anything."

He backs toward the door, giving Grace one last glance before slipping out into the hall.

I sink back into the chair beside her bed, dragging a hand down my face. It's been more than eighteen hours since Emi's news story. The full moon is tomorrow. And yet no one's made a move on our house. Zephyr's monitoring for any online chatter, but hasn't heard a thing.

Maybe I should call Harris and ask him to send anyone he has—hell, *everyone* he has—down here. Build a fucking wall of Rangers so strong around my wife that no one and nothing can *ever* get through.

Leaning forward, I brush my knuckles over Grace's hand. She doesn't stir, and I focus on the steady rise and fall of her chest.

"I got you, darlin'," I murmur, the words rough and low enough I won't wake her. "Don't care who tries to get close, don't care what it costs me—there's nothin' I won't do to keep you safe. Not now. Not ever."

CHAPTER SEVENTY-FOUR

AJ

Nurse Elaine pokes her head in the door. "Mr. Stone? I'm goin' off shift soon. How's our girl doin?"

I get to my feet, doing my best to stifle my groan. "Any chance dinner might come with some heat to it? Grace barely ate breakfast this morning. She's got a strong aversion to bland food."

I don't tell the nurse that it's PTSD. That near as we can figure, the mostly empty room with the plain wood walls she spent three goddamn years in didn't come with salt, pepper, or any sort of flavor to whatever meals she was allowed.

"Not much I can do about that, I'm afraid. Bland is the order of the day around here. But I won't say anythin' if you smuggle in a bottle of hot sauce. There's a grocery store right around the corner." She offers me a wink, and with a quick check of the monitors, rushes off to her next patient.

I glance over at Parker, sitting cross-legged in the corner, the glow from her laptop screen tinging her cheeks.

"Go," she says. "I'll sit with Grace. She won't wake up alone."

"I can't leave her." Fear practically chokes me. As long as I'm at her side, I know she's safe. Alive. Healing. It doesn't matter how much I trust Parker. She ain't me.

"AJ, when was the last time you even took a piss? You're no good to her half-dead yourself." Parker closes the laptop with a heavy click, sets it on the window sill, and yawns as she stretches her arms over her head. Then she points at the door. "So here's the deal. You go. You grab hot sauce. And while you're at it, queso and chips too. I'll nuke it downstairs and she'll actually eat. Don't argue."

She's right. Dammit. She's right. If only that made it easier to walk out the door.

I'm in the middle of the hot sauce aisle when my phone buzzes in my pocket. One glance at the screen, and I drop the bag of chips in my hand.

Perimeter Breach - Backyard Cam

Connor's message follows in under ten seconds. *"Possible movement off the deck."*

Fuck.

I'm already moving, shoving my way past a guy debating salsa brands like his life depends on it. Taking off at a run, I make it out the sliding doors, across the street, and back to the hospital in under two minutes.

The elevators in this place are too damn slow. Stairs it is. I nearly collide with Hardison as I burst out onto the neuro floor.

"They're—" I'm still moving, almost to Grace's room, when Nate grabs my arm.

"You're not running point from her bedside, man. Grace doesn't need a live action suspense movie playing out in her hospital room." He turns me around, prodding me past the nurses' station. "Last room on the right is empty. We can work without spooking her. Parker's got her."

Marvin rounds the corner before we make it to the end of the hall. That damn belt buckle shines like the sun amid his black pants and dark gray shirt.

"Somethin' goin' on?" he asks.

"No time," I snap. "Post yourself outside Grace's door and don't fucking move until I relieve you. Got it?"

"Yeah. Sure. But if you need any help—"

Hardison glares at him. "Help is you on doorstop duty, man. Don't improvise."

I slide my comms device into my ear and mutter, "Talk to me."

Grace

For the first time since my surgery, the pencil feels steady—right—in my hand. Steadier than my thoughts. Parker's gone over the alphabet with me half a dozen times today. She's always slow. Always patient. And when I make it from A to Z without fumbling, she smiles so wide, my own lips curve too.

But the shadows have started creeping in at the edges of my vision. Whispers I can't understand echo against my skull. They're ghosts. Memories I can't touch, even now.

So while she sits in the chair next to my bed, her eyes closed, I draw.

For weeks now, I've tried to get this one image from my head to the page. I could see fragments of it, but whenever I tried to piece it together, all the lines and curves blended into what might as well have been a child's first scribble.

This time, it's clearer. Or, at least parts of it are. The lanterns. The altar. The cult members gathered to watch me die. I turn the page, try to find another angle. This one is better. In front of one of the poles is a man. Average height. A little overweight. Short hair, thinning on top. And at his waist, a large belt buckle.

I switch to drawing *just* the buckle. A man riding a bull. His arm raised high in the air, hat in hand. But it's the lettering around the outside that's always confused me. The brightness of it. The ugliness of it.

Fort Worth Rodeo

I can't say the words. They'd come out all jumbled—nothing but an incomprehensible mess of vowels and consonants.

Oh, my God. It all makes sense now.

Why I couldn't draw it before. Maybe even why I can now.

My brain took all the shapes—the man, the bull, the hat, the letters—and jumbled them all together.

My surprised gasp startles Parker, and she sits up with a jerk. "Shit. I'm tired. AJ went to get you queso. Store bought, but it'll still be better than the food in this place."

I grin and sign. *"Love q-u-e-s-o."*

She laughs, the sound soft, almost gentle. But after a glance at her phone, her head tilts, and her muscles stiffen.

"AJ's on with Connor. Might be a couple of minutes," she says, too quickly.

Shit. Something's wrong. I reach for her hand, and she squeezes my fingers.

"Hey. Don't worry. Marvin's right outside, and I ain't goin' anywhere."

My heart stutters. No. Not him. I shake my head, try to force the words out. "Marvin... Bad." But all that escapes is a mess of broken sounds.

Frustrated, I shove the sketchbook at her, then jab the page.

Parker frowns. "Lanterns?"

Why can't she understand? *Dammit.* She's looking at the wrong image.

I lean over, almost losing my balance as the vertigo pitches the whole room sideways, but manage to flip to the drawing of the buckle.

Her eyes widen. "Wait—"

The door opens, and Marvin ambles in, all calm, an easy smile on his face. "AJ'll be back soon. Just figured I'd come check on the two of you. See if you needed anythin'."

My breath saws in and out of my throat, the terror hitting so hard, the edges of my vision dim.

Parker leaps out of her chair, but she's a second too late. The butt of Marvin's gun whips across the back of her skull, and she crumples to the floor with a strangled moan.

"Nnnnnn!" I try to haul myself out of bed, but the world tilts, and I land next to Parker in a heap.

I blink up at Marvin with tears in my eyes. He pulls open the door. "All clear."

Two men dressed in blue scrubs rush in with a gurney. I kick at them, but they grab me, slam me down, and tighten straps over my chest, my arms, my thighs, and my ankles. One of them pulls a syringe from his pocket.

I open my mouth to scream, but the other wraps his hand around my throat and squeezes. Hard. The needle stings my arm. I buck and thrash, my body desperate for air. But within seconds, a dull warmth spreads through me. My arms and legs are so heavy. I barely feel the IV ripped from the back of my hand.

"Take her too," Marvin orders, jerking his thumb at Parker's limp body.

No. Not Parker!

The taller of the two men grabs the wheelchair in the corner of the room, hauls Parker up by one arm, and dumps her into the chair. Zip ties tighten around her wrists before he throws a blanket over her from chest to toes.

Marvin yanks my sketchbook from the floor, and rips the

last page free. "Throw this drivel away. Somewhere no one can find it."

The ceiling swims above me, the drug turning the world soft and shimmery.

Elevator. We're going up. Oh, God.

Cold night air crashes over me as a door slams open. The inky black sky is alight with stars. Rotors thump overhead, deafening, rattling my bones.

Parker stirs, coming awake with a feral scream. She lunges for me, but one of the men in scrubs punches her in the face, then throws her onto the deck of the helicopter.

I'm fading. Darkness closes in. The gurney jolts, the straps biting tighter each time.

"Careful with her, Brother Vincent," one of the nurses mutters, shifting his grip.

"Why? Prophet just needs her alive for the ceremony tomorrow. It don't matter if her brain's hopelessly scrambled."

Brother Vincent.

The memory hits me so hard, it steals my breath.

The night I ran away. Brother Vincent and Brother Malone chasing me. The ropes biting into my wrists. Dragging me from a horse when I could no longer run—or even stand.

Metal clanks against the helicopter's frame as they shove me inside and lock the wheels into place. My chest heaves. The drug's fog thickens, but adrenaline fights it back.

"Prophet is waiting," Marvin barks. God, his voice sounds so far away. "He wants Nova purified before the ceremony tomorrow night."

The words echo in my skull, terrifying in their finality.

The rotors scream louder, drowning out all other sounds. The floor vibrates under me. Harder. Faster. Until the world tilts, and the helicopter lifts off.

The city lights fade away—along with any hope I'll ever see AJ again.

CHAPTER SEVENTY-FIVE

AJ

Hardison shuts the door behind us, then plants himself against it, arms crossed, like this is any other shift on any other day. Except for his eyes. The flecks of green in his gold irises are practically glowing as he scans the room, then cuts his gaze back to mine with a weight I don't like.

Not panic. Not even fear. Just a tight focus that says something's coming, and we don't know if it's a rain shower or a goddamn hurricane.

I slip the comms device into my ear. "Talk to me. Jas? Connor? What's goin' on."

"Two headed for the back deck," Jasper says. "One hidin' behind the shed. The fourth is comin' in from the front."

I cast a quick gaze to the door. Hardison hasn't moved. If I didn't know better, I'd wonder if he was breathin'. The man's got two gears: deadpan smartass and serious as a heart attack. And right now, he ain't crackin' jokes.

"Copy that," I mutter. Something about this feels...*wrong*.

On my phone screen, I cycle through the various security feeds. I should have sent Hardison for Parker's laptop.

There they are. Two guys, dressed all in black, marching up the stairs to the deck like they own the whole fuckin' place.

Connor cuts in. "Are these jackoffs *trying* to get dead? I've seen Girl Scouts with better op-sec."

"Don't dis the scouts, man," Hardison says. "Some of those badges are serious business."

I glare at him. This ain't the time for jokes. "Girl scouts are welcome to ring the doorbell. These guys aren't. Make 'em regret every one of their life choices." My tone's sharper than I intend, but I don't care. Grace's safety depends on this being over. Fast.

The two on the back deck walk right up to the door and try the goddamn handle.

"Hey, assholes," Jasper calls. The doggie door opens, and my brother fires four shots, right to their kneecaps. The men drop with guttural curses and cries, grabbing their legs and rolling around like Jas just kicked them in the nuts.

Another two shots, and Connor's voice rumbles in my ear. "Three down. One to go."

Flipping to the camera covering the front of the property, I watch the last man hesitate. He glances at the front door, then back at the road.

Do it. Put one goddamned foot on the step and see what happens, asshole.

The guy adjusts his grip on his gun and races up the stairs. He hurls himself at the door, shoulder first, but rebounds like he just hit a brick wall. Even on the tiny screen, it's obvious he's not tryin' again.

Jasper opens the door and draws down on the idjit. "Drop the gun or I drop it for you."

The pistol hits the wood. Jasper spins the guy around, zip tying his wrists before marching him through the house, all the way to the back deck where the two guys with no knees lie face down, whimpering something about blood loss and hospitals.

"Find out who sent them—and do it quick," I snap.

"We ain't amateurs, AJ," Jas mutters.

Connor crouches next to his captive, who's bleeding from not one but *both* arms. "You idjits gotta be the worst infil crew I've ever seen. My grandmother could've made it farther, and she's been dead for ten years."

"Yeah, because that's the fucking point." Hardison grabs my arm, real fear in his eyes. "They were only there to waste our time."

Grace.

He's half a step behind me as we bolt for the door, race down the hall, and burst into Grace's room.

Her bed is empty, the sheets spilling onto the floor. Parker's laptop is in two pieces. Next to it, a partial footprint smeared in blood.

Fuck!

A weak groan from behind me has me pulling my gun.

Marvin.

He's slumped against the wall, a bright red goose egg swelling at his hairline.

"Where. Is. Grace?" I roar, hauling him to his feet. My fists ache with the overwhelming need to rearrange his anatomy in a way that would *not* support life.

"Parker," he manages. "She...took...Grace. Said...she had to. That some prophet guy...was her savior. I tried to stop her, but she" —he winces— "she's stronger...than she looks."

"Don't you dare," I growl. "Don't you *dare* put this on her."

I shove Marvin toward Hardison. Gone is the snark, the lazy grin, all traces of sarcasm. What's left is nothing but ice and steel. He secures Marvin in a headlock so fast, the bastard barely gets a breath in.

"Try that again," Hardison grits out. "And if you so much as say her name, I'll end you right here."

Marvin claws weakly at Nate's arm. I slam a knee into his groin for good measure. He folds, whimpering like the coward he is.

"Parker would die before she let anyone *touch* Grace," I spit, terror and rage battling for control. In the end, rage wins. "She wouldn't leave her side for five fuckin' minutes. You think you can sell me that bullshit? No. This was you. All you."

"I'd...never..." he wheezes.

"Last chance, asshole. Tell me where Grace is, or I let Hardison here snap your neck like a dry twig."

Marvin chokes, then...laughs.

"In twenty-four hours, Nova's sacrifice will bring salvation to the entire Blessed Flock. You can't touch me, Stone. Nothing can. Not now. Not ever."

"Her name is *Grace*." I press the SIG to his temple hard enough he flinches. "And the only one dying tonight is *you* if you don't talk."

"Cap," Hardison cuts in, his voice sharp. "Not here. Not in this building. We take him somewhere private. And then we make him beg."

I grit my teeth so hard my jaw pops. "We don't have time for private. Grace—"

"Has twenty-four hours." Hardison's voice dips so low, it's barely a guttural whisper. The emotion in it...I've never heard from him before. "Hopefully Parker does too. You want answers? We take him somewhere he can scream."

Marvin gives a wet, rattling laugh that makes me want to peel his skin off his bones. I shove the barrel harder into his temple, but before I can threaten to end him, Jasper's voice cuts in over comms.

"AJ." Rage grinds the words ragged. "If Marvin's a member of the cult—"

The truth detonates inside me. My knees give out. I hit the edge of Grace's bed, then the floor, and the sheets—*Christ*—the sheets still smell like her. Her shampoo. Her skin. I bury my face in them and choke back the scream tearing at my throat.

Hardison doesn't flinch. Doesn't soften. He just says what I can't.

"It's been him. The whole goddamn time. Intel from his CIs sent you and Jasper on that stakeout. That's why you and Grace weren't out of town that weekend."

"I'm gonna fuckin' kill him," Jasper grits out.

He'll have to get in line.

Three goddamn years. Marvin knew. He knew where she was. Knew what they were doing to her. And he came to work every fucking day. Sat across the table from me. Pretended to care.

Hardison shoves Marvin to the floor, then drives a boot into his ribs. I don't stop him. Hell, I give him a sharp nod. Because right now, there's no daylight between his fury and mine.

"Cap," Hardison says, his voice so calm, he could have just ordered coffee and donuts instead of broken a man's ribs, "get up. We've gotta work the scene—and fast—before the night shift nurse checks in. Then we can make this son of a bitch piss himself a hundred times over before morning."

He holds out his hand.

I force myself up, but something crunches under my boot. Reaching under the bed, I find Grace's sketchbook. There's a page ripped out, the edge jagged.

"She never tears the pages," I whisper.

Hardison gives Marvin another kick, then picks up Grace's pencil. With quick, practiced strokes, he shades the blank page until we can see the last image my wife drew.

Fort Worth Rodeo

We turn as one. The world's ugliest belt buckle has always been Marvin's pride and joy. His great uncle's. Or so he said.

Below the words, Grace captured it all. The curve of the bull rider's arm. His hat held high. The animal's horns.

Grace has been trying to draw this goddamn belt buckle for more than two weeks. But she could never finish it. Never understand what she was seeing.

She *knew.* Somewhere in the wreckage of her mind, she knew. Behind the buckle—the man *wearing* the buckle—she drew one of the poles with a lantern swinging in the breeze.

I'm gonna be sick. "You son of a bitch!" I snarl, slamming the sketchbook so hard against Marvin's chest, his entire body jerks. "*This* is why you took Parker. Because she saw this and she recognized your goddamned belt buckle."

Hardison steps in before Marvin can open his mouth. He grabs the offending belt buckle and uses it to haul the asshole up and slam him back against the wall.

"One question, fucker," he growls, his voice utterly lethal. "Is Parker alive? Yes or no."

Marvin smirks, but it falters when Hardison jerks him again, hard enough to rattle his teeth in his skull.

"She's alive," Marvin gasps. "Prophet didn't want her dead. He wanted her...saved." His lips curl. "Said he was ready for his fifth wife."

Hardison's gaze turns feral. "If he hurts her—if he *touches* her—there won't be enough left of either of you to bury."

Marvin's bravado cracks just a hair. His eyes widen, and he swallows, the sound loud enough we can hear it. Hardison shoves him to the floor with a disgusted snort, then looks at me, hard edges and something dangerously close to fear. "AJ, Parker's...family. If this goddamn Prophet takes what little soft she's got left, we'll lose her. Even if she survives."

I can't see past my rage. "Get him up. We're goin' somewhere no one can hear him scream." I grab Grace's sketchbook, the only part of her I have left. "And Nate? If he so much as *looks* at you funny..."

Hardison smiles—actually smiles. "I'll make sure he can never look at anyone ever again."

CHAPTER SEVENTY-SIX

AJ

WE HAUL Marvin out of the trunk like the sack of shit he is. Nate *knows a guy* who used to run this auto shop on the edge of town. But with half the sign's letters missing, weeds pushing through the cracked asphalt, and the lingering stench of decay mingling with the smell of oil and rust in the air, the guy hasn't been here in years. Neither has anyone else.

It's the perfect place for a man to disappear.

Jasper and Connor wait just inside the door, arms crossed over their chests.

I never thought the two of them looked much alike, but right now, they wear the same expression we all do. Rage.

Marvin hasn't said a fucking word since we dragged him into the hospital stairwell. Every flight, Hardison "dropped" him at least once. His knees will never be the same.

"I reckon this should do him just fine," Jasper says, waving his hand at one of the old repair bays.

I slam Marvin into a battered, rusted tool chest. Wrenches

scatter to the concrete with a metallic crash. He groans, curling in on himself as best he can with his hands cuffed behind his back.

"Find me a goddamn chair," I snap.

"Got a better idea, Cap." Hardison punches one of the buttons for the hydraulic lift system, and a chain thuds down from the ceiling, one link at a time. "The chair is for *after* we break both his legs."

Connor and Jasper pin Marvin's arms while Hardison swaps the cuffs to the front. I catch the bastard's weight, snap the chain around the cuffs, and hit the hydraulics until he's stretched tall, his toes brushing the concrete floor.

I step in close. "Where. Is. Grace?" Each word lands with a sharp jab to his ribs.

Marvin wheezes but forces a smile. "She belongs to Prophet. She always has. She always will."

Hardison leans in, shaking his head slowly. "Man, you keep talking like that, and I'm gonna start believing you *want* us to get creative."

Connor snorts. "Ain't much left to get creative with."

"Don't sell me short," Hardison fires back. "My imagination's just gettin' started."

I press my forearm against Marvin's throat, enough to shut him up. "Well, *you* belong to us. And I promise you, Prophet ain't half as scary as we'll be if you don't start talkin'."

Marvin doesn't flinch when I take a step back. "You expect me to believe two decorated Rangers, a former FBI agent, and Lieutenant Boy Scout over there are gonna torture me?"

Shoving his hands into his pockets, Hardison gets right in Marvin's face. "See, here's the problem. You're betting on us playing by the rules. On being scared to push too far." His eyes narrow, a lethal calm settling in his tone. "You put your hands on Parker. I don't have rules anymore."

Jasper circles behind Marvin, his voice quiet, dangerous. "AJ's the best of us. But you got no idea what losin' the love of your life can do to a man." He pulls a blade from his back pocket. It snaps open with a metallic click.

With a sneer, Marvin meets my gaze. "Do your worst."

Hardison's eyes narrow. "Oh, he did *not* just say that."

I glance at my twin. He shrugs as he passes me the knife. And I drive it deep into the fleshy part of Marvin's shoulder.

He screams, his toes scraping across the metal.

"That's one. For every minute Grace is gone, you'll get another," I say, yanking the knife back out and wiping it on Marvin's shirt sleeve. "Where is she?"

He chokes out a laugh. "Long gone. We have people everywhere. You know how easy it was? Gettin' her out of the hospital? Took all of a minute. Into the elevator, up to the roof, and on a helicopter headed for sunrise. You'll never find her."

Hardison whistles. "East, huh? See, that's progress. Couple more minutes, and you'll be giving us GPS coordinates and Prophet's blood type."

Marvin spits at the man, but it lands far short of Hardison's boots. "You think you're gonna scare me? I'm a senior cleric of the Blessed Flock."

Connor's lips curl in a humorless smile. "You ain't seen scary yet, asshole."

Jasper folds his arms, his voice flat. "When we get tired of askin'...*that's* when the scary part begins."

I grab Marvin's jaw, force his eyes to mine. "Where's the goddamn ceremony? Tell me, or I swear to God, I'll put you in the ground right now."

Jasper grabs his shoulder from behind, digging his fingers into the wound.

Marvin groans through the pain. "Even if you *did* find her, you'd never make it past the gates."

Hardison chuckles, the sound dry as dust. "Yeah, we know all about the ghost guns, shit-for-brains. Did you think we'd be goin' in there alone? You and your *brothers* aren't gonna have any use for them when we're done. Last I checked, ghosts couldn't pull triggers."

Marvin's eyes dart from me to Hardison and back again.

"Someone slipped," I grit out. "Whoever dumped Grace's body in the middle of the Mexican countryside left a fragment of a firin' pin in the bag with her."

"No...there wasn't anything in there," he gasps. "Just...her."

I barely manage to rein in my shock. Then again, why should I be surprised? The bastard arranged for her kidnapping and lied to my face for three goddamn years.

I meet Jasper's gaze over the asshole's shoulder. "I think it might be time to tell the world how Grace was *really* found. And who was personally responsible for confirming the cult's connection to the Cordova cartel."

Jasper comes back around to stand next to me, his phone in his hand. "Say the word, AJ, and I'll call Emi. She can be on the air in twenty minutes. Probably less."

Marvin's bravado cracks into pieces. "No! If Jefe finds out... I was supposed to make the problem go away. Not—"

Connor cuts him off, his voice razor-sharp. "Oh, he's gonna find out. Tell us what we need to know, and maybe we'll do you a solid and throw him in jail for the rest of his life *before* he carves you into tiny pieces."

Marvin sags against the cuffs, sweat dripping down his temple. He shakes his head. "Nova's sacrifice will save me. Even from Jefe."

Hardison barks out a laugh. "Save you? Man, your Prophet's been feeding you fairy tales like candy." He turns to me, disgust curling his lip and nothing but ice in his gaze. "AJ, this fool's had so much Kool-Aid, he's more red dye number five than man now. I say bring the pain."

An hour later, no one's hands are clean. Marvin's blood slicks the floor. Both of his eyes are swollen half-shut, and he's not so much breathin' as gaspin'.

I step back and let Hardison take over. The man drives a fist into Marvin's kidney hard enough the bastard loses what was left of his last meal. "Fuck. Now you've done it. These are my favorite boots. Give up the Blessed Flock's location, or you get to see what happens when I run out of patience."

Marvin tries for a sneer, but it crumbles when Connor leans in close and whispers something I can't quite make out. Whatever it is drains all the color from the asshole's face. But he still ain't talkin'.

Jasper doesn't even raise his voice. Just takes his phone out of his pocket and taps the screen. "Emi? How fast can you get on the air?" A second later, his lips curve into a smile. "That's what I thought. Go for it, sweetheart. This idjit needs a little... motivation."

Marvin chokes out a weak, "No. Please..."

"Please?" I snap. "You think I give two shits about your beggin'?" I step closer, my shadow swallowing him whole. "Not a chance. Not with Grace and Parker still out there. You want mercy? Earn it. Tell. Me. Where. They. Are."

Tears cut through the grime on his cheeks. His bluster is gone, his defenses stripped bare. He's nothing but a man drowning in his own fear.

"There's a compound." Desperation turns his voice brittle. Thin. Like a bundle of dry twigs waiting to snap. "Just east...of Shafter..."

I tap the comms unit in my ear. "Zephyr? Did you get that?"

"Searching the flyover footage now," she says. "I lost the helicopter less than three miles from Austin Memorial. No transponder, no flight plan. But based on air speed...they could have made it to Shafter...well...right about now."

I grab Marvin's blood-soaked shirt and yank him so close, I

can smell the fear on his breath. "You think your *Glorious One* can save you? If your *Prophet* harms even a single hair on their heads, I won't just kill you. I'll carve off a piece of your body for every fuckin' day my wife suffered. And only *then* will I put a bullet in your brain."

CHAPTER SEVENTY-SEVEN

Grace

THE HELICOPTER JERKS, the roar vibrating all through me, every *whomp* of the blades pulsing against my skull.

Shadows and colors start to sharpen. Whatever they gave me is wearing off. I wish it wasn't. Because now, my whole body is paralyzed with fear.

Cold air stings my cheeks when the doors open. The scent of manure fills my nose. Dust and dirt. The cloying stench of oleander.

Hands clamp around my arms. Someone—I can't see well enough to know who—cuts through the straps holding me down.

I'm hauled up, dragged out of the helicopter. Rocks bite into my feet through my fuzzy purple socks. Isabel's gift. I'll lose those soon. Along with my favorite pajamas. Forced back into the white dress I wore for three long years.

Tears well in my eyes. I try to make my legs work, but they're too heavy. Too weak. The men jerk me forward, and a voice I've heard in so many of my nightmares is suddenly right in front of me.

"Blessed evening, *Nova*."

I blink up at the man, and memories come flooding back to me. Pain. Fear. Soul-crushing despair.

Brother Malone.

Shit. He wants an answer. I *have* to answer or he'll hurt me. But I can't.

"Breaking the rules already? I told Brother Marvin it was a mistake to wait so long to return you to us. You will answer me when I speak to you!" His hand clamps down on my shoulder, squeezing hard enough I see stars. With a tiny whimper, my shaky legs give out completely. If it weren't for the other two holding me up, I'd be face down in the dirt.

"She can't, asshole!" Parker shouts. Two more of Prophet's clerics muscle her forward. Zip ties cut into her wrists, but her legs are free, and she fights with everything she has, twisting and kicking. One of her boots catches the guy on her right in the shin hard enough that he falls, taking her down with him.

She's up again in a heartbeat, ducks her shoulder, and tries to ram the brother holding my left arm. But before she reaches me, she's caught around the waist and thrown to the ground.

Brother Malone chuckles as he stalks forward and plants his boot in the center of her chest. "Two hundred and sixteen of us. One of you. Brother Marvin said you were smart. Guess he doesn't know what he's talking about."

"Fuck you, asshole," Parker manages, each word punctuated by a pained gasp. Brother Malone shifts more of his weight forward.

"*Stop!*" That's what I want to say. But it comes out garbled, the word shattering on my lips.

Parker makes a small, pained sound.

He's going to break her ribs. Or her breastbone.

"St....st..." It's the best I can do.

"What's wrong with her?" Brother Malone asks, finally removing his boot so Parker can breathe.

The glare she gives him could freeze Hell itself. The clerics haul her to her feet, and Malone grabs her chin hard enough to bruise. "Rule number one. Women do not speak unless spoken to. Rule number two. If a brother asks you a question, you answer."

"Fuck...you...and your...rules," Parker wheezes.

His hand flies, hitting her cheek with a sickening *crack*.

"Rule number three. Members of the Blessed Flock are not allowed to swear," he growls.

"Good thing...I'm not one...of them." Parker stands up a little straighter. "Grace can't speak. Because you assholes stole her from her hospital bed twenty-four hours after she had fuckin' brain surgery."

Brother Malone hits her again, but this time, with a closed fist. She slumps forward, blood dripping from her mouth.

"Bring them," Brother Malone snaps. "Prophet says the preparations for tomorrow's ceremony need to start immediately."

Terror steals my breath in an instant. The clerics on either side of me clamp down on my arms, half-carrying, half-dragging me past the barn. The horses spook as the helicopter lifts off again, stamping and tossing their heads. The blades stir the air so fast, dust stings my eyes.

Parker. Where is Parker? I twist, straining against the men dragging me up the hill.

She staggers between two clerics I don't know—or can't remember—her eyes glassy, her lip split and swollen. She looks wrecked—but she's still fighting. I see it in the way her shoulders set, the way she keeps jerking against their grip, like if she just times it right, she'll break free. Her gaze locks on mine, hard and steady, before she drops her eyes to her hands, zip tied in front of her.

I follow her gaze. Her fingers are moving. Slowly. Carefully.

A-J W-I-L-L C-O-M-E.

AJ will come.

God, I want to believe her. But the memories claw at me—sentry towers, men with AK-47s laughing in the darkness. If AJ comes here...they'll kill him. They'll kill him because of me.

My throat burns. Tears streak hot down my cheeks. My arms feel like stone, my fingers thick and useless, but I force them to move. I can't let my last words on this earth be nothing but broken sounds from my broken brain. I point to her, then start to form letters.

N-O G-I-V-E U-P.

Don't give up.

Parker sees it. She jerks her chin at me, fierce, protective even now when all hope for me is gone. Her lip trembles but her eyes—God, her eyes burn. She understands. She won't stop.

They drag us higher, toward the glow at the heart of the compound. The altar looms ahead like a sadistic beacon, ringed by lanterns and a trench of open flame. My stomach heaves. Every instinct screams at me to run, but I can't. All I can do is stumble forward, and pray Parker finds a way out.

I half expect them to tie me to the altar and leave me there until tomorrow night. But Brother Malone takes a hard left, and we're forced to follow.

My body remembers this path, even if my brain hasn't caught up yet.

Nausea crawls up my throat. I can't let them lock me in that room again. But...what choice do I have?

Memories slam into me with every breath, every step across the warped floorboards. Some are only fragments. Others...in full technicolor.

The house smells the same. Like sweat and oleander. The rough plank flooring snags on my socks. Up the stairs, down the hall, past Prophet's bedroom, to a door where padlocks dangle open on two thick hasps, like they've been waiting for me.

One of the clerics shoves me inside. My legs give out, and I twist at the last second, collapsing onto the narrow bed instead of the floor. The lumpy mattress provides almost no cushion, and I stare up at the plain wooden ceiling with tears in my eyes.

I choke on a broken sob. Almost a word.

No.

They drag Parker in next. She thrashes, landing a solid kick to somewhere vital, but the two men muscle her into the corner anyway. Her chest heaves, and her gray eyes flash with pure fury.

Heavy footsteps thud down the hall. Familiar. Terrifying.

I scramble back on the bed until my spine hits the wall, curling inward, trying to make myself as small as possible. It won't help. There's nowhere for me to go. But still, I try. My knees come up tight to my chest, arms locked around them like that will somehow stop Prophet from hurting me.

"Blessed evening, Nova." His voice is almost tender. Reverent. "Welcome home."

"That isn't her name, asshole," Parker snarls. She springs up, her hands balled into fists, but Brother Malone is faster. He catches her with an arm around her waist and throws her back against the wall. Her left leg slides out from under her, and she crashes to the floor.

"It is her only name," Prophet says, the edge to his voice sending a chill down my spine. "And she knows it. Don't you, Nova?"

Tears clog my throat. I nod, though every part of me wants to scream.

"Grace, no. You're not his. You were never his!" Parker scoots closer to the bed and clamps her fingers around my ankle like an anchor. Her voice is raw, frantic. "Promise me, Grace. Promise me you won't give him the satisfaction."

For a heartbeat, I think I can. I think I can be strong for her. But then Prophet's hand shoots out, closing around her throat. He hauls her upright like she weighs nothing. Parker kicks, claws, fights with every ounce of fury she has left, and finally, spits in his face.

"Defiance is expected. For a time. But a week in the box will cure you of that spirit." Prophet's tone is too calm. Calm is always followed by pain. "What did Brother Marvin say her name was?"

"Parker Elmore," Brother Malone answers.

"No more. Now, you are Sister Willow. Soon, you will be my fifth wife."

My lungs seize. Sister Willow. God, no. Please, no. Not Parker.

Parker thrashes, wheezing as Prophet tightens his grip. And then it hits me—the memory slamming into me so hard, my entire body shudders.

The sound. The endless, droning vibration, so low it rattled every bone in my body, yet so loud my skull felt like it was cracking apart. No melody. No words. Just an unrelenting frequency tearing through my chest until my heartbeat wasn't *mine* anymore. The air itself vibrated until I couldn't tell where my body ended and the noise began.

And the lights. Always on. Blinding. White-hot. Hours blurred into days. The suffocating heat of the day and the biting, bone-deep cold at night. No silence. No darkness. No escape.

A week will destroy her.

It destroyed me.

Something inside me fractures. She's only here because of me. Because she wouldn't leave my side. Because she thought she could protect me.

Prophet shoves Parker at Brother Malone. "Take her. When I release her, she'll beg me for the sacred honor of being my wife."

"No!" The cry rips from me, broken and jagged, but the closest thing to an actual word I've managed. I reach for Parker, but my arms are weak, my body too heavy, my chest crushed under the weight of what Prophet is about to do to her.

"Grace!" she screams, kicking and bucking as Brother Malone drags her toward the door. Her voice cracks, fury giving way to raw terror. "Don't you let him win! Promise me! Grace!"

Her voice fades as Brother Malone hauls her down the corridor, but I can still hear the echoes of her rage, the pounding of her boots against the wood for several long moments, until finally, a door slams below us.

And then the silence crushes me.

Prophet turns his gaze to me, his eyes burning with a kind of devotion that makes my skin crawl.

"It's time to prepare for the ceremony."

"Wh...?" It's too early. If he's waiting for the full moon...it's *tomorrow.*

The door creaks open. A cleric stands in the hallway, his arms crossed over his chest. One of Prophet's wives enters, her dark pink dress brushing her toes and a bundle of white fabric in her hands. A dress. Silk. Plain. Like the one I was found in.

"Strip," Prophet orders. "The rags of your old life sully the purity the Glorious One demands. Put on the dress, then lie down on the bed." His smile sharpens. "If you refuse, Brother Vincent will *help* you."

My hands shake so violently, I can't grip the hem of my pajama top. But all it takes is one step by Brother Vincent and I force myself to work the buttons open.

I peel my clothes off, a piece at a time. Each one hits the floor like a blow. My skin prickles with shame as I drag the dress over my head.

It fits so well, it's like it was made for me.

Because it was.

I lie on the bed, braced for him to tie me down. Or drag me into the darkness and bind me to the altar. My breath catches with each shift of his shadow.

He snaps his fingers. One by one, his wives rush in, silent, their arms loaded down with flowers. Oleanders.

Prophet arranges them himself. Carefully. Deliberately. As though he's building a shrine. The air thickens with their cloying sweetness until every breath scorches my throat. Until the weight of the scent presses down on my chest. Until I can't breathe without choking.

He smooths a hand over the blooms near my hip, almost tenderly. "Blessed night, Nova," he murmurs. "Sleep well. Tomorrow you will ascend in glory and fulfill the destiny the Glorious One has chosen."

The door slams shut. The locks *thunk*.

I sob until my body shakes, until there's nothing left but raw sound. Rage claws its way up next, jagged and wild. But too soon, my strength is gone, leaving only silence and the suffocating sweetness of oleander.

CHAPTER SEVENTY-EIGHT

AJ

THE FOREST SMELLS like pine and damp earth. Any other time, it'd be refreshing. But now...it's nothing but the scent of a fresh grave.

Static crackles over comms. The reception out here is shit, but the tech Pritchard sent is straight out of a Tom Clancy fever dream. Four tactical drones, enough firepower to blow up a small city, and a satellite hub to connect us to Zephyr. God only knows how he managed to get the two large crates to Odessa so fast.

Connor finishes dragging the last of the camo netting over the three ATVs behind us. This is as close as we dare get to the compound. Here, the trees hide us from view, but less than a quarter mile away, it's nothing but open prairie with the occasional weeping willow or oak. Nowhere to hide.

The glow of the drone's monitor paints Hardison's face in a ghostly green light, making his hard angles even sharper.

"If you don't slow down," Zephyr says, her voice whisper-quiet in our ears, "they're going to spot the drone and this whole operation goes sideways."

"I *am* going slow," Hardison mutters. "This is me out for a Sunday drive."

The sound she makes is something between a snort and a laugh. "Hardly. I'm taking over, Nate."

He throws his hands up. "Oh sure, by all means. Just remember, when you crash it, I get to say 'I told you so.'"

"Here we go," Zephyr says. "Two sentries on the northwest and northeast towers. They've got AKs. Plus floodlights. Good ones. You try to approach on foot, they'll pick you off from half a mile away."

"Fuck. Check out the south side." I stop pacing to peer over Hardison's shoulder.

"Where do you think I'm going next? Patience, grasshopper."

I ball my hands into fists.

Don't piss off the tech goddess. We need her.

It takes her almost ten minutes to skirt the edges of the compound. It's that fucking big. "No floodlights on the southeast tower. Southwest though...same setup as the other three."

"Because they think no one's stupid enough to scale that cliff face," Connor mutters, leaning against the ATV.

"Yeah, well, guess we're gonna draw the short straw." Nate shakes his head. "Nothing like a little breaking and entering at four a.m. to get the blood pumping."

Four a.m. Grace has been gone almost ten hours. My mind won't stop running worst-case scenarios. All the ways this Prophet asshole could have hurt her—and Parker—in that amount of time.

"Taking the drone in deeper now," Zephyr says. "Keep your eyes peeled."

Jasper and Connor huddle around the monitor with us. The drone's night vision is state-of-the-art, and the image is so crystal clear, it's like watching a movie. A terribly boring movie with a life-and-death test afterward.

Greenhouses. Barns. A low, squat, gray building in the distance... So much of the topography mirrors Grace's sketches. When the drone flies over the center of the compound, I lose my breath completely.

Fuck.

There's the altar. The lanterns are lit, and around it, the remains of a fire smolder in a kind of sick and twisted moat.

"Find her window," I hiss. "That's where she'll be."

"You don't know that," Connor says, his hand steady on my shoulder. "We're hopin' that's where he's put her. We don't know for sure."

I turn and glare at him. "She's in there."

Jasper shifts beside me. "If she is, Parker's likely nearby. She's his leverage to keep Grace in line."

Hardison spins around, shoving Jasper with an almost feral growl. "She's a *person*. Not a poker chip this asshole gets to toss on a table."

My brother's right. But so is Nate. "Stand down. Both of you. Jas, don't you *ever* call Parker leverage again. Even if that's exactly what she is to their damn *Prophet*."

Jasper blows out a breath. "Fine. But we're splittin' hairs here. And we still don't know where the fuck she is."

"Zephyr, how close to Grace's window do you think you can get the drone?" I return my gaze to the monitor, watching the drone make its third pass over the altar.

"If I dip much lower, even running dark, someone could see it," she says.

Fuck.

"We should go in now. Hit 'em hard and fast. Before sunrise." I'm already moving toward the ATVs when Connor grabs my arm.

"And walk straight into a kill box? AJ, they've got AKs on

every tower, choke points at the gate, and God knows how many men inside. We go now, we'll have no cover. The best time to move is right before the ceremony. Eight thirty, eight forty-five tonight. Maximum chaos."

"That'll be too late." The words tear through my heart like jagged knives. "The poison could kill her long before the blade does. The fucker knows he failed last time. What if he gives her twice as much? What if he cuts her throat rather than just stabbing her in her side? What if he's already done it...?"

Hardison clears his throat. "Cap—"

"No!" My shout is too loud. Even here, almost ten miles from the compound, the sentries, *my wife*, I know I'm being reckless as fuck. But I don't care. "Every minute we wait, is a minute closer to Grace dyin'. And once Grace is dead...Parker's next."

For several long moments, the only sounds come from the forest. The skitter of the occasional squirrel. The hoot of an owl. The whisper of tree branches in the light breeze.

Then Hardison pipes up, his tone light but the words obviously forced through a clenched jaw. "Well, gentlemen, glad we're all in agreement—storm the death cult at dawn, die a glorious death, and maybe our heirs get a movie deal out of it all." He taps the monitor, right over the Prophet's house. "If we want to live long enough to have a say in the casting decisions, we need intel from inside."

Connor pulls off his black cap, runs a hand through his hair, and tugs it back on again. "How, exactly, do you propose we do that?"

Hardison glances at me and shrugs. The move would be casual if anyone else did it. But for him...it's tension personified. "Get a message in. To Grace. To Parker. Both if we can. Tell 'em to stall any way they can."

"You planning on walking up to the gate and passing them a goddamn note?" I ask.

With a small shake of his head, Hardison blows out a long, slow breath. "We got a perfectly good drone in the air right now. You say Grace is in that bastard's house? Let's find out."

Zephyr cuts in. "And if I get too close trying to see in that window? You lose the element of surprise. Be damn sure you're willing to take that risk."

I pin my gaze to the screen. The drone is hovering a good twenty feet over the roof. All the windows are dark. Grace could be in there. Alone. In pain. Afraid. Or...she could be anywhere.

"Cap." All the humor has vanished from Hardison's tone. "This is a huge fucking risk. But it's also our best chance."

Connor blinks, almost startled. "Jesus. He's not even being sarcastic anymore."

Hardison doesn't look away from me. "That's how you know I'm right."

Grace

The light from the nearly full moon slashes across the end of the bed. The cloying scent of oleander clings to my lungs, suffocating me even through the sheet I hold to my mouth and nose.

The thin, scratchy blanket wrapped around my shoulders is my only source of warmth. Of comfort.

My thoughts chase themselves in jagged, broken loops.

Parker screaming as they dragged her away.

The bright lights, gnawing hunger, and ear-splitting sounds inside the box.

The ceremony.

The poison. Cramping muscles. Pounding head.

Lying on cold stone.

Ropes holding me down.

The chanting. The lanterns. The blade piercing my side.

Another sob rips from my throat. I don't have any more tears to cry. I'm so dehydrated, my tongue sticks to the roof of my mouth. But the last time I tried to make it to the bathroom for water, I collapsed, landing in a pile of oleander blooms. If I'd had anything in my stomach, I would have lost it right then.

I pin my gaze to the window. It's only an illusion of freedom, but I'll take an illusion over my own spiraling thoughts.

Something flickers red just beyond the glass. But then it's gone again.

I rub my eyes, then wince as I catch the edge of the incision at my temple. When I look again, it's gone. Until...it's not. This time, it's not just a single pulse. It's a whole series of them. A pattern.

No. It's not possible. I'm hallucinating. Or...am I?

Dragging the blanket with me, I crawl over the carpet of flowers, my knees aching, my palms crushing the blooms, until I can curl my fingers around the sill and pull myself up.

Pressing my palm to the glass, I strain to see what's out there.

It's all black. Almost...delicate. With four circular rotors moving so fast, they're only vague blurs.

My heart stutters in my chest. I force my fingers to bend.

Make a fist. Thumb pointed up. A.

Move the thumb across the fist. Pinky finger out. Draw a J.

The red light blinks once.

Tears blur everything. I didn't think I had any left, but for AJ...apparently I do.

I point to my chest. Then cross my arms. Then point to the drone.

I love you.

Another flash.

The drone drifts closer. One edge presses right against the

glass, and a low sound seeps through the pane. At first, it's only a subtle vibration, but then—

"Grace."

AJ's voice. It's so faint, I have to press my ear flat to hear it.

"Coming for you. During the ceremony."

No. No, no, no.

I wave my hands, desperate to make him understand. If he waits until the ceremony begins, it'll be too late. The poison…

"Stall. Need fifteen minutes. After it starts."

I shake my head, too hard, too long. A wave of dizziness almost takes me down. But I grab on to the sill, straining to hear.

"No other option. Where's Parker?" AJ asks.

I pull back enough to sign *B-O-X.* then point to the edge of the group of houses. I never told AJ about the box. I couldn't remember anything beyond the sound and utter despair.

"Love you. Always."

The drone rises, higher and higher, until I can't even see a tiny speck of black against the pre-dawn sky.

The silence filling the room is unbearable now. I crumple to the floor, clutching the blanket around me, and press my back to the wall. Relief and terror twist together until they're practically *one* emotion.

AJ's here. But if I have any hope of seeing him again, I have to survive long enough for him to get to me.

I'm too weak to fight Prophet. Or Brother Malone. Or… anyone. I try to muffle my sobs in the blanket, but I'm cracking into pieces, and they're so loud, I'm petrified Prophet will hear them. That he'll somehow know about AJ. About the drone. And that will not only be *my* end, but the end of everyone I love.

CHAPTER SEVENTY-NINE

Grace

THE HARSH CLANG of the morning bells drags me from a haze of exhaustion. My head pounds, and my stomach won't stop twisting itself into knots.

I've been lying on this wretched bed, working on my words for hours. Nothing complicated. The simplest sounds. Broken syllables I might be able to use to convince Prophet I'm dying *now*. He won't like that. He'll call his father.

Not long after the drone flew away, I remembered Abe. How he was kind to me. How he wanted to help me, but didn't know how.

"P-poh-suh. Poh-sun. Siii...sick." I hold onto the brief moment of triumph like it's the most precious thing in the world. Right now, it is. Those two words might be enough. At least for Prophet.

Abe... Maybe he'll have a pen? Or maybe...he'll just know what I need.

Footsteps thud on the stairs. Two sets. Like always. Prophet and Brother Malone.

I burrow deeper under the thin blanket, and as the heavy steps get closer, I start to shake. It's only partially an act. I'm terrified Prophet will see right through me. Or that he won't care.

The heavy locks *thunk*, and the hasps open with a metallic screech.

"Blessed day, Nova," Prophet says, a hint of reverence in his voice. Brother Malone follows him into the room, sets a tray down on the desk, and retreats back into the hall. But he doesn't leave. He never does. In case I manage to find a burst of strength or decide to claw Prophet's eyes out.

God, I wish I could. But I'm so tired and dizzy, I'd probably end up with my fingers poking into the man's ear instead.

"Sit up," Prophet orders. "You need strength for the ceremony tonight."

I moan softly, then roll my eyes as far back in my head as I can force them.

He sighs, dragging the heavy, uneven chair closer to the bed and lowering himself into it. "I failed the flock last time. I see that now. I should never have allowed Jefe to dictate the timing of your sacrifice. But tonight...the Glorious One will be pleased. My wives have picked *all* the oleander flowers in the greenhouses. The holy wine will be twice as strong. I will slit your throat, letting your blood bathe the sacred ground beneath the altar until not a single drop remains in your body."

He's almost apologetic. I'd laugh if I didn't need him to believe I'm too close to death to move.

I squeeze my eyes shut. If I can't get Abe here, if I can't delay, AJ won't have time. He'll die. Along with Connor. Jasper. Hardison. And Parker...Parker's still in the box. By the time anyone else comes, I'll be dead, and she'll...she'll be gone too.

Another weak moan, and I tighten my throat so it sounds like I can barely breathe.

Prophet scoops up a spoonful of eggs and holds it close to

my lips. I don't have to fake the gag. The scent—mixed with the oleander I can't get away from—sends bile rushing up my throat.

I turn onto my side and vomit.

The chair legs scrape over the floor. "Nova?"

I let my head hang half off the bed. The position sends a drum beat slamming against the inside of my skull.

"Si...si... Poh-sun." The words are only half formed at best. But with a shaking hand, I try—unsuccessfully—to push some of the flowers away.

Prophet grabs my shoulders and shoves me onto my back. His eyes narrow on me. "Poison? Is that what you're trying to say?"

I nod and clutch my stomach harder.

He barks out a laugh. "Not poison. Purification. You are still resisting me, Nova. You know that is not allowed."

I roll my eyes back a second time. "Huur...ts." The word escapes on a sob.

Prophet's grip tightens on my shoulders, his face inches from mine, his tone so sanctimonious, I want to vomit all over again. "You will *not* defy me, Nova. You will eat, or I will force the food down your throat."

My vision blurs. The stench of the flowers is everywhere. Prophet pries my jaw open and shoves some of the eggs into my mouth. "*Eat!*" he shouts.

His sharp command, the bruising grip on my jaw, and three *years* of conditioning conspire against me. I swallow automatically, but the taste—God, the taste—sends the food right back up onto his hand.

"Brother Malone!" Prophet shakes the eggs from his fingers in disgust. "Send for my father. Now! If she dies before the ceremony, the Glorious One will not be pleased!"

The door slams shut, rattling the bare wooden walls. Prophet paces in front of the bed. I feel each heavy step deep in my chest. I want to cower, to pull the blanket over my head to hide from his angry gaze, but I have to make him believe I'm too weak to move.

His eyes track every ragged breath. Every tremor in my limbs. "If you think this weakness will spare you, Nova, you are mistaken."

If I have my way, Prophet, *this weakness will spare me, but end you.*

For endless minutes, the only sounds in the room are his boots striking the floorboards and my wheezing.

Until Brother Malone's steps rush back down the hall, and the door slams open.

"Father Abe," Prophet snaps.

The man who steps over the threshold is a stranger and not at the same time. My only memories of him are of his voice. And how gentle he was with me. How he'd call me Grace if he knew no one would overhear.

But he looks so much like Prophet, I can't meet his gaze.

He shuffles closer, his fingers trailing over the flowers, pausing on the wilt showing at their edges. His nostrils flare. "She's weak," he says. "If you expect her to make it to the ceremony, all these flowers must go. Now."

Prophet stomps closer. "The blossoms will purify her."

"They'll kill her in under an hour if you leave them here. Son, I believe every word you've ever written. You know I do. The Glorious One requires his Nova to be breathing when her blood is spilled."

Abe reaches for the bandage over my temple. I whimper, try to turn my head away, but fear locks my muscles up tight.

"Look at her, Prophet." Gently, he pulls the bandage away. "Her surgery was less than forty-eight hours ago. The incision hasn't even started to heal. If you want her strong enough to take the holy wine and complete her sacrifice, you'll let me treat her."

"Fine," Prophet snaps. "I will send my wives up to bring the anointed flowers to the altar. Brother Malone will be right outside. Treat her quickly. You still have to mix the holy wine for tonight. Twice as strong as last time. I want it ready by eight."

"Yes, Prophet," Abe says, his eyes downcast. "Twice as strong."

The door shuts—almost softly—and the sound of his boots fades away.

Only then do I draw an easy breath.

Abe listens for another minute, then carefully lowers himself down into the chair. "Grace, I am sorry." His lower lip wobbles slightly. "When he found out you were alive...he kept me in the box for three days. Until he learned it was hypothermia that saved you."

Tears prick at my eyes. I fumble for Abe's hand, and squeeze once. How could Prophet be so cruel as to torture his own father?

Floorboards creak beyond the door. Abe jerks his arm back as Prophet's four wives, clad in identical pink dresses, file into the room. Their eyes never meet mine. They move like ghosts, scooping up armfuls of blossoms, their skirts brushing against the bed frame. Petals scatter across the floor, bruised and torn. When they leave again, the air is a fraction clearer, though oleander still sickens me more with each breath.

Abe lingers at my side, studying me the way a man might study a wounded foal. His gaze drifts to the mess at the side of the bed, the sour bile streaked over a few crushed blooms, the sharp tang of vomit mixing with the flowers. His jaw tightens.

He moves quickly into the bathroom, the faint rush of water following. The sound nearly breaks me—I want it so badly. My mouth aches with dryness, my tongue thick and useless. I claw for the word, but all that comes out is a pitiful sob. "Terr..."

Abe kneels beside the bed, a washcloth in his hands with

steam still rising from the white fabric. His brows knit. "What did you say, my dear?"

"Th–thir—" The syllable fractures against my cracked lips. My hand trembles as I mime lifting a cup.

Understanding dawns in his eyes. He sets the cloth next to me, disappearing again, then returns with a glass filled nearly to the brim.

He has to steady it at my lips. I gulp too fast, choking, water spilling down my chin. I could weep at how good it tastes. It's the only thing untainted by the horrors of this place.

"Slowly, Grace. Slowly," he murmurs. Once I've had half a glass, he sets it down and retrieves the washcloth.

With a gentle touch, he cleans the bile from the corner of my mouth, dabs at the sheets, and finally, swipes the soiled cloth across the floor.

When he finishes, his gaze flicks to my temple. "You need a fresh bandage. May I?"

I manage the smallest nod.

He digs in his leather bag, coming up with a roll of gauze, some medical tape, and a small brown bottle. The antiseptic stings, and I hiss out a breath.

"I know. I'm sorry," he murmurs as he presses a fresh square of gauze to the wound and tapes it into place. "But if this gets infected..." His hands start to shake, and he jerks them away. "It...won't matter. Because my son..." A tear carves a silent trail down his cheek.

I can't let him spiral. Not when this is my only chance. "A... A...J." The letters are almost clear, but does he have any idea what they mean? "C...cuh...ming."

Abe blinks, as if he can't possibly have heard me right. "AJ?" His voice is barely audible. "That's your husband? The Ranger?"

I nod hard enough to make my skull throb. "Cer...em. Nee...

Lih...vve." I pound a weak fist against the mattress, frustrated when the word collapses into nonsense.

Think, Grace. Find another way.

With shaking hands, I reach for his sleeve, yank his wrist closer, and trace clumsy letters against his palm.

D-E-L-A-Y.

His mouth opens, closes. He glances at the door like he expects Prophet to burst in any second. Then he leans close. "I can't delay the ceremony, Grace. Even if I could, the ritual wine —the oleander—at the concentration my son wants... It will stop your heart long before the blade touches you."

I try again to make him understand, pressing harder this time.

1-5 M-I-N.

"Fifteen minutes?"

"Uh...huh." My voice cracks. Tears burn hot down my cheeks. "AJ..."

Abe's breath hitches, and for a moment I think he might collapse right there. "He knows where you are?"

Fear slices through me, sharper than any blade. What if I've just sealed my fate? And AJ's? What if the days Abe spent in the box broke him? Oh, God. I didn't think this through. The brief glimpse of hope fades in an instant.

"Grace, he'll die if he tries anything. The sentries...they'll see him coming. They'll kill him."

The concern in his voice is so real, I think—I hope—he's still the kind man who helped me hold onto the last shred of my life I would have otherwise lost. My name.

I take his hand again, dragging my finger across his palm.

H-E-L-P.

B-O-X.

His brows knit. "Help...box? Oh, fuck. The girl. The one Malone said was causing trouble. She's in the box?"

I nod. "Fend. Fr-end."

Fresh sobs claw at my chest. I press both hands to my mouth, terrified my weeping will bring Prophet storming back.

Abe's eyes darken, and a tremor ripples through his body. "Listen to me, Grace. My son was dead to me the minute he declared me mentally incompetent and dragged me here against my will. What walks these halls is rot in a man's skin. I will not let him break another soul—not yours, not that girl's. Not while there's still breath in my body."

His conviction, the absolute truth of it in his voice and in his eyes, cuts through my terror with bright, warm hope.

Abe leans in and lowers his voice. "I'll try to see to her. But...my son doesn't trust me. He hasn't—not once—since he found out you were alive. He'll send Vincent to watch me mix the ritual wine. If I try to weaken it, and he catches on, it'll be the end of me."

I shake my head hard enough, it feels like the room tries to throw me sideways into the wall. "Nd...me...too."

For a heartbeat, the silence between us is unbearable. Then Abe nods once, resolve hardening his expression. "I'll do whatever I can. For you. For the girl in the box. I promise."

Abe reaches into his leather bag and pulls out a small vial. He unscrews the top, then pours a dark liquid into a tin cup. A bitter, acrid scent burns my nose.

"It's not much. Charcoal and a mix of roots. The oleanders have been poisoning you for hours now. My son doesn't understand how toxic they are. But this will help slow what's already in your system. And it'll give you a little extra strength for tonight."

He presses the cup into my hands. The first sip nearly chokes me, but I force it down and take another. Then another.

When the cup is empty, he caps the vial and slides it under my pillow. "Take the rest when the sun sets. Not before." Abe covers my hand with both of his. "Now rest. He won't come for you until close to nine." For a long moment, he doesn't move.

But eventually, he rises, takes the water glass back into the bathroom, and refills it before setting it next to the bed. "I'll tell Malone you need to rest. That I've given you a sedative. Sleep if you can."

By the time he opens the door, his whole demeanor has changed to a beaten, weary old man.

For the first time since Prophet locked me in this room three years ago, I think maybe...I might survive this.

CHAPTER EIGHTY

AJ

HARDISON MOVES like a man who's already lost patience with subtlety. He ducks behind one of the ATVs, his fingers flying over the satellite phone while Zephyr taps into the line.

The weight of what we're about to do—this deal we're making with a devil—presses down on me. I don't know how to justify it, but I know at the end, Grace will be alive, in my arms. And Parker will be free.

"Nothing says good life choices like dialing up a cartel boss for a friendly chat," Hardison says.

"Friendly?" My brows shoot up. "Ain't nothin' about this that's friendly."

Connor adjusts his rifle strap across his chest, jaw tight. He hasn't said a word in ten minutes, but the way his eyes keep flicking toward me, I reckon he's thinking the same thing I am —this is insane.

But Grace is inside that compound, and insane is the only card we've got left.

Zephyr's voice is thin and tinny over the tiny earbuds. "You'll have Reyes in three, two, one..."

I picture my wife's face. The way she squints when she's trying to make a joke land. How she rested her cheek against my chest that first night home, so relaxed I thought my heart would stop. That's why we're doing this. *She's* why we're doing this.

The doc answers, his voice low and measured. "Dr. Alejandro Reyes. Who is this?"

"Doc, it's AJ."

There's a long pause. Long enough, I wonder if he's going to talk to me at all. "Is Grace all right?"

I close my eyes for half a beat, because even through the crackle of the sat phone, I hear the worry in him. The man who cut into her skull in a clinic that had no business handling brain surgery, and who kept her alive long enough for me to get to her. "She's hangin' on. But she ain't safe, Doc. The man who...almost killed her... He's about to try again. And this time, he won't fail. That's why I'm calling. You saved her. You gave me my wife back." My voice cracks, the desperation leaking through no matter how tightly I grit my jaw. "I need your help again. One more time."

Hardison mutters beside me, "Cue the part where we dial up Satan's second cousin."

Connor cuts him a look sharp enough to peel paint, but I don't flinch. "You know Miguel Sandoval," I say, forcing my voice to steady. "You run his clinic. And you swore that he was a good man. That he'd never condone...anything that was done to Grace."

Reyes lets out a short breath, half-sigh, half-laugh. "He is the head of the cartel, AJ. His hands will never be clean. But yes. He is, at his heart, a good man."

"I ain't askin' for clean," I say. "I'm askin' for someone willing to straddle the line between good and evil...for the right cause. The Cordova Cartel is runnin' a ghost gun operation out of land owned by a cult called the Blessed Flock. Their leader, who insists his devotees call him Prophet, has Grace in their compound now. Stole her right out of the hospital in Austin less than thirty-six hours after she'd had a craniotomy."

"Dios Mio. Only a monster..." Reyes lets out a string of curses in his native tongue.

"In twelve hours, he's gonna poison her all over again, then bleed her out so his *flock* can have eternal life. The cult's lands run from Alpine all the way to the U.S./Mexico border. Right to Sandoval's territory."

"And this is why you want to speak to Miguel? You think he can...somehow put a stop to these zealots? Even though they are not even in the same country?" Reyes's thin laugh grates, but he's got a point.

"I think Cordova's been sending a fuckin' tsunami of guns into Mexico. Undercutting Miguel's operations, making him look weak. You know the next step is to try and wipe Sandoval off the map."

Reyes is silent for a moment. "Miguel does not want a war."

"Cordova does. If Sandoval looks like he can't stop one, he's already lost."

"What are you proposing?" Reyes asks.

"Sandoval shows up at the front gates tonight. Loud and ornery. Provide enough of a distraction, enough chaos, for us to get Grace—and Parker—out of there alive. Once we're clear, he can go in, guns blazin', and take all of Cordova's manufacturing lines. All the 3D printers, supplies...everything."

Static hisses while Reyes thinks, and I swear my heart's gonna pound out of my chest.

"Do you understand what you are asking of me?" He sighs, the sound carrying years—if not decades—of weight. "To call him...to vouch for you? It is no small thing."

"I know." I ball my free hand into a fist. "Doc, you found her.

Kept her breathin' when I didn't even know she was alive. I'll never forget that. I got no business askin' you for a damn thing. But I'm callin'—beggin' you because I'm out of options. And Grace is out of time."

"Miguel trusts me. Even though I hid Grace's existence from him until you were back in the United States. I explained how fragile she was. But also, her strength. The purity of her soul."

"Doc...please." My chest is tight enough I can hardly breathe. If he says no...we're fucked. Grace and Parker will die. And I'll have nothin' left in this world but a dog who'll, once again, lose her person.

"I will make the call. He will listen, at least. But I can make no promise that he will be willing to help."

"Alejandro—"

"Make no mistake, AJ. Miguel is not a savior. He is not a man you control. He is a man you unleash."

Hardison leans closer to the receiver, whispering, "So basically, we're trading one devil for another?"

I glare at him, then steady my voice. "Understood, Doc. Just give me a chance. Give *Grace* a chance to live. Again."

There's a soft rustle on the other end, followed by the sound of a chair scraping. "For Grace," Reyes says at last. "Always for Grace."

Those three words soften something feral in me. Something I thought might be gone forever. I picture Reyes in his clinic. His weary smile. The way he cared for Grace. Protected her. Even from me until he was certain I could be trusted. He'll do this for Grace. And maybe...we'll have a chance.

After a few moments, there's a click, and a new voice rumbles over the line. Measured. Ancient in a way. The voice of a man who knows loss.

"This is Miguel Sandoval. Alejandro says you come to me for a favor?"

"More of a...trade. My name is AJ Stone. I'm a captain with

the Texas Ranger division. I won't waste your time with my resume. I reckon you can find that out on your own. My wife, Grace, and one of my lieutenants, Parker Elmore, were kidnapped by some assholes callin' themselves the Blessed Flock. They're in deep with the Cordova Cartel, manufacturin' ghost guns on cult lands that they send right into Mexico. But their leader is convinced Grace is the key to his *eternal salvation*. He's plannin' on sacrificing her tonight. Nine p.m. I've got an infil team ready to go, but these bastards are prepared for anythin'."

"That is an interesting story, Captain Stone. But I do not know what you need from me," Miguel says, his tone warning me he's growing weary of listening.

"We need a distraction. Noise. A show of force at eight-fifty-five p.m. Big enough that their Prophet stops the ceremony and to distract his sentries so they never see us comin'."

"Tonight?" He laughs. "The United States is not my territory, Stone. And if I were to make it so, it would take weeks—if not months—to prepare such an invasion."

"We've done the work, Miguel. We can send you drone footage of the entire compound. Provide intel on every possible escape route. All you have to do is show up. Threaten this Prophet asshole. His whole fuckin' flock. Do anything but burn the place down. Once we get what we need—Grace and Parker —you can have the 3D printers, whatever you find in the cult's coffers, everything in the compound."

"I want the head of the Cordova Cartel."

"I can get him there," I say before Jasper, Connor, or Hardison can argue with me. "I'll get Jefe to show his face. You can have him too for all I care."

After a long beat, Miguel hums. "You can summon a rival to my doorstep? How will you do that, Captain Stone?"

"That's my business, Miguel."

Miguel is quiet long enough I can almost hear crickets. "You would bring two predators into a single cage. You understand what that means?"

"I do. But there are rules, Miguel." This is the moment when we win or lose. Right here. Miguel could call for my head as easily as most men would order a club soda.

His dry laugh worries me, but there's no turning back now. "Go on."

"You promise me that no woman or child—no matter how deep their indoctrination—will be harmed by your people. You promise me that Grace, Parker, and my four-man infil team will be safe and free to walk out of there. Do that, and I don't give a damn about anything else."

"I lost my family to men like Cordova," Miguel says at last, his voice rough with grief and a lifetime of blood. "I am not blind. Those who traffic in suffering should never be tolerated. Your terms are acceptable. I will not harm the women or children. My men will be punished if they do. As for Cordova's head—I want him to know the meaning of fear. I will take his machines. I will take his pride. If he is foolish enough to come, I will take him."

I let the anger out of my chest in a single, ragged exhale. "Thank you. Eight-fifty-five. On the dot. If you're a minute late, my wife is as good as dead."

Miguel's voice softens in a way that almost sounds like pity. "You are a dangerous man to ask this favor of me, Captain Stone. Do not expect me to be your saint. Expect me to be efficient."

"Efficient is exactly what I need." I sweep my gaze over the men who've been standing at my side for weeks now. Jasper. Connor. Hardison. Each of them nod in turn.

On the other end, Miguel's voice takes on a low, dangerous edge. "For your women," he says, "we will make it swift. For Cordova...we will make it unforgettable."

When the call drops, we sit in the thicket of trees with the radio static buzzing in our ears, the knowledge of what we've asked and what we've been given forging a new kind of quiet. My stomach is hollow and heavy all at once.

Hardison pockets the phone like it's contraband and looks at me, his face a map of too many lost nights. "We just rented time from a man with better reasons to kill than to forgive. Hope he's in a charitable mood."

"I hope he keeps his word," I say, because hope is all I have right now. "And if he doesn't..." My voice hardens. "We burn the world down around him."

CHAPTER EIGHTY-ONE

AJ

A SUBTLE BEEP in my ear is all the warning I get before Zephyr chimes in with an update. "Jefe is primed. I sent him the footage of the trigger assembly *and* Marvin's...err...confession. Indicated Marvin was on his way to the compound, and spun the story about Prophet believing that since Grace survived the last time, she's to be revered. Not murdered."

Hardison tugs on a black, long-sleeved t-shirt and pulls his gloves from his pocket. "Good. Poke the bear. But only a little. Because they're bigger and meaner, and think we taste great with some ketchup. Too much and this could backfire on us in a heartbeat."

"Marvin's confession was a deep fake," Zephyr says, a hint of exasperation in her tone. "None of you are implicated. All Jefe saw was Marvin boasting to one of his buddies about how the boss would never find out he failed to make sure Grace was dead. Or that he was the one who left the trigger assembly in the bag."

"The jig is up the second Jefe sees Marvin." Hardison cracks his knuckles, one at a time. "Dude is gonna look like roadkill for weeks."

Connor grimaces. "He can't walk into the compound under his own power. Not tonight, anyway. We could arrange a drop at the edge of cult property, but that puts whoever makes it at risk."

Zephyr breaks in. "Um, hello? Tech genius here. Marvin doesn't need to be anywhere near the compound. I can spoof his phone so if Jefe does trace it, he'll think Marvin's dead center at that altar."

Hardison's expression goes flat. "Time for moral calculus class. If we hand him to Jefe, Marvin is gonna point the finger right at us. Maybe Jefe believes him, maybe not. But even if he does, he isn't going to let Marvin live. He's too much of a liability. He'll gut him for sport before Sandoval even gets there. And in the end, he's the reason we know where Grace and Parker are.

"Option two. We could give him to the feds. Connor might be able to pull some strings to shut him up. Or we make sure he knows if he keeps his mouth shut, he'll end up in a much better prison than if he tries to implicate us.

"And behind door number three... We keep him off the board entirely until Grace and Parker are safe. Then" —he shrugs— "we decide what justice looks like when we're not bleeding out from every artery."

I drop my head into my hands, scraping my fingers over my scalp hard enough to feel the bite of pain. "We don't hand people over to monsters."

"Says the man who strung Marvin up by his wrists and drove a knife into his shoulder," Hardison says softly.

Fuck.

He's right. My hands will never be clean. How the hell am I

supposed to face my wife and tell her what I had to do to get her back?

"If we turn him over to Jefe, I won't be able to look Grace in the eye ever again," I say. "We've all done things on the job we regret. But last night, I crossed a line. One I won't ever cross again. He's secure for now. He's got water, a handful of protein bars, and a half ton of sheet metal covering the repair pit we left him in. Once Grace is safe, Connor can call some of his buddies to come get him. If he names me...I'll take the heat. I won't let it come down on the rest of you."

"Fuck that," Jas says. "Whatever happens, you don't face it alone, AJ. Not now. Not ever."

"All for one and one for all," Hardison chimes in. "Look at us. The Four Musketeers. Which one of us is D'Artagnan?"

"That'd be you, dumbass," Connor says. "You're the youngest."

Hardison looks almost offended. I chuckle, but when I blink, I see the terror in Grace's eyes through the drone's high-resolution camera. She'd want me to be ruthless. But not vengeful. I have to give her that.

"We need to move. It's at least a five-hour hike to the top of the cliff if we expect to stay out of sight," I say and heft my ruck-sack onto my shoulder.

Hardison follows suit. "All right. Let's go break into a cult and try not to get ourselves killed. Sound fun?"

Connor snorts. "Fun would be different."

"There's somethin' wrong with both of you," Jas says. "When this is over, we're *all* gonna need a few sessions with a *very* trustworthy shrink."

We move, silent and tight, each of us heavy with choices we can't unmake.

AT EIGHT FORTY-TWO, we crawl on our bellies to the edge of the cliff. The world narrows to ropes and belays and the handful of weapons we've each strapped to our bodies.

Connor goes through his checklist like it's a standardized test. Hardison is more zen about his preparation. Jas and I mirror one another, checking our carabiners, tugging on gloves, patting each holster and testing each rifle strap.

There's a beep, and Zephyr's voice is whisper-quiet in my ear. "Sandoval's men are visible on the east road. Four trucks, headlights off, moving like molasses. They'll be at the gate in ten," she says.

"Great. I was worried we'd have more time to second guess all our life choices." Nate grins, but it doesn't reach his eyes.

We hook in. The ground looms two hundred feet below us. Loose gravel falls like rain.

Connor goes first, the rope singing through his glove. He moves like he's done this a hundred times before, even with a bum leg. Jasper follows, but he's slower. The explosion that almost killed him destroyed his right rotator cuff.

Hardison casts a quick look up at me before he steps off. "If we survive this, Cap—" But he drops before he can finish the sentence.

The wind slaps my face as I push off. Mid-descent, my earbud beeps again.

"Sentries just spotted them. Towers are on high alert, but the two closest to you are focused on Sandoval's men. Get a move on."

"Copy," Connor says, his voice as calm as always. He hits the ground first, drops into a crouch and scans for threats. Jasper lands two breaths later. He cuts for the first tree, rifle up. Hardison weaves back and forth like a ping pong ball until he finds his own tree to hide behind.

I hit the ground with a roll, breath ripping out of me, and take off at a run. There's no path. Just rocks and tumbleweeds.

No cover. But Zephyr's drones are in the air, and she calls out updates every minute.

We haven't slept. My lungs burn, my calves are trying to murder me, and my hands want to shake. But I tighten my grip on my M4.

I'm coming, Grace. Hold on just a little longer.

CHAPTER EIGHTY-TWO

Grace

ALL DAY, I've kept up the ruse. Lie in the narrow bed, moan and convulse whenever Brother Malone checks on me, then wait until his footsteps fade away to crawl to the bathroom and drink another glass of water.

My left eye is bruised and swollen from the surgery, and the pain slicing through my skull is sharp enough, it takes all my energy not to cry. But whatever Abe gave me this morning has left me feeling stronger.

Close to sunset, he returned with a bowl of broth for me. I couldn't even look at it. But then he produced a roll from his pocket, and that tasted like heaven. I finished the last of the bitter charcoal tincture not long after. But if Abe can't dilute Prophet's *holy wine,* I doubt it'll be enough to save me.

I watch at the window until my neck burns from the sheer effort of holding my head up, praying I'll see Parker. That Abe will be able to get her out of that damn box. But the one time I saw him shuffle in that direction. Brother Vincent stopped him. They argued for a full two minutes. Eventually, Abe walked away, his head bowed, shoulders hunched, and returned to the barn.

Not long after darkness blankets the compound, the clerics light the lanterns, then toss kindling into the pit all around the altar and set it ablaze.

It takes less than ten minutes for the flames to rise a good five feet. The air tastes of smoke, the sickly sweetness of oleander, and my own fear.

I wish I could hear AJ again. I whisper his name into the dark until my throat is raw, but my voice is clear.

They come for me like they did before. Brother Malone and Brother Vincent. They don't care that I'm shaking in the bed. Each man takes an arm so they can drag me down the stairs, my bare toes catching splinters from the rough boards.

We stop in Prophet's living room. One of his wives comes in, holding ropes braided with so many oleander flowers, I can barely see the white and gold threads.

My hands are tied in front of me, tight enough my fingers go numb almost immediately.

A crown of red, white, and pink oleander flowers is forced down on my head. It scratches against the fresh wound from my surgery, and I whimper a little.

Abe slips in, his gaze pinned to the floor. The cup of "wine" is so dark, it's almost green. He passes it to Prophet. "Twice as strong. As you requested. The rest is at the altar."

"How long will it take at this concentration?" Prophet asks.

"Minutes. But when she goes into convulsions, you will need to spill her blood quickly." Abe's dark eyes meet mine. Do I imagine his nod?

Brother Malone yanks my head back by my hair, and Prophet pours the drugged grape juice down my throat.

I don't fight him. There's no point. It wouldn't buy me more than thirty extra seconds of life.

Terror seizes my muscles. If Abe failed, I'm going to die with AJ close enough to watch.

"Bring her," Prophet says, and Brother Malone tosses me over his shoulder. The oleander starts to work its way through my system. The stomach cramps are first. So sudden and violent, I'd vomit if I had the strength. Then my legs and arms join in. I cry out in pain, but no one cares.

Two of the other clerics—including Prophet's son—lay stone planks across the flames. Brother Malone carries me over the fire, then dumps me onto the altar with all the care one would show a sack of potatoes.

My arms are bound tightly over my head. My ankles tied down. The heat of the flames licks at my feet. The smoke stings my eyes.

Like a slow tide, the poison steals the world away. Cramps squeeze from my calves, up to my thighs, my back, my chest. My fingers clench against the ropes. The world starts to spin in soft, lazy arcs. Every one takes more from me.

White lights explode in my vision. Then the dark spots follow. Soon, I can see nothing but a dozen different shades of gray.

My heart flutters in odd patterns. Sometimes fast. Sometimes slow. Sometimes skipping beats entirely. Then slowing into a molten rhythm that weighs my entire body down.

My breath saws weakly in and out of my chest.

Where are you, AJ?

I try to call his name, to beg for help, but the words collapse on my tongue. It hurts everywhere at once. Like someone turned my body inside out.

Prophet crosses the flames with a large wicker basket. He reaches inside and grabs a handful of oleander blooms, then scatters them over my feet. Time and time again, he does this until my entire body is covered with them. Then he slides his hand under my neck, lifts my head slightly, and forces me to drink the rest of the poison.

Before he can add more blooms to the altar, a low, dark sound starts rumbling all around me.

The flock's chanting turns to shouts. The lanterns sway in the breeze. This is it. I'm going to die. He'll slit my throat in seconds.

But then...his gray silhouette disappears. I try to follow him with my eyes, but I can't see past the flames.

Something's wrong. Or...maybe something's right. My stomach cramps, and I start to retch. I turn my head and vomit, sour bile and the bitter, choking taste of oleander and grape juice.

I don't stop until there's nothing left. The cramps start to fade. My head clears just enough for me to think. To see.

Warm fingers cover mine. "Use this," a voice whispers, and presses something cool and hard into my palm. But then the warmth disappears, and I wonder if I imagined it. Except...I can *feel* the thing. *Oh, God.* It's a pocket knife.

On the other side of the flames, I can see them now. Prophet and Jefe. They shout at one another, barbs landing like hard stones. I can't make out the words, but they're loud enough to hurt. Brother Malone steps in, trying to mediate, but one of Jefe's men fires a shot into the air. Everyone takes a step back immediately.

This is it. *This* is what AJ was talking about.

Focus, Grace.

I pry the blade open with shaking fingers and jam the tip between the strands of rope. My arms are as heavy as lead. The knife scrapes and cuts my palms. Each pull threatens to shatter me, but the first strand finally snaps.

I clench my teeth and saw faster. My shoulders scream. My chest is raw, my lungs burning, and for a moment, I'm not sure I can go on. Until the ropes give way. I struggle to sit up, to focus on the ties holding my ankles down. These are thinner, and they snap in seconds.

I roll sideways. The world tilts, stars blooming at the edges of my vision. And then I fall. Off the altar and onto the hard-packed earth behind it. The heat from the moat scorches my back, but I'm so weak, I can barely move.

Shots snap like dry branches. The sound makes my blood run cold, even though my shoulders are about to blister.

Prophet moves like a feral animal. He leaps the flames, rolls over the altar like an action movie star, and wraps his hand in my hair. "You cannot escape your fate, Nova! You are mine!"

Hauling me to my feet, he pins my arms to my sides and presses a knife to my throat.

"I will have my salvation! The Glorious One will show me the way to eternal life once your blood has soaked his holy altar."

I still have the cheap pocket knife in my hand. There's no strategy. No brilliant plan. Only me, a three-inch blade, and a desperate, animalistic need to survive.

I drive it backward, aiming for anything that might cause him pain. It sinks into his thigh. Warmth spurts over my palm. A hoarse sound spills out of him. But he doesn't let go.

His blood soaks into the back of my dress. But it's not enough. He's still standing. Still pulling me closer to the altar.

"Grace!"

The sound of AJ's voice is a lifeline. I grab onto it, hold it tight, and pray.

CHAPTER EIGHTY-THREE

AJ

"Grace!"

I press myself flat against one of those goddamn poles Grace drew time and time again. The lanterns overhead swing wildly in the breeze. Connor, Hardison, and Jasper are fanned out around the altar. We all agreed. Unless there's no other choice, Prophet is mine.

The bastard still has the knife held to Grace's throat. If I make a move, he'll use it, and she'll bleed out in seconds.

Sweat beads on her skin. Her muscles tremble so violently with the simple act of holding herself upright, I'm afraid she'll impale herself on the blade before he gets the chance to kill her.

One wrong move, one twitch, and it's over.

Jefe has half a dozen of Prophet's men tangled up in some twisted dance of chaos. Shots ring out. Cartel and cult members alike fall.

I can't take my eyes off Grace. She's all that matters.

Movement flickers at the far side of the altar.

Oh, my God.

Parker. She's barefoot, wearing a pink dress so long it skims the ground. Her cheeks are stained with dirt and tears, hair plastered to her face, eyes glassy and unfocused. Her fingertips are bloody, but in her hands, she holds a three-foot piece of metal. Her entire body shakes violently. How the hell is she still standing?

She flicks her gaze in my direction. A hint of that fire I know so well still remains. Even if it is buried down deep. With a nod, she crouches out of Prophet's view, rips a long strip of fabric from her dress, and winds it around the metal bar. Then she thrusts it into the flames.

Smoke curls upward in thin, gray wisps as the cloth catches.

Fucking hell. She's gonna set the asshole on fire.

I want to tell her to stop. That he could jerk and kill Grace. But Parker knows what she's doing. Always has. Always will. Even now when she looks like she hasn't slept in weeks.

She almost drops the bar as she stands, but after two shaky steps, she thrusts it at the man, catching the bottom of his robes.

It takes a moment. One long, agonizing moment. He's still whispering to Grace, and tears stream down her cheeks. I can hear her tiny whimpers, even over the crackle of the flames.

But then, he screams, jerking Grace against him and twisting toward Parker. He doesn't get a chance to see her face. Only the burning end of the bar as it connects with his temple.

"Hope you like Hell," she spits out. "Because it's comin' for you."

The stench of smoke and burning flesh hits me. Acrid. Rotten.

Parker took out his eye.

The asshole lets go of Grace, and she crumples to the ground.

My heartbeat roars in my ears. I narrow my eyes and raise my gun. Everything else—the chaos, the smoke, the screaming —drops away.

I take a deep breath. Let it out slowly. And pull the trigger.

A neat hole in his forehead is quickly swallowed up by the flames. He staggers back, his body unable to catch up with his brain. He's already dead. Flames lick at his robes, bright orange against the black cloth.

Hardison is on Parker before she can even *think* about falling. One arm under her knees, the other at her back, hauling her off her trembling feet. She coughs, smoke rolling from her nostrils, eyes squinting against the haze.

"Seriously," Hardison says, half-awed, half-sarcastic. "This ugly pink dress, no shoes, and you *still* lit a bastard on fire?"

Parker smirks, coughs, and shakes her head. "He...couldn't take...the heat."

I jump over the flames to get to Grace and gather her in my arms. Her body trembles against mine, tiny and fragile, but alive. Warm. Real. I press my lips to her hair, breathing her in, feeling the tremor of fear still clinging to her. "I love you. I've got you," I whisper.

Tears streak her face, hot and sudden. "Got. You," she gasps, clutching me like she'll never let go.

All around us, the chaos is only getting worse.

"AJ! Over here!" Jasper calls. He points to a stone plank over the flames. *Fuck.* How did I miss that before? I carry Grace to the other side, and the six of us skirt the edge of the fray and race down a gentle hill. As soon as we're out of sight of the worst of the fighting, I drop to my knees and cradle Grace against me.

"Cap?" Hardison half carries Parker over to us. Up close, I can see the pain in her eyes. She's wrecked, in some of the same ways Grace is. Smoke still curls around her like she's some small, fire-breathing avenger. "Can we make like trees now and get gone? If we stay any longer..."

"We die." I stare through the smoke and the bodies toward the road that leads to the front gate. "It's gonna be a long walk. A long, dangerous walk."

"A...J..." Grace curls her fingers in my black t-shirt, tugging slightly until I meet her gaze. "Gr...zuh. Gr...ah..zuh."

"Garage?" I ask. "With vehicles?"

"Yes." Even that simple declaration is still muddy. Still broken and jagged from her lips. But it's so much clearer than anything she could say twenty-four hours ago, I think...maybe she'll be okay. Maybe we got lucky.

"Where, darlin'?"

She tries to lift her hand, but her arm shakes, and she lets it fall with a little whimper.

An older man with white hair steps out from the shadows. My brother and Connor draw down on him, and he raises his hands. "The garage is a quarter mile past the barn," he says. "The gray building. Go quickly while my son's clerics are... otherwise engaged."

"Your son?" Jasper grabs the man's arm, forces him to his knees, and jams his SIG against the guy's temple.

Grace tugs on my shirt again, hard, then starts moving her fingers. "Darlin', I don't know all the letters—"

"She's saying, 'Kept alive.'" Connor lowers his gun slightly. "He kept you alive?"

With a shuddering breath, she nods, then lays her palm over my heart. If that's not code for *please believe me*, I don't know what is.

I hold her close, my eyes narrowed on the old man. "That smoking pile of garbage is your son, yet you saved Grace's life? How? Why?"

"Zeke trapped me here years ago. I'm an old man, Captain Stone. And he has—had—an army. But when Grace told me you were coming, I realized I had one chance to save my soul. To defy him in a way that mattered. So I slipped her the knife. Tainted the juice in the hopes it wouldn't stay down. And"—he glances at Parker, limp in Hardison's arms—"slid a piece of metal through the floor of the box so that girl would have a fighting chance."

Nate stares down at his partner, at her bloody fingers, her soot-stained cheeks, and tightens his arms around her. "Cap, we gotta take him with us."

I motion for Jas to let the old man up. His brows lift, but he takes a step back.

"I sure hope you can run," I say. "Because we ain't stickin' around."

The old man shakes his head. "No. My place is here. The wives and children...they're innocent, Captain Stone. And they need me," he says. "You'll send someone for them, won't you?"

"Yes. But...not until tomorrow. What happens next... Get them somewhere safe... Indoors. Away from any of the men. You hear me?"

Tears tumble down Grace's cheeks. She reaches for the man, and he grasps her fingers briefly. "Your life is yours again, Grace. Live it well."

In the next second, he's gone. Melting back into the shadows.

"Zephyr? Where's this goddamn garage?" Connor asks.

The hacker's voice is like a whole fuckin' choir of angels in my ear. "Northeast of you. Wait for ten seconds, and you'll have a distraction."

They're some of the longest seconds of my life.

"Now. Everyone move!" The order shakes us all loose. Connor goes first, Jasper close behind. Hardison carries Parker next, and I hold Grace close, bringing up the rear.

One of the drones flies over our heads, and a second later, Zephyr calls out, "Get ready for a big boom, folks."

"Parker, it's gonna get loud," Hardison warns.

She flinches, while Grace winds her arms around my neck and buries her face against my chest.

The percussion blast is strong enough I feel it all the way down to my toes. Grace jerks in my arms, a tiny whimper escaping her lips.

The effect is immediate. Men scatter, the gunfire dies down, and the battlefield collapses into silence and smoke. Thank God the women and children ran for their homes the second the shooting started.

Prophet is nothin' more than a smoldering heap of burnt skin and blood, and my body unclenches a fraction. We're safe. We should *be* safe. As long as Sandoval kept his word.

Inside the garage, more than a dozen vehicles wait. Jasper beelines for a white van.

"No!" Grace cries, panic sharp in her voice, clawing at me like the van itself might swallow her whole. "Took...me."

Jasper stops inches away, frowns, then scans the place again. "Not the van, then." He points at a newer pickup, clean, with a backseat. "That'll have to do."

Connor climbs into the bed, rifle at the ready. Jasper swings behind the wheel. Hardison and I get Grace and Parker into the back seat. We wedge in tight, me supporting Grace, Hardison bracing Parker.

Nate shoots me a sideways glance, lips twitching. "No offense, Cap, but if Parker drools on me, you're swapping."

Parker rasps, "Not...my...best look."

"Sweetheart, it's top five," Hardison says, squeezing her shoulder gently.

Grace leans into me, murmuring broken syllables I have to piece together. "Safe. Home?"

"Yeah, darlin'. Home," I say and press a kiss to her hair. It smells faintly of oleanders, and, *fuck*. Will the scent ever truly leave her now?

We rattle through the gate. Connor's voice carries, sharp and commanding, calling out in Spanish. It's a phrase Sandoval told him to use if we encountered one another. For a breathless second, I think they're gonna shoot us anyway. Until the men stand down.

Miguel steps forward. Tall, broad, the kind of man who's spent his life under sun and war. Black hair streaked with gray, bronze skin lined from years of carrying other men's burdens. His eyes are sharp, flinty, the sort of stare that could cut a weaker man in half. If I didn't know a little of his history, I'd be worried we were trading one devil for another.

Reyes steps out from behind him with a bag slung over his shoulder.

Thank fuck.

"Which one of you is Stone?" Miguel asks.

"I am." I shift Grace a little closer to me. "The compound's clear. Prophet's dead. Most of his strongest fighters too. Women and children should be safe in their homes. Along with the Prophet's father. He saved Grace's life. Parker's too. Leave him be. You'll have some stragglers, but nothing you and your men can't handle. The FBI will send for the survivors. Get them deprogrammed, contact any families missing them. But not until tomorrow. Clear out by noon, and you'll be good."

Miguel frowns, like he doesn't quite trust me.

"Zephyr," I say, "give him eyes."

A second later, the feed from the drones pings onto Miguel's tablet. He watches as Zephyr toggles through aerial sweeps—the burning altar, the dead all around it, the cartel trucks abandoned.

Miguel gives a single, curt nod, then gestures to Reyes. "See to them."

The doctor doesn't waste time. He goes to Parker first, who's leaning against Hardison like he's the only thing keeping her upright.

He checks her pulse, and his eyes narrow at the shredded skin on her hands. The burns on her lower legs. "Fluids, oxygen, pain management," he mutters.

Then, his gaze turns to Grace. For a moment, he just looks at her, almost in awe. "It is good to see you again, my dear."

Grace's lips tremble. She manages a broken, "Ray...yez."

Reyes squeezes her shoulder gently, careful. "Sí. It's me. You're safe now."

"She had another craniotomy just two days ago," I explain. "A bone fragment broke off inside..." I swallow hard, the realization of how close I came to losing her hitting hard.

"Aphasia," Parker adds, then coughs weakly.

Reyes nods, understanding flashing across his face. "To be expected. May I examine you, Grace?"

She nods, but keeps one hand fisted tightly around my shirt.

The doctor pulls out a small flashlight, aiming it at her pupils. She flinches, then steadies when I start rubbing her back. He listens to her lungs, frowning at the faint wheeze. Then he carefully peels back the edge of the bandage at her temple.

One stitch has popped, and a bit of blood has soaked into the gauze. Reyes's mouth hardens. "This needs attention tonight to avoid infection. Parker's hands too. They both need fluids. I can clean, re-stitch, start antibiotics. What they need most is rest."

He straightens, turning back to Miguel. "They cannot stay here. Nor would I advise the long trip back to Austin tonight. I can take them across the border to Ojinaga. The clinic there will not ask questions when I demand rooms and supplies."

Miguel studies him, then me. Finally, he gives a short nod. "Captain Stone, you are a formidable man. You have my respect. And guaranteed safety until you return home. But after that, I never want to see you in my territory again. Understood?"

"Got it." I press a kiss to Grace's forehead. "Give me a minute, darlin'? Just one, I promise."

"O...kay." The look in her eyes almost stops me. But when Reyes steps forward to brace her, she relaxes and lets him help her into the back of a large SUV.

Miguel and I stare at one another for a long moment. Two men who've lost, fought, and won in the end. "I'll always be a Ranger, Sandoval."

"And I will always be cartel. But we understand each other, yes?"

"More than that, I think." I offer him my hand. His grip is strong—as is mine—but not crushing. "You gave me my wife back. Twice. That's a debt I can never repay."

"Then you are lucky I forgot my ledger at home," Miguel says with a small smile. "Now go, before one of my men insists I start a new one."

CHAPTER EIGHTY-FOUR

Grace

I DON'T REMEMBER MUCH from the ride to the clinic. AJ's arms around me. The steady beat of his heart under my ear. The smells of smoke and sweat. Parker trembling beside me with Nate's arm around her shoulders.

But now, there's pain as AJ helps me out of the SUV, through the darkness, and into an older clinic that smells like disinfectant.

Reyes tries to get Parker and me into separate rooms, but she grabs my hand and holds on tight. "No. I want to stay with Grace. Please?"

He nods, and relief loosens some of the tightness in my chest. Nate looks stricken as she staggers into the room without him. AJ refuses to leave my side, and I'm grateful for his strength.

Parker lets Reyes clean and bandage her hands, give her oxygen, and set up an IV, though her jaw never unclenches. Her gaze is haunted, a look I feel deep in my soul.

When it's my turn, I sit quietly, my hand held tightly in AJ's.

Reyes swabs the angry line of stitches on my temple, then adds two more to replace the one that popped when Prophet forced the crown of oleanders onto my head.

I stay still, only a single whimper when the needle slides into my skin.

After Reyes has applied a fresh bandage, started an IV, and given me a couple of pills that he says will help with any lingering effects from the oleander, he leaves, promising to return to check on us soon.

I tap AJ's arm and mime writing. I'm so tired of trying to make my words come, but there are things I need to say. To him. But especially to Parker.

It takes him a beat, but then he rummages in the little nightstand and comes up with a pad of paper and a pen.

"Go? Need time with Parker."

His shoulders stiffen, and for a moment, I think he's going to argue. But then he nods. "We'll be right outside."

The door shuts softly, and I turn to Parker. Oh, God. She sits on the edge of her bed, staring down at her hands. Tears stain her cheeks, but she doesn't make a sound.

I don't trust myself to get up, but I pat the bed to get her attention. As if she's just remembered I'm in the room, her haunted gaze snaps up, she swipes at her cheeks, and grabs her IV pole.

It's awkward at first, both of us trying to figure out how to hold one another without ripping out our IVs. But eventually, she has her arms around me, and we both sob until we have nothing left.

"Grace," she says, and a shuddering, wheezing breath escapes her. "The sound..." Her whole body is shaking now. "I can still hear it... I screamed. So loud, but no one came. I couldn't even think...except that I really *would* lose myself. That he was right. I would beg...by the end."

I fumble for the pad, my tears blurring the shaky words I manage to scribble.

"*You survived. You're here.*"

She squeezes her eyes shut and presses her forehead against my shoulder. "It was only a day...but..."

I write slower this time, taking the care Parker deserves. "*I know. First time. Right after he took me. Four days. Then, year later. Tried to escape. He caught me. Eight days.*"

Her breath hitches, raw and wheezing. "Oh, God, Grace. I'm...sorry. I don't... How?"

Parker clutches my hand like I'm the only tether she has to reality. I remember that feeling. Even with so many other holes in the past three years—in my entire life—I remember the box. And how it broke me.

I try again. "*AJ. Knew he was out there. Knew I had to get back to him.*"

Parker chokes on a sob, swiping her free hand over her cheeks. "I didn't know how they'd find us. *If* they'd ever find us." Her voice quivers, thin and raw, like she just confessed something shameful.

"They...did," I whisper, the words almost clear. "Nev-rr stop look-king."

Parker sniffles, blinking fast, her chest hitching like she's trying to swallow everything down. "I know. I know they would've searched forever if they had to. But in there—God, Grace—it felt endless. Like time didn't move. Like I was already gone, and the world just didn't know it yet."

I squeeze her fingers harder, wishing I could pour strength into her veins. "You...here," I murmur, slow and broken, but true. I wrap my arms around her again, pulling her close. "Safe."

"Safe," she echoes, as if the word itself is a miracle.

WHEN THE MEN come back in, eyes scanning like they expect an ambush even here, Parker's composed again. Fragile, but steady.

"You will stay here tonight," Reyes says firmly. "IV fluids, monitoring. Tomorrow you fly."

I look to AJ, hoping he'll understand how very much I want to go home. But he's nodding. "Whatever's best for them," he says as he moves to sit next to me and takes my hand. "You'd still be in the hospital at home if...that bastard hadn't... It's one night, darlin'. And I'll stay with you the whole time."

Nate drops into the chair next to Parker's bed, stretching out his legs like he owns the place. "Guess that makes me your bodyguard-slash-entertainment for the evening. Don't worry, I do birthday parties too."

Parker's lips twitch, a ghost of a smirk breaking through the exhaustion. "Pretty sure you'd eat the cake before the party even started."

Nate presses a hand to his chest. "Words can wound, Lieutenant Loose Cannon. But you're not wrong."

She stares down her nose at him, brows lifted slightly, but her tone is soft, almost needy. "You're really workin' hard to keep your own nickname, Lieutenant Last Nerve."

"No one's ever accused me of being lazy," he says, puffing out his chest. But in the next breath, he rests his hand on Parker's forearm, lowers his voice, and grits out, "I'm staying. No arguments."

"He doesn't get near the cake. Or any of the food. Not until everyone else has eaten," Connor says from the corner, arms crossed, a pistol strapped to his hip. "There wouldn't be anythin' left."

Nate glares at him. "Bleeding out from verbal shrapnel here, and not one of you bastards is calling for a medic? Doc? You're responsible for triage, right?"

Reyes looks at us like he can't quite tell if we're joking or concussed. "I...will check on the food. You all need to eat. Then rest."

After the doctor leaves, Jasper returns to his post, standing sentry only inches from the door, and smirks at Nate. "You'll live. Ain't a bullet that can take you down, much less a truth bomb."

AJ pulls me close, shifting so we're both propped up against the pillows. We reek of smoke. Of burnt oleanders. Of exhaustion and fear. But we're together. Our whole family is together.

———

HALFWAY THROUGH A MIDNIGHT snack of tamales and fresh fruit, Parker turns her gaze to me. "That man—Prophet's dad? How did he even know I was in the box?"

My throat tightens, and I squeeze my eyes shut. It takes all my focus to force the words free. "Abe. Told...himm."

"Abe?" AJ asks. "That's his name?"

I manage the smallest nod, then rest my head on my husband's shoulder. I hope Abe is safe. That the FBI will help him—help everyone Prophet trapped there.

Parker coughs weakly. Nate picks up a cup of water and angles the straw toward her, but she waves him off. "I don't know when Abe shoved that piece of metal through the wall. I was so out of it, it could have been there for hours. But I saw a tiny crack in the fabric. And a single rough board—must've been how he got it to me—and I started pryin' at them when it was still daylight. Took me until the ceremony started to open a hole big enough to crawl through."

"Smart." Pride roughens Nate's voice. "Stubborn as hell, but smart."

Connor and Jasper make a plan to stand guard in the hall, trading shifts every two hours, leaving just the four of us alone in this room.

Parker nods off immediately, with Nate watching over her. AJ pulls the covers up over us, wrapping his arms around me so I can lay my head on his chest.

"I love you," he whispers against my hair.

"Love. You." The words come easier now. Not perfect, not whole, but mine. "So much."

His heartbeat is steady under my cheek, a rhythm I thought I'd lost forever. My eyelids grow heavy, the warmth of him wrapping me in something that feels like peace. Real peace.

For the first time in my broken memory, I let go, knowing when I wake up, I'll still be...me. Still be held. Still be...safe.

EPILOGUE

AJ

TWO WEEKS. It's been two weeks since we pulled Grace out of hell. Since I put a bullet in Prophet's skull. Since I shook hands with an angel in devil's clothing and lived to tell about it.

Watching Grace as she sets the table, I can't believe so little time has passed. The physical and speech therapy have done wonders for her. She still stumbles over her words more often than not, and has days when the vertigo leaves her off balance and migraines knock her flat. The doctors say this is her new normal, and I've made my peace with it. Grace...still struggles with it sometimes.

"Done," she says, standing back to survey the table, a hint of pride in her voice. "I only dropped one fork this time."

I wrap my arms around her from behind and press a kiss to her neck. "Darlin', you could drop every single one of 'em, break every plate and glass, and I'd still love you every bit as much as I do right now. You know that, right?"

"I do. Today's a good day. It's...impor-prr...*shit*. Im-por-tant." She turns in my arms, tipping her head back so she can meet my gaze. All her bruises have finally faded. Yesterday, Emi—with Jasper as their bodyguard—took her to the salon to get her hair cut, and she came home with such a smile on her face, I almost broke down the second I saw her.

"You look beautiful." I tuck a lock of her hair behind her right ear—she doesn't like it if I get too close to the scar at her left temple—lean down, and capture her mouth with mine.

The kiss starts out soft. Hesitant. Gentle. We haven't done much more than this since the night before her surgery.

I don't want to push her too far, too fast. So for now, it's kisses, long showers, soaking together in the tub—the kind of touches that build a bridge back to what we had, one quiet minute at a time.

Grace parts her lips as soon as I take the kiss deeper, but it's *her* tongue that probes mine. Her hips that start a subtle swivel that drives me wild.

"Fuck, darlin'. Tonight. After everyone leaves. I...I want you so damn bad it hurts."

Her palm settles against my cheek. "I need you too, Aaron."

The doorbell forces us apart. Before long, Jasper and Emi, Parker, Hardison, Connor, Isabel, and Veronica join us around the table, enjoying extra spicy enchiladas, tamales, and fresh queso, and laughing like only family can.

Halfway through dinner, Hardison pushes his chair back with a scrape and gets to his feet, lifting his bottle of Shiner. "All right, before Jasper starts licking the bowl of queso, I'm making this official." He glances at Parker, then tips his bottle toward me. "Thanks to Cap—sorry, *Chief* Stone here, Parker and I managed to stumble our way into the esteemed rank of Captain. Which is wild, 'cause between the two of us, we've probably broken more laws than Harris has rules posted on his office wall."

Parker snorts into her water glass. "Speak for yourself. I've only broken half as many as you."

"Lies and slander," Hardison shoots back, hand pressed over his heart. "Anyway, here's to promotions we probably didn't deserve, and to surviving the next six weeks until AJ takes pity on us and comes back from his leave of absence to boot Harris into retirement."

There's more laughter, the easy kind that makes the room warmer, but when I glance at Parker, I catch the shadows still lingering in her eyes. She's smiling—even jabs Hardison in the ribs when he bows and starts asking me when it's *his* turn for a nice, long, leave of absence—but I'm not sure she'll ever be whole again.

But she's got Grace to talk to when the nightmares get too bad. And while I know Grace would give anything to take those memories away from Parker, having someone who understands—even a little—has been good for her too.

After dinner, when everyone else heads into the living room where we've set up the poker table by the fireplace, Connor pulls me aside. "You can consider Marvin a non-issue from here on out."

I almost choke on my whiskey. The day we landed back in Austin, Connor and Jasper went straight to the abandoned garage to have a little *chat* with the human piece of garbage before the FBI took him into custody. They warned him that if he didn't stick to the "official" story—that a couple of Jefe's guys beat the shit out of him—he'd find himself in lockup with a couple dozen Cordova Cartel members. And Connor would personally show each one of them the deep fake of the confession that sent Jefe to the compound that night.

"Did someone get to him?" I hold my breath, unsure I want to know the answer. Not truly.

Connor takes a long sip of his drink, as if he's about to go into battle. "The dumbfuck was bein' transferred to the cushy country club I promised him. He jumped outta the van at a red light, tried to play Frogger across three lanes of traffic, and got pancaked by a goddamn bus. His last words were apparently, 'The Glorious One will save me!'"

"A bus. After everything, a *bus* took him out." I want to laugh. Hell, I do chuckle briefly. After all the sleep I've lost worryin' about what he'd say under interrogation, this...is almost comical.

"Yup. Some Glorious One." He shakes his head.

"Oh, I dunno." Jas wanders over to refill his drink. "I think Marvin gettin' thrown under a bus is pretty damn glorious."

I turn my gaze to the living room. Grace shines like the sun. She, Emi, and Isabel are trying to convince Parker to watch some rom-com at their next girls' night, while Veronica plays with Belle in front of the fire.

Parker's hands are still a little shaky as she divvies up the poker chips. She sits next to Grace, and they trade a quick look —a moment of connection between two women who've been pushed to the edge and survived.

"All right," I say, taking my seat next to Grace. "Whose money is my wife takin' tonight?"

"Not mine," Hardison declares, leaning back in his chair and flashing a grin. "I've been running numbers in my head all week. Got odds, probabilities, whole-ass spreadsheets up here." He taps his temple. "Grace doesn't stand a chance."

My wife quirks a brow and flicks a chip into the center of the table with practiced ease. "Bold. You'll regret it." Her voice is steady, her eyes sharp—like this part of her never went anywhere.

Parker shakes her head, sliding her own stack closer. "He'll regret it in about ten minutes. Tops."

Connor smirks, already riffling through his cards. "Hell, I'll give it five. And that's generous."

The game rolls on, laughter and trash talk filling the room, Grace playing with a sly confidence that's almost dangerous.

By the time the last hand is dealt, Hardison's groaning dramatically, half his stack gone. "I call foul. You trained her. That's the only explanation." He points at Jas, then Parker. "Y'all are in cahoots."

Grace just smiles, sweeping the chips toward her side as Parker snorts.

When everyone starts gathering their things, Parker yawns, hiding it behind her hand. Hardison notices instantly. "All right, c'mon. I'm drivin' you home before you hustle me outta gas money too."

She rolls her eyes, but lets him take her bag without argument.

The rest of the family filters out with hugs, promises, and a few more jokes, until it's just me and Grace again.

We move through the quiet routine of bedtime. Grace struggles with her pajama top, her tired hands fumbling with the buttons, and mutters a frustrated, "Stupid...cloth...thing."

I step in gently, drawing her closer and planting a kiss to her forehead. "When you first came back to me, you needed me to do this for you every night. And a part of me...well...I knew once you didn't anymore...I'd miss it." I do up the last button and kiss the curve of her neck. "You don't have to struggle, darlin'. Not with me. Not unless you want to."

Her words falter as she peers up at me. "Long nii... But... good."

"It was good. But we ain't lettin' Jas make the queso ever again. If Emi's too busy, we go with store-bought."

She laughs. "D-damn straight."

We slip under the covers, her body curling naturally against mine. She tucks her face into my chest with a sigh, and I trail my fingers over her back in slow, gentle circles.

"Love you," she murmurs, the words soft but clear.

"Love you too, darlin'."

Within minutes, her breathing evens out, sleep stealing her

away. I hold her tighter, letting the weight of her against me be the last thing I feel before I drift off beside her.

———

Grace

The sunlight hitting the back deck is warm, though Parker and I both have blankets wrapped around our shoulders while Belle runs along the shore of the lake, barking at demons only dogs can see.

AJ hovered like a storm cloud until I pushed him toward the door with a grocery list and a hard, fast kiss.

"I need to be able to do this. To remember who I am with you and *without you."*

He'd nodded, and if Parker weren't here, I think he'd probably be calling every five minutes to check up on me.

She came over with a couple of Deluxes from Whataburger—and *three* orders of fries. We ate at the kitchen counter, not really talking, but just enjoying the freedom of an ordinary meal on an ordinary day.

I need more of those. Some of my memories are clearer now. My mom's cookies cooling on the counter. The smell of cinnamon and sugar melting into the air. Her smile. But other pieces of me are gone—like pages torn from a book—and I'm not sure I'll ever get them back.

Parker slides her gaze to me, concern furrowing her brow. "You're quiet," she says finally, then picks up the tennis ball Belle dropped at her feet and throws it halfway across the lawn.

"I...'membered more." The words don't like to come when I'm stressed. Or afraid. Sometimes not even when I'm happy. But at least they come well enough I can communicate what's really important.

She swallows, hard enough for me to hear it. "Want to talk about it?"

I tell her about the time I tried to escape. About running so far and so long in the pouring rain. About being so cold, I couldn't feel my cheeks. About Malone and Vincent catching me, and what came next.

"Eight...uh..." I try three times to finish the sentence, but I can't form the words. So I make the sign for "*days,*" then spell out *B-O-X*.

The sob that tears from Parker's throat cuts through me like a knife. I scoot to the edge of my chair and wrap my arms around her.

"It's so stupid," she whimpers, clinging to me like I'm the only thing anchoring her to this reality. "I was only in there for a day. *One* day. But you, Grace...*God.*" Her voice breaks, and she sucks in a jagged breath, like she's trying to hold the rest inside, but her body betrays her—trembling, rigid, desperate. I smooth my palm along her back until I feel her start to relax, just a fraction.

"You're not weak," I whisper against her hair, thankful the words don't shatter on my tongue. "You're here. That matters."

She shakes her head, pulling back, her eyes wet and unfocused. "It's not just the box. It's what came with it. What I knew was waiting." Her throat works, a convulsive swallow, and then the truth rips out of her, ragged and raw. "I knew what Prophet planned for me. And I...I lost it. I thought, if *you* couldn't escape, if someone as strong as you couldn't get out, then what chance did I have?

"I keep thinking it shouldn't be this hard. Twenty-four hours. You survived so much worse. But the ringing in my ears, the silence when it stopped, the way I thought I was disappearing into myself—I don't know how to come back from that."

There's so much I want to say to her. But I know my voice

won't hold. Not with something this important. So I grab the notebook on the table and start to write. *"You did come back. You survived. And you don't have to go through this alone."*

She presses her lips together, then lets out a shuddering breath. "I've been thinking about seeing a therapist," she admits. "Haven't told Hardison yet. He'll fuss. But I think I need it."

I nod, my throat aching with pride. With relief. With the knowledge that we're both still fighting. And I tell her how strong I think she is. How important she is to me. How I'm always here. Even if sometimes it has to be with a piece of paper and a pen.

Eventually, Belle demands Parker cuddle her, and it heals us both just that much more.

Later, when Parker stands at the door, her bag slung over her shoulder, I pull her into a hug. She clings tighter than I expect, tighter than she probably realizes. When I finally let go, her eyes are a little less haunted, a little more alive.

"See you soon," she murmurs.

I nod, watching her walk down the path. My heart feels steadier, my feet firmer beneath me. Because I know, whatever comes next, the bond between us—the pain, the survival, the sisterhood forged in fire—will keep us both moving forward.

AJ's ARM slides around me the moment I crawl into bed, pulling me into the solid heat of his body. His chest is warm against my cheek, his scent filling my lungs.

And that's when I break.

The tears rush up so quickly, I don't have time to stop or hide them. My body convulses, ugly sobs tearing out of me like I've been split open. I clutch at his arms, like if I don't hold on tight enough, I'll lose him, lose this...lose us.

AJ doesn't flinch. He rocks me like he's done this a thousand times. Like he'll do it a thousand more if that's what I need. His breath stutters against my temple, and I realize he's crying too. Not the quiet, controlled kind. Real tears, hot and wet against my skin.

"Grace," he murmurs, voice raw but steady. His arms band tighter around me. "I've got you, darlin'. I've got you. Let it out."

I can't stop. I don't want to. Weeks—years—of holding myself together unravel all at once. I can only manage broken fragments of words. "Cold. Alone. Lost." My throat shreds more with each syllable.

His hand cradles the back of my head, his lips brushing my temple. "Not anymore. You're not alone. You're not lost. You're home. With me."

I sob harder at the conviction in his voice, but the scent of him, the strength of him, roots me. His heart thunders under my cheek, steady and alive. He's alive. I'm alive.

When I can finally speak, my throat raw, I whisper, "I don't know how to deserve this. You. Us."

AJ eases back just enough to tilt my chin up. His eyes are wet, shining in the low light, but steady as always. "You don't earn love, Grace. You give it. You live it. And we've both bled for it. So don't you dare tell me you don't deserve it."

A fresh wave of tears blurs him, but this time they're not grief. I reach up with shaking hands and frame his face.

"I love you," I choke out, the words raw and desperate.

He touches his forehead to mine. Our tears mix together, and we cling to one another. "I love you more than anything in this world," he says. "More than my own life."

His mouth finds mine then, and the kiss is salty, messy, trembling, but so very, *very* real.

Suddenly, I need us to be closer. As close as two people can possibly be. I need proof that this is real. That we're here together.

You're home. You're safe. You're loved.

His words always come back to me when I need them most.

I tug at him with desperate hands, and he comes willingly, trailing kisses over my skin, worshipping me, telling me how beautiful I am. How strong. How perfect.

The need in me shifts, the ache so sharp, there's only one thing that can possibly fill it. My tears won't stop, not even when he slides deep inside me. They pour from me as freely as my love for him. Each sob is a release. Each caress stitches me back together. He whispers to me the whole time—my name, his love, promises he doesn't have to make but does anyway because he knows I need to hear them.

When we come together, I collapse against him, utterly spent, but lighter. Freer. He draws slow circles along my spine, and for the first time in so long, my entire being stills. But it's not the quiet of loneliness. It's the quiet of peace.

"You're my heart, Grace," he murmurs against my hair. "Every beat, it's yours."

I smile through the last of my tears. "Always."

His arms tighten around me, his breath steady and sure. I drift into sleep with him wrapped around me. And for once, the shadows don't come for me. There's only love.

Thank you for reading Stone's Throw.

GRACE AND AJ's journey was about surviving the unthinkable, finding themselves again, and proving that love can survive even the darkest and toughest of times.

But the L.A.S.T. Defense world is far from over.

You won't want to miss *Flint's Strike*—Parker Elmore's story.

A Texas Ranger Captain with scars she's hidden for years, Parker has always been the unbreakable one. But when a man carrying burn scars of his own crashes into her world, she'll be forced to face a truth she's avoided for years: surviving isn't the same as living.

Her walls won't protect her this time.

And his love may be the thing that saves them both.

 Preorder *Flint's Strike* today!

THIS ISN'T THE END.

Want more of Grace and AJ—more passion, more heartbreak, more healing? And some sneak peeks at scenes from Parker and Hardison's perspectives?

I've written a library of **bonus scenes** just for you.

Subscribe to my newsletter today, and the next chapter is yours.

IF YOU LOVED CONNOR, Isabel, Zephyr, Jasper, and Emi in this book, you can read their books now!

Connor and Isabel find their happy ever after in Rogue Survivor.

Zephyr and her guy (Ronan) are from Protecting His Target.

Jasper and Emi's story is Blade's Edge.

Happy reading!

ACKNOWLEDGMENTS

This book hit me in ways I'm still only starting to comprehend. Grace's journey, finding her way after losing every part of herself—everything that made her...*her*...

Well, I feel like I was finding myself right along with Grace and AJ.

Life hasn't been easy the past few years. I've had challenges I didn't anticipate, and there are likely a few more on the way. Finding moments of joy, of peace, of focus? It's been so hard.

The mantra that AJ repeats to Grace over and over again is one that I've actually started using myself.

You're home. You're safe. You're loved.

If it helps, I hope you'll use it too.

This book wouldn't be what it is without some very important people.

Michelle

I had no idea how much I needed you. Your perspective. Your fresh take on words. Your willingness to work on a book that ended up being *twice* as long as it was supposed to be. Your support of my decisions *and* all the times you challenged me. Whatever success this book has...it is in no small part due to you. Not only your editing, but also, your friendship. All my love.

Jane

You're always there for me. Your insights are always spot on, and you are my Texas guru. Most importantly, you're my friend and I love you.

My author friend group

My life, my writing, and my sanity are all better for having found my people. We don't see one another often enough, but know that you're always in my heart.

ABOUT THE AUTHOR

Patricia D. Eddy is a USA Today bestselling author who writes romance for the beautifully broken. Fueled by coffee, wine, and *Doctor Who* episodes on repeat, she brings damaged heroes and heroines together to find their happy ever afters in many different worlds. From military to paranormal to BDSM, her characters are unstoppable forces colliding with such heat, sparks always fly.

Patricia makes her home in Seattle with her husband and very spoiled cats, and when she's not writing, she loves working on home improvement projects, especially if they involve power tools.

Her award-winning *Away From Keyboard* series will always be her first love, because that's where she realized the characters in her head were telling their own stories—and she was just writing them down.

facebook.com/patriciadeddyauthor

x.com/patriciadeddy

instagram.com/patriciadeddy

bookbub.com/profile/patricia-d-eddy

tiktok.com/@patriciadeddyauthor

ALSO BY PATRICIA D. EDDY

L.A.S.T. Defense

Blade's Edge

Stone's Throw

Flint's Strike

Reaper's Kiss

Away From Keyboard

Dive into a steamy mix of geekery and military prowess with the men
and women of Hidden Agenda and Second Sight.

Breaking His Code

In Her Sights

On His Six

Second Sight

By Lethal Force

Fighting For Valor

Finding Their Forevers (a holiday short story)

Call Sign: Redemption

Braving His Past

Protecting His Target

Defending His Hope

Trusting His Instincts

Saving Their Forever (an Away From Keyboard novella)

Guarding His Heart

Gone Rogue (an Away From Keyboard spinoff series)

Rogue Protector

Rogue Officer

Rogue Survivor

Rogue Defender

Rogue Operator

Rogue Mission

Dark PNR

These novellas will take you into the darker side of the paranormal
with vampires, witches, angels, demons, and more.

Forever Kept

Immortal Hunter

Wicked Omens

Storm of Sin

Gabriel's Gambit

Elemental Shifter

Pick up the COMPLETE Elemental Shifter series for thrilling tales of
werewolves and magic.

A Shift in the Water

A Shift in the Air

A Shift in the Earth

A Shift in Fire

By the Fates

Check out the COMPLETE By the Fates series if you love dark and steamy tales of witches, devils, and an epic battle between good and evil.

By the Fates, Freed

Destined: A By the Fates Story

By the Fates, Fought

By the Fates, Fulfilled

In Blood

If you love hot Italian vampires and and a human who can hold her own against beings far stronger, then the In Blood series is for you.

Secrets in Blood

Revelations in Blood

Holidays and Heroes

Beauty isn't only skin deep and not all scars heal. Come swoon over sexy vets and the men and women who love them.

Mistletoe and Mochas

Love and Libations

Targets and True Love

Restrained

Do you like to be tied up? Or read about characters who do? Enjoy a fresh COMPLETE BDSM series that will leave you begging for more.

In His Silks

Christmas Silks

All Tied Up For New Year's

In His Collar

www.ingramcontent.com/pod-product-compliance
Lightning Source LLC
Chambersburg PA
CBHW010018200726
48283CB00015B/2957